SEDUCED BY MOONLIGHT

a novel

LAURELL K. HAMILTON

BALLANTINE BOOKS • NEW YORK

A Ballantine Book
Published by The Random House Publishing Group

Copyright © 2004 by Laurell K. Hamilton
Excerpt from *A Stroke of Midnight* by Laurell K. Hamilton copyright © 2005 by Laurell K. Hamilton

Published in the United States by Ballantine Books, an imprint of The Random House Publishing Group, a division of Random House, Inc., New York, and simultaneously in Canada by Random House of Canada Limited, Toronto.

Ballantine and colophon are registered trademarks of Random House, Inc.

www.ballantinebooks.com

ISBN 978-0-345-44359-5

Manufactured in the United States of America

First Edition: February 2004
First Mass Market Edition: January 2005

19 18 17 16 15 14 13

To J
because he promised
and he always keeps his word

ACKNOWLEDGMENTS

Darla Cook, for being a sounding board, watcher at the gates, nag (her word not mine), and kindred spirit. Karen Wilbur, who got to read this book early. One of these years I'll be between books on your birthday and I'll actually have to buy you a present. To Shawn Holsapple and his Cathy, kindred spirits all. Sharon Shinn, who gave her expert feedback as the wonderful writer she is. Deborah Milletello, who I don't get to talk to nearly enough. Mark and Sarah Sumner, who I don't get to see enough of either. Never enough time to be with friends. Rhett MacPhearson, who is still writing delightful mysteries. Lauretta, I hope we get our families together for a trip sometime. Marella Sands, fine writer, and Tom Drennan, where's that book?

Chapter 1

A LOT OF PEOPLE LOUNGE BY POOLS IN L.A., BUT FEW OF THEM are truly immortal, no matter how hard they pretend with plastic surgery and exercise. Doyle *was* truly immortal and had been for over a thousand years. A thousand years of wars, assassinations, and political intrigue, and he'd been reduced to being eye candy in a thong bathing suit by the pool of the rich and famous. He lay at the edge of the pool, wearing almost nothing. Sunlight glittered across the blue, blue water of the pool. The light broke in a jagged dance across his body, as if some invisible hand stirred the light, turning it into a dozen tiny spotlights that coaxed Doyle's dark body into colors I'd never known his skin could hold.

He wasn't black the way a human being is black, but more the way a dog is black. Watching the play of light on his skin, I realized I'd been wrong. His skin gleamed with blue highlights, a shine of midnight blue along the long muscular sweep of his calf, a flare of royal blue like a stroke of deep sky touched his back and shoulder. Purple to shame the darkest amethyst caressed his hip. How could I ever have thought his skin monochrome? He was a miracle of colors and light, strapped across a body that rippled and moved with muscles honed in wars fought centuries before I was born.

The braid of his black hair trailed across the edge of the lounge chair, fell over the side, and curled beside him on the concrete like some patient serpent. His hair was the only thing that seemed black on black. There was no play of colors, only a gleam like a black jewel. It seemed as if it should have been the other way around, that his hair should have held the highlights and his body been all one color, but it wasn't.

He lay on his stomach, head turned away from me. He was pretending to be asleep, but I knew he wasn't. He was waiting. Waiting for the helicopter to fly over. The helicopter that would contain the press, people with cameras. We'd made a deal with the devil. If the press would just stay away enough for us to have some privacy, we'd make sure that at pre-arranged times they had something newsworthy to take pictures of. I was Princess Meredith NicEssus, heir to the throne of the Unseelie Court, and the fact that I'd surfaced in Los Angeles, California, after a three-year absence was big news. People thought I'd died. Now I was alive and well, and living in the middle of one of the biggest media empires on the planet. Then I'd gone and done something that was even better tabloid fodder.

I was looking for a husband. The only faerie princess born on American soil was looking to wed. Being fey, especially a member of the sidhe, the highest of the high royals, I wasn't allowed to marry unless I was pregnant. The fey don't breed much, and the sidhe royals breed even less. My aunt, the Queen of Air and Darkness, would not tolerate anything less than a fertile match. Since we seemed to be dying out, I guess I couldn't blame her. But somehow the tabloids had gotten wind that I wasn't just dating my bodyguards, I was fucking them. Whoever got me with child, got a wedding. Got to be king to my queen.

The tabloids even knew that the queen had made it a contest between me and her son, my cousin, Prince Cel. Whoever got a baby first, won the throne. The media had fallen on us like a cannibalistic orgy. Not pretty, not pretty at all.

What the tabloids didn't know was that Cel had tried to have me assassinated more than once. They also didn't know that he'd been imprisoned by the queen for six months as punishment. Imprisoned and tortured, for six months. Immortality and an ability to heal almost anything does have some downsides. Torture can last a very, very long time.

When Cel got out, he'd be allowed to continue the contest, unless I got pregnant first. So far, no luck, and it wasn't for lack of trying.

Doyle was one of five bodyguards, the queen's own body-guards, who had volunteered, or been volunteered, to be my lover. Queen Andais had had a rule that her bodyguards gave their seed to her body, or nobody. Doyle had been celibate for centuries. Again, immortality, if it goes wrong, can have some downsides.

We'd chosen one of the most persistent of the tabloids and made our arrangements. Doyle thought it was rewarding bad behavior; the queen wanted us to show positive images to the media. The Unseelie Court of the sidhe has a reputation for being the bad guys. We can be, but I'd spent my fair share of time at the Seelie Court, the bright and shining court that the media think is so perfect, so joyous. Their King Taranis, the King of Light and Illusion, is my uncle. But I'm not in line to that throne. I had the bad taste to have a father who was full-blooded Unseelie sidhe, and that is a crime for which the glittering throng has no forgiveness. There was no prison that I could go to, no torture I could endure, that would cleanse me of this sin.

They can say that the Seelie Court is a beautiful place, but I learned that my blood is just as red on white marble as it is on black. The beautiful people made it very plain at a young age that I would never be one of them. I'm too short, too human looking, and, worse yet, too Unseelie looking.

My skin is as white as Doyle's is black. Moonlight skin is what I have, a mark of beauty at either court, but I am barely five feet tall. No sidhe is that short. I have curves and am a little too voluptuous for the sidhe—that pesky human blood, I guess. My eyes are tricolored, two shades of green and a circle of gold. The eyes would be welcome in the Seelie Court, but not the hair. It's blood auburn, sidhe scarlet, if you go to a good salon and get the dye job. It's not auburn, and it's not human red. It's as if you took good red garnets and spun the jewels out into hair. It has one other nickname among the glittering throng—Unseelie red. The Seelie have red hair, but it's closer to human red, orangey, golden, true auburn, or true red, but nothing as dark as mine.

My mother made sure that I knew I was less. Less beautiful, less welcome, just less. She and I don't talk much. My father died when I was younger, and there is rarely a day that I don't miss him. He taught me that I was enough, beautiful enough, tall enough, strong enough, just enough.

Doyle raised his head, showing the black wraparound sunglasses that hid his own black eyes. The light glittered off the silver earrings that graced almost every inch of his ears, from lobe to pointed tip. The ears were the only thing that gave away the fact that Doyle wasn't pure Unseelie sidhe. Contrary to popular literature, and every wannabe fey with ear implants, real sidhe do not have pointed ears. Doyle could have hidden the ears and passed for pure sidhe, but he almost always wore his hair back so that this one imperfection showed. I think the earrings were so you wouldn't miss them.

"I hear the helicopter. Where is Rhys?"

I didn't hear anything yet, but I'd learned not to question Doyle; if he said he'd heard something, he had. His hearing was better than a human's, and better than most of the rest of the guards. Probably something to do with his mixed heritage.

I sat up and looked back toward the wall of glass that led into the house. Rhys appeared in the sliding glass doors before I could call for him. His skin was the paleness of mine, but there the sameness ended. His waist-length hair was a mass of tight white curls framing a face that was boyishly handsome and would be forever. His one eye was tricolored blue, cornflower, and winter sky. His other eye was gone, lost long ago. Sometimes he wore a patch to cover the scars, but once he realized that I didn't mind, he seldom bothered. The scars trailed down his face but stopped short of his kissable, pouting lips. For sheer shape of the mouth, his was the prettiest. He was five foot six, the shortest full-blooded sidhe I'd ever met. But every inch of him that showed was muscled. He seemed to try to make up for the lack of height by being in better shape than the rest of the guards. They were all muscular, but he was one of the few who really took the weight lifting seriously. He was also the only one with wash-board abs. He had the towels he'd gone for, in front of those abs, and lower, and it wasn't until he dropped the towels beside my chair that I realized he'd left his bathing suit in the house.

"Rhys! What are you doing?"

He grinned at me. "Bathing suits this small are like lies. It's a way for humans to be nude without being naked. I'd rather just be naked."

"They won't be able to print the pictures if one of us is nude," Doyle said.

"They'll print my ass, just not my front."

I looked up at him, suddenly suspicious. "And just why won't they be able to see the front of your body?"

He laughed, head back, mouth wide, a sound so joyous it seemed to make the day brighter. "I'll be hiding myself against your gorgeous body."

"No," Doyle said.

"And are you going to do anything picture-worthy?" Rhys asked, hands on his hips. He was totally comfortable nude. His body language never changed no matter what he was, or wasn't, wearing. It had taken two days' worth of arguing to get Doyle into the thong bikini bottom he had on. He'd never participated in the court's casual nudity.

Doyle stood, and the front of the suit was tiny enough, and close enough in color, that I could see Rhys's point. If you didn't know how magnificent Doyle looked nude, you might think this was it, at a glance. From the back he looked almost as nude as Rhys.

"I am wearing this, and I am in public view."

"You're cute," Rhys said, "but if we want the tabloids to stop trying to snap pictures through the bedroom windows, we need to play fair with them. We need to give them a show." He spread his arms wide when he said the last, turning his back to me so I got the full view of the back of his body. The view was better without the bathing suit to break up the clean, muscled lines of him. He still had a wonderful ass, unlike some bodybuilders, who've taken the lack of body fat to a point where there is nothing soft on their bodies. You need a little softness to hide the lines of muscles, or it just looks wrong.

I could hear the helicopter now. "We're running out of time, gentlemen. I do not want to go back to having the photographers camped out in the trees outside the wall."

Rhys glanced back at me. "If we don't give the first tabloid a good show, they'll tell the rest that we lied, and we'll have them climbing all over us again." He sighed, and not as if he was happy. "I'd rather flash my ass to the entire country than have another photographer break his arm falling off the roof."

"Agreed," I said.

Doyle took a deep breath in through his nose and let it out slowly through his mouth. "Agreed." How little he liked it showed in the lines of his body, the way he stood. If he couldn't act better than this, Doyle would have to be excused from future photo opportunities.

Rhys came to the foot of my lounge chair and knelt on all fours, with his hands on the chair arms. He was grinning at me, and I knew he'd find a way of enjoying this. It might be duty, and he might prefer to just shoot the helicopter out of the sky, but he'd play fair, and he'd find a way to make it fun, if he could.

I gazed down his body, because I couldn't help it. I couldn't not look at him dangling there, close enough to fondle, close enough for so much. My voice was a little less than steady when I asked, "Do you have a plan?"

"I thought we'd make out."

"And what am I supposed to be doing?" Doyle asked. He sounded disgusted with the entire situation. He loved being my lover, loved the possibility of being king; he hated the publicity and everything that went with it.

"You can take one end, I'll take the other."

The helicopter was close now, perhaps hidden only by the line of tall eucalyptus trees that bordered the estate. Doyle flashed a smile, white and sudden as lightning in the darkness of his face. He moved with that liquid grace and speed

that I could never match, and was suddenly kneeling beside
my shoulder. "If I must, then I would have the sweet taste of
your mouth."

Rhys darted a quick lick across my bare stomach that
made me writhe and giggle. He raised his face enough to say,
"There are other tastes just as sweet." The look in his eye, his
face, held a heat and knowledge that stole the laughter from
my throat and sent my pulse racing.

Doyle brushed his lips across my shoulder. The movement
brought my gaze to his, and there was that same dark knowledge. A knowledge born of nights and days of skin and
sweat and bodies, of tangled sheets and pleasure.

My voice came a little shaky. "You've decided to play.
What made you change your mind?"

He whispered against my cheek, and just his breath hot
against my skin made me shudder. "This is a necessary evil,
and if you must parade yourself for the media, then I will not
abandon you." That flash of a smile came again, like a surprise across his face. It made him look younger, almost like
someone else entirely. It had only been in the last month or so
that I'd known Doyle had a smile like that inside him. "Besides, I cannot leave you to Rhys. Goddess knows what he
would do out here on his own."

Rhys ran a finger along the edge of my bikini bottom.
"Such a tiny piece of cloth. They'll never see it if we're
careful."

I frowned at him. "What do you mean?"

He dropped lower on the lounge chair so that his face was
above that tiny piece of cloth, his hands sliding under my
slightly raised thighs until those hands came up over my hips
and hid the bright red cloth of the bikini bottom. He lowered
his face just over my groin, and his hair spread across my
thighs like a curtain.

I didn't have time to protest, or even decide if I was going
to. The helicopter cleared the trees, and that was how they
found us. Rhys with his face buried in my groin, his legs bent
at the knees, feet kicking slightly over his bare ass, like a
child with a piece of good candy.

I thought Doyle would protest, until he pressed his face into my neck and I realized he was laughing. Silently, shoulders shaking. He eased me back onto the lounge chair so that I was lying down again, still laughing, but hiding it from the cameras.

I started to smile and was glad my sunglasses were back in place. The smile started to turn into a laugh as the helicopter circled overhead, close enough to chop the water of the pool and send Rhys's hair tickling along my skin. My hair flared in the artificial wind like bloody flames.

I was laughing full out now, which made things besides my shoulders shake.

Rhys licked across the front of my groin, and even through the cloth it slowed the laughter, brought a catch to my breath. He rolled his eye up the line of my body, and the look was enough; he didn't want me laughing. He set his teeth into the cloth and grazed me delicately with his teeth. The sensation made me shudder, spine bowing enough to spill my head backward and open my mouth in a throaty gasp.

Doyle squeezed my shoulder, brought me back into my head a little. I was still shaky and had trouble focusing on his face. "I think we have had enough of a show for one day." He laid one of the towels across my stomach. He handed the other one to Rhys.

Rhys looked up at him, and I saw the thought to argue cross his face, but in the end he simply began to get up, spreading the towel as he moved so that the cameras didn't get a glimpse of the bikini bottoms. I'd half expected him to flash the camera, show the joke, but he didn't. He very carefully covered me with the towel, while the helicopter swirled overhead and the wind beat our hair around us. On his knees, he was fully exposed, and I wondered if there'd be photos with him politely fuzzed out, or whether they'd sell them to the European papers and not worry about it.

When I was covered completely, from thighs to just under the red bikini top, he scooped me up in his arms.

I had to shout to be heard above the sound of wind and machinery. "I can walk."

"I want to carry you." He seemed so serious when he said it, and it cost me nothing to let him do it.

I nodded.

Rhys carried me toward the house with Doyle walking a little behind and to one side of us. Doyle was being a good bodyguard, bringing up the rear, but he was also walking to one side, instead of directly behind us, so that he didn't ruin the photo opportunity.

He stopped at his chair and scooped up a third towel, then moved smoothly toward the house. I caught a glimpse of the gun wrapped in that towel. The helicopter circling overhead never knew that any of us was armed. They also couldn't see Frost standing just inside the sliding glass doors, hidden by a spill of drapes. He was fully dressed, and very fully armed. I think the reason I didn't mind the media games so much was that if no one tried to kill me, it was a good day. When that's your criterion for a good day, what's a few helicopters and some racy photos? Not much.

Chapter 2

FROST WATCHED RHYS CARRY ME INSIDE WITH ANGRY GREY eyes. Frost had been the one guard who voted against our treaty with the press. He would guard us while we did such foolish things, but he would not participate. His dignity would never have stooped so low.

He was handsome in his anger, but he was always handsome. Goddess had made it so that he couldn't be anything else. He was all cheekbones and flawless lines that would make a plastic surgeon cry with envy. Skin like snow, hair like silver frost glittering in moonlight, broad of shoulders, slim of waist, narrow-hipped, long of leg and arm. Clothed he was handsome; nude he was breathtaking.

He watched us walk across the cool tile floor with a look like a petulant child. He was the moodiest of the guards. The first to anger, the last to forgive, and he pouted. It seemed the wrong word for a warrior who had defended his queen for more than a thousand years, but it was the right word. Frost pouted, and it made me tired to see it. He was amazing in bed, a wondrous warrior, but shoveling his emotional shit was nearly a full-time job. There were days when I wasn't sure I wanted the job.

"The Goblin King has called on the mirror," he said in a voice as sullen as his eyes.

"How long ago?" Doyle asked.

"He's talking to Kitto now."

Doyle started toward the far bedroom, then stopped and glanced down at what he was wearing—or rather wasn't wearing. He sighed heavily, then padded barefoot across the tiles. He remarked over his shoulder, "If Meredith were dressed thus, it might gain us some advantage, but Kurag does not care for a man's flesh."

"That is not true," Rhys said, and the bitterness in his voice made me turn and look at him. I was still in his arms, so that just turning my head was somehow intimate. "The goblins love a bit of sidhe flesh."

Doyle stopped long enough to frown at him. "I did not mean to feast upon."

"Neither did I," Rhys said.

That stopped Doyle firmly on his bare feet, so dark against the white and blue tiles. "What are you saying, Rhys?"

"I am saying that there were many goblins who had never tasted the pleasure of sidhe flesh, male or female, and there were those who did not care that it was male." He rubbed the side of his face against my neck and shoulder, a comfort gesture.

"Kurag . . ." Frost began, but he couldn't finish the sentence. The anger at Rhys, or the reporters, or whatever, was gone. His face displayed the outrage they were probably all feeling.

I stroked Rhys's curls, so soft, and molded myself more tightly in his arms. I drew my fingers down the curve of his neck and shoulder. When the fey are anxious, we touch each other. I think humans would do it if their culture didn't confuse touch with sex so often. Touch can lead to sex, but at that moment I just wanted to hold Rhys and take that look off of his face.

Doyle came back a few steps, one hand on a slender hip. "Are you saying that Kurag . . . outraged you?"

Rhys raised his face from the curve of my neck. "He never touched me, but he watched. He sat on his throne and ate snacks as if it were a show."

"We have all had to sit through entertainments at our own court, Rhys. No one speaks of it, but how many of our fellow guards have agreed to a little one-on-one together for the queen's pleasure, if it would free them of the celibacy even for an hour or two?"

"I never did it." His hands convulsed around me, fingers digging in painfully.

"Nor I," Doyle said, "but I did not fault those who did."

"Rhys, you're hurting me," I said softly.

He put me down, gently, carefully, as if he didn't trust himself. "It would be one thing to choose it. It is another to be bound and . . ." He shook his head.

I let the towel fall to the floor and touched his arm. "Rape is always ugly, Rhys."

He gave a smile so bitter that it made me hug him, to comfort him and so I wouldn't have to see that look on his face.

"A lot of the guards don't agree with that, Merry. You're too young, you don't remember what we're like during a war."

I stayed clinging to him, trying to will him happier just by pressing my skin against his. I didn't want to know that my guards had done horrible things. No, that wasn't it. I didn't want to know that the men I shared my bed with had done horrible things. Then I remembered a conversation that I'd overheard months ago.

I pulled back enough to look into Rhys's face. "I remember this conversation, Rhys. You said you'd never touched a woman who didn't welcome your touch. Doyle said, outright, that the penalty for the queen's guards to touch any woman but the queen still applied to rape. You go to any other woman and it's death by torture, for you and the woman."

Rhys's face was suddenly paler even than normal.

It was Frost who said, "Not all the Unseelie sidhe warriors are members of the Queen's Ravens."

I looked at him. "I know." I felt like I was missing something. I stepped back from Rhys completely, so I could look at all three of them easily. "What am I not understanding here?"

"That nothing of which Rhys is accusing the goblins is something that members of the Unseelie have not done," Doyle said. He shook his head. "I must go and speak with Kurag." He seemed about to say something, then stopped and simply turned and walked toward the hallway and its string of bedrooms.

I looked at both the other men, still feeling as if they'd stopped the conversation early, as if there were secrets they would all keep to the death. The sidhe are big ones for secrets, but I was their princess, and perhaps one day their queen. That they kept secrets from me seemed a bad idea.

I let out a breath, and even to me the sound was impatient. "Rhys, I told you once that the goblin culture may not give you a choice on sexual contact, but they do let the 'victim' set the rules. They can demand intercourse, but you can dictate how much damage they can do to you."

"I know, I know," he said, avoiding my gaze and starting to pace the room. "You've told me before that if I had known more of their culture I wouldn't be short an eye." He looked at me, and the anger was back, but it was directed at me now.

He didn't have any right to be angry with me. Rhys was totally reasonable on almost every topic, except the goblins. The goblins were my allies for two more months. For two more months, if the Unseelie happened to go to war you would ask me, not Queen Andais, for goblin aid. Moreover, my enemies were the goblins' enemies for two more months. I believed, and Doyle believed, and Frost believed, oh, hell, even Rhys believed that it was this alliance that had kept the assassination attempts to a bare minimum.

I was in the middle of trying to negotiate for more time on that alliance. We needed the goblins. We needed them badly. Every time I thought Rhys had worked through his issues on the topic, I was wrong.

"You're right on one thing, Rhys, the goblins do not see same-sex sex as a bad or a shameful thing. If it's the way you swing, it's the way you swing. They also are much more likely than the sidhe to be opportunistically bisexual. If they have a chance to enjoy something they've never had, or something they may never get again, they'll take it."

Rhys had gone to the huge bank of windows that looked out over the pool. He gave me a view of his lovely backside, but his arms were crossed and his shoulders hunched with his anger.

"But just as you can negotiate for no damage done to your body, you can negotiate on the sex of your partners. There are some even among the goblins who are simply too heterosexual to be interested in exploring the possibilities. If you'd negotiated, then no male could have touched you."

Frost made some small movement, as if he wanted to go to Rhys. He gave me a look that wasn't entirely friendly.

Rhys's voice brought us back to him. "Do you delight in reminding me that my worst nightmare was my own doing? That if I hadn't been an arrogant sidhe who couldn't be bothered learning about any people but my own, I might have known that I had rights among the goblins. That even the victims of torture have rights." He turned, and rage filled his single blue eye with light. That circle of sky blue, the ring of winter sky, and that brilliant line of cornflower around the pupil blazed. The separate colors literally glowed with his rage, and a faint milky light began to flit behind his skin. His power raised with his anger.

There was a time when I'd feared Rhys when he was like this, but I'd seen his anger too often to fear it. As Frost with his pouting, so Rhys with his anger; it was just a part of them. You accepted it and moved on.

If Rhys had suddenly blazed to life like some pale sun, then I'd have been worried. But this was a small display; it meant nothing.

"You're still being arrogant about their culture, Rhys. You act as if what they did to you is nothing that could ever have happened in the high courts of the sidhe. If the Queen of Air and Darkness bid it, or the King of Light and Illusion wanted it, it would be done. And the sidhe have no laws protecting the victims of torture. You're just tortured. The goblins may do more torture, maiming, and rape than the sidhe, but they've got more laws in place to protect the people who end up on the wrong end of the punishment. You get fucked over by the sidhe, and they fuck you any way they want to. So you tell me, Rhys, which race is the more civilized?"

"You cannot compare the sidhe to the goblins," Frost said, his voice dripping with that arrogance that has been more than one sidhe's undoing. I guess if you've been the ruling class for a few thousand years, you forget what it's like to be ruled.

"You can't honestly mean that you prefer the goblins' world to ours," Rhys said, and his surprise was overcoming his anger.

"I didn't say that."

"What did you say?" he asked.

"I'm saying that this attitude the sidhe have that nothing and no one is as good as they are isn't necessarily so. My father used to say that the goblins are the foot soldiers of the sidhe armies. That without the goblins as our allies the Unseelie would have been destroyed by the Seelie centuries ago."

"The goblins and the sluagh," Rhys said.

The sluagh were the nightmares of the Unseelie court. They were all that was most frightening, most monstrous. All fey, sidhe or no, feared the sluagh. They were the Unseelie's version of the wild hunt, and there was nowhere you could hide, no place you could run to, that sluagh would not find you. On rare occasions it had taken years, but the sluagh never give up unless called off by the Queen of Air and Darkness. The sluagh were the queen's big scary gun. It is said that even King Taranis himself fears the sound of wings in the dark.

"Yes, the sluagh, those of our kind that most sidhe would rather not admit even belong in faerie, let alone that we could share a bloodline or two."

"We are not related to those creatures," Frost said.

"Their king, Sholto, is half-sidhe, Frost. You've seen him. His mother was Unseelie sidhe."

"Him, perhaps, but not the rest."

I shook my head. "The sluagh are the Unseelie, Frost, more than the sidhe themselves. Our one strength as a court is that we take in anyone. The Seelie Court keeps rejecting anyone who isn't good enough for them, and that has been the Unseelie's strength for centuries. We take in the fey they don't want. It's what makes us different from them; better, I think."

"What do you want from us?" Rhys asked, and he wasn't so much angry now as puzzled.

"Kurag is like a schoolyard bully. He only continues to pick at you because he gets such nice reactions from you. If you could act as if it didn't bother you, then he'd tire of the game."

Rhys hugged himself tighter. "It isn't a game to me."

"It is to him, Rhys. It's wonderful that you've overcome your feelings enough to sit beside me when I speak with the goblins, but truthfully, I spend so much time worrying about your feelings that I'm not as focused as I need to be."

"Fine," he said, "I won't go in with you. Consort knows, I'd rather not have to see his ugly face."

"When you're not there, Kurag spends time asking after you. He keeps asking, *Where's my delicious guard? The pale one.*"

"I didn't know he did that," Rhys said.

I shrugged. "He does."

"Why didn't you tell me?"

"Doyle said it would just upset you, and there wasn't anything you could do about it." I closed the distance between Rhys and me, laid a hand on his crossed arms. "I disagree. I think you're stronger than Doyle knows. I believe that you can swallow this hurt, and help me turn the tables on Kurag."

He looked suspicious. "How?"

I dropped my hand from his arm. "Never mind, Rhys." I turned toward the hallway.

"No, Merry, I mean it. How could I help you negotiate with . . . him?"

"Doyle's right, if I lose most of my swimsuit it will make it easier to negotiate with Kurag. He's a terrible letch."

Rhys shrugged. "And where do I come in?"

"Put on a robe and flash some of that gorgeous white flesh if Kurag gets stubborn. If you could keep your temper, no matter what he said, you beside me like this would distract him, not because of sex, but because all goblins love the taste of sidhe flesh. One of the things the goblins hated the most about making peace with the sidhe was that they couldn't eat us anymore."

"You ask too much," Frost said.

I looked at that handsome, arrogant face and shook my head again. "I haven't asked anything of you, Frost."

"How can you ask Rhys to sit there and let a goblin think of him as food? It is beneath us."

"If Kurag agrees to lengthen the alliance, I'll be beneath a lot of goblins." I'd said the last almost to be cruel. I was tired of hearing how much they hated my plan.

Frost's face showed the disgust he felt. "The thought of any sidhe woman giving herself to goblin men is repulsive. The thought of a princess of the blood, and a future queen, lying with them is beyond anything I have words for. Even Queen Andais has never stooped so low to gain the goblins' favors."

"Kitto is half-goblin and half-sidhe, and for better or worse I brought him into his powers, full-sidhe powers, through sex. No one thought that any goblin half-breed could be full-sidhe."

"Their blood is not pure enough," Frost said.

"I may hate it," Rhys said, "but Kitto's magic is the magic of our blood. I've seen him glow with it." He looked suddenly tired. "Kitto's not even half bad for a goblin."

"Merry," Frost said, and took a step toward me. "Merry, please don't do this. Don't say that you will bring over more of the goblin half-breeds. You have not seen them. Few of them are as fair as Kitto. Most are much more goblin-like than sidhe-like."

"I know, Frost."

"Then how can you offer yourself?"

"First, I want the alliance lengthened, at almost any cost. Second, the sidhe have been dying out for centuries, but if Kitto can be full-sidhe, then maybe other half-sidhe could be brought into their full powers. It would mean that the Unseelie Court would suddenly be stronger than it has ever been."

"The queen is excited about Merry bringing Kitto to us," Rhys said. "The queen wants Merry to try other half-breeds in her bed."

"And what if one of them gets you with child?" Frost asked. "No sidhe will accept a half-goblin king."

"At this point, Frost, I'd settle for just being pregnant. It's been four months of sharing my bed with all of you, and there's no child. I think I'm going to worry about winning the race first. Then I'll worry about who sits beside me."

"The sidhe will not accept a goblin king." He said it with such finality.

"I hate the plan as much as Frost does, maybe more," Rhys said, "but it's not my lily-white body that's being bartered over." He took a deep, shaking breath, as if he pulled the air from the soles of his feet to the top of his head. He finally said, in a voice so calm that it was empty of all emotion, "If you can agree to fuck them, I guess I can flaunt myself in front of their king."

"Rhys!" Frost looked as shocked as that one word sounded.

Rhys gazed at the bigger man. "No, Frost, it's time. Merry is right." He looked at me, and the ghost of his usual grin flickered on his mouth. "How distracting to Kurag will it be to see me nearly nude?"

"About as distracting as this." I ran my hands over the mounds of my breasts where they lay barely contained in the red bathing suit. My hands slid lower, down my ribs, my waist, to frame my hips. Rhys's gaze followed my hands like a starving man. Nude as he was, he couldn't hide how watching me touch my body affected him.

He was one of those men who looked small until he grew, and then you knew he wasn't small in anything but stature. It was Rhys's laugh that brought my gaze back to his face. "Consort thank you, I love seeing that look on a woman's face."

A human would have blushed to be caught staring, but my cheeks held no heat as I raised my eyes to meet his laughter. If I had not stared at Rhys's lovely body, it would have implied that he wasn't worth noticing. My eyes held all the heat that would have blushed across my face if I'd been just a little more human, a little less fey. The heat in my eyes sobered his face, drenched his tricolored eye in heat of its own.

He had to clear his throat to say, "As distracting as all that, my, my." A smile flashed across his face. "So you're the tits and I'm the ass?"

That made me laugh. "That's one way to put it."

He stepped closer to me, letting his eye linger in one of those looks that is almost more intimate than a touch. A look that made my skin begin to glow, softly, as if I'd swallowed the moon and it was shining underneath my skin. It raised the hair along my body, caught my breath in my throat. All this from a look.

I had trouble focusing on him as he smiled down at me. "To see your body react to my gaze like that"—he let out a shaking breath—"I'd face a thousand ogling goblins to watch the play of light under your skin."

My voice came out breathy, very early Marilyn Monroe, but I couldn't seem to help it. "Why is it that you're the only one who can do that with just a look?"

His smile quirked into a grin, and his gaze slid briefly toward Frost, who was scowling at us both. "I could say it was because I'm the best lover you have." He held up a hand, as Frost took a step forward. "But I'd rather not have to fight a duel later."

"Then why?" I breathed.

The humor faded, replaced by a depth of emotion, intelligence, everything, that Rhys had managed to hide for centuries. A month ago, more by accident than design, Rhys had recovered powers that had been stripped from him centuries ago. All of the guards had recovered lost magic, but it was Rhys who had recovered the most because it was Rhys who had been stripped of most of his power. The price for the fey coming to the United States after they'd been kicked out of Europe was that there were to be no more large-scale fights among us. If we went to war against one another on American soil, they'd exile us, and we were out of countries that would take us. The answer to keep that from happening had been the Nameless: a creature made up of the wildest magic the sidhe of both courts had left. But as with all spells dealing with wild magic, it was unpredictable. Some sidhe had barely lost any powers; others had been nearly stripped dry. The Nameless wasn't the first time the sidhe had done this. The first time was trying to stay in Europe after the great human–fey war. That one didn't take, but Rhys had lost a lot in the first great spell. The Nameless had taken most of the rest. Rhys had been transformed from a major deity to one of the less powerful of the sidhe. He'd lost so much; he would no longer allow anyone to mention his old name. Out of respect, and horror that it might have been one of them, all the sidhe honored his wish. He was simply Rhys now, and what he had been was lost.

A month ago he'd recovered himself. He was simply more. He could call light into my skin by looking at me. I wasn't sure if he was truly more powerful magically, or if it was the nature of his magic. I thought the former, rather than the latter, because he was a death deity and not a fertility god. Surely my body should have reacted more to life than death.

His voice came soft and low. "What do you want me to do?"

For a moment I couldn't think what he meant. It took all my concentration not to buckle at the knees. "What?" I asked.

Frost made a disgusted noise. "She's power-drunk. Rhys, you really must be more careful."

"It's been almost seven hundred years since I had this much power. I'm a little rusty."

"You enjoy how you affect the princess," Frost said. He was closer now, but it would have been too much effort to turn my head to look at him.

"Wouldn't you?" Rhys said.

Frost hesitated, then said, "Perhaps, but we have no time for it, Rhys."

I felt Frost's strong hands on my arms as he turned me slowly to face him. "Find robes for both of you while I fix this."

I thought I heard Rhys move away into the room, but I wasn't sure. I was too busy staring at Frost's chest. His white shirt was buttoned all the way up to the rounded collar. I knew what lay under that tightly buttoned cloth. I knew the swell of his chest as I knew my own hand. I felt heavy and thick—not just thickheaded, but as if the hand I raised toward him was heavier than it should have been.

He caught my hand before it touched his chest. My red fingernail polish seemed brighter against his white skin, like startled drops of blood. "If there were more time"—he spoke low, just above a whisper—"I would wake you from this befuddlement with a kiss, but I would not trade one bemusement for another." He bent close, whispering against my face, "And if my kiss has not the power to befuddle you, I do not wish to know it."

I started to say something romantic and silly, like his kiss was always magical, but his hand where it touched mine had gone cold. Ice, his hand was like ice. If I'd been thinking more clearly, I'd have jerked back before he finished, but of course if I'd been thinking clearly Frost wouldn't have done what he did. Cold shot through my body, a cold to freeze the skin and ice the blood. A cold so intense that it stole my breath, and when I could breathe again, it came from my lips in a white fog. I jerked free of him, and he let me go. I was no longer befuddled. No, I was clearheaded, and shivering with cold.

I fought chattering teeth to get out, "Damn it, Frost, you didn't have to freeze me."

"My apologies, Princess, but like Rhys, I have not had my full power in centuries. I am still relearning the niceties of it." His grey eyes were full of snow, as if the iris of each eye were one of those snow globes that you shake up to see the snow fly. Almost every other sidhe I'd known glowed with power, and Frost could glow with the best of them, but when he called cold, his eyes filled with snow. Sometimes I thought that if I gazed into those grey, snow-flecked eyes long enough I'd see a landscape done small, see the place where he'd begun, see a time before I was born.

I looked away. My nerve broke every time, because I wasn't entirely sure where those winter eyes would lead me, or what secrets they might reveal. There was something in the snow that frightened me. There was no reason for it. No logic to it, but I did not like the snow.

If I'd been human I'd have accused myself of being unnerved by the strangeness of it, but I wasn't human enough for that, and Goddess knows I'd seen stranger things than snow fall in someone's eyes.

I was already warmer. The cold never lasted long, but I didn't like it. He had used it as foreplay once in our lovemaking, and though interesting, I didn't want to repeat it. To hide the fact that I was unnerved by his magic in a most un-sidhe-like way, I said, "Why is it that only Rhys's magic bemuses me like that?" I didn't meet his eyes as I asked. Eventually, his eyes would return to their normal grey.

"None of us had lost as much as Rhys, and he was once a deity to rival any."

That made me look up. His eyes held a sense of movement, but were grey again. "None of you talks about what it was like before."

"It is hard to speak of that which is lost, and can never be regained."

"Are you saying that Rhys was more powerful than any of the rest of you?"

"He was the Lord of Death himself. Death followed at his step, if he willed it. When he was great among us, Meredith, none could withstand us."

"Then why didn't the Unseelie destroy the Seelie?"

"Rhys was not always Unseelie."

That surprised me. "He was Seelie Court?"

Frost nodded, then frowned. He frowned so much that if he'd been able to wrinkle, he would have had grooves in his forehead and around his mouth by now, but his face was smooth and flawless, and always would be. "Rhys was a power apart. He was the ruler of the land of the dead, and that is not truly Unseelie *or* Seelie. He was welcome at the shining court, but he was truly a thing apart, as were some of

the rest of us. The system of two courts of the sidhe is rela-
tively recent. Once there were many courts. The humans
chose to call those of the fey who were beautiful and did
them no harm *Seelie*. Those they found ugly, or harmed
them, they named *Unseelie*. But it was not so clean a line."

"Like the goblins and the sluagh, now?"

"More like the goblins. The King of the Sluagh is a noble
of the Unseelie Court. They are no longer truly separate.
King Kurag holds no title among us; nor does any sidhe hold
title in his court."

Rhys came back in with a white terry-cloth robe belted
around his body. It was long enough that it came nearly to his
ankles. It would have draped the floor on me. His white curls
looked darker against the white of the robe, the difference
between fresh snow and ivory. Shades of white.

He held the robe that matched my bikini. It was red, and
meant more to decorate the body than to cover, so that most
of the robe was sheer, like seeing your skin through a haze
of fire.

Rhys looked from one to the other of us. "Why do you both
look so solemn? Nobody died while I was gone, did they?"

I shook my head. "Not that I know of." I took the robe and
slipped in between the patches of silk and the scratchier
sheerness. The next robe I got was going to be just silk, or
satin, something that didn't feel like it was catching on my
skin as I moved.

"So what do you want me to do once we're in talking to
Kurag?" Rhys asked.

"Just flaunt yourself—maybe flash your ass or upper
thigh. They're supposed to be two of the prime cuts of meat
that you can carve off our bodies."

Rhys put his head to one side, as if thinking. "Will it
bother him to see meat he can't taste?"

"It will be a little bit of torture, and I don't use the word
lightly. The worst thing you can do to a goblin is show him
something he wants and deny it to him. Showing Kurag his
wildest desire when he knows he can't have it, it'll drive
him mad."

"Or make him so angry he walks away from the negotiations," Frost said.

"No, Frost, if we make Kurag lose control that badly, he won't walk away. He'll respect the fact that we beat him this round. He'll try to find something else to distract us for next time, but he won't hold it against us. Goblins love a good game of one-upmanship. He'll be flattered that we went to the trouble."

"I do not understand the goblins," Frost said.

"You don't have to," I said. "My father made sure I did."

Frost looked at me, and there was something I couldn't read on his face. "Prince Essus raised you as if he was grooming you to rule the courts, yet he knew that Cel was heir, and not you. If Cel had produced even one child, the queen would never have offered you this chance."

"You're right on that."

"Why do you think he taught you to rule, if you were never going to mount the throne?"

"My father was secondborn and never going to rule, yet his father raised him to be a ruler. I think he raised me the only way he knew how."

"Perhaps," Frost said, "or perhaps, Prince Essus did not lose all his prophetic abilities when the rest of us did."

I shrugged. "I don't know, and I don't have time to worry about it."

Doyle came to the front of the hallway. "Kurag is willing to talk to you, Meredith, but he is not happy about it."

"I didn't expect him to be."

"He fears your enemies," Frost said.

"That makes two of us," I said.

"Three," Rhys said.

"Four," Doyle said.

Frost shook his head, his hair glittering like a curtain of Christmas tree tinsel. "Five. I fear for your safety. If we lose the goblins' threat, Cel's allies will move against us."

"Then we're agreed," I said.

Doyle was looking from one to the other of us. "What have we agreed to?"

"I'm going to play hors d'oeuvre for the Goblin King," Rhys said.

Doyle's black-on-black eyebrows rose nearly to his hairline. "I have missed something."

"Rhys is going to help me negotiate with Kurag," I said.

"Help how?" Doyle asked.

Rhys dropped the robe off one pale shoulder, flashing down to one tight nipple. He grinned and shrugged back into the robe.

Doyle raised dark eyebrows. "Do not take this in a spirit in which it is not meant, but you have been a stumbling block to our work with Kurag. He has chided you, fully clothed, and you have practically foamed at the mouth like an ill-used dog. What makes you believe you can do . . ." He seemed to be searching for a word. He finally settled for, "What makes you believe you can stand up to Kurag's teasing on this day?"

"Today, I'll be teasing back. Merry said that Kurag is like a schoolyard bully, and she's right. Besides, if Merry can do it, so can I." He looked suddenly fierce again. All the humor had gone, leaving his face bleak. "Though I'd much rather kill goblins than negotiate with them."

"Funny," Doyle said, "that's exactly what King Kurag said about the sidhe only moments ago."

"Perfect," I said. "Let's all go and irritate each other."

Doyle led the way down the hallway. He looked terribly nude from the back. I realized that Kurag would have more than just Rhys and me to ogle. I wondered if Doyle thought of himself as a potential sex partner, or as a meal? I guess that all depended on how Kurag felt about sidhe men, and if he preferred dark meat to light.

Chapter 3

I HEARD KITTO'S VOICE IN THE HALLWAY LONG BEFORE WE GOT to the bedroom. I couldn't hear everything he said, but the tone was pleading, and the voice that answered him wasn't Kurag's. It was Kurag's queen, Creeda. Over the last month I'd learned to truly dislike her.

Kitto stood in front of the mirrored dresser, drawn up to every inch of his four-foot height. He was the only man I'd ever taken to my bed who made me feel tall. The bare back he showed us was perfectly masculine, with a swell of shoulders, chest, a narrow waist, just done small. From the front he looked human enough, but from the back, without his shirt, you could see the scales. They were bright and iridescent, a glittering rainbow of color that ran down the middle of his back on either side of his spine. I knew that they spread out onto either side of his very upper buttocks. The rest of him was a white perfection of skin like mother-of-pearl. His Seelie mother had been raped by a snake goblin in the last great goblin war.

I noticed that his curly black hair had grown long enough to trail over his neck where the scales began. He'd need a haircut soon if he were to maintain the goblin tradition of doing nothing to hide his deformities.

He was saying, as we entered, "Please, Goblin Queen, do not make me do this."

She sat in the mirror, not a reflection, but as clear as if she sat just in front of us. She wasn't much taller than Kitto, and her hair was long and black, but where his hair was silken, hers looked as dry and harsh as it truly was. She had more eyes scattered about her face than I could count. That along with a nest of arms around her middle gave her the look of some great spider. A smile split the wide lipless mouth and flashed fangs enough to make any spider proud. She had only two legs and two breasts. If those had been multiples, she'd have been the epitome of goblin beauty.

Seeing the female goblins always made me wonder why the goblin men wanted sidhe women. Maybe it was more of a power thing than a sex thing, like most rapes.

The queen, Creeda, leaned toward her side of the mirror, filling our vision with her dozens of eyes and that oddly off-center mouth. There was a nose in there somewhere, but it was so overwhelmed by everything else that you had to concentrate to notice it. "You will do what ye're told," she said, and her voice had taken on that whining growl we'd all begun to dread.

Kitto's small hands went to the top of his shorts, and he began to slide them down.

"Stop, Kitto," I said, making sure my voice was clear and cheerful, and that my face didn't show how much I disliked Creeda.

Kitto pulled his shorts back into place and turned to me, the gratitude on his face so plain that I hurried to make sure he wouldn't turn toward the mirror again. I drew him against the side of my body with one arm and placed my other hand against his soft hair. I pressed his face gently into the curve of my neck and shoulder so he wouldn't turn and look at Creeda. If she once understood how truly afraid of her he was, she'd make the Summerlands into a wasteland to have him at her mercy.

"You have interrupted," she whined.

I smiled, and knew my face was pleasant, even bright and shiny. I'd been relearning a lifetime of polite lies that had kept me alive as a child in the faerie courts. You had to be able to lie with your face, your eyes, your entire body language, to maneuver through the politics of the courts. I wasn't always perfect at it, but the goblins were less noticing of such things. The true test was always my aunt, the Queen of Air and Darkness: She noticed everything.

"Greetings, Goblin Queen. I am so sorry that I have kept you waiting."

She snarled at me, flashing a mouth full of fangs, as if she had more of them than she needed, like she had eyes. I wondered if she had trouble eating without molars. I knew beyond doubt that her bite was poisonous. Of course, so was Kitto's, but his one pair of fangs was retractable. Creeda's were not.

Her face was a mask of fury as she mouthed her pleasantries. "Greetings, Meredith, Princess of the Sidhe, I have enjoyed my wait. Truly, if you have other things to do, Kitto and I will be busy for a little while longer." She shifted most of her eyes to stare at Kitto with a hungry look. But there were too many eyes, and they were too randomly placed for her to turn all of them his way. Some moved independently to watch as Rhys and Doyle entered the room behind me.

I smiled harder. "Whatever do you mean?"

"If he is truly sidhe, as you claim, I want to see him nude and shining."

A deep voice spoke off camera, as it were, out of sight of the mirror. "All our talking hinges on Kitto being sidhe. There are creatures of faerie who do not glow with magic during sex. Goblins are one of those creatures." Kurag moved into view. He wasn't as tall as most sidhe, but he was broader. His shoulders were nearly as wide as Doyle was tall. Some of the bigger goblins are among the bulkiest of the fey. After looking at the queen, Kurag's three eyes seemed underdone. His skin was the old yellow of bad wounds; of paper when it's rotten enough to break in your hands. He was covered in lumps, bumps, and warts, each considered a beauty mark among the goblins.

One large lump on his right shoulder held an eye. A wandering eye, the goblins called it, because it wandered away from the face. Kurag's other eyes were a yellow that bordered on orange, but the eye at his shoulder was lavender, with a spill of black lashes to frame it. There was a mouth on his chest, to one side, that matched that lavender eye, lovely lips, and straight, almost human-looking teeth. The small pair of arms on the side of his body near the eye and mouth waved at me.

I waved back and said, "Greetings, Kurag, Goblin King. Greetings also to Kurag's twin, Goblin King's Flesh." The stray bits were part of a parasitic twin trapped in the goblin's body. The mouth could breathe, but not speak. The eyes and hands moved independently of Kurag. When I was a child, I'd played cards with the hands while my father and Kurag did business. I was sixteen before I realized that it was a whole separate person trapped inside the other male's body. At sixteen Kurag had shown me both his own manhood and that of his twin. He'd thought the idea of two penises would impress me. He'd been wrong.

I'd never truly been comfortable around Kurag after that. The thought of one thinking being trapped in the body of another, unable to speak or choose his own way, or even his own sexual partners, had filled me with a horror that no other trick of genetics among the fey had ever quite exceeded.

From the night I'd realized that the extra bits were a different person, I'd greeted them both. To my knowledge, I was the only person who did so.

"Greetings, Merry, Princess of the Sidhe." He looked at his queen, and she scampered down from the great wooden chair. She made sure he didn't have to look at her twice. Kurag was not above hitting her if she was slow to do his bidding. In fact, he wasn't slow to hurt anyone who displeased him. The goblins feared him, and they feared little.

He settled himself into the chair. It creaked under his thick bulk. I don't mean to imply that Kurag was fat; he was not. He was just solid. "We have talked and maneuvered this last moon span, but it was Creeda who said it. If Kitto is not truly sidhe, then we talk for nothing."

"We have told you he is sidhe. The sidhe may try to trick, but we are forbidden to lie outright."

"Let us say we wish to see it with our own eyes." He wore

that look that said he was a lot smarter than he appeared, and a lot less ruled by his desires. There was a shrewd mind in that powerful body. Most of the time he hid it, but today he seemed strangely serious, businesslike. I wondered what had happened to take the teasing out of Kurag.

I almost asked, then knew it would have been a mistake. One fey does not admit to another that he is so easy to read. It simply isn't done, especially if one of them happens to be king. It is never wise to let any king know that you see too deeply into him.

"What did you have in mind, Kurag?"

His gaze switched from me to Rhys, who had moved up to stand to one side of me. "I see our white knight." This was usually Rhys's cue to say, *I'm not your white knight.* Today he just smiled.

Kurag frowned. I don't think he liked his insult being ignored. He held out a great yellow hand, and his queen came to him. He picked her up one-handed as if she were light as air, and sat her on his lap. "Creeda longs for a taste of sidhe flesh. She didn't get to fuck the white knight when he was here."

I felt rather than saw Rhys stiffen beside me. He wasn't going to be able to pull this off. I'd asked too much of him. Damn it.

But I'd underestimated Rhys.

He sat down on the bed. I glanced behind to see that he sat leaning forward, making the top of the robe gape, framing his chest, white surrounding white like a piece of smooth ivory wrapped up in a cloud. He propped his heels on the underpart of the bed so the robe parted in the middle, not showing much flesh, but giving the promise that only a little more movement would flaunt his legs, his thighs, all of him.

A small sound drew me back to the mirror. Creeda was making a high, thin noise in her throat. I think it was supposed to be provocative. It came out as an animal sound, but not a sound of any animal that had ever worn fur. There was something definitely insect-like about the noise.

"You gonna flash us?" Kurag asked.

Rhys just smiled.

Kurag's eyes narrowed. I watched the first flush of anger start across his face. In that moment, I realized that Rhys's teasing could backfire, badly.

Doyle stepped into the heavy silence. He pushed away from the post of the bed where he'd been leaning, watching the show. He came to stand on the far side of Rhys, even though there was room to stand on my other side. He was far less dressed, damn near naked, but neither Kurag nor his queen teased Doyle. He was still the Queen's Darkness or, simply, Darkness. The goblins can say what they like, but they were afraid of the Dark, just like everyone else.

"The time for our trip grows near, Kurag, Goblin King, and we need to know if we are visiting your sithen. Is Princess Meredith to grace the goblins' court, or not?" He leaned his long, dark body against the dark wood of the bed-post. He usually stood at attention, but I think he, like Rhys, was playing with the goblins. His arms were crossed over his chest so that the nipple ring glittered against his arm. Even his legs were crossed at the ankle. The bathing suit was so close to the color of his black skin that he looked nude. I knew just how much more compelling he looked with that last bit of cloth gone, but the goblins didn't.

Creeda was making that high-pitched noise again. She reached out with three of her hands, as if she'd try to touch the Darkness.

Kurag pulled her hands back, hugging her to him. A set of her hands moved to caress him. It might have been a nervous gesture, or she might have been so moved by the sight of the men that she needed sex. In goblin culture if you needed sex, you just took it, wherever you happened to be or whatever you happened to be doing. It made business meetings with them odd.

"Prove that Kitto is sidhe. Prove it beyond doubt."

"If we prove it," I said, "you agree to our proposal?"

He shook his great head. "No, but if he is not sidhe, then our talks are finished."

I let some of my impatience with them show. "So, what,

Kitto puts on a show for you, and we gain nothing from it? I don't think so."

The queen's hands had found Kurag's groin through his pants. Kurag ignored it, as if nothing were happening. "I think all our talks have been for nothing. I still don't think the princess has the balls to do what you're pressing her to do, Darkness."

"I am pressing her to do nothing, Kurag. Princess Meredith decided this path on her own."

Kurag shook his head. "I know you would not lie outright, but I also know that a woman besotted with a man will do much from a hint. It doesn't have to be an order. A word here, a word there." His eyes lost focus for a second, and he pushed the queen's hands away from his body. She struggled to keep her nest of hands on his groin. He squeezed her thin arms in his huge hands like a bouquet of flower stems. Only when pain crossed her face did she release him. He held the pressure for a second longer, as if he meant to crush her arms, then let her go.

She sat in his lap, rubbing her arms with some of her other hands. She looked sulky, like a child told, *No*. I'd have been angry. Creeda saved her anger for other things.

Doyle finally answered, "I have done nothing to persuade the princess, except remind her she will someday be queen."

"It is not certain she will be queen. Cel could still be king."

Doyle pushed away from the bed to stand straight and perfect, as he usually did. "Have you ever known me to stand at the side of the loser of such a contest?"

Kurag took in a great breath of air, then let it out slowly. "No." He didn't look happy about it.

"Then enough stalling. We have offered you a fair bargain."

Kurag's gaze flicked to me. "Is the Darkness your voice, Merry?"

"No, but when I agree with everything he's saying, I don't see a problem with letting him finish."

"So he will finish the bargaining."

I sighed. "No, that is not what I meant, and you know it.

We will bring your warriors into their full power. Think of it, Kurag: Goblin warriors with sidhe magic in their veins."

"There are those who fear goblins with such magic," he said.

"I am not one of them."

He frowned, then stared at me. I let the silence draw out. I learned long ago that most people can't abide silence. They feel compelled to fill it. I waited, and finally he spoke. "Why are you not afraid? All that has kept the goblins from conquering all of faerie is the magic of the sidhe. Give us that to match our strength in battle, and none will stand before us."

"And if the goblins go to war on American soil, you will be cast out, not just from faerie, but from the last country that will tolerate you." I shook my head. "Centuries ago when we warred one upon the other, then perhaps I would fear, but not now. You like it here, Kurag. You like it far too much to risk it all, especially when you can't guarantee victory."

"There are those among the sidhe who will fear us gaining their magic."

I nodded. "I know, but that is not your problem. That is mine." Truthfully, I didn't think that bringing over half a dozen goblins to sidhe would tip the balance of power. Half-sidhe didn't usually survive to childhood among the goblins. When grown and in our power, we are hard to kill, but as children we are fragile things. Goblins come from the womb hard to kill.

He ran his big hands down the much smaller queen, the way you'd pet a dog. "You risk much, Merry."

"How much I risk is my business, Kurag. I offer you a chance at what the goblins have been denied for millennia. I offer you sidhe magic. No one else can give you that. Cel cannot. Only me, and those who stand with me."

"An extra month for each goblin you make sidhe is too much. A day extra."

I leaned forward, forcing my own robe to gape, and knew that the red satin framed my breasts as if they were white jewels. I'd never have tried this on another sidhe. I was far too human to appeal to most of them, but for the goblins, I could be beautiful. "A day extra is insulting, Kurag, and well you know it."

His gaze was solidly on my cleavage. He licked his thin lips with a large, rough tongue. "A week then."

Creeda stroked his face, half of her eyes on me, half on Kurag. For whatever reason, I made the Goblin Queen nervous. Kurag had proposed marriage once upon a time, but I think it was desire for sidhe magic in the goblin bloodline more than true desire for me. Oh, Kurag would fuck me if I'd let him, but that wasn't much of a compliment. Kurag would probably have fucked anything if it held still long enough.

I sat up straighter and began to fuss with the robe as if I were hot. "Why not a year for each of the ones I bring over? Yes"—I looked up from undoing the sash of my robe—"yes, I like that. A year for each of them, and that includes Kitto." I opened the robe to frame the rest of my body. To show clearly how little I was wearing.

"No, no year. If you stripped naked for me, you could not get a year."

I smiled up at him, putting the shine into my tricolored eyes, two shades of green and a circle of gold. "And you cannot bargain me down to a day."

He laughed then, a deep, rolling belly laugh. It held all the unfettered joy that the goblins had—and that the sidhe seemed to be missing these years. There was other masculine laughter from out of sight of the mirror. I knew Kurag and Creeda were not alone. I wondered whom he trusted enough to hear us bargain.

"You are your father's daughter, Merry, I'll give you that. You know your worth."

I looked down, playing coy, because I didn't want him to see my face clearly. I was thinking too hard, and wasn't sure I could keep it off my face. I needed to get Kurag to agree to what we wanted. All he had to do to keep me from succeeding was simply say no. I needed him to say yes. The question was how to overcome his natural caution about interfering in sidhe business. How could I get him to agree to something he didn't want to do? Or maybe was afraid to want.

I let the robe fall to the floor. "How much can I be worth, if you will not sell sky and earth to see me nude? If I were truly beautiful, you would not have said it." I gave him a face that was questioning, and I put the doubts that I had around the sidhe into my eyes. My own mother had been the worst of my critics. It had only been a few months ago that I'd realized she'd been jealous of me. That I realized my mother looked more human than I did. She had the height and the slenderness of figure, but her hair, her skin, her eyes, they were human. Mine weren't.

Kurag read the doubt in my eyes, and I watched his own gaze cloud over. "You do doubt yourself." He sounded almost awed by it. "I've never met a sidhe woman who didn't believe she was Goddess's gift to males."

"Those same women tell me I am too short to be beautiful—" I traced my hands across my breasts—"they say my breasts are too large"—I traced down my waist to my hips—"that I curve in places they do not"—I traced down my thighs. Sidhe women don't have thighs. I let my hair fall across my face as I moved, so that my eyes gazed at him half hidden behind the scarlet of my hair. "They tell me I am ugly."

He spilled out of his chair, dumping his queen to the floor. He roared, "Who says these things? I will crush their jaws and see them choke on their own lies!"

The outrage on his face, the trembling rage of him—I took it for the compliment it was. I realized in that moment that Kurag might want me for more than just politics or supernatural bloodlines. In that heartbeat, I thought that maybe, just maybe, the Goblin King loved me, in an odd sort of way. I had expected many things today, but not love.

I don't know why, but I suddenly realized there were tears trailing down my face. Crying because some goblin had offered to defend my honor? I gazed up at Kurag, and I let him see what was in my face, my eyes, all of it. Because I realized that I still didn't believe I was beautiful. The guards wanted me because to be without me was to be celibate. They pursued me so they might be king. None of them wanted me for me. Maybe that was unfair, but how would I ever know why they came to my bed? I looked at Kurag and knew that here was a man who'd known me since I was a child, and he thought I was beautiful, and worth defending, and he would never bed me, never be my king. Knowing that anyone adored me, just for me, meant something. Something I had no words for, but I let Kurag see that I valued it. That I valued him, and how he felt about me.

"Merry-girl, don't cry, Consort save me from that," Kurag said, and his voice was softer, though still rough.

Kitto came up from the floor where he'd been sitting so he could lay his mouth against my cheek. His tongue flicked out, caressing my skin, the twin tips tickling along my cheek. When I didn't protest he licked my cheek, drinking in my tears. The goblins considered most body fluids precious and not to be wasted. I understood what he was doing, and frankly, just then, almost any touch would have done. I slid my arm across his shoulders and leaned into his body as he licked my tears away.

Rhys was behind me, on his knees, on the bed. He hugged me from behind. And because Kitto and I were so close, he was forced to hug Kitto as well. Only those of us in the room understood what a breakthrough it was for him to willingly come that close to Kitto. Just his willingness to do it made me feel better.

"Not a year, Merry, not even for your tears. Not even for that look on your face." Kurag still stood, so wide that he seemed to fill the mirror. He loomed over us, partly because the mirror was raised, and partly because he was standing too close to the glass on his side.

Kitto had drunk me clean on that side of my face. He had to turn the front of his body more firmly against me as he tried to reach my other cheek. He was pressed tight in the circle of Rhys's arm and my body. I expected Rhys to open his arm enough to let Kitto move to the other side of my body, but he didn't. He kept us pressed together in the crush of his arms. The moment I realized we were effectively trapped, unless Rhys released us, my breath caught, my pulse speeding against my throat.

My voice breathed from my body full of that pulse, and that sudden awareness. "Are my tears worth a month, Kurag?"

Kitto twisted against the strength of Rhys's arms. It forced Kitto's body hard against mine, but it was Rhys's whisper against my hair, "Turn your face to him," that made me turn so that he could reach the other cheek.

Kitto's tongue caressed my cheek, his breath almost hot against my skin. Rhys tightened his arms, and it was like being bound in chains of flesh and muscle. I couldn't concentrate, couldn't think.

"A fuck and a food to turn any goblin's head," Kurag said, and his own voice was low, growling, but not with anger.

I whispered, "Rhys, please, can't think."

He loosened his arms, but only enough to give the illusion of freedom. I knew the game, but the middle of political negotiations was not the time for it. Part of me wanted to tell Rhys to let us go, but part of me loved the feel of his arms around us, the solidity of his body pressed against my back, the whisper of his breath against my hair. I knew that Kitto liked few things better than being ordered around, being given no choices. It made him feel safe. It was comforting, but for me it wasn't safety I was seeking.

I managed to focus on Kurag, but I knew that my face showed some of what I was feeling. I kept waiting for Doyle to interfere, to stop this unseemly display, but it was as if the room held only Rhys, and Kitto, and me.

"Let me show you what a real goblin can do for you, Merry," Kurag said. His gaze slid to Rhys. "Let me cut off a choice piece of flesh. It'll grow back if it's done right. For that I'd agree to almost anything."

It was Rhys who said, "You left Kitto out of the bargaining." His voice was almost husky.

"He is a goblin, and I can do to him what I choose, when I choose."

"I don't think so," I said.

"He's sidhe now," Rhys said, in that deliciously low voice. "He was anyone's meat once, but that has changed."

"He is still as he was. He still craves someone to dominate him. I fear no one who seeks a master."

I found my voice, and it was almost normal again. "Yet you talk about cutting up someone who is his master. What logic is that, Kurag?"

"I do not need his permission to take what I want from Kitto. I can take what I like from any goblin if he has not the strength to keep it from me." He pointed at Kitto. "And he is not that strong."

I said, "There are many kinds of strength, Kurag."

He stepped back from the mirror and sank into his chair once more. He was shaking his head. "No, Merry, there is only one kind of strength: the strength to take what you want."

"And the strength to keep it," a male voice said out of sight of the mirror.

Kurag flashed a frown in the direction of the voice, then turned back to me. "Let me fuck you, and taste the white knight, and I'll agree to a month for every goblin you make sidhe."

Rhys let me go, slowly, almost reluctantly. If he'd had trouble touching Kitto so closely, it didn't show. Kitto had cleaned the last of the tears from my face and stood pressed against the front of my body.

"I can't help you break your marriage vows, no matter how loosely you hold them. Our laws forbid it. As for my guards, all my guards, they are not meat." I kissed the top of Kitto's head.

"Then we can have no bargain." For a second I saw the relief of that decision on his face.

Doyle's voice fell into the silence like some deep, heavy bell, the purring beat of his voice playing along my skin. "I was there when the goblins were stripped of their magic, Kurag. I remember your wizards. I remember that there was a time when the goblins' magic was as feared as their physical power."

"And who slaughtered every wizard and witch among us?" There were the beginnings of anger again.

"I did," Doyle said. I'd never heard two words so empty of emotion, so carefully nothing.

"And it was sidhe magic that sucked the magic from our veins."

"That was not an Unseelie spell, Kurag. We meant to win the war, not to destroy you."

"That bastard Taranis did not destroy us. Him and his shining folk who did the spell. They sucked our magic, and they kept it. Don't believe otherwise, Darkness. That shining bunch of hypocrites kept what they stole."

"I put nothing past the King of Light and Illusion," Doyle said.

Kurag stared at Doyle for a second or two, then spoke slowly, even though I could still see the anger on his face. "You helped take our magic. Why would you help give it back?"

"I did not agree that it should be taken the first time. I had no problem with killing your people. They were slaughtering us. If their spells had stayed in place, it might have gone badly for the sidhe."

"We'd have won, and owned all your shining asses."

Doyle shrugged. "Who can say what will happen in a war? But I say this now: We can offer you back some of the magic that was stolen away."

I whispered against the curve of Kitto's ear, "Shine for him, Kitto."

Kitto raised his head to meet my eyes with his own. His face was so solemn, as if he didn't want to do it. I wanted to ask why not, but I couldn't ask in front of Kurag because I didn't know what answer Kitto would give. I'd learned long ago that in the middle of negotiations, you never ask a question you don't know the answer to. The answer is so likely to hurt you.

Kitto said, in a small voice, "I'm afraid."

I understood then. Anger, lust, all sorts of emotions could make the magic flare, but fear, strangely, could kill it. It depended on the kind of fear. If it was that mind-numbing, panic-inducing kind of terror, you just couldn't concentrate around it. But a little fear could help you bring it on, and sometimes your greatest fears could manifest your greatest powers. Still, especially at the beginning, when the magic was new, you never knew which way fear would work for you.

Kitto couldn't draw his magic because he was scared to death of Kurag and Creeda. He was too terrified to think clearly, let alone do magic.

I cupped his face in my hands. "I understand." I glanced behind me at Rhys, and sighed. Rhys had played a good game up to now, but that one forceful hug was the most physical interaction he'd had with Kitto. Asking Rhys to help me do what amounted to foreplay with Kitto was asking too much. My white knight, as Kurag put it, had done his duty for the day.

With his face still cupped in my hands, I laid a gentle kiss on Kitto's mouth.

"What's this?" Kurag asked.

I raised my face enough to see his face. "I want Kitto to call his magic, but he fears you too much."

"What use to the goblins is such frail magic?"

"In the beginning of your powers, you sometimes need help drawing them."

Doyle added, "It is like any other weapon, Kurag. Someone new to the sword may hesitate in battle, or be unsure where to strike the blow."

He frowned, settling into his big chair as if it were suddenly less comfortable. "I don't do magic, but if you say it's like a weapon, then so be it." I could tell by his face that he'd gotten our meaning, though.

Creeda hopped back into the frame of the mirror. Kurag picked her up absently, as if she were a pet that had asked to be taken onto his lap. "Shine for us, Princess, shine for us,"

Creeda said in an eager voice that still held a touch of that high, mechanical whine.

Kurag cuffed her gently on the side of the body. She rolled her eyes up to him. "What? You wanted me to make the little one shine."

Looking at Kurag, fighting to keep his face neutral, I realized that it was one thing for Creeda to have her fun with Kitto, but another to include me. In that moment, I knew two things. One, I had the advantage of Kurag in any negotiations; two, the other goblins would notice, if they hadn't already, and they'd see it as a weakness. The goblins don't have a hereditary monarchy. You become king because you are strong enough to slay the old king. No Goblin King ever dies quietly in his sleep. They all feared Kurag, but if they sensed one weakness, they'd suspect there were others. Goblins, like sharks, sniff for blood.

"Will the rest of us miss the show?" The male voice that had commented earlier spoke off camera again.

Kurag sent a baleful look in the direction of whoever it was. "The princess doesn't do shows." He turned back to me. "Or has that changed since you got your harem?" He'd managed to get his face back into a belligerent blankness, using anger to hide whatever he was thinking.

"To ease Kitto's fears, I will caress him."

There were shouts and sounds from beyond the mirror. They were typically masculine sounds, and wouldn't have been out of place in most bars on a Saturday night.

Kurag ignored them, as he should have, but the effort showed in his big hands, the set of his shoulders. His queen tensed, as if she were poised to leap to safety.

"It will not be much of a show by goblin standards, or even by Unseelie standards, but I will ease his fears and open him to his magic."

"I've seen him shine, Merry. I believe he's sidhe. I believe he has magic in him. But not the kind of magic that will help on a battlefield. And that is the only kind of magic we need."

"You say that, Kurag," Doyle said, "because the goblins have never known any other kind of magic."

"I say it because it is true." His eyes were more orange than yellow, colored with his anger.

"Do you want to see him shine with the magic that could be yours, Kurag?" I asked, and I dropped my voice a little. I admit to using his attraction to me against him. If we could gain the goblins for near-permanent allies, we could keep most of our enemies at bay. For the lives of those I held dear, for the future of the Unseelie Court itself, I could manipulate a king.

He gave a gruff nod. Creeda clapped her many hands together, those that had mates to clap, and bounced like a child on his lap.

I looked at Kitto. I asked him with my eyes if he was ready. He mouthed, *Yes.* I kissed him gently on the mouth, not as foreplay but as a thank-you, and as an apology for making him do something he didn't want to do.

I could feel the reluctance in his body and I was torn. I knew Kitto well enough to put him in the right mind-set quickly, but if I did it in front of the goblins they'd know how to do it, too. I knew how to make Kitto shine, because I was his lover and his friend. If I went slower and did more things, with the touches that were truly his favorites lost in many touches, then Creeda would not have the keys to his body. It would take longer, but I didn't want to help Creeda torment him. I would do my best to see that Creeda never got her hands on him, but I knew too much of royal politics to be certain I could keep him safe. You do not lightly refuse a queen, any queen.

I made my decision, and drew Kitto into my arms.

Chapter 4

I SAT ON THE EDGE OF THE BED WITH KITTO IN MY LAP, HIS LEGS straddling my body as if I were the boy and he the girl. His shorts were stretched tight across the firm roundness of his buttocks, and my hands cupped that firm flesh through the cloth. I held him in my lap while my mouth explored his face, his neck, his shoulders. I bit gently at his shoulder, and he shuddered against me. Even through the cloth, I felt him grow firm. I kept one hand on his buttock, to keep him from falling, but the other I trailed up his back. I played on the rainbow scales on his back and found the line of naked skin that traced up his spine. I caressed a fingertip up that long, smooth line of skin, and it brought his breath shivering, flung back his head, put his face up to mine with his eyes closed and his lips half parted. But still he did not shine.

He was beautiful as he sat in my lap, but there was only the magic of bare skin and delighted flesh. He did not glow with power.

"Make him glow, make him glow!" Creeda cried, as if she had waited as long as she could to exclaim.

At the sound of her voice, Kitto wilted, both with the slump of his shoulders and the lowering of his head, and the press of him against my stomach lessened. It was as if just the sound of her voice made him remember unpleasant things. The goblins do not see marriage vows the way we do, and both partners are allowed certain freedoms. Whatever child results from whatever liaison is raised by the married couple as their own. There's no shame or screams of being cuckold. Maybe that's why there's no hereditary monarchy. But whatever the custom, I hadn't known that Kitto had ever been Creeda's pet.

Kurag said, "Hush, Creeda." But the damage was done.

Kitto wrapped his legs around my waist like a child clinging for comfort. He hugged himself to me and buried his face against my shoulder.

I looked up at Kurag. "I didn't know your queen knew Kitto that well."

"She didn't."

I patted Kitto's back and wasn't sure I believed him, but I couldn't think of a good reason for him to lie. "Then I don't understand his level of fear around her."

"Creeda, like most of our women, is eager to try a goblin who is also sidhe. He will have his choice of females at the banquet." Kurag didn't look particularly happy about it, and I wasn't exactly sure why, but it didn't matter, not really.

"Goblins will rape an enemy, or a prisoner, but they do not rape each other," I said.

Kurag looked past me to Rhys. "Your pale prince knows just what we do to prisoners." He gave an ill-tempered leer, as if he was happy to be back on ground he enjoyed. He liked teasing Rhys.

Rhys moved on the bed behind me. He'd been very still during the scene with Kitto. "I know I was a fool, Kurag. The princess has told me that I could have saved myself a great deal of pain, if I'd known what to ask for."

Kurag's leer faded into a frown. "A sidhe admitting he is a fool, it's a miracle."

I glanced back just enough to catch Rhys's nod. "We are an arrogant race, but some of us can learn from our mistakes."

"And what have you learned, pale prince?"

"That before we arrive for any banquet at your court we'll be very clear on what can happen to us, and what can't. To all of us, including Kitto."

"Now, that's arrogant," Kurag said. "No sidhe can deny the goblins access to another goblin."

I added, "If Kitto doesn't want to be with the women, then he can say no."

"I will have a taste of him," Creeda said.

"Not if he says no," I said.

"I will have him," she said, leaning toward the glass.

Kitto cringed in against me. "Control your queen, Kurag," I said.

"Why, she's one of hundreds who feel the same, Merry."

I held Kitto closer. "He might not survive the attentions of hundreds of goblinesses."

Kurag shrugged. "We're immortal. We heal."

I shook my head, but it was Rhys who answered. "No, we won't give Kitto over to that."

"He is mine," Kurag said, that grumbling roar trickling into his voice. "I have given him to Merry, but he is still mine. I am his king, and I say what will and what won't happen to him."

"Kurag," I said, and when those nearly orange eyes were upon me, I continued. "I know your laws. You do not rape your own people, not unless they have broken some law and you have deemed it fit punishment for the crime."

"There is one exception to the rule, Merry."

I must have looked as puzzled as I felt. "I know of no exception to this rule." Silently, I thought, *Except that to refuse your ruler is a dangerous thing.*

"I thought your father made sure you were versed in our ways."

"So did I," I said, "but you do not force yourself on each other; there's no need. There is always some willing partner close at hand."

"But if one of us sells his body for safety and shelter, then he gives up the right to refuse his body to anyone. Only his protector can dictate who can touch him, and who cannot."

I was still frowning.

Kurag sighed. "Merry, did you not wonder how I was so sure Kitto would go with you, and do what you wanted?"

I thought about that, then answered, "No, if our queen had

bid one of her guard go with me and do what I wanted, he'd
have done it. It's not our law, but it's unhealthy to refuse the
queen. I assumed that it was the same with your people."

"I gave you Kitto because I knew his protector had grown
tired of him. We are a hard people, Merry, but I had no desire
to watch Kitto be torn apart if he could not find someone to
take him in. A good king watches over all his people."

I nodded. Kurag was crude, lecherous, ruled by his temper
at times, but no one had ever accused him of not tending his
people, all his people. It was one of the reasons that he'd
never faced a serious challenge to his kingship. He was hard,
but fair. Half his people feared him, and the other half loved
him, because he kept them safe.

"I didn't know that any goblin needed that kind of protection," I said. Kitto went very still against me, and I could almost smell his fear. Fear of what I'd think of him now.

"The fate of a half-sidhe among us is not pretty, Merry.
Most die young before they come into that famed sidhe
magic. But there are many among us who long to have a
sidhe in our bed. A lot of your half-breeds end up trading
their flesh for safety."

He was talking about prostitution, a concept unheard of
among the fey, at least in faerie itself. Outside faerie, well, an
exile has to make a living, and there were a few who made it
that way. But even then, it was more a way to make the fey's
usual joys pay off. We are a traditionally lusty lot, and sex is
sex to some of us. No judgment, just truth. But the goblins
did not even have a word for prostitute. A more alien concept
for their society would have been hard to come by.

"But there is always sex among the goblins. Don't most
goblins think that one sexual partner is much like another?"

Kurag shrugged. "All goblins are voracious lovers, Merry,
but it is the addition of more tender meat to ours that has
given rise to trullups. Those who cannot protect themselves,
and have no other skills to offer. They are not craftsmen;
they do not make anything, or sell anything. They have only
one skill, so we allow them to trade that skill for what they

need." He didn't look happy about it, as if it somehow offended him, offended his idea of how the world should run.

"We would have killed such weaklings, but once they
found shelter with someone who was strong enough to keep
them safe, we had to let it bide."

"There can't be many among you like this," I said.

"No, but almost all of them are sidhe-sided." He glanced
off to the side of the mirror. "Though not all sidhe-sided are
weak." He made a motion, and two men stepped into view of
the mirror. At first glance I would have taken them for sidhe,
Seelie sidhe. They were both tall, slender, with long yellow
hair, and handsome the way that the sidhe sometimes are,
with full, generous mouths and a line from brow to cheek to
chin that reminded me of Frost. Their skin was that delicate
gold the Seelie Court calls *sun-kissed*. It's rare among them,
unheard of among us. But a second glance and you saw the
eyes, too large for the face, oblong like Kitto's, and a solid
color that gave no white to the eye, only a dark round of
pupil lost in a sea of green for one, and red for the other. The
green was the color of summer grass. The red was the color
of holly berries in deep winter. They were bulkier than
sidhe, too, as if they'd done more weight lifting, or the goblin genetics allowed them to simply carry a little more muscle mass.

"This is Holly and this is Ash. Twins left at our doorstep
by some Seelie woman after the last great war. They are
feared among us." For the King of the Goblins to say this in
an introduction was the highest of praise for a goblin warrior—and something of a warning for us, I think.

The one with the red eyes glared at us. The one with the
green had a much more neutral look to him, as if he was still
deciding whether to hate us. His brother seemed to have already made up his mind.

"Greetings, Holly and Ash, one of the first among Kurag's
warriors," I said.

The green-eyed one answered, "Greetings, Meredith,
Princess of the Sidhe, wielder of the hand of flesh. I am

Ash." His voice was pleasantly neutral. He gave a small bow as he spoke.

His brother turned to him and looked as if he'd strike him. "Do not bow to her. She is nothing to us. Not queen, not princess, nothing."

Kurag was out of his chair and nearly on top of Holly before he could react. Holly actually put his hand on the knife at his belt, then hesitated. If he drew the blade, then Kurag could take it as mortal insult, and the fight would be to the death. Once he drew the blade, it was Kurag's choice. I had a second to see the confusion on his face, then Kurag's hand was a blur, and the younger goblin was on the floor near the chair. Blood flashed in the light like an odd crimson jewel on his golden skin. The blood was almost the same color as his eyes.

"I am king here, Holly, and until you are goblin enough to say different, my word is law."

Holly smeared the blood from his chin onto his sleeve and spoke, still sitting on the ground. "We are not trullups. We have done nothing by our laws that enables you to send us to her bed, to anyone's bed. We need no protectors for our flesh." He coughed and spat blood on the floor. It was an insult among the goblins, wasting blood. He should have drunk it. "We have proven ourselves goblins first, and sidhe not at all, yet you would trade us away to this pale sidhe. We have done nothing to deserve this."

Kurag moved forward in a slow-motion stalk, as if every muscle fought against every other muscle. He wanted to tear Holly apart; it was plain on his face. We watched him try to master his rage.

Ash made a small movement. I wasn't sure what he'd done, but it attracted the eye. The knife at his belt was still sheathed, but he'd done something.

It was Doyle who called, "Kurag, this will be difficult enough without reluctant bed partners."

Kurag looked up at us. "They are too young, Darkness, they do not remember what we were. If Holly understood what we once were, what we could be again, he would go eagerly."

"Are most of your half-sidhes from the last great war?"

Kurag nodded. "Most of the old ones are dead. Sidhe-sides didn't last long among us until we made them trullups."

"We have never been trulls," Holly said.

Ash stood almost smiling at Kurag's back, but one of his hands was hidden against the side of his body. Creeda was behind the throne, and I caught the flash of a blade held in her many hands, but not the hands on the side facing Ash. Had he drawn a blade? Whatever he'd done, Creeda didn't like it. Truthfully, neither did I.

"Enough of this, Kurag," I said. "I will not force myself on anyone. If Holly does not want to be sidhe, then so be it."

"But I want to be sidhe," Ash said in that easy voice that matched the slight smile, and left his green eyes empty and pleasant. He was a born politician, was Ash. His smile widened, but was somehow sad. "My brother and I have never disagreed on anything until this. But I will be sidhe, and Holly will, too."

Creeda was almost close enough to be sure of what he held out of sight. He moved his hand into view. I saw Creeda tense. I felt Doyle and Rhys tense around me. Ash's hand was empty. But I would have bet almost anything that it hadn't been a second ago.

My voice was a little breathy as I asked, "Come and be sidhe then, Ash. Why drag your brother if he is unwilling?"

"Because I will it so," Ash said, and the pleasantness was replaced by an arrogance that you saw only on the face of a sidhe. Oh, yes, Ash was one of ours. He survived among the goblins, but he was ours.

Holly was on his feet now, keeping the big wooden chair halfway between Kurag and himself. He had his back to us, so I couldn't see his face, but I heard his voice, something close to fear or some other harsh emotion I couldn't name. "Brother, do not do this to us. We do not need the shining ones. We are goblin, and that is better."

Ash shook his head. "We have survived together, Holly, and we will continue to survive together. I have heard the tales of our storytellers. I have glimpsed what once we were, and you and I will bring those glory days back to the goblins." He walked toward his brother, walking around Creeda as if she weren't there. She hissed at him as he strode past. The blade in her hand flashed silver but she put it away, in a sheath that was lost to sight among her nest of arms.

He got to Holly and laid a hand on his shoulder. "I will stand by you in all things, even your anger at our king, but do not get us killed when we are about to go on to such glory as the goblins have not seen in more than two thousand years." Somewhere in that speech was his acknowledgment that he wouldn't have let Kurag kill Holly; that he would have backstabbed the king before he'd have allowed that.

Holly made a violent motion to point toward us, his arm flailing. He shot a glance our way that was venomous in its hatred. "They left us to die. How can you go to their beds?"

Ash grabbed his brother's arms, fingers digging in deeply enough that you could see it from a distance. He shook him, just a little. "These sidhe did nothing to us. None of them is mother or father to us."

"How can you be sure?"

"Look at them, Holly, look at them with something other than your hatred." He actually turned his brother around to face us, and the look on that one's face was such a mixture of pain and rage that it was hard to meet. "There is no golden skin and hair among them. They are Unseelie sidhe, and they did nothing to us."

Holly looked almost ready to cry. Something I thought I'd never see on a goblin's face. Kitto cried, but that was Kitto. He'd ceased to be a goblin to me, and was simply himself. No matter how sidhe Holly looked, he was still a goblin to me. Genetically he was half-sidhe, but culturally and morally he was goblin. I'd treat him that way until he convinced me otherwise.

"I do not believe that this goblin can shine like a sidhe," Holly said, his voice angry and desperately stubborn.

"Make him shine, Merry," Kurag said. "He needs convincing."

"If we have your guarantee that Kitto will not be meat for every goblin who wants a taste of sidhe flesh, then I will make him shine for you. Without that guarantee, I think his fear may prevent it."

Kitto shivered against me. He'd turned his head enough to peek at the mirror again, but he clung to me limpet-like, as if afraid the tide would drag him away.

"No," Holly said, and tore away from his brother's restraining hands. "No, if he gets safe passage then all the trulls will want it." He shook his head, making his blond hair fly.

"Sadly, I agree with Holly, Merry. If one gains it, then it is a slippery slope."

I frowned at them, then said, "I am his lover. Does that make me his protector?"

Kurag looked like he wasn't sure what to say. Ash shook his head and said, "She doesn't understand what she's asking."

Kurag looked at Doyle. "Darkness, the princess is sidhe, but she is not you, or even the pale prince. She has not the strength of arm to withstand every goblin who will want to taste Kitto."

"She has spoken," Holly said. "She is his protector, let it stand."

"Yes," Creeda said, "let me be the first to fight her when she comes. I will have Kitto, and if I get to cut that pure flesh, so much the better."

I knew then I'd misspoken, but wasn't sure how to undo it.

"We will not bring the princess to your hall if she must spend all night fighting duels," Doyle said. "We would be poor bodyguards indeed to do that."

"Holly is right. If I grant Kitto safety, then the others like him will want the same. We are a more democratic people than you, and I am more ruled by my people's voice than any sidhe ruler." He shrugged his massive shoulders. "It works well for us, but Merry is not goblin. She would not survive the night."

"Are sidhe such fragile things?" Holly said, voice full of scorn.

"Don't make me cuff you again," Kurag said.

"I'm mortal," I said.

Holly's face showed his surprise, but it was Ash who spoke. "We thought that was an evil rumor bandied about by your enemies. You are truly mortal then?"

I nodded.

Ash looked perplexed. "Then you would die protecting the trulls."

Rhys moved up behind me, his arms sliding over not just me, but Kitto as well. He leaned his chin on the top of my head but let his hands wander over the smaller man's back.

"We are his protectors," Rhys said. His voice was very clear, and empty of emotion.

Kitto glanced up at him, and I was thankful that no one in the mirror could see the look of shock on his face. Rhys didn't look at him, just kept that blank face toward the mirror and Kurag.

For once the goblin king was speechless. I think we all were. Well, not all.

Creeda jumped up on the chair so she could get a better view, or be better viewed. "Did we give you a taste for goblin flesh, white knight?"

"Kitto is sidhe," Rhys said in a flat voice, "so say I."

"So mote it be," Doyle said.

There was a ringing in the air, not of actual bells or anything you could hear with your ears, but the words had weight and reverberated through the room. Kurag's face showed that he sensed it, too. Something important had happened. Something fated, some piece of prophecy had either begun or been changed so completely that the fates of all had changed in that moment. You can feel the weight of it, but you never truly know what it means, not until it's too late to do anything to change it. It could be days, or years, before we knew what had happened in those few words.

There was a sound from deeper in Kurag's room. It was a clattering noise with an edge of slithering, like a many-legged snake. I didn't know what the sound was, but Kitto went pale, bloodless in my arms, his body suddenly limp. If I hadn't been holding him, he'd have fallen to the floor. Rhys was on his knees, his hands on my shoulders, but kneeling tall behind me. I could feel the tension singing through his hands.

I wanted to ask what was wrong, but I didn't want us to appear weak in Kurag's eyes. Then Kurag answered the question for me, even unasked.

"I didn't call you yet." Kurag was angry, but there was an edge of resignation to it. As if the anger were mainly formality. Real anger, but he didn't have much hope it would help things. I'd never seen Kurag so . . . defeated.

A voice came just out of sight of the mirror. It was high and hissing, and first I thought *snake*, but it held that metallic buzzing to it that Creeda had, and there was no snake goblin in the queen. The voice said, "You wanted to show me off, didn't you Kurag? Show the princessss that not all are asss ssidhe ass Holly and Asshh."

"Yes," Kurag said, and turned to the mirror. He looked solemn. "Know this, Merry: Not all sidhe-sides have taken after their sidhe parentage. Before you agree to this, you should see what will come to your bed." He looked at Rhys now, but that teasing edge was gone. "And not all our half-breeds are male."

"Don't do this, Kurag," Rhys said, and his voice was empty, but that emptiness was full of something, something that frightened me.

"She is part sidhe, white knight, and she wants her chance at bedding you again."

That clattering, slithering noise came closer, as if something were crawling and dragging itself along at the same time.

Kitto was making a high-pitched noise deep in his throat, a helpless keening. I held him tight, and it was as if he couldn't feel me. His body still lay limp in my arms, as if he was withdrawing into himself.

"What's happening?" I asked.

Rhys said one word, a name, with such hatred that it hurt to hear it. He said the name just as something crawled up on Kurag's great chair. Something that looked as if it had been sewn together from different nightmares.

"Siun."

Kitto screamed.

Chapter 5

KITTO'S SCREAMS WERE HIGH AND PITEOUS LIKE THE SOUNDS A baby rabbit makes when the cat's got it. He scrambled out of my lap, across the bed, to fall over to the other side.

Frost rushed into the room with a gun in one hand, and a sword in the other. He searched for an enemy, then just frowned at us all when there was nothing to shoot. "What's happened? What's wrong with Kitto?"

"Doesn't my little trullup want to greet his master? Have you forgotten everything I taught you, Kitto?" the thing on the chair said.

Doyle had gone to kneel by Kitto, and was trying unsuccessfully to soothe him. I heard the deep voice through the screams, but when Kitto finally found his words again, it was to say, "No, no, no, no, no." Over and over and over.

I'd tried to turn and help Kitto, but Rhys's hands had tightened on my shoulders. One glance at his face, and I knew that Kitto wasn't the only one who needed help. I didn't know what to do, but I stayed where I was, with Rhys kneeling so that his body touched the back of mine. I stayed there so he could lean against me and not fall over.

I turned back to the goblin in the chair and waited for my eyes to make sense of it. At first it looked like a huge black, hairy spider. A spider the size of a large German shepherd. But the head had a neck, and there was something vaguely human about the mouth; it had lips and fangs. There were huge black legs on either side of the bloated body that were pure spider, but the two hands that stuck out of the front of it weren't. It seemed to have eyes everywhere, and every one

of them was tricolored in rings of blue. It raised up as if trying to get more comfortable on the chair, and flashed a
glimpse of pale breasts. Female. I couldn't bring myself to
call it a woman.

I never thought I'd see anything among the fey that I truly
thought was nightmarish. I was Unseelie sidhe; we were the
stuff of nightmares. But Siun was a nightmare for nightmares. If she had been a little less of one thing, and a little
more of the other, it would have made her less terrible, but
she was what she was, and there was no saving it.

That strangely shapely mouth, caught in the midst of all
that black hair and those eyes, spoke. "Rhysss, how very,
very good to ssee you. I still have your eye in a jar on my
shelf. Come visit us again. I'd love a matched pair."

I felt a shiver run through Rhys, as if his entire body trembled in some unseen wind. His voice came out empty like a
shell tossed on a beach, echoing with its loneliness. "If you
didn't want us to agree to this treaty, you should have just
said so, Kurag, and saved us all the time and energy."

I patted his hand that still gripped my shoulder, but I'm not
sure he felt anything in that moment.

"Frost," Doyle said, "tend to Kitto."

Frost sheathed his sword and holstered his gun, moving to
kneel beside Kitto. In day-to-day arrangements Frost and
Doyle argued, but in an emergency all the guards obeyed
Doyle. Centuries of habit were hard to break.

Doyle spoke as he moved to stand beside us. "What is your
intention with this, Kurag?"

Siun said, "I wanted to see the pretty sidhe."

"Shut up, Siun." Kurag said it without looking at her, as if
he just expected her to do it. Surprisingly, she did.

"I felt Merry deserved to see what you were offering her
up to." Something close to his usual leer crossed his face.
"Besides, Darkness, it won't be Merry in Siun's bed."

"It won't be anybody," Rhys said.

Doyle touched his arm. "You cannot intend that she will
bed either Rhys or Kitto again."

"You volunteering?" Kurag asked.

Doyle blinked at him, unreadable. "What are you saying, Kurag?"

"If I agree to an extra month for every goblin you make sidhe, then you must agree to bring over every sidhe-side who wants to try it."

Doyle's black gaze flicked to Siun, then up to Kurag. "Why are you fighting this, Kurag? Why don't you want magic in the veins of the goblins again?"

"I'm not fighting it, Darkness, I'm agreeing to it, on certain conditions. I'm even giving Merry her month per goblin whom she brings over."

Doyle made a small gesture toward Siun. "To insist that we bed all who come our way is an insult."

"Would she be like this if one of your people hadn't raped one of ours?"

"Her mother wasn't raped," Rhys said, and his voice was still empty, still horrible to hear.

Kurag ignored the comment, but Doyle said, "What do you mean, Rhys?"

"She bragged that her mother had raped one of us during the last war." His hands dug into my shoulders until it almost hurt. "Don't blame this particular horror on the sidhe, Kurag. The goblins did this to themselves."

It was plain on Kurag's face that he had known the truth. "You have lied to us, Kurag," Doyle said.

"No, Darkness, I said, *Would she be like this if one of your people hadn't raped one of ours?* I made it a question, not a statement of fact."

"That is splitting the truth a wee thin," I said.

Kurag looked at me. He nodded. "Perhaps I have learned from the sidhe just how thin the truth may come."

"What's that supposed to mean?" Rhys said.

Doyle held up his hand. "Enough of this. Either we are going to agree to Kurag's terms, or we walk away and have the goblins for another two months, and only two months."

"I'll give you time to talk among yourselves," Kurag said. He raised a hand as if he'd wipe the mirror.

"No," Doyle said, "no, if we give you time you'll come up

with some other reason to avoid this agreement. We do it now, today."

I looked at Doyle and could read nothing from his face, or his body. He was the untouchable Darkness, the left hand of the queen. The figure I'd feared as a child. Though admittedly I'd never seen him this unclothed. The Queen's Darkness wore clothes from his neck to his ankles to his wrists, all year, all weather. Once to see Doyle's bare arms had been tantamount to him being undressed in public, but here he stood wearing only the tiny black thong, and somehow clothes or no clothes, he was still the same untouchable, unreadable, frightening Darkness.

"Which of you will bed Siun?" Kurag asked.

"I will," Doyle said.

I was the one who said, "No."

"None of us touches her," Rhys said.

"We will make this agreement, Rhys," Doyle said.

Rhys was shaking his head. "No, I swore that I'd kill Siun when next we met. I swore blood price on it."

"You swore blood price?" Doyle asked.

Rhys only nodded.

Doyle sighed. "We agree to trying to bring over all the half-sidhes you have, Kurag, but this Siun must answer to Rhys when we come to your court."

"What if she kills him?" Kurag asked.

"Then the blood price is satisfied. We will not seek vengeance for it."

"Done," Kurag said.

"And after I have killed Rhysss," Siun said, "I will have his trull, my Kitto. I will ride him till he shines underneath me." She glared at Rhys with her dozen eyes, all ringed with blue, sky blue, cornflower, and violet. The eyes were lovely, and belonged in a different body. "Thisss one wouldn't shine for me. If you'd have glowed underneath me, I wouldn't have taken your eye."

"I told you then, and I tell you now. You can force yourself on me, but you can't make me enjoy it. You're a lousy lay."

She swarmed off the chair and was suddenly filling the mirror, as if she'd grown larger, all those legs reaching for us, those hands, and that strange half-formed mouth. She battered at the glass with her limbs and shrieked, "I will kill you, Rhysss, and the princessssss will not save Kitto. I will have him, and I'll make him sssshine for me!"

Kitto screamed from the far side of the bed. We all turned and looked at him. His face was pale, his blue eyes huge in his face. He flung out his right hand as he screamed, "Noooo!"

Rhys flung us both off the bed a second before I felt the spell shiver through the air above us. It was as if the glass had melted, and Siun began to slide through that melting. Head, one arm, her other arm flailing, searching for something to hold on to. She slid farther, fighting the fall, and not able to stop it.

Kitto put both hands in front of him as if to ward her off, and he screamed again, wordless this time, pitched high with terror.

Rhys pressed me to the carpet, covering my body with his. There was more screaming, and not all of it was Kitto's. Doyle's voice said, "Let the princess up, Rhys." He sounded puzzled.

Rhys went to his knees, looking around the room, then staring toward the glass, and it was Doyle's hand that helped me to my feet.

Frost was holding Kitto, rocking him as you'd comfort a child. I turned to look where Rhys was staring.

Siun had stopped sliding through the mirror. Half her long black legs were on this side of the glass, and the other half were still back with Kurag. One of her hands reached into this room; the other was beating on the glass on the other side, as if trying to break it. She was cursing low and steady. She tried to struggle free, flashing her breasts in the sunlight, but she was trapped. If she'd been mortal, she'd have died, but she wasn't mortal, and she wasn't dying. She was just stuck.

Doyle went close to the glass, but stayed out of the reach of Siun's struggling legs. "It seems solid now."

Kurag spoke on his end of the glass. "Now isn't this a bitch of a predicament?"

"Yes," Doyle said.

"Can you fix it?" Kurag asked.

Doyle glanced at Kitto, who seemed nearly catatonic in Frost's arms. "It was Kitto's magic. He could reverse it, if he understood how. But no one else in this room can do this."

"What by the Consort's horns did Kitto do?" Kurag was close to the mirror on his side, looking at it, but carefully not touching the glass.

"Some sidhe can travel through mirrors, and most can speak through them. Though I've never heard of any who could travel over this many miles." Doyle was studying the mirror and the trapped goblin as if it were a purely academic problem and he was trying to figure out how it worked.

"Can Kitto undo it?"

"Frost," Doyle said, "ask Kitto if he will free her from the mirror, send her back."

Frost spoke low to the smaller man in his lap. Kitto shook his head violently, huddling in against Frost. "He's afraid that if he opens the mirror again, she'll fall through into this room."

"Just push her back this way," Kurag said.

Frost answered, "He says she can stay in the mirror until she rots."

"She won't rot." Kurag turned back to Doyle. "She's not mortal, Darkness, she won't die." He tapped the glass lightly. "This will not destroy her."

"Well, she can't just stay in the mirror like this," I said. I wasn't sure what we were going to do, but I knew just leaving her there wasn't an option.

"Actually, Meredith, she could," Doyle said.

I shook my head. "I don't mean that it's not possible, Doyle, I mean it's not acceptable. I don't want her in my bedroom mirror like some living trophy mounted on a wall."

"I understand." He looked at the trapped goblin. "I will

entertain suggestions, but in honesty, I do not see an easy solution."

"Could we break the mirror?" Kurag asked.

"That would likely cut her into pieces."

"It won't kill her," Kurag said.

"No, no breaking," Siun said.

Everyone ignored her.

"But it might leave one piece on your side of the mirror and one on our side of the mirror," Doyle said. "Can your goblins heal such a terrible wound?"

Kurag frowned. "They won't die of it."

"But once we cut her in two, can she be put back together, or will she live bisected?"

Siun started to push and pull harder. "No breaking the mirror, damn it!"

I couldn't really blame her for that, but it was one of those problems that even among the fey was so peculiar you couldn't really be horrified by it, not yet. Seeing her stuck in the mirror didn't even seem quite real.

"Well, if we can't break the mirror, I'm damned if I know what to do," Kurag said.

Holly came up close to the glass. He touched Siun's body where it went into the glass. He didn't hurt her, but she complained as if he had. Holly's voice came out awed: "Kitto did this. I saw him. I felt the magic race across my body like crawling wind." He traced his hands around Siun where she entered the mirror.

"Ssstop touching me," she said.

Holly looked out at us. "I will agree to what my brother wants. I will come to the princess, if there is a chance to gain such power." He gazed at the mirror, and Siun's body. Then his crimson eyes found mine. "We will come to you, Princess." He looked at me, and there was something close to lust in his gaze, but it wasn't the lust of flesh. It was the lust for power. It's a colder wanting, but it can lead to warmer things, hotter things, dangerous things.

"We will see you all at the banquet, Holly," I said. Saying *I look forward to seeing you* would have been a lie.

"We will see you there," Ash said.

"Let us be clear, Kurag," I said. "A month for every goblin we make sidhe."

"Agreed," he said.

"And let us also be clear on this," Doyle said. "There are other ceremonies that can bring sidhe into their power. Not all of them are sexual."

"Blood combat, you mean?" Kurag said.

"That, and the great hunts, the great quests."

"There is no more great hunt, Darkness, and the quests are over. We have not the magic for either."

"Perhaps, Kurag, but I want the options open to us."

"If it does not cost them their lives, then you may bring my goblins over as you see fit. In truth, Holly is not the only one who would rather not bed a sidhe." He grinned then, a pale imitation of his usual leer. "None of you has enough extra body parts to be handsome."

"Oh, Kurag," I said, "you ol' flatterer."

"I want one thing very clear," Ash said. "For my brother and I it will be sex with Princess Meredith, or nothing."

"Brother, we do not have to do this," Holly said.

Ash shook his head, his blond hair sliding around his shoulders. "I want it." He looked at his brother, and something passed between them, some message that I couldn't read. "I will lie with her, Holly, and where I go, you go."

"I don't like it."

"Don't like it, just do it," Ash said.

Holly gave a small nod.

Ash smiled at us. "We will see you at the banquet, Princess."

"Agreed," I said.

"What about me?" Siun half screamed, half whined.

I shrugged. "I have no idea how to fix this."

"Nor I," Kurag said.

"I know how to fix it." Rhys rose from his knees to stand over Siun. She slashed at him with her spined legs. He jerked out of reach, and laughed. It was a strange laugh, pleasant and unpleasant at the same time.

"How?" Doyle asked.

"I claim blood price on Siun here and now."

"Killing her will not rid her from the mirror," Doyle said.

Rhys nodded. "Yes, it will." He stood over the goblin, just out of reach of her one arm and frantic legs. "I saw this done once on purpose to trap an enemy. Once he was dead, the mirror closed and each side of the glass got the parts on its side, but the mirror was whole."

Siun struggled, beating against the glass, her spined legs making great white scratches in the varnished wood of the vanity. "No," she said.

"The last time we were together it was me who was trapped and helpless. I don't think you like it any better than I did."

She lashed out at him, the black spike on the side of one leg striking the wood so hard it stuck, and Siun had to struggle to free the leg.

"Temper, temper, Siun," Rhys said.

"Damn you, Rhysss."

"If she curses any of us," Doyle said, "then we will trade curses with the goblins. The sidhe are much stripped of their power, but you still do not want to trade curses with us, Kurag."

"If she curses again, you can cut off her ungrateful head," Kurag said.

Siun's scream sounded more from anger and frustration than fear. I don't think she feared death here and now. I couldn't blame her. There were very few things that could cause death to the immortal of the fey. It took a great deal of magic invoking mortal blood, or a special weapon. We were fresh out of both.

Rhys stepped out of reach of Siun's struggles and turned to Kitto. "Frost, give Kitto your short sword."

Frost looked at Doyle. Kitto didn't even bother looking up.

"What are you about, Rhys?" Doyle asked.

Rhys walked around the bed to Frost and Kitto. He knelt so that he was at eye level with the smaller man. He stroked Kitto's hair until he turned his head and looked at Rhys. "I was with her for only a few hours, Kitto. I cannot imagine what it was like to belong to her for months."

Kitto's voice came hoarse, but clear. "Years."

Rhys held the smaller man's face between his hands, and pressed their foreheads against each other. He spoke low, and I could no longer understand all the words; only the tone was still clear: persuading, sympathetic, cajoling.

"Do not ask this of him, Rhys," Frost said.

Rhys looked up at the bigger man, his hands still holding Kitto's face. "The only way to cleanse yourself of a fear is to face it, Frost. We will face it together, he and I."

Kitto nodded, his face still held between Rhys's hands.

"Give him your short sword, Frost, or I'll go fetch him one." There was something in Rhys's face, some command, some strength that hadn't been there before. Whatever it was, Frost responded to it. He sat Kitto on the edge of the bed and stood up. He reached underneath his suit coat and came away with a sword that wasn't much longer than a large knife. In Frost's hands it looked too small. He offered it hilt-first to Kitto.

Kitto hesitated, then reached a tentative hand for it. The guards had been teaching him weapons skills. He had some, but goblin tactics relied on strength and body mass. It wasn't the right approach for someone Kitto's size. He was learning to use his body the way it was meant to be used, but he was still hesitant in practice, as if he didn't trust himself yet.

He wrapped his small hands around the hilt, and it was big enough for both of them to hold it, one above the other. He stared down at the naked blade as if it might turn in his hands and bite him.

Rhys knelt out of sight and came back up with a sheathed sword from under the bed. We kept weapon caches throughout the house, just in case. But I guess there wasn't anything short enough to fit Kitto's hands under the bed.

Rhys walked back around the bed with a hand on Kitto's shoulder, half guiding and half pushing. Kitto began to hang back as they rounded the bed. The short sword drooped in his hands.

Siun began to yell, "Kurag, my king, you can't let them do this."

"Calling me king will not help you now, Siun."

"Help me, Kurag, help me. Would you ssstand idly by while ssidhe ssslay your goblin?" She held out the one white hand that was on his side of the mirror as far as it would stretch, beseeching.

Kurag sighed. "Is there anything I can offer you, white knight? A wergild price to replace her life."

"I won't die, Kurag," Siun said. "They can cut me up, but I won't die!"

"She's right, pale prince, you cannot truly slay her."

Kitto had stopped, refusing to go closer to Siun than the last corner of the bed. Short of Rhys picking him up bodily and carrying him the last few feet, Kitto was not getting closer.

Rhys left him where he was and moved to the mirror, just out of reach of Siun's struggling limbs. He stared down at the trapped goblin, and there was a distant look on his face, a remembering. "Leave the killing to me, Kurag," he said.

"Name something I am willing to offer, pale prince, and I will pay wergild for her. Surely there is something you would trade for?" Kurag had stepped just behind Siun. He stroked her black-furred back, a soothing gesture.

"Her life is all I want, Kurag," Rhys said.

A look of both pleasure and worry crossed Kurag's face, as if he wasn't sure whether it would be too much. His voice was careful as he began, "The life of one of the male goblins who enjoyed your company. Would that be worth Siun's life?" He kept his face and voice as neutral as he could, but there was an eagerness to his orange-yellow eyes that said he enjoyed Rhys's discomfort. I doubt that Kurag had watched Rhys used by men for the sex show, but for the power, for the sight of the mighty thrown low, oh, yes, Kurag had enjoyed that.

Rhys's face clouded with the beginnings of anger, but he smoothed it away. He turned a thoughtful face to Kurag. "Is there some male in particular you'd offer in Siun's place?"

Now it was Kurag's turn to look thoughtful. "You remember any names?" His smile was close to his usual leer.

"Most wanted me to know who it was that would use me. I remembered Siun's name."

Kurag nodded, and his face sobered again, almost as if he'd said something he would take back if he could. There had to be a male among those who'd been with Rhys whom Kurag hated, or saw as a threat. That was the only thing that made sense. For the Goblin King to admit that anyone was a threat meant it was serious, maybe even dangerous. Goblins did not assassinate each other. It was considered cowardice. A king who resorted to letting others do his killing could be executed. But if Rhys did it now, as a wergild price, then Kurag would be blameless. Still, the fact that Kurag had suggested the name—that would be taken badly. So he stopped short of names. He would not name.

"Then name someone, white knight, name someone."

Rhys shook his head. "If you had asked me to name the one goblin I wanted most to kill, it would be Siun." He gestured at the trapped goblin as he said the last. "No one else's death will satisfy."

"What if the Goblin King could offer something other than a death?" Doyle asked.

Kurag looked at Doyle, but Rhys had eyes only for Siun. "What would you have, Darkness?"

Doyle allowed himself a small smile. "What would you offer?"

Rhys shook his head, and I knew what he was going to say before he said it. "No, Doyle, no, I want this death. I won't trade it away." He looked back at the tall, dark man, met Doyle's unhappy gaze. "I am sorry, but not for politics. I won't trade this death away for just politics."

"And if it could gain us some advantage for Meredith?"

He frowned, then finally shook his head. "No." He looked at me, where I stood almost forgotten by the bed. "I'm sorry, Merry, but I will have this death." He turned back to Doyle. "Trust me, Doyle, Siun dead will help us more than Siun alive."

Doyle made a push-away gesture. "As you will."

Rhys held his hand out to Kitto, who still stood frozen by the bed. "Come on, Kitto, let's do this."

Kitto was shaking his head over and over. "Can't," he finally said.

"Yes, you can," Rhys said. He waggled his hand at him. "Come."

Doyle held his hand out to me. "Come, Meredith, let's put you out of the line of—fire." He hesitated over the last word as if he would have said something else. I went to him, stepping carefully between Kitto and Rhys, and the naked blade in Kitto's hand.

Rhys unsheathed the sword in his hand and flung the empty sheath toward Doyle, who caught it without looking, with his free hand. The other hand stayed in mine, and there was the faintest dew on his palm. Doyle was nervous. Why?

I was missing something. I had no idea what, but if it made Doyle nervous, it was probably a bad thing to miss. I was princess here, which meant I was supposed to be the ruler, but as so often seemed to happen, I was out of my depth. If I hadn't had the touch of Doyle's hand in mine, I would never have suspected he was nervous. That meant the goblins didn't know it at all. We needed to keep it that way.

Rhys raised the long silver blade up over his head for a great downward strike. Siun pleaded, "My king, my king, help me!"

"I offered you his sex and his flesh, Siun. I didn't tell you to maim him." Kurag stroked her furry back one last time, then stepped back. "If you can kill sidhe, do it, but don't fuck them up and leave them alive, because they never forget, and they never forgive." He looked at Rhys. "She's yours." He didn't sound happy about it, but he wasn't brokenhearted, either. I don't think he cared for Siun one way or the other. He'd tried to save her because she was one of his people, nothing more.

Siun tried to plead with Rhys, but to raise her one arm up to him she had to stretch her body upward. Her pale breasts flashed, and a look came over Rhys's face, a look that I never, ever wanted to see directed at me. "Do you remember what you made me do with those?" he asked, in a voice that seemed to burn through the room.

"No," she said, and she held out that arm, opened that mouth, and begged.

"I do," Rhys said, and the blade flashed down. The sword bit into the back of her body with a sound like cracking plastic, and that sound alone let me know that whatever skeletal system Siun had, it wasn't sidhe. But the blood was still red. Rhys chopped at her like you'd fight a tree that couldn't fight back. One of her black legs with its dagger-like spurs slashed through his robe to the skin beyond. The second slash was down his side, and it made him hesitate, clutching at the wound.

Kitto was suddenly there, his clean silver blade catching a leg before it could slice at Rhys. He severed the leg with one blow, and it went spinning onto the carpet at our feet. Doyle moved me farther away from them, and I didn't argue.

Frost started to cross the room, to join the fight, I think. Doyle stopped him with the sheath of Rhys's sword, held like a barrier. He shook his head twice, and Frost stood beside us, one hand holding his other wrist, as if he had to hold something if he couldn't fight.

Kitto was screaming, a high, maddened wail. It was a battle cry of sorts, but the battle cry of the damned, the lost, the wounded, risen up to smite their masters. The sound raised the hair at my neck and made me huddle against Doyle's body. He hugged me to him, wordless, his eyes on the fight.

Rhys stepped back from the body. He leaned against the wall, favoring his wounds, letting the gore drip down his sword. The front of his robe was soaked with Siun's blood and his own. A splatter of crimson stained the side of his face and his white hair. He didn't seem tired; he had just stopped fighting. Was he hurt?

Kitto alone struggled with the goblin, chopping and slicing, whittling her away a piece at a time. She'd tried to protect her head, rolling it under her body in a way that no human shape could have done, but Kitto split her head wide in a fountain of blood and thicker things. And still she lived.

Kitto was covered in blood and gore nearly from forehead to feet. His blue eyes looked so blue, it was like watching blue fire pool in a mask of blood.

I looked at Rhys, who was just leaning against the wall. He had to be hurt. I started to go to him, but Doyle held me back, shook his head.

"We have to help Kitto then," I said.

Doyle just shook his head, his face grim.

I grabbed his arm. "Why not?" I turned back to watch Kitto struggling with the dagger-like legs that slashed and fought even as he cut them away. The goblin could still hurt him badly.

For the first time I wished Doyle had been wearing a shirt, so I could shake him by it. "He'll get hurt."

Doyle hugged me against his body, and it wasn't exciting as it had been earlier, with Rhys, it was irritating. "Let me go."

He leaned close and whispered against my face, "It is Kitto's kill, Merry, let him have it."

I stood pressed to his body, and didn't understand. It wasn't Kitto's kill, it was Rhys's. Then I looked at Rhys standing there, doing nothing. He watched Kitto. I remembered then what I'd forgotten. When my first hand of power had come in unexpectedly, Doyle had made me give true death to the hag I'd accidentally turned into a mass of living flesh. The hand of flesh is just that, it can take flesh and turn it inside out—a leg, an arm, a whole body. He gave me the choice of killing her, or leaving her like some inside-out ball of flesh forever. She'd never die, just remain. Even with a sword that was capable of giving death to the immortal, the blood had soaked through my clothes to my underwear. I'd been covered in it. When it was done, Doyle had informed me that you needed to bloody yourself in combat after the first hand of power manifests so that it would come again, a sort of blood sacrifice. I'd hated him for making me do that. I hated him and Rhys now, for doing the same to Kitto.

Kitto gave his war cry until his voice broke. He chopped and sliced on the body until he couldn't raise his arms higher than his waist, and fell to his knees on the blood-soaked carpet. He gasped for air, and it was almost loud enough to drown out Siun's high-buzzing scream.

Rhys looked at Doyle, who nodded. Rhys pushed away from the wall and walked wide around what was left of the goblin. He knelt in the blood and hugged Kitto to him. I wondered if he was saying the same ritual words that Doyle had spoken to me that night.

Rhys got to his feet and saluted Kitto with his own bloody sword, then turned to what was left of the goblin. "You have made a mess of her," Kurag said, "but she will not die for you."

Rhys held his sword loosely in one hand, the other hand held out toward the main body that was left. He touched her furred back with his finger, and spoke one word, his voice clear and ringing like a soft bell. *"Die,"* he said, and the body stopped moving. The pieces on the floor that had been wriggling lay still. It was as if Rhys pressed a button. He said, *Die,* and she died.

Doyle made a sound like a quiet hiss, and I forgot to breathe for a second or two. No sidhe could kill by just a touch and a command. Our magic didn't work that way.

"Consort bless us," Frost whispered.

There were hushed oaths from the younger goblins, but Kurag's voice when it came was deep with weariness. "The last time I saw you do that, it was before the last great war, white prince," he said.

Rhys stood there in his bloody terry-cloth robe, splattered with gore, and said, "Why do you think the goblins almost won that one?" There was a look on his face, a set to his body, that I'd never seen before. It was as if he took up more room than his physical form; as if he were taller than the room could hold, and his presence filled everything for a moment. It was as if all the air had become Rhys's magic.

The moment passed, and I could breathe again, and the air felt sweet and cool, and better than it had a moment ago. I leaned against Doyle's body for support, as if my knees were weak. A second ago I'd been angry with him for forcing Kitto to fight alone; now I huddled against him. I think I would have clung to anyone in that moment. I needed the touch of other flesh, other hands.

Once the goblin was dead, the corpse fell into pieces on either side of the mirror. The mirror was whole again. The goblins agreed to everything we wanted. Rhys blanked the mirror and turned, his robe more red than white. The blood had stained his white hair and skin, like red ink sprinkled on him. Where the blood touched his skin and hair, the red seemed to glow. That shining blood began to vanish, as if his very skin absorbed it, until he stood straight and clean, and untouched, except for the bloody robe. His blue eye was a whirl of colors, like looking into the center of some sky-colored storm.

Doyle used the sword sheath in his hand to salute, and Frost drew his long sword. They both touched their foreheads, but it was Doyle who said it. "Hail, Cromm Cruach, who slew Tigernmas, Lord of Death, for his pride and his crimes against the people."

Rhys raised his bloody sword, saluting them in turn. "It's good to be back." His solemn bloodstained face broke into his usual grin. "Blood makes the grass grow, rah, rah, rah."

"I always thought it was sex that made the grass grow," Galen said from the doorway, and we all turned around to look at him. Except for Kitto, who seemed lost in the blood-covered aftermath of his powers coming online.

Galen moved into the room just enough to lean against the wall. He looked tall and cool, from the top of his short, curling pale green hair—with its one tiny braid that played over his shoulder like an afterthought—to his broad shoulders, slender waist, and hips in their cream-colored suit. The white open-necked shirt brought out the slight green tint to his skin so that he looked more like the fertility god he would probably have been, had he been born a few hundred years earlier. His long legs in their loose slacks ended in brown loafers worn without socks. He leaned against the wall, arms crossed, a smile shining from his face that lit his grass-green eyes like jewels, not from magic, but from sheer goodwill—sheer Galen. He looked cool and pleasant, like some pale green liquid that you knew would quench whatever thirst you had.

I went to him, partly to bestow a welcoming kiss, and partly because I could rarely be in a room with Galen and not touch him. Touching him was like breathing; I'd done it so long, I didn't remember how to stop—not and live. The fact that he and I had been lovers for a month and I'd just finished bleeding our hopes of a child away had been both painful, and a relief. I loved Galen, had loved him from the time I was twelve or thirteen. Unfortunately, now that I was all grown up I finally realized what my father had tried to tell me years ago. Galen was strong, brave, joyous, my friend, and he loved me, but he was also the least politically savvy sidhe I'd ever met. Galen as king would be a disaster. I'd lost my father to assassins when I was young. I didn't think I could live through losing anyone else to them, especially not Galen. So part of me wanted to have him in my bed forever, my lover, my husband, but not my king. But my king would be whoever got me pregnant. No baby, no marriage; it was the way of sidhe royalty.

I wrapped my arms around Galen, sliding my arms underneath his jacket, where it held the warmth of his body, pulsing against my arms even through his shirt. I cuddled my face to his chest as his arms held me close. I hid my face from his gaze, because more and more lately I couldn't keep the worry out of my eyes. Galen was hopeless politically, but he understood my moods better than most, and I didn't want to explain these particular facts of life to him, not just yet.

His voice rumbled through his chest against my ear. "Maeve is back from her meeting with the heads of the studio. She's having a crying fit in her room."

Doyle said, "I take it the meeting didn't go well."

"The studio isn't happy that she's pregnant. Publicly they're thrilled, but behind closed doors they're pissed. How is she going to do her next movie, which is a very sexy role with nudity, when she'll be three or four months' pregnant at the time?"

I drew away from him enough to look up into his face.

"Are you serious? As much money as she's made these people over the last decade, and they can't let one movie slide?"

Galen shrugged with his arms still wrapped around me. "I only report the news, I don't explain it." He frowned, and the happiness slipped out of his eyes. "I think if her husband wasn't dead . . . I mean, they seemed to imply that she could get pregnant some other time."

I gave him wide eyes. "An abortion?"

"They never said it out loud, but it was there in the air." He shivered and hugged me so close I couldn't see his face anymore. "When Maeve reminded them that her husband was dead barely a month, and this would be the only chance she had to have his baby, they apologized. They said they never meant to imply any such thing. They sat there and lied." He kissed the top of my head. "How could they do that to her? I thought she was their big star."

I hugged him tighter, pressing myself against his body as if I could take that hurt out of his voice. "Maeve dropped two movies while her husband died of cancer. I guess they were looking forward to having their cash cow back at work."

Galen laid his chin against my hair. "I couldn't imagine doing what they did to her today, to anyone, for any reason. They were all hints, and looks, and never just saying what they meant, and then outright lies." He shivered again. "I don't understand that."

And that was the problem. Galen truly didn't understand how anyone could be so mean. To survive in most arenas of power you must first understand that everyone lies, everyone cheats, and no one is your friend. The paradox is that not everyone lies, and not everyone cheats, and some people are your friends. The problem lies in the fact that one smiling face and handshake looks much like another, and when you're surrounded by consummate liars, how to tell the truth from the lie, friend from foe? Better to treat everyone professionally, pleasantly, smile, nod, be friendly, but never be friends. Because there is no way to tell who is on your side, not really. Galen couldn't grasp that concept. I needed someone who could.

I turned my face enough to see Doyle standing on the other side of the room. He was cool and dark, but he reminded me not of a drink that would quench my needs, but rather a weapon that would protect all I loved.

I stood there wrapped in Galen's arms, but my eyes were for Doyle, and Frost watched us all. Frost, whom I'd begun to love for the first time. Frost who had finally figured out he needed to be jealous of Galen, and had always been jealous of Doyle. The fey are not supposed to be jealous in the way humans are, but glancing into Frost's grey eyes, I was beginning to think that perhaps the sidhe had become more human than they realized.

Chapter 6

THE GOLDEN GODDESS OF HOLLYWOOD LAY CURLED INTO A
ball on top of the satin comforter that covered her round
king-sized bed. It was the bed she'd shared with the late Gordon Reed for more than twenty years. I'd suggested that
maybe she could move to a new bedroom until she got over
some of her grief. She'd given me a look so scathing that I'd
never suggested it again.

Her suit jacket, the color of goldenrods, lay forlorn on the
floor. The boots—made of leather so soft, it seemed to still
breathe on its own—were scattered, as if she'd thrown them
when she undressed. She was still wearing the slacks that
matched the jacket, and the copper-colored vest that had
been the only shirt she'd worn. The headband that had
matched the vest, perfectly, was the last thing dropped by the
bed. Her hair lay free and disarrayed across the edge of the
bed. The hair was still the color of soft butter, which meant
as upset as she was, she was still wasting magic for her glamour. The glamour that had let her pass for human for a hundred years since she was exiled from faerie. For fifty of those
years she'd been the golden goddess of Hollywood, Maeve
Reed. For untold centuries before that she'd been the goddess Conchenn.

Behind the closed door of the bedroom her personal assis-
tant was in tears, wringing her hands, helpless. Maeve had
kicked her out. Nicca had stood next to the door with his long
brown hair and pale brown skin. Even his eyes were brown.
He looked the most human of all the guards, when you
couldn't see the wing-shaped marks on the back of his body,

like the world's most elegant tattoo. There but for genetics Nicca would have had real wings. He apologized for being on this side of the door, but Maeve had clung to him a little too forcefully. She hadn't exactly made a pass, but she probably would have responded to one. Nicca thought discretion the better part of valor. I didn't blame him.

Maeve had been a goddess of love and spring. She was still more than capable of turning the charm on. *Charm* in the original sense of the word, a magic. She was alone in her big bed for the first time in decades. She was lonely, and she was a being of heat, the new life after the long winter. You can fight your basic nature, but under stress, it gets harder. Maeve was under a lot of stress.

The sound of her soft crying filled the room. I walked barefoot toward her. I'd tied my red peekaboo robe tight but hadn't taken time to change. Doyle and Rhys had stayed at the guesthouse to dress and help Kitto clean up. It left me with Frost standing rigid by the door, but he wouldn't come near the bed unless I made him. He didn't care for Maeve's teasing. Frost had been celibate for eight hundred years, give or take. He had coped with that punishment by not flirting, not playing any games. He'd been his namesake, cold, icy, frost.

Galen also stood by the door, but he was at ease, smiling. If Maeve had made polite overtures to him, he hadn't mentioned it. Either she'd started on Nicca only when they were alone in her bedroom, or Galen just didn't think it was important. I agreed with him. Nicca's panic had been odd, come to think of it.

I was beside the bed before I thought to wonder why Nicca had been so upset, or what she might have done. I said her name softly: "Maeve." I repeated it twice more, and there was no reaction. I touched her shoulder, and the crying increased, growing from something quiet to something that shook her shoulders, made her body quiver with its force.

I bent over her, hugging her, resting my cheek against the silk of her hair. "It's all right, Maeve, it's all right."

She twisted against me, turning so that I had to draw back to see her face. She'd dropped some of her glamour, because her eyes weren't the human blue that the movies saw, but the brilliant tricolor that was real. The wide outer edges were rich deep blue, and there were two thin circles around her pupils: one melted copper, the other liquid gold. But what made her eyes like no others was that the gold and copper trailed out across the blue of her irises like streaks of metallic lightning. Her eyes were lightning-kissed, as if the Goddess Herself had decreed she would have the most beautiful eyes in the world.

I stood by the bed, staring down into those eyes, lost for a moment in the wonder of them. Her tearstained face looked almost desperate. Had she lost control of her own glamour; had she not meant to show her eyes?

She grabbed my wrist, and I could feel the pulse in the tip of each of her fingers like tiny separate hearts, beating against my skin. I suddenly knew why Nicca had panicked. Maeve rose to her knees, hand still wrapped around my wrist. On her knees she was tall enough to bring our faces close together. I stood there immobile, frozen, not with indecision, but with power. Maeve's power.

It was as if a warm spring breeze trailed across my skin. I threw my head back and let that wind blow my hair away from my face. I opened my eyes and gazed down at Maeve, and watched the rest of her glamour fade away, as if the golden glow of her skin rose through her body. Her suddenly white-blond hair danced in the warmth of her power. Those glittering lines in her eyes flashed like a spring storm come to blow away the winter's sloth. It was as if my very skin lifted away like an old coat grown too tight. I felt like some animal that had shed its shape for something lighter, something that should have been able to fly.

My skin glowed as if I'd swallowed the moon. The stray bits of my hair that danced around my face glowed like garnets and rubies spun out into something glittering and alive. I felt my eyes begin to glow, and knew that they shone as if

some hand had cut an emerald, a piece of jade, and the gold
that held them together, and set them with his own personal
fire.

Her power stripped me of all my glamour, even the last
bits that I kept almost constantly. The dark hand-shaped scar
just under my breast, over my ribs, bloomed to life, like a
dark imperfection against all that glowing light. That scar
marked where another Unseelie sidhe had tried to use her
magic to crush my heart. She'd broken my ribs, torn muscles, but not the muscle she wanted to tear. I knew that if the
black hand mark over my ribs was visible, the marks on my
back would be, too. They were scars, but not the kind of
scars that a human would understand, or even most fey. Another duel gone bad, where a fellow Unseelie had tried to
force a shape change on me in the middle of the fight. It
wouldn't have killed me. He had been playing with me.
Showing off his superior magic, and my lack. I'd driven a
blade into his heart, and he'd died. He'd died because the rituals surrounding duels were based on blood rituals: his and
mine. Mortal blood makes immortals weak. It's an old bit of
magic, and it was all that had saved me.

I hid my scars even in the midst of magic. Imperfections
aren't popular among the sidhe. Being stripped bare of that
last bit of hiding made me try to pull away from her, brought
something of myself back. I had closed my eyes because I
did not want to see the look of revulsion. I was able to say,
"Maeve," but when I opened my eyes, I found her face almost touching mine. I had a moment of staring into her eyes
from so close that they seemed to fill the world for a moment,
a glittering, broken world full of storm and wind and color.
She licked her lips, and that one small movement drew my
gaze. I'd never noticed how full her lips were, how moist,
how pink. Her mouth glistened like some succulent pink
fruit, and I knew that it held warm juice that would run down
my mouth, my throat. I could almost taste it, almost feel it.

I tasted her breath upon my mouth, so sweet, like new
grass fresh-sprouted from the earth. Our lips touched, and
the world was suddenly filled with the perfume of blossoms.

I was drowning in apple blossoms as if I'd fallen into some enchanted orchard, where it was always spring, always new, always possible.

I saw Maeve sitting under a tree in full blossom. There was a hill behind her, and she wore a gown the green-gold of new leaves, with hints of white linen at her bosom and wrist. The linen seemed to glow like white feathers in the sunlight. Her hair fell to her knees like a fall of white frothing water. Her skin was carved of the sunlight itself; golden and shining so bright I could not look upon her, yet even as I felt my eyes begin to burn, I could not look away.

It began to snow. The warmth began to fade, and the blossoms fell from the tree in a shower of white and pink, and the snow dotted the grass. Cold, it was so cold. I was lying on my back, staring up into Frost's face. He looked worried, and his eyes held that falling snow. I stared into that snow, and again I had the sense that there was someplace behind the snow. That if I stared long enough I'd see it. But I wasn't afraid this time. I knew he'd called me back, saved me somehow. I felt his strong hands on my arms, the press of his body against mine, and I wasn't afraid.

I saw Frost standing at the foot of a snow-covered hill, except the hill was his cloak, a cloak of snow, that moved with him. His hair glistened like ice in the sun, and his skin was the brilliance of snow when the sun dances on it. A brilliance that would blind as surely as staring at the sun itself.

The cloak of snow opened, as if Frost had spread his arms, and there was a soothing darkness underneath all that white. It was a still winter's night when the world waits, holding its breath. I stood in that soothing darkness, and I wasn't cold, though I knew that I was ankle-deep in the snow. The moon rode full overhead and the snow lay white and glistening, but so much gentler than in the light of day. A figure seemed to form from the blue shadows of that winter silence. Smaller even than I, but not by much, with long thin arms and legs, longer than they should have been, if he had been human. But of course he wasn't human, had never been human.

He was dressed in rags, but those rags sparkled in the

moonlight to shame the brightest diamond. His skin was the blue of snow shadows in the moonlight. His face was that of a lovely child. His hair streamed behind him the color of silver frost. He held out a hand toward me that was so long-fingered, it held extra joints. He touched my cheek with those slender fingers, and his touch was warmer than it should have been. I stared down into those grey eyes, and smiled.

He turned from me then, and went dancing barefoot upon the snow. Where he passed, the snow remained pure and untouched, as if he weighed nothing. I understood now why we were here in the silent night. He was frost, truly frost. The hoarfrost that rimes the world, but only if it's still. Such delicate work cannot survive a stout wind.

I watched him dance away across the shining snow until he melded with a patch of blue moonshadow and vanished.

I came to myself one more time. Frost was still holding me, but this time there was no snow in his eyes; they were just grey, the grey of a winter's sky. His voice came strained, a whisper, as if he was afraid to speak. "You grew so cold. I was afraid . . ." He let whatever he was going to say trail away, then he pushed himself off me, abruptly, and walked away. He walked across the room, through the door, and left it swinging open behind him.

Galen crawled across the bed to sit beside me. He didn't touch me, though, which seemed odd. "Are you all right?" He wasn't smiling when he asked.

I had to think about the question, which usually meant no, I wasn't all right. Something had happened, but for my life, I wasn't sure what. It took me two tries to speak, and even then my voice sounded hoarse and strange. "What happened—" I swallowed, coughed, tried to clear my voice. "—just now?"

Maeve spoke from the far edge of the bed. "We're not entirely sure."

I looked at her. She was still the goddess Conchenn with her lightning-kissed eyes, long white-blond hair, and golden skin, but she didn't glow. She was gorgeous but her power had left her, for now.

She looked embarrassed, which you don't see in god-

desses that often. "It's my fault. I wanted the comfort of another sidhe's touch. I tried to seduce Nicca and it didn't
work." She gave me an arrogant face, but it left her eyes uncertain. "I'm not accustomed to being turned down by anyone I really want. I thought you might share one of your
men." She looked down again, then up, and she seemed more
determined than arrogant now. I didn't know if all actresses
did this, but Maeve Reed could go from one emotion to another at the blink of an eye, and they all seemed real. I didn't
know if she'd always been this moody, or if it had been the
job that had made her that way. "I know it was stupid and
thoughtless. You gave Gordon and me the chance to have a
child. Your magic, and Galen's, did that, Merry. I am an ungrateful wretch, and I am sorry."

"It's okay," I said, and still my voice sounded strained. My
throat was actually sore. I frowned up at Galen. "Why is my
throat sore?"

He glanced back, and Maeve met his eyes. They had one
of those moments that said, more clearly than any words,
something had happened, something I didn't remember, and
it had been bad.

"Just tell me." I raised a hand and touched his arm.

He jerked as if I'd bit him and moved out of reach. "Don't
touch me, Merry, not just yet."

"Why?" I asked.

"Look at the coverlet," he said, "near your head."

I turned my head and found a wide wet spot on the off-
white bedspread. I frowned, and didn't understand, until I
touched the wetness and found ice crystals in the water. I
frowned up at Galen. "Why is there melting ice on the bed?"

"Because you threw it up."

I stared at him, and wanted to ask if he was kidding, but
one look at his face and I knew he wasn't. "How, why?"

"That's the part we're not entirely sure of," Maeve said.

"Tell me the parts you are sure of."

She walked around the edge of the bed until she stood opposite me, but she made no move to get on the bed, or come
closer. "I tried to seduce you, and it worked, a great deal bet-

ter than I'd planned. I forget sometimes that you're part human. I used the power I'd use for another sidhe, another deity."

I nodded, and even that hurt my throat. "I remember that part, but then it changed, became something else. I saw you sitting under a tree, and it hurt my eyes to look at you."

"No mortal can look full upon the face of a god and survive," Galen said.

"What?" I asked.

Maeve leaned against the bed. "I was Conchenn for a moment. I was what I had been. I think I'd almost made myself forget. The loss of faerie is a new wound, Merry, compared to having lost my godhead."

I was getting a headache. "I'm not following this."

"Let me." Galen looked serious, determined, very un-Galen. "Maeve used her powers, or what was left of them, as the goddess Conchenn to try to seduce you. But you brought on more power. You brought her into her godhead again."

I gave him wide eyes. "I thought that once you gave up being a god you couldn't get it back."

"So did I, until today," Maeve said.

I frowned at her. "Besides, only the Goddess can make you a god."

"I believe that is still true," Maeve said. "But perhaps anyone can be a vessel for Her power."

"Not just anyone," Galen said. "If just anyone could have done it, it would have happened centuries ago." He looked at Maeve as if she'd been rude.

"You're right. You are right. I will not belittle the gift. I know the touch of the Goddess when I feel it."

"What goddess?" I asked.

"Danu." She said the word in a whisper that seemed to echo through the room.

I closed my eyes and took a deep breath, let it out, counted slow, took another breath. I opened my eyes. "I'm hearing things," I said. "I thought you said, *Danu*."

"I did."

I shook my head, and didn't even care that it hurt my

throat. "Danu is the Goddess whom the Tuatha De Danaan, the children of Dana, are named after. She's the Goddess. She was never personified."

"I never said she was a person," Maeve said. "I said that she gave me my godhead, and she did."

I frowned at her, the headache starting to pound between my eyes. "I don't understand."

"In the first treaty we ever signed with the Formorii, both sides worked the first weirding magic. We lessened ourselves lest our two races destroy the land that we now shared. Danu, or Dana, agreed to distance Herself from us for the great spell to be done." Maeve's eyes shimmered, and it was tears, not magic. "I don't think that any of us understood what we were giving up. Except perhaps Danu Herself." She sat on the edge of the bed and let the tears fall. This time I didn't think it was a bad day at work and baby hormones. I think she sat in the Southlands, on the edge of the Western Sea, and wept for a Goddess who had never seen America.

Chapter 7

DOYLE ENTERED THE ROOM AT A RUN, STILL WEARING NOTHING but the thong, his shoulder holster flapping loose over his bare chest, gun naked in his hand, and his power riding before him like a storm. Rhys was at his back, wearing white dress slacks and an unbuttoned shirt, a gun in his hand, no holster in sight. Rhys's power marched into the room on whispers, half heard.

They both stopped in the doorway, looking for something to shoot, I think. Nicca nearly ran into Rhys as he came through the door. He was more out of breath than either of the other two; of course, he'd had to run back and forth from the guesthouse to the main house, twice. He panted as he leaned against the doorjamb. "Not assassins. Magic . . . gone bad."

Doyle and Rhys visibly relaxed. Doyle holstered his gun, though he had to use his other hand to steady the holster because the straps weren't buckled on as they were supposed to be. Rhys just stood there, the gun slowly lowering beside his thigh. Both their powers receded like the ocean pulling back from the shore, like feeling it go down from def-con 1 to def-con 3.

I just lay on the bed and watched them, because trying to sit up had hurt my chest. It felt as if I'd swallowed something down the wrong way. Something very big and very solid, so that I ached all around my ribs. Other than that I didn't feel bad. It seemed like I should feel tired if I'd actually done what Maeve and Galen had said I'd done. Shouldn't you be tired when you make a god? If that's what had happened.

Since that was impossible, I was still waiting for an alternate theory that I could buy. If anyone could come up with one, it would be Doyle. For a high royal of the court of faerie, he was a very practical man.

He came to stand beside the bed. I realized that he was wet from the waist down as if he'd waded in the swimming pool, but there was no smell of chlorine. I remembered Kitto, then. He'd been helping the little goblin clean up. I'd forgotten about him coming into his hand of power today. A future queen shouldn't forget things like that, should she? Maybe I wasn't thinking as clearly as I thought I was.

"Kitto, how is he?" I asked.

Doyle smiled. "He's fine. A little confused, but he'll be fine." The smile faded around the edges. "How are you?"

I frowned. "Not sure." My voice still sounded harsh, but it was getting better, sounding more like me. "I thought I was fine, but I'm not sure I'm thinking as clearly as I think I am. Does that make sense?"

He nodded and turned to Maeve and Galen. "What happened?"

They both started to talk at once, and he held up a hand. "Ladies first." He motioned her away from the bed, and they went to the far side of the bedroom to talk. The bedroom was almost bigger than my old apartment, so there was plenty of room for privacy. Rhys gave me a smile, then trailed them so he could hear.

That left Galen with me. He still hadn't touched me. I badly needed to be touched, to have that reassurance. "Why won't you touch me?"

He smiled down at me, but his hands were clasped in his lap. "Believe me, it's hard not to, but you touched Maeve and this major goddess energy came down, then Frost grabbed you to stop Maeve from using you, and it happened again, with him."

"Maeve using me?"

"We thought she'd called out her major-goddess-seductive powers on you. It wasn't until Frost used his power to break what we thought was her hold on you that we realized something else was happening." He started to reach out to touch my arm, then put his hand back in his lap. "I can feel how badly you need comforting, and Consort knows I want to hold you right now, but I'm afraid that if I touch you, it'll happen again."

"I don't buy that I brought on anyone's godhead," I said.

He nodded. "I know, but Maeve says she's had it done to her before. She should know what it feels like."

"I'm mortal, Galen. I'm the first sidhe ever to be born mortal, no matter how much mixed blood they had. Mortal hand cannot bring on immortal power. It's not logical."

He shrugged. "If you have a better explanation for what just happened, Merry, I will be happy to hear it." His green eyes, the color of summer grass, grew anxious. "I thought for a moment, Merry—" He shook his head, and bit his lip, before he could finish. "—I thought we'd lost you." He leaned over me, as if he'd kiss me, but was careful not to touch. "I thought I'd lost you."

I raised my hand to touch his face, and Doyle called from across the room. "Not yet, Princess. Let's be cautious until I've heard Galen's half of the story."

I lowered my hand reluctantly. I didn't like it, but it wasn't worth the risk, not yet. "Fine."

Galen smiled at me as he slid off the bed. "Just for now, Merry, just for now." He walked across the room toward the huddled group. He had a way of walking as if he danced, danced to some music that only he could hear. Sometimes when he held me, I could almost hear it; almost.

Nicca came to stand at the foot of the bed. He'd regained his breath, but he still looked scared. Intellectually, I knew he was centuries older than Galen, but he seemed younger than the other guards. Age in years doesn't always tell the tale. He looked very young, and very worried as he leaned his six-foot frame against the edge of the bed. His hair fell in a shining brown curtain nearly to his knees. He'd left it loose, and his deep brown dress slacks and suit jacket peeked through the richer brown of his hair. The hair framed the moss green of his T-shirt, so that I was more aware than normal of how nice his chest was. The T-shirt was silk, a gift from Maeve. She'd given all the men silk tees in varying colors to complement their skin tone. She'd given me a shopping spree at her favorite stores, on the theory that as a woman I'd be happier picking out my own clothes, and the men would rather have the choices made for them. She was half right. Though everyone had taken the gifts, they then traded the colors around among themselves until everyone was happy.

The moss-green shirt had originally been Galen's, but it looked better on Nicca, brought out the rich brown of his skin. It had just made Galen look green. That rich brown body in its tailored suit sat down on the far edge of the bed. He flipped his hair out of the way without thinking about it, the way a woman would. "You look better than you did a few minutes ago." His voice held an edge of shakiness.

"How did I look?"

He blinked at me and turned away as if he knew how easily his thoughts played across his face. "Pale, very, very pale." He looked back at me with what I think was supposed to be a poker face, but wasn't. There was too much tightness around his eyes, too much worry in their perfectly brown depths. He glanced toward the far side of the room. The huddle had broken up, and everyone was walking this way.

Doyle looked down at me, his face inscrutable darkness. I'd have played poker with Nicca or Galen any day, but never Doyle. When he didn't want me to read his face, I couldn't.

"Meredith, Princess, we need to understand what is happening, but I cannot think of a way to guarantee your safety and still explore this problem."

I tried to read something from his dark face, and couldn't. "What does that mean, exactly, Doyle?"

"It means that we must experiment, and I do not know what will come of those experiments."

"Experiment how?" I asked.

"Maeve believes that you have reawakened the true magic within her—her godhead, for lack of a better term. She was once a goddess in truth, so you have only returned what was lost. But Frost was not a deity, and to him you have given powers that never flowed within his body." He managed to look grim without ever having changed expression.

"She told me the theory. She even mentioned a goddess name to go along with it, but Doyle, I am not Danu. I am so not a deity. How could it possibly be true?"

"When we fought the Nameless and it spilled wild magic on all of us, I believe there were powers that needed a goddess-shaped vessel to hold them. Maeve had been taken to safety by the time the fight ended. You were the only goddess-shaped vessel, Meredith. You were the closest the power could find to what it needed."

I blinked up at him. I was tired of lying on the bed. If I was going to have to listen to tricky philosophical theories, the least I could do was not be flat on my back. I tried to sit up, winced, but kept at it. Nicca started to help me, but Doyle waved him back, then seemed to think better of it and motioned him to help me.

Nicca touched my arm, helped steady me, and it was just a warm touch. There was no magic to it, except the touch of skin to skin. Nicca fluffed pillows behind me so that I could sit propped up. When nothing happened at that first touch, he touched me where he needed to, until I was comfortable, or as comfortable as I was going to get.

"If Nicca's touch had caused another gathering of power, I don't know what we would have done, but if Nicca can touch you with impunity, then I think we should see how safe the rest of us are." He motioned, and Maeve stepped up beside him.

"Touch her."

Maeve looked at him as if she weren't accustomed to being ordered around. Then she took a deep breath and had to crawl on the edge of the bed to reach me. Maeve was not a short woman, and that spoke to how truly large the bed was.

She hesitated a moment, searching my face.

"Do it," I said.

She did. The palm of her hand was warm and dry and soft, but nothing more. There was no pull of magic to it. We both looked at Doyle, with her hand still pressed to my shoulder. "Nothing's happening," she said.

"Try a little flare of power," Doyle said.

"Do you think that's safe?" Rhys asked.

"We need to know," Doyle said.

"She's been through a lot today. As long as we can all touch her, I think we can wait on experimenting with power."

Doyle turned so that they were facing each other beside the bed. "It is your night with the princess tonight, Rhys. Do you really believe you can be with her and it not be a thing of power?"

Rhys glared up at him, the hand without the gun forming a fist. He was quiet for almost a full minute, then finally, reluctantly, he said, "No."

"None of us can be with her without it being a thing of power, Rhys. We must know now, while there are more of us to help, if our magic will bring this on again. Whatever it is."

"I have told you what it is, Doyle," Maeve said. "Why will none of you believe me?"

"I do not doubt you, Maeve, but godhead was always given as a gift, something earned. It was not accidental. Meredith did not bring this upon you and Frost deliberately." He looked at me, and raised an eyebrow. "You didn't, did you?"

"It would never have occurred to me to try," I said.

He turned back to Maeve, as if that satisfied him. "We must understand what brought this on, because we cannot afford to lose Meredith, even if it made the rest of us gods on high."

"Well then, you're going about it wrong," Maeve said.

Doyle looked at her, and I'd seen many a court noble wilt under that gaze. Maeve didn't even flinch. She put her arm around my shoulders and snuggled closer to me, a smile playing on her lips. "Danu's power wasn't called until we were kissing."

"Please stop saying that name," I said. I just couldn't keep hearing that the magic of the Goddess was inside me, even a little bit. I know in theory that we are all the Goddess, or rather images of Her divine perfection. Theory is one thing, though; actually having that kind of power and being able to use it is entirely different.

"Why?" Maeve asked, and she looked genuinely puzzled.

Galen raised his hand. "Ooh, I can answer this one."

Maeve turned puzzled eyes to him.

"Merry's creeped out that the Goddess climbed inside her."

"That's not it," I said.

"That the power of the Goddess is inside you," he said, and the teasing softened as he said it.

"Maybe awed more than creeped out," I offered.

"You should be honored," Maeve said, hugging me.

"I am honored," I said, "but this particular honor almost killed me."

Maeve's face looked suddenly solemn. "Yes, and it would have been my fault."

"No," I said.

"I played you with my magic, Merry. I tried to seduce you because all the men keep turning me down for you." She kissed the top of my head. "I thought, *If you can't beat them, join them*." She hugged me tight enough that I couldn't see her face when she said, "I want sidhe flesh, Merry. I want a glow to match my own to throw shadows on the walls in the dark." Her voice was fierce.

"Will you settle for a kiss?" I offered, my voice muffled against her shoulder.

She leaned back enough to show me a smile. "If it comes with magic, yes."

"I guess if it doesn't come with magic, we won't know if the Goddess energy will remanifest."

She smiled and raised a perfectly arched eyebrow. "I suppose not."

"Was it a kiss with power that did Frost as well?" Doyle asked.

"Yes," Maeve and Galen answered in unison.

"Frost freed her from Maeve's power, and then it was as if he couldn't help himself." Galen looked out into the room, as if he were visualizing what had happened. "This look came over his face just before he bent down and kissed her." He blinked and looked back at Doyle. "He looked bespelled."

"Where is he now?" Doyle asked.

No one knew the answer. "Queen's curse take it," Doyle said, "Nicca, Galen, find him, bring him here."

Nicca turned for the door, but Galen hesitated. "What if Merry needs us?"

"Go," Doyle said, "now." And the way he said it brooked no argument.

Galen gave me a last glance, then joined Nicca at the door, and they went through it at a jog.

"He just didn't want to miss the show," Rhys said.

"What show?" I asked.

He grinned at me. "Two of the most beautiful women I know locked in an embrace. There are people who would pay to watch."

I shook my head. Sitting by Maeve Reed, the epitome of Seelie beauty, I didn't feel beautiful. Something must have shown on my face because Maeve touched my chin, raised me to meet her eyes. "You are beautiful, Merry, and having once been a goddess of beauty, I should know."

"I look too human," I said softly.

"Why do you think our men have been stealing human women away for centuries? Because they're ugly?" She shook her head, and there was a soft chiding in her face. "Merry, Merry, know your worth." That gold light began to pulse inside her skin, as if someone had lit a candle deep within her and the light was growing closer, flowing through her body, until she glowed like the sun stretched inside her skin. The power shivered over me, sped my pulse, brought my own pale light gloaming through my skin so that I rose moon to her sun.

Her hair began to move in the wind, that warm wind. Her eyes filled with light, and again it was like staring into the heart of a spring storm, flashing with lightning, ripping the heavens apart, but instead of rain, it was her power that fell upon me. I turned my face up to that power as if it truly would rain down upon me.

Her hands curved over my bare skin, as if the bathing suit wasn't there. She held me in her arms, and I went willingly, my own hands sliding up the warm skin of her bare arms. It seemed wrong that she wore so many clothes. We needed to touch more skin than this. I realized that I was sensing Maeve's skin-hunger. Her need for sidhe flesh to cover her own. I remembered the hunger all too well, and it had only been satisfied for me four months back. So long, so lonely. I couldn't tell if it was my feelings or hers, and I knew that that was part of her magic. To project her needs and make them my own.

I reached for the buttons on her vest, but they were too small, too hard to open. I got two fistfuls of cloth and yanked. The buttons went flying, making small sounds as they hit the walls, the bed, and the men.

Maeve gasped, eyes wide, and drowning with need. Her breasts were pointed with large round nipples that seemed to shine as if they'd been carved of some thick, red jewel. I ran my hands over her bare stomach. The white glow of my hands made the golden glow of her skin pulse and fade, growing brighter at my touch, fading slightly as I moved my hands around the warmth of her waist. My hands slid upward until my thumbs and fingers rested just below her breasts. If a man had touched me here, my breasts would have hung over his hands, but Maeve's were small and tight, and still untouched.

The glow of her magic pulsed under my hands, bright and brighter, as if she had started to burn just underneath her breasts. She moaned, "Please!"

I realized in that moment that I'd pushed clear of her need, no longer feeling it as my own. I was deep in power, but about this one thing I was clear. If I touched her, it would be my choice.

I gazed up at her, head thrown back, eyes half closed. Her need still rode the air like some musky perfume, but now I could breathe it in and not drown. I stared at the bright gold of the power under my hands, and wondered what it would feel like to have that much power brushed across my breasts. This much I could give her.

I said, "Kiss me, Maeve."

She opened her eyes enough to look in my direction, but she couldn't focus; she was already half gone from the touch of magic and skin.

I repeated, "Kiss me."

She lowered her head, and I waited, waited until our mouths touched, then I caressed my hands upward over the mounds of her breasts. She pressed her mouth harder against mine, and the kiss became something deep and urgent, then my hands slid to the hardness of her nipples, and it was as if the world exploded. Power rocked us backward onto the bed so that she fell on top of me and my hands were locked on her breasts, as if I'd put my hands on a live wire and now couldn't get free.

Part of me didn't want free. Part of me wanted to sink into the golden glow of her, and be lost. She rose above me, quivering, shrieking, jerking against my hands where they seemed melded to her flesh. She ground her hips against mine, and if I'd been male, she'd have hurt me. But I wasn't male, and some part of my magic kept her amazing orgasm from jumping to me. The power pulsed wave after wave through my body while Maeve danced above me, but that ultimate pleasure was hers and hers alone. Somehow it seemed right. She'd waited so long.

She opened her eyes in the midst of it all, and she must have seen my face, understood that I was giving to her, but not taking, and she didn't like that. She pressed her hand to my stomach, and my white glow intensified under her touch. It was like being touched by spring's warmth, something heavy and rich that shivered and throbbed against my skin. I had a moment to wonder if that's what my hands felt like on her breasts when she slid her hand down the front of my bathing suit, and slid her finger between my legs. The moment that throbbing, pulsing power thrilled along my flesh, the orgasm burst from my body in waves, as if her touch were a stone thrown into a deep lake, and each ripple was an-other ring of pleasure, and where the stone slid downward pleasure followed. It was like being caressed and mined with sex all at the same time.

I came back to myself still on the bed with Maeve col-lapsed on top of me. I couldn't hear her ragged breathing for the pulse in my own ears, but I could feel the rise and fall of her chest as she struggled to breathe, as we both struggled to breathe past the pounding of the pulses in our throats.

When I could hear again, it was her frantic breathing and ragged laugh that came first. Then it was Rhys's voice: "I don't know whether to applaud or cry."

"Cry," Galen said, "because we missed the entire show."

I turned my head, and it seemed to take a lot more effort than it should have. I ended up staring at the room through a mist of Maeve's pale blond hair. I swallowed and tried to speak, but that was still beyond me.

Galen, Nicca, and Frost were just inside the door. Rhys and Doyle were by the bed, but not close enough to be acci-dentally touched.

Maeve found her voice before I did. "I'd forgotten, forgot-ten. Goddess bless me, I'd forgotten what it could be like with another sidhe." She rolled off me slowly, awkwardly, as if her body wasn't working right. She turned to look at me, a smile on her face even as she struggled to focus her eyes. "You were wondrous."

I managed to whisper, "Remind me the next time I ask for a kiss to be more specific."

That made her laugh, which made her cough. "My throat is dry."

Funny, so was mine.

"Nicca," Doyle said, "go get the ladies some water."

As Nicca left the room, he walked wide outside the door as if someone were standing on the left-hand side of it. It was Galen who said, "There's a tree in the hallway. I think it's an apple tree. It burst through the stone floor just inside the pool area, and by the time we got upstairs it had made a hole in the floor up here."

Rhys walked over to peer at the tree in the hallway. "The blossoms are opening."

The smell of apple blossoms began to drift in through the door.

Doyle stared down at us, at me. "How do you feel?"

"Better. My throat doesn't hurt anymore."

He offered me a hand, and I took it, let him lift me from Maeve's bed. My knees wouldn't hold me, and only his arm around my waist kept me from the floor. He picked me up, cradling me against his bare chest. I was too spent to do much more than lie there. I had an urge to play with the silver ring in his nipple, but it seemed too much effort. I was suddenly tired. Tired in a good way, but tired nonetheless.

He carried me out into the hall, past the pink-and-white mass of blossoms that almost filled it. I was drowning in the scent of apple blossoms again, and for a moment power flared through me, a strong pulse that made Doyle stumble.

"Be careful, Princess, I do not wish to drop you."

"Sorry," I mumbled, "didn't mean to."

I noticed the unevenness of the stairs, and got a glimpse of the grey tree trunk before we got to the sliding glass doors, but the last thing I remembered was a flash of blue water and sunlight from the pool. Then I closed my eyes, snuggled against Doyle's chest, and gave up the fight. Sleep swept up and over me, as complete and deep as any I could remember. Do the gods sleep well at night? I think, maybe, they do.

Chapter 8

I DREAMED. I STOOD ON A HILL WITH A ROUNDED TOP AND gazed down upon a vast open plain. There was a woman beside me, but I couldn't see her face. She wore a grey cloak; or it was black, or perhaps green. The harder I tried to see her, the thicker the shadows around her grew, until I knew that I wasn't meant to see her. Her face was hidden in the shadows of the cloak's hood. I couldn't tell her age, though I thought she was not young. She had the feel of someone who had seen much, and not all of it happy. One thing I was sure of: I did not know her.

She held a staff in her hand, so ancient that it was black and shiny with use. She motioned outward with her empty hand toward the plain. Doyle strode across the grass with hounds roiling around him, huge black hounds with eyes of fire. The Gabriel Ratchets, Hell Hounds, curved like shadows and smoke around him. They gathered close to him so he could rub an ear, stroke a head, thump a chest bigger around than I was. He was smiling and at ease, and in a breath they vanished. Galen was there, and where he walked trees sprang up, entire forests spread, and children appeared in the woods, chasing after him, tugging on his arms. He touched their heads, chucked them under the chin, played tag among the trees and flowers. One of the little boys touched a tree, and his palm glowed golden. Nicca stepped out of the trees, and wherever he walked flowers sprang up. He met Galen, and the children, and they played. Far across the plain, away from the happy scene, Rhys appeared. He was at the head of a vast army, and somehow I knew that the warriors at his back were dead. But when he looked at me he had two good eyes; the scars were gone. Somehow I knew this wasn't glamour, that he'd been healed. He had a hammer in his hand, and it shone with a light of its own. There were bodies on the ground, wounded. He touched them with the butt of the hammer and they rose, healed.

The lady turned me to face away from all of that, to find Kitto. He was shining, and fully sidhe, but it was a group of goblins at his back. He raised his hand, and light so white and pure that it blinded like lightning shot from his palm to rake through the army they faced. The goblins chanted his name like a prayer. I saw from a great distance, but still could see snakes in the grass among the opposing army. Poisonous snakes struck the enemy, and I knew that they did so at Kitto's bidding. The enemy broke apart, fleeing in panic, and the goblins gave chase to cut down those who remained.

The woman moved, brought my attention back to her. Her staff stood in the middle of the hill, stuck into the earth, and as I watched, it grew into a great spreading tree, so old and ancient that its trunk had split and it had died. She put her hand in the opening of the trunk, and when she withdrew it, she held a shining cup, a chalice formed of silver and set with precious stones. The chalice began to shine the way the skin of a sidhe shines when power is running through him. The shine became a glow, until the chalice was like a star sitting in her hands, a glowing, pulsing star. Light seemed to spill out of it, as if light could be liquid and held in a cup.

She held the cup out to me. "Drink." That one word echoed through the plain. It never occurred to me to say no. It never occurred to me to question her. I put my hands over hers where they held the cup, and found her skin soft, and fragile with age. She was old, much older than I'd thought. We raised the cup to my lips together, and the light inside it was so bright that for a moment I could see nothing but golden light, so warm, so comforting, so perfect. I drank from the cup, and it was like drinking power, drinking light.

She lowered the cup, and my hands were still upon hers. Her hands had changed. They were young, strong, with clean, delicate fingers. Wind spilled across the hilltop, rustling in the leaves. I looked up and found the dead tree thick with summer leaves. The trunk had healed except for a small knot that my hand would barely have fit inside. A bird began to sing high up in one of the branches. A squirrel scolded us from nearer the ground.

She squeezed my hands, and I caught a glimpse of her face. For a moment it was me, then she smiled, and I knew it wasn't my face inside the hood, yet it was.

I woke gasping in a strange bed in the dark, my heart thudding. I felt good, refreshed, and frightened all at the same time.

Rhys turned to me, his white hair gleaming in the moonlight. "Merry, are you all right?"

I started to say *yes*, then felt something beside my hip. I reached under the covers and touched something hard and metallic. I jerked the sheet back and there, gleaming softly in the moonlight, was the chalice from my dream.

Chapter 9

THIRTY MINUTES LATER WE'D ALL GATHERED IN THE KITCHEN, including Sage. If he'd been larger than a Barbie doll he'd have been handsome, if your taste ran to the slender yellow-skinned variety, but I had to admit the yellow-and-black swallowtail wings were pretty. He could make himself nearly my height, a form of shape-shifting less surprising than those of us who could take animal form, but it was a rarer gift to change from tiny fey to human-sized fey. He was what you might call an ambassador for the Unseelie demi-fey, and their queen, Niceven. I'd struck an alliance with them. They'd agreed to stop spying for my cousin Cel and his allies, and start spying for me. They still spied for my aunt, Queen Andais, but then she was supposed to be my ally, too. There were days when I wondered about that, but not tonight. Tonight we had enough problems without worrying about who Andais really wanted to be her heir.

The chalice sat in the middle of the tiled kitchen table, looking terribly out of place in the stark white modern kitchen. Doyle had brought a silk pillowcase to spread on the table, but even the bit of black silk wasn't enough to make the chalice look at home. It sat in the glow of the overhead lights looking like what it was, an ancient relic of power that just happened to be sitting on a breakfast nook table barely big enough for the four chairs that framed it. The cup needed at the very least a large dining room table, with acres of gleaming hardwood and shields and weaponry mounted on the walls. The cat clock on the wall with the moving tail and eyes didn't match the cup, but it did match the white canisters with black-and-white kittens painted on top of them. Maeve had never owned a cat, but I'd bet her decorator did.

Galen had made coffee and tea, and hot chocolate. We all sat huddled around our respective hot liquids and stared at the gleaming cup. Nobody seemed to want to break the silence. The ticking of the clock just seemed to emphasize the quiet.

"Once it was a cauldron," Doyle said, and I wasn't the only one who spilled tea down the front of his or her robe. Galen fetched paper towels for everyone who needed one. Frost cursed softly but with feeling under his breath as he mopped at the front of his grey silk robe. We all had silk robes, monogrammed with our initial. They'd been gifts from Maeve. We'd go out to work for the day, and we'd come home to packages.

Sage didn't get presents. I think it was half that he was demi-fey, and most sidhe treated them as if they were the insects that they resembled. It was one of the reasons they made such excellent spies: No one really paid them much attention. The other was that Maeve didn't know he could make himself bigger. She was hungry enough for fey flesh that she might have thought better of him if she'd known. She might not have cared, for the Seelie are pickier about the fey they call lovers. But the fact that some of Niceven's people could shift larger was a very closely guarded secret. As far as we knew, those of us in this room were the only sidhe who were aware of it.

Sage sat on the end of the kitchen cabinet, swinging his tiny legs in the air. His wings fanned slowly behind him, as they often did when he was thinking. He lowered his tiny, handsome face carefully over the mug beside him, being careful not to get his nearly shoulder-length butter-yellow hair in the foam of the hot chocolate. All the little fey seem to have a sweet tooth. He was wearing a tiny skirt made out of what seemed to be pale blue gossamer, as if it had been sewn by spiders, so fine was the cloth. Sage didn't wear many clothes, but what he did was of finer weave than any silk.

My silk robe was crimson, but lucky me, I'd managed to

pour more hot tea down my chest than on the robe. It burned, but not much, and silk once stained is ruined. My chest would clean up just fine. "What do you mean, it used to be a cauldron?" I asked.

Rhys answered me. "One day they went into the sanctuary and instead of a black cauldron that looked as ancient as it really was, there was this shiny new cup." He hadn't bothered with a robe at all. He stood naked in the kitchen, mopping at his bare chest. He pointed toward the chalice with the coffee-stained paper towel.

Doyle sat to my right, wearing black jeans and nothing else. "The King of Light and Illusion thought the cauldron had been stolen. He nearly went to war with our court over it." He leaned toward the table, his cup of tea still untouched in his hands. "But it hadn't been stolen. It had merely changed."

I sipped my own tea. "You mean the way the Black Coach of the wild hunt started its existence as a chariot, then changed to a coach when no one drove chariots anymore, and now is a big black shiny limousine?"

"Yes," he said, and finally took a drink of his own tea. His eyes never left the chalice, as if nothing else really mattered.

"The wild magicks have a mind of their own," Kitto said from where he huddled in the chair to my left. He held his mug of hot chocolate between both his hands the way a child will drink from an overly large cup. He had his knees tucked up to his chest, and the legs of his satin night shorts were just a thin strip of burgundy cloth.

"What do the goblins know of relics?" Rhys asked. There was a hint of his old hostility.

"We have our items of power," Kitto said.

Rhys opened his mouth, and Doyle said, "Stop. We will not squabble tonight, not with one of the sidhe's greatest treasures returned."

That shut everybody up again. I'd never seen all of them at such a loss for words. "I would think all of you would be celebrating. Instead you act as if someone has died." I knew why I was scared. I'd been around magic all my life, but I'd never had anything follow me home from a dream before. I didn't like it. Greatest treasure or not, the idea that things in my dreams could become real and cross over to the real world was a very frightening thought.

"You still don't understand," Doyle said. "This is *the cauldron*. The cauldron that can feed thousands, and never go empty. The cauldron from which the dead warriors can rise again, alive the next day, though robbed of their speech. This is a thing of elemental power for our people, Meredith. It appeared among us one day, like the Black Coach, like so many things just appeared. Then one day it vanished, and we lost our ability to feed the masses of our followers, and for the first time we watched them starve." He rose and turned, pressing his hands against the window's dark glass, leaning his face so close to it that it looked as if he meant to kiss the darkness outside. "We were not in the country when the great famine hit, but if we had still possessed the cauldron I would have strapped it to my back and swum to Ireland." For the first time I heard a burr of brogue in his voice. Most of the sidhe pride themselves on having no accent. I'd never heard Doyle sound like anything or anywhere in particular.

"Are you talking about the great potato famine?" I asked.

"Yes." His voice was almost a growl.

He was mourning people who had died nearly two hundred years before I was born. But the pain was as real to him now as if it had been last week. I'd noticed that the immortals carry all the strong emotions—love, hate, grief—for longer than a human lifetime. It's as if time moves differently for them, and even sitting beside them, living with them, my time and their time weren't the same.

He spoke without turning around, as if he spoke more to the darkness outside than to us. "What do the gods do when once they could answer the prayers of their followers, then suddenly they cannot? One day they simply have to watch their people die of diseases that only weeks before they could have healed. You are too young, Meredith, and even Galen; neither of you really understands what it was like.

Not your fault. Not your fault." He spoke the last in a whisper to the glass, his face finally pressed gently to it.

I got up from my chair and went to him. He flinched when I touched his back, then moved away from the glass enough for me to slide my arms around his waist, pressing my body against his. He let me hold him, but he didn't relax against me. I tried to give comfort, but in a way, he wouldn't take it.

I spoke with my cheek pressed to the warm smoothness of his back. "I know that there was more than one cauldron. I know that there were three main ones. I know that they all changed form, and became cups. My father blamed it on all the King Arthur stories about the Holy Grail. If enough people believe something, then it can affect everything. Flesh affects spirit." Somewhere in my matter-of-fact talking, Doyle began to relax against me. He began to let the hurt go, a little.

"Yes," he said, "but the first cauldron given was the great cauldron that could do all that any could do. There were two lesser cauldrons. One could heal and feed, and the other held treasure, gold and such." The way he said the last words showed clearly that he didn't think that gold and such were worth nearly as much as healing and food.

"There were more cauldrons than that," Rhys said.

Doyle pushed away from the glass enough to turn his head and look behind him at the other men. I stayed wrapped around his back. "Not real ones," Doyle said.

"They were real, Doyle, they just weren't given to us by the gods. Some among us had the ability to make such things."

"They could not do what the great cauldrons could do," Doyle said.

"No, but they didn't disappear when the gods withdrew their favor, either."

Doyle turned, and I had to let him go so he could pace back toward Rhys. "They did not withdraw their favor. We gave up the power to work directly with them. We gave them up, they did not give us up."

Rhys held up his hands. "I don't want to have this argument, Doyle. I don't think a few centuries will make the fight any more fun. Let's just agree to disagree. All we know for certain is that one day the great relics began to vanish. The things that the fey had made themselves, from their own magic, remained behind."

"Until the second weirding magic," Frost said. It was the longest sentence I'd gotten out of him since this afternoon. I'd tried to speak to him in the hall, and he'd been curt and avoided me. I was the one who had nearly died, but he was the one throwing the fit. Typical Frost.

"Yes," Nicca said in his soft voice, "and then the items we'd wrought ourselves began to break, or just stopped working. It was as if the spell drained them."

I knew that Nicca was centuries old, but I kept forgetting until he said something that forced me to remember.

"I don't think everyone would have agreed to the second weirding if they'd known what would happen to our wands, our staffs." Nicca shook his head, sending his deep brown hair glimmering in the lights. "I wouldn't have agreed."

"Many of us would not have agreed," Doyle said.

"If that's true," I said, "then how did you all agree to the weirding that made the Nameless? That was the third weirding, so you all knew what to expect. You all knew how much you could lose."

"What choice did we have?" Rhys said. "It was either give up more of our power or be exiles without a country."

"We could have stayed in Europe," Frost said.

"And what," Doyle said, "be forced out of our hollow hills to buy houses and live next door to humans? To be forced to intermarry with humans." He looked back at me and said, "I don't mean to insult the princess, but a little mixed blood is one thing; to be forced to marry humans is something else. Those who remained behind in Europe had to sign treaties to give up their culture." He spread his arms and hands wide. "Without their culture and belief a people do not exist."

"That's why they did it," Rhys said. "It was a way of destroying us that didn't smack of genocide."

"The humans were not strong enough to kill us all," Frost said.

"No," Rhys said, "but they were strong enough to bring us to the treaty table and force a peace that more than half of every race of the fey thought was unfair."

"I know the facts of what happened," I said, "but this is the first time I've ever heard any of you talk about the exile with this much emotion."

"We left Europe to save what was left of faerie," Doyle said. "Now that cup sits on the table, and it will all begin again."

"What will begin again?" I asked.

"The Goddess gave us her gifts, the Consort gave us his gifts, then one day they were gone. How can we trust that whatever gift we are given will not abandon us at our hour of need?" Pain, anger, frustration, hope, all fought across the darkness of his face.

"I think you're borrowing trouble," I said. "I think that we should figure out if the cauldron still does what it used to do before we worry about it disappearing again."

Rhys shook his head. "It never worked just because we wanted it to. It feeds us when we need to be fed. It heals when we need healing. The high holy relics are not sideshow entertainment. They only work if there's need."

"It's a matter of faith," Nicca said. "We have to have faith that it will help us when we need it." He didn't sound happy about it when he said it.

"Faith," Rhys said, so full of emotion that his voice was lower than normal, thick with things unsaid. "I gave that up a long time ago, Nicca. I'm not sure I can pick it back up again."

"I think we all believed we were truly gods," Doyle said, "equal to any. When the first lessening happened, we learned different." He strode to the table and looked almost as if he was going to pick up the cup, but he didn't. "We learned the difference between playing gods and being gods." He shook his head. "It is not a lesson I want to learn twice."

"Me, either," Rhys said.

"I was never more than I am right now," Frost said. "I learned different lessons." He didn't sound any happier about his lessons than the rest did about theirs.

My father had made sure I knew the cold facts of our history, but he'd never complained, never spoke of the pain I was seeing now. I'd known intellectually that the sidhe had lost much, but I hadn't really understood. I probably didn't understand even now, but I would try. Goddess help me, I would try.

"Didn't the children of Dana demand that the goblins not be gods to the humans?" Kitto asked. "Wasn't that your rule in the very first peace treaty with us? Is it that much different from what the humans have done to all of us?"

Rhys turned toward the smaller man. "How dare you compare—" He stopped in midsentence and shook his head. He rubbed his free hand across his face as if he was tired. "Kitto's right," he said.

The surprise showed on all our faces, even Doyle's. "Did you just agree with Kitto?" Nicca asked.

Rhys nodded. "He's right. When we first landed, we were as arrogant, and as determined to break the goblins' power, as the humans are of us."

"I'm not sure it's arrogance on the humans' part," I said. "I think it's mostly fear that another fey-and-human war might decimate Europe."

"But it's still arrogance to think that they can dictate rules of conduct to a civilization that existed millennia before their ancestors stopped living in caves," Rhys said.

To that I could add nothing, so I didn't try. "I concede the point."

He grinned at me. "You're not going to argue with me?"

I shrugged. "Why should I? You're right."

"You know, you have a mighty democratic way of thinking for the heir to a throne."

"I was raised for ten years out among the democratic American humans. I think it helps keep me humble." I smiled at him, because I couldn't not smile. Rhys had that effect on me, sometimes.

"I hate to break up the lovefest," Galen said, "but what are we going to do about the cauldron, chalice, whatever?"

Galen was hopeless at politics, but he was very good at being practical. "What is there to do?" I asked.

"Well," he said, and his smile faded around the edges, "do we tell anyone?"

Everyone suddenly got even more serious. "He's right," Doyle said. "We need to decide whom we will tell, if anyone."

"Are you thinking of withholding this information from the queen?" Frost asked.

"Not withholding, but simply not sharing just yet." He motioned at Kitto. "We have had a very busy day and night, Frost. Kitto has come into his hand of power. A hand of power that hasn't been seen among us since the second weirding."

"By the way," I asked, "what is his hand of power called? I mean, mine is the hand of flesh and the hand of blood, but what do you call the mirror thingie?"

"It is called the hand of reaching," Doyle answered, "because it reaches between two points of communication and brings people across from one point to the other. The hand of reaching, because it reaches out to people."

"Logical, when it's explained," I said.

"Most things are logical when they're explained." He sounded almost normal, but his face showed the strain of all the unanswered questions. Of questions perhaps not only unanswered, but unanswerable.

"The queen will want to know of Kitto's new power," Frost said.

"I have told her already," Doyle said.

"And Rhys's coming back to his godlike powers?"

Doyle nodded. "She knows."

"When did you have time to tell her all this?"

"When you went with the princess to the main house to see Maeve."

Frost frowned. Then something very like fear flashed through his eyes, before he gained control of it and gave a handsome blank face to Doyle. "Does she know the rest?" His voice was more uncertain than his eyes.

"That Meredith seems to have brought Maeve back into her godhead, and perhaps given you godhead for the first time? Or the part where Meredith almost died doing it? Or do you mean have I told her that the princess seems now to have the gift of magical dreaming? Or maybe you wonder if the queen knows we have the chalice. Which of those things are you wondering about, Frost?"

"He didn't mean to make you angry," I said.

"I don't need you to defend me," Frost said.

"What is wrong with you, Frost? You've been acting mad at me since I woke up."

He looked down at the kitchen island in front of him. He hadn't come closer to us than that, or perhaps it was me he avoided.

"How can you ask me that? I am your guard, your Raven, sworn to protect you from all harm, and I nearly killed you today."

I walked over to stand beside him. I reached out to touch him, and he jerked away. "I don't want to hurt you again."

"You saw the end of what Maeve and I did together, Frost. I think I can touch your hand and be safe."

He shook his head, using his long silver hair to hide his face and most of his body from me. His hair had always been the incredible color of Christmas tree tinsel, but tonight it seemed even shinier than normal. I reached out to touch that shining hair and found that it was damp.

He pulled back again, stepping away so that I couldn't touch him. He put his back to the kitchen cabinets and hugged himself. "When your cries woke us, I was covered in ice." He shook his head. "No, not ice, frost. I woke up covered in a rime of frost. It melted almost immediately, but it was thicker in my hair. My hair crackled like frozen tree branches when I first moved." He looked frightened.

I reached out to him again, and he moved away. "No, Meredith, I don't have control of these powers. It's not a matter of relearning what I knew once. These aren't my magicks." He looked at me with wide, frightened eyes. "I don't know how to be a god, Meredith. I've never been one before."

"We'll teach you," Rhys said.

"What if I don't want to learn?" Frost asked.

"That is a different problem, my old friend," Doyle said. "The Goddess gives where She will, and it is not ours to question why or where."

The fact that Doyle had been doing that very thing a few moments ago seemed to have escaped his notice—or maybe Doyle was the only one allowed to express doubts about the Goddess. Whatever the logic, or lack of it, no one pointed it out to him.

Chapter 10

"WE HAVE TO TELL THE QUEEN THAT WE HAVE THE CHALICE," Rhys said.

"No." Doyle shook his head hard enough to set the heavy braid of his hair swinging.

"She will be pissed if we keep this from her, and I for one do not want to spend another night in the Hallway of Mortality." The Hallway of Mortality was the torture chamber for the Unseelie Court. Christians once thought the Unseelie were demons from hell. If any part of our court was the punishing hell that came to be after Dante's *Divine Comedy*, it was the Hallway of Mortality.

"Nor I," Frost said.

"Me, either," Galen said.

"No," Nicca said, "no."

I leaned against the kitchen cabinets and looked at Doyle. He had been the Queen's Darkness for more than a thousand years. Her left-hand man. Her ultimate assassin. He was loyal to her, though lately he'd begun to be loyal to me. But it still wasn't like him to keep something this big from the queen, especially since eventually she would find out. She was the Queen of Air and Darkness; everything said in the dark would eventually float back to her. And words like *cauldron*, *chalice*, and such would prick her interest. It was just too big a secret to keep forever.

"Why don't you want to tell the queen?" I asked.

"Because this is not our relic. This cauldron belonged to the Seelie Court. We nearly went to war over its disappearance centuries ago, when Taranis suspected us of stealing it. What would he do if he knew we actually had it?"

"The queen would never tell him," Galen said.

Doyle gave him a look of such withering scorn that Galen took a step back. "Do you truly think that there are no spies among us? We certainly have spies at the Seelie Court; I must assume that Taranis has the same among us." He motioned at the gleaming cup, sitting so innocently on the table. "This is simply too large a thing to keep secret. It will get out once it is known outside this room. We must think what to do when that happens."

"What do you mean?" Frost asked.

"Taranis will demand the cup back. Do we give it to him? And if we don't, are we willing to go to war for it?"

"We cannot give it to Taranis," Nicca said.

We all turned and stared at him. It was so unlike him to be adamant about anything, and totally out of the question for him to say something so decisive and so potentially disastrous.

"Even if it means war?" Doyle said.

Nicca paced closer to the table. "I don't know, but I do know this: Taranis has broken our most sacred taboos. He's been hiding his own infertility for at least a century, because he exiled Maeve for refusing to marry him on the grounds that he was infertile. He has knowingly condemned his own court to a fading of their power, their fertility, and everything they are. When he feared Maeve would reveal his secret to us, or had already, he freed the Nameless. He set loose our most feared powers to stalk the land, yet he didn't have the power to control it. Innocents died because of that, and Taranis seems not to care. We were here to save Maeve and slay the Nameless, but without us here, she would be dead, and the Nameless might have laid waste to Los Angeles. If the humans found out it was sidhe magic that did it, the consequences could have been devastating for us. Who knows how the human government would have reacted. This is the last country that will accept free sidhe, without restricting our culture, our magic, us." Nicca had a small glow to him as he spoke, as if his words had power to them.

"We all agree that what Taranis has done was selfish and not deeds fit for a king," Doyle said, "but he is king. We cannot accuse him of his crimes, and see him punished."

"Why not?" Kitto asked, still huddled in his chair, sipping his hot chocolate.

"He is king," Doyle repeated.

"Among the goblins, if you know the king has broken our laws, you can confront him in open court. It is our way, and our law."

"The sidhe are not so straightforward," Doyle said.

"Yes, it is what has allowed you to best us for centuries, the fact that you are more devious than we are."

I glanced at Rhys, and something on my face must have shown because he said, "I'm not going to argue with him. The sidhe are more devious than the goblins. Goddess knows that the sidhe are more devious than any of the fey."

"So good to hear a sidhe admit the truth," Sage said.

I looked at the little man on the counter. He looked so harmless sitting there with his oversized mug of cocoa. There was even a rim of chocolate foam around his mouth so that the illusion of childish innocence was even stronger than normal. The demi-fey traded on the fact that they looked cute. I'd seen a flock of them tear the flesh from Galen's body while he lay chained and helpless. Prince Cel had ordered them to do it, but they'd enjoyed the feast.

He half fell and half pushed himself off the cabinet to hover in midair. "This is all moot, my sidhe friends, for I must tell Queen Niceven. It is all well for you to think of concealing things from your queen, because Merry may yet be queen in her stead, but Niceven's hold upon her court is secure, and I cannot chance her anger." He fluttered to the edge of the table, landing as if he had no weight, though I knew he actually weighed more than he appeared to. It always seemed like it should be the other way around, but there was substance to Sage that you could feel when he walked on your body.

He moved toward the chalice, and Doyle put a hand out,

almost but not quite in front of him. "You see enough from where you are."

Sage put his hands on his slender hips and stared up at the much larger man. "What do you fear, Darkness, that I will steal it away, take it back to my court, my queen?"

"It is a sidhe gift, and it will remain in sidhe hands," Doyle said.

Sage sprang into the air, fluttering around the overhead light like some great moth, though in truth there was more of butterfly than moth to him. "But I still must needs report this to Queen Niceven. You can debate all you wish about telling your queen, but because I must tell mine, you might as well tell yours."

"We will be at the courts tomorrow night," I said. "Can you wait that long to tell your queen?"

"Why should I wait?" he asked, and came to hover in front of my face so that the wind of his wings danced in my hair.

"Because it would be safer for all of us, including your people, if fewer people know of the chalice."

He pointed a finger at me. "Tut, tut, Princess, logic will not win me. I stayed away today though your magic called me like the love song of a siren." He lit upon the table in front of me. "I did not come because I have witnessed all the amazing sidhe sex I ever wish to see, since I am not invited into your bed. I am not really much of a voyeur."

"I agreed to share blood with you once a week, Sage. That was the price of alliance with your people. I've kept my end of the bargain."

He paced in front of me on tiny butter-colored feet that matched the yellow of his wings. "Blood is a fine thing, Princess, but it does not take the place of a good thrusting." He leaned his hands on my hand, as if I were a fence, and gazed up at me with tiny black eyes. "Let me in your bed tonight and I will tell no one until we arrive at the courts."

I moved my hand quick enough to make him stumble, and he took to the air, his wings an angry blur. "Are you really still trying to make a bid to be my king, Sage? I thought we had been clear about this."

He got near enough to my face that I heard the whir of his wings. Real butterfly wings didn't make that noise. He sounded like an angry hummingbird. "Yes, originally my queen wished to make a bid to put me on the Unseelie throne as her puppet, but Flora save me, Princess, I don't care about that anymore."

"What do you care about?" Doyle asked.

Sage turned in midair and rose high enough to look at both of us. "I want sex. I want to lie with a woman again. Is that so hard a thing to believe?"

"No," Doyle said.

"No," I said.

It was Kitto who said, "The demi-fey don't care about sex any more than the goblins do, not if they can have power and blood."

Sage turned and stared at the goblin who had become sidhe. "Your kind still roasts us on spits and thinks us a delicacy. Forgive me if I don't give your opinion much weight." The sarcasm was thick in his voice.

Kitto hissed at him, and he hissed back.

"Enough," Doyle said. "What would you take to keep our secret until we arrive at the courts tomorrow night? Do not ask again for sex with the princess, for that is not going to happen."

Sage crossed his arms and did a very good imitation of a child's pout, complete with the chocolate mustache on his mouth, but I'd seen him with my blood smeared across his tiny mouth too many times to fall for it. He acted cute because it was what was left to the demi-fey, but he wasn't. He was dangerous, treacherous, lecherous, and spiteful, but not cute.

"How about the blood of a god?" Rhys asked.

Sage turned in midair like some fantastic helicopter to face Rhys. "Are you offering Maeve's blood, or Frost's?"

"Mine."

He shook his head. "You are no god."

"My power has returned. Doyle called me Cromm Cruach again this day."

Sage turned to Doyle. "Is this true, Darkness?"

Doyle nodded. "I give you my word that I called him Cromm Cruach this day."

Sage hovered in front of Rhys so that the white curls moved around Rhys's face. He went close and closer until his body almost touched Rhys. He darted in and licked Rhys's forehead, then darted away before Rhys could catch him, or swat him. Though Rhys didn't try for either. Galen would have, but Galen had the same reason to hate the demi-fey that Rhys had to hate the goblins, and it had been much more recent.

"You don't taste like a god, Rhys. You taste good, powerful, but not a god."

"When's the last time you tasted a god?" Rhys asked.

Sage fluttered over toward Frost, though he stayed out of reach. Frost wasn't tolerant of unwanted touch from anyone. Centuries of forced celibacy had made him most un-fey-like in that regard. I could touch him, but few others could.

"Let me taste your skin, Frost. No blood, not yet."

Frost scowled up at the little man, and shook his head. "I am no one's blood whore."

"What does that make me?" I asked, and my voice was as cold as my anger was hot. I'd had about all I could handle of Frost's moods for one day. I was the one who'd almost died; when was it my turn to be in a mood?

Frost looked confused. "I didn't mean . . ."

I walked toward him. "If I'm willing to donate a little blood for the cause, then what makes you too good to do it?"

He motioned at the hovering demi-fey. "I do not want that laying its mouth on me."

"I do it once a week, Frost. If it's good enough for a princess, it's good enough for you."

His face was the arrogant mask he wore when he was hiding what he was thinking. "Are you ordering me to do it?" His voice was very cold, and I knew that here could be something that would drive a wedge between us, maybe for a day, maybe forever. You never knew with Frost.

I stepped close to him, and when he jerked away, I let my hand fall to my side. "Not exactly, but I am asking you to please do this. Please help us."

"I don't want to . . ."

I touched his lips with my fingertips and he let me. His breath was warm on my skin. "Please, Frost, please, it is a small thing. It hurts only a little, and Sage is very good at glamour. He can make it hurt not at all."

"I have not agreed that Frost's blood will buy my silence," Sage said. "I have not tasted him. He may be no more godling than Rhys."

"Both of us," Rhys said, "both Frost and me, and all you do is wait to tell your queen until we arrive at the courts in person." Rhys moved so that he was staring up at the small hovering man. "The blood of two sidhe nobles for less than twenty-four hours of silence. It's not a bad deal."

Sage slowed his wings enough that you could see the eyes of red on the inside of them, and the blue iridescence that matched the broader blue stripe on the outside. It was almost as if he floated rather than flew toward where Galen stood.

Galen leaned with his back to the far cabinets, arms crossed. The look on his face was as hostile as it ever got. "Don't—even—ask." His voice held a note of enraged finality that caused Sage to sink for a moment toward the floor, like a human might stumble.

He regained his height, then added more so he was close to the ceiling, out of reach. "But you were so tasty."

Galen looked at me. "Why don't we just bespell him for twenty-four hours?"

"Tempting as it is," I said, "Niceven might consider hostile magic on her proxy to be a violation of our treaty."

"It would solve the problem," Rhys said.

"Very well," Sage said. "For a taste of Frost and a taste of the white knight, I will agree to hold my tongue until I see my queen."

"In the flesh at her court," I added.

He whirled up near the ceiling like some lazy bird. He laughed and came to hover near me. "Are you afraid I will cheat?"

"Say the words, Sage," I said.

He gave me a smile that said he would do what I wanted,

but he would be a pain in the ass while doing it. It was his way. In fact, it was the way of a lot of the Unseelie demi-fey. A cultural thing, perhaps.

He put his wee hand over his tiny chest and stood straight in midair, toes pointed downward. "For the blood of both men, I will wait to tell my queen about the chalice until face-to-face and true flesh to true flesh we are." He darted upward, so that I had to crane my neck to keep track of him near the ceiling. "Satisfied?"

"Yes," I said.

"I have not agreed to this," Frost said.

"I'll be there," Rhys said.

I slid my arm through Frost's arm, over the silk and the pull of his muscles. "I'll be there, too."

"Frost," Doyle said.

The two men looked at each other and something passed between them, some knowledge, some comfort. Whatever it was, it softened Doyle's face, made him seem more . . . human.

Frost nodded. "What if the new magic tries to harm Meredith again?"

"Rhys will be there to see that that does not happen."

Frost opened his mouth as if he would say something more; then he stopped, closed his mouth, and gave one sharp nod. "As my captain commands, so will I do."

The rest of the guards seemed to forget sometimes that Doyle was the captain of the Queen's Ravens, then suddenly they'd remember. They'd use a title long disused. The respect was always there, and the fear, but the titles came and went.

"Good," Doyle said. "Now that that is settled, we have other business to discuss. Once our respective queens know of the chalice's return, it will come to Taranis's attention. What do we do when he demands its return?"

I glanced around the room, tried to read their faces, and couldn't read most. "You aren't seriously thinking about keeping the chalice once Taranis asks for it? It would be a fight, if not an outright war."

"We cannot give it to him," Nicca said. "He no longer deserves it."

"What do you mean, Nicca?" Doyle asked.

"He is not . . ." Nicca seemed at a loss for words, then finally spread his hands wide and said, "He is not worthy to wield the chalice. If he were worthy, it would have come to him—but it hasn't. It came to Merry."

Doyle sighed loudly enough that I heard it halfway across the room. "And that is yet another problem. If Taranis fears that his hold as king is slipping because of his infertility, then to have the chalice appear to another sidhe noble, especially one half-Unseelie, will only feed his fear."

"He should be afraid." Rhys came to stand beside me, on the other side from Frost's solid presence. "Bringing Maeve and Frost to godhood, maybe that's just her being the only goddess-shaped vessel, just like Doyle said." He put his arm around my waist, hugging me a little to him, while my arm was still linked with Frost's. It made his hand bump into Frost, and I felt the bigger man tense. Rhys didn't seem to notice, but gazed out at the other men. "But the chalice coming to her, that's not just because she's the right sex for the power. The cauldron was originally given to men, not women. What if it came to her because she's the only sidhe noble fit to be its caretaker?"

"I don't think that's it," I said.

"Why isn't it?" Frost said.

I looked up the length of his own body to meet Frost's gaze. "Because I'm mortal. I'm not even full sidhe by some standards."

"By whose standards?" Frost said. "All those would-be gods who stand around and talk about the glories of the past?"

"The Seelie Court does sound like someone's high school reunion," Rhys said. "They talk about the old days when they were younger, stronger, better. The nostalgia is deep."

I frowned up at him, then glanced back at Frost. "Fine, yes, by the standards of the people who lost the chalice in the first place, I don't count. But regardless, Frost, Taranis will never accept that we have the chalice, not without a war."

"She's right," Rhys said, "because all the Seelie will think that with the chalice back, they could regain their powers."

"And with that logic," Doyle said, "if the Unseelie have it, then we could regain ours."

"I don't think that's true," Frost said. "I have not regained my powers. I have acquired powers that belonged to sidhe I once called master. And the chalice did not give me these powers, Merry did."

Rhys hugged me close. "Our queen will be pleased, but Taranis won't."

"He would be, if he thought she could do for him what she's done for Frost," Doyle said.

Rhys's face showed a moment of absolute panic, before he covered it with a grin and a joke. "I don't know which is more dangerous, that he thinks he can use Merry to regain his lost vitality, or that her new powers would make her a strong queen."

"A rival, you mean," Doyle said.

Rhys shook his head. "No, not a rival. Even if Merry could bring all of us into our full power, it wouldn't help her in a fight. There is still right of combat among sidhe nobles, and the king is just another noble to some of our laws." He gazed down at me. "I know you have two really nifty hands of power, but I've seen Taranis in a duel." He kissed my forehead, and spoke with his lips against my skin. "You would lose."

"The last time Taranis fought a duel was before the third and final weirding," Doyle said. "Who's to say what powers he still possesses, and what was lost?"

Rhys looked at him. "She would die."

"I have no intentions of our princess fighting the King of Light and Illusions in personal combat, Rhys, but do not give him more power than he has. We all lost things with the weirdings. Some of us are just better at hiding it."

"Maybe," Rhys said, arms still holding me close as if he was afraid Doyle would whisk me away for a duel right that moment, "maybe I do overestimate Taranis and his court, but maybe you give them too little credit."

"Do not mistake me: They are very dangerous, and very powerful. Their court holds more magic than ours. They still have the great tree in their main hall, and it still holds leaves, though colored with autumn now. Their power is still there." Doyle shook his head and sat down at the table, resting his chin on his arms so his face was even with the goblet. "We are not ready to accuse Taranis of his crimes. Maeve cannot testify to them because she is exiled, and an exile may not give testimony against another member of faerie. Bucca-Dhu's testimony about helping Taranis release the Nameless could so easily be used against Bucca himself."

"What do you mean?" Nicca asked.

"You've seen what Bucca has become. He was once one of our great lords—a leader of the Cornish sidhe when there were enough of us to have many courts. Now he is like some misshapen dwarf. The Seelie will not want to believe he is who he says he is, and even if they do believe that, they could try him with his own words. If he says that Taranis is guilty then he himself is guilty as well. Taranis could simply deny, and force them to execute Bucca for the crime. Someone is punished for the crime, the mystery is solved, and the only witness to Taranis's part in it is dead. It would be very neat."

"Sounds like him," Rhys said.

"But Bucca has the queen's own protection," Nicca said. "He is being guarded at this moment by the Unseelie."

"Yes," Doyle said, "and the queen told none of Bucca's guards why he was being guarded, yet the rumors have already begun."

"What rumors?" I asked.

"Whispers about the Nameless and who would gain from its attack on Maeve Reed. The rumors are only in the faerie courts, but the attack was on all the major news sources, and some of the sidhe of both courts keep up with the human news." He stared at the cup while he spoke, as if mesmerized by it. "Most know that Taranis personally had her exiled. The rumors are already beginning. If he'd had other magicks that could have slain Maeve from a distance, I think he would have used them. The Nameless may not be able to be traced back to him directly, but it is a major power, and everyone now knows that whoever released it, it was used to hunt Maeve."

"His very fear will be his undoing," Frost said.

"Perhaps," Doyle said, "but a cornered wolf is more dangerous than one in the open. We do not want to be around Taranis when he feels himself out of options."

"Which brings me back to why he wants me to visit the Seelie Court," I said. I pushed away from the comforting weight of both men. There were too many questions, too much happening, for a mere hug to make it all right. It was very human and very un-fey-like of me, but I just didn't want to be held right that moment.

"He says he wishes to renew your acquaintance now that you are about to be heir to the Unseelie throne," Doyle said.

"You don't believe that any more than I do."

"It has the kernel of truth, or it would be an outright lie, and we do not lie to each other."

"Maybe, but a sidhe will omit so much of a truth that it might as well be a lie," I said.

Sage laughed, and it was like the ring of golden bells. "Oh, the princess does know her people."

"We bought your silence," Doyle said. "Let it be true silence for this discussion, unless you have something of true worth to add." He stared up at the little man, who was circling lazily near the ceiling. "Remember this, Sage: If the Unseelie Court falls, you will be at the mercy of the Seelies, and they will never trust you."

Sage came to stand on the edge of the table, his handsome wings folded back from his shoulders. He gazed up at Doyle—though with Doyle's chin resting on his arm on the table, they were nearly the same height. "If the Unseelie fall, Darkness, it will not be the demi-fey who suffer the most at the hands of the Seelie. They distrust us, but they do not see us as a threat. They will destroy all of you. We will be swatted like flies on a summer day, but they will not see us as worth destroying utterly. We will survive as a people. Can the Unseelie say the same?"

"That is as may be," Doyle said, "but wouldn't it benefit your people to do more than survive? Survival is better than the alternative, Sage, but merely surviving can get tiresome."

"More half-truths and omissions to trick me, is that it?"

"Believe what you like, little man, but I tell you truth when I say that the fate of the demi-fey of one court is tied to the fate of the sidhe of that court."

They stared at each other, and it was Sage who took to the air and broke the staring contest. I'd never doubted who would break first. "The princess is right, Darkness, none of the sidhe can be trusted."

Doyle raised himself up from the table enough to shrug. "That this is true of many of us, I cannot argue with." He looked across the room at me. "I would give much to know Taranis's true purpose in inviting you to the Seelie Court. No one seems to know why he's doing it. His own court is amazed that he wants you back. That he would throw a feast for a mortal."

"He is my uncle," I said.

"Has he ever acted like an uncle to you before?" Doyle asked.

I shook my head. "He almost beat me to death as a child for asking about Maeve Reed's exile. He doesn't give a damn for me."

"Why not just refuse the invitation?" Galen said.

"We've been over this, Galen. If we refuse the invitation, then Taranis will see it as an insult, and wars, curses, all sorts of unpleasantness among the sidhe have begun over things like that."

"We know it's a trap of some kind, yet we're still walking into it. That makes no sense to me."

I looked at Doyle for help. He tried. "If we go at Taranis's invitation, then he is guest-bound to treat us well. He cannot challenge any of us to a personal duel, or cause us harm, or allow harm to come to us while we are his guests. Once we step outside his mound, his court, then he can challenge us on the spot, but not inside his own court. It is too old a law among us for even his own nobles to stomach a breach in it."

"Then why are we so worried about taking enough guards inside the court to keep Merry safe?"

"Because I could be wrong," Doyle said.

Galen literally threw his hands up. "This is crazy."

"Taranis could be crazy enough to try to do harm on the spot. His court could be more corrupt than I know. Prepare for what your enemy can do, not what they will do."

"Don't quote at me, Doyle." Galen was pacing up and down one side of the kitchen as if he needed to use up some of the nervous energy floating around the room. "We are endangering Merry by going to the Seelie Court, I know it."

"You do not know it," Doyle said.

"No, I don't know it. But I feel it. It's a bad idea."

"Everyone agrees it's a bad idea, Galen," I said.

"Then why do it?"

"To find out what Taranis wants," Doyle said, "in the least dangerous way."

"If going to the Seelie Court and standing next to the King of Light and Illusion is the least dangerous way, I'd like to know what the *most* dangerous way would be."

Doyle finally stood and walked toward Galen, who was still pacing the kitchen. He stopped the pacing by simply standing in front of Galen, forcing him to stand still. They stood and looked at each other, and for the first time I felt something between them. Some test of wills that had happened with Doyle and Frost, Doyle and Rhys, but never Galen.

"The most dangerous way would be if we refused Taranis's invitation and gave him an excuse to call Meredith out for a duel."

"It's been centuries since anyone's dueled over matters of court etiquette," Rhys said.

"Yes," Doyle said, but his gaze never left Galen. For the first time I was aware that Galen and Doyle were the same height, and Galen's shoulders were actually a touch broader. "But it is still an acceptable reason to give challenge. If Taranis wants Merry dead, it would be perfect. She could not refuse him outright, because to do so would force her into exile. A sidhe noble who refuses challenge, for whatever reason, is branded a coward, and cowards cannot rule at either court."

Galen's shoulders rounded a little, as if he slumped. "He wouldn't dare."

"He released the Nameless to slay one sidhe woman, for fear she would whisper his secret. I think Taranis would dare anything."

"I didn't think . . ." Galen started.

"No," Doyle said, "you did not."

Galen stepped back from him. "Fine, I'm stupid, I don't understand court politics, and I don't understand being that devious. I'm useless at strategy, but I'm still scared for Merry to go into the Seelie Court."

Doyle gripped his arm. "We are all worried about that."

They had a moment when their eyes met, and then it was okay between them again. Had Galen been challenging Doyle in small ways for a while, and I just hadn't noticed, or had this been the first? As challenges went, it was mild, but even a mild challenge from Galen was something I'd never seen. He just wasn't a leader. He didn't want to be. But for fear of my safety he'd stood up to Doyle.

I went to Galen and hugged him from behind. He rubbed his hands over my arms, sliding the silk of my robe up so he could touch my skin. He was wearing only the dress slacks he'd started the day in, so that I had the warm skin of his stomach against my hands. "I can't tell you it will be all right, Galen, but we're going to do our best to have enough muscle and political allies on our side to make even Taranis hesitate."

"I don't like that part of the plan, either," Galen said. "You cannot agree to sleep with all the half-goblins."

I started to pull away from him, and he caught my hands, held me pressed against his stomach. "Please, Merry, please, don't be mad."

"I'm not mad, Galen, but I am not going to argue about this

with anyone else. I mean it. We have our plan, it's the best we can do, and that is that." I pulled my hands out of his grip, and he didn't fight me. I turned to Doyle. "The chalice complicates things, but it doesn't really change anything."

He gave a small nod. "As you say."

"What if Merry keeps the chalice on the grounds that the Goddess gave it to her?" Nicca said. He'd gone to kneel by the table so he could look at the goblet more closely.

"I don't think divine intervention is a good enough reason," Rhys said.

"But it is our tradition," Nicca said. "They may have messed the story up and confused it with other stories, but *Whosoever pulls this sword out of the stone is rightful king* is still true. The Ard-Ris of Ireland had a stone that would cry out at the touch of the rightful king."

"There are those who believe that when the Ard-Ri was no longer chosen by the stone, that is when the Irish lost to the English," Doyle said. "They forsook their heritage, their great magic, and the line of true kings was broken."

I looked at him. "I didn't know you had Fenian leanings."

"You do not have to be a Fenian to understand that the English have tried to destroy the Irish through any means—political, cultural, even agricultural. The Scots were treated badly, but the Irish have always been the special whipping boys of the English."

"The Irish fight among themselves, that's why they keep coming up short," Rhys said.

Doyle gave him an unfriendly look.

"It's the truth, Doyle, they're still killing each other over who crosses themselves when they bend a knee to the Christian God. You don't see the Scots, or the Welsh, slaughtering each other over a matter not of which god they pray to, but of how they pray to the very same God. I mean, that's a crazy reason to kill each other."

Doyle let out a breath, then said, "The Irish have always been a hard people."

"Hard, and melancholy," Rhys said. "They make the Welsh look cheerful."

Doyle actually smiled. "Aye."

"Can Merry actually claim the right to keep the chalice on the grounds that it chose her?" Galen asked. "I'm not old enough to remember anybody getting to be king because some stone cried out, so will this actually work?"

"It should work," Doyle said, "but I can't say that the Seelie Court will bow to tradition. It has been so long since the great relics have been among us that many have forgotten how we acquired them in the first place."

"Forgotten because they wish to forget," Nicca said.

"Perhaps, but just saying Meredith owns the vessel because it came to her from the hand of the Goddess Herself will take some convincing."

"How do I prove that the Goddess gave me the goblet?" I asked.

Doyle waved a hand at the table. "The fact that we have the goblet is the proof."

"We prove that the Goddess gave me the chalice by simply having the chalice in my possession?" I asked.

"Yes."

"Isn't that a circular argument?"

"Yes," he said.

"I don't think they're going to buy that."

"I am open to suggestions," Doyle said. Doyle was the master strategist, so whenever he asked for suggestions on a plan, it made me nervous. When he didn't know what we were doing for certain, it didn't usually bode well.

"Whatever we decide, Merry must keep the chalice," Nicca said, "and that means that our queen can't have it, either."

"Oh, shit," Rhys said. "I hadn't thought of that."

I looked at Doyle. "You talked about spies, but that's really why you don't want her to know, isn't it?"

He sighed. "Let us just say that I do not know what she will do when she finds out. The reappearance of the chalice was most unexpected, and the method by which you gained it is also unexpected." He shrugged. "I do not know what she will do, and I do not like not knowing. It is dangerous not to know."

"I'm only her heir if I get pregnant before Cel gets someone else pregnant. She's still my queen, and if she demands the cup of me, I'm duty-bound to give it to her, aren't I?"

Doyle seemed to think for a moment, then nodded. "I believe so, yes."

"Merry must keep the chalice," Nicca said.

"You keep saying that," Rhys said. "Why are you so sure of it?"

"It vanished once because we weren't worthy to keep it. What if Merry hands it over to someone else who isn't worthy, and it goes away again?"

"I think our queen would allow Merry to keep the chalice on that logic alone," Doyle said. "She would not risk the loss of it again."

"If Taranis forces us to give him the chalice and it vanishes again," Galen said, "then it would be the ultimate proof that he isn't worthy to lead."

"And we might prevent him from taking the goblet by that logic," Doyle said, "but only in a private audience. We cannot by hint or faintest action allow anyone to guess that we do not think he is worthy to be king."

"Not my court, not my problem," I said.

"We will try very hard to keep it from being our problem," Doyle said. "Now, I think a little sleep is in order for all of us. We are leaving for the courts in less than a day, and there is much to do."

"What do we do with the chalice? We can't just leave it here on the table," I said.

"Wrap it in the silk and take it to the spare bedroom. Put it in a drawer beside you."

"We're not going to lock it up in the safe? The guesthouse does have one."

"I think that anyone who might want to steal it would have little trouble tearing the safe out of the wall."

"Oh," I said. "Maybe I've been too long out among the humans. I keep forgetting how very strong some of us can be."

"I think, Princess, you had best not be forgetting things like that. Once we return to the high courts of faerie, you will

need to remember just how dangerous everything and everyone can be."

"Is the discussion finished?" Sage asked from midair.

Doyle looked around the room, meeting everyone's
solemn face. "Yes, I believe it is."

"Good," Sage said. "I'm due some blood, and I want it
now."

I heard Frost take a breath to argue, and I knew the sound
so well that I said, "No, Frost, he's right. We bargained, and
sidhe who don't keep their bargains are worthless."

"I will not go back on our bargain, but I do not like it."

I sighed. I'd been feeding Sage once a week for a month,
but Frost had to open his own lily-white vein once, just once,
and it was a major problem. I loved Frost when I was in his
arms. I even loved Frost when I was looking at his beauty, but
I was beginning to not love Frost when he pouted; to not love
him when he made simple things so much harder than they
had to be. It made me question whether I had ever been in
love with Frost, or had it just been lust? Or maybe I was just
tired. Tired of it always being my blood and my body on the
line. It was Frost's turn to take one for the team, and I really
didn't want to hear any whining about it, no matter how delightful he looked while he did it.

Chapter 11

RHYS FLUNG HIMSELF ONTO THE BED, SETTLING HIMSELF ONTO his side, and plumping the pillows so that he was half sitting against the headboard. One knee was up, the other half bent so that he flaunted himself to all of us as we came into the room. The grin on his face did not bode well; it was the look he usually wore when he was going to tease. Frost did not respond well to teasing, and that was an understatement.

"No teasing, Rhys, I mean it. I am tired, it's late, and it's been a very weird day." I opened the bedside table and tried to put the chalice into the drawer. It didn't fit. The drawer was too shallow. I cursed softly under my breath. "Do you think it would be all right just sitting by the bed wrapped in the silk?"

"Probably," he said.

I sat the silk-wrapped cup beside the lamp, and somehow wanted it both farther away and closer. It made no sense, but I wanted to hold it in my hand, have it touch me, so I'd know it wouldn't vanish, and I wanted to hide it in the bottom of a drawer, bury it under clothes, and never have to touch it again. I settled for putting it on the floor beside the bed, half hidden under the dust ruffle. If someone broke in, it wouldn't be immediately apparent, and if I needed to grab it quickly, I could.

"You're so touchy tonight," Rhys said. "Not used to having hot lesbian sex, are you?"

I glared at him. "It was a privilege to bring Maeve to her first sidhe-on-sidhe orgasm in a century, but you know I didn't do it on purpose."

"Looked pretty on purpose to me," he said, still grinning.

Fine, he was going to be difficult. "You're just jealous that I got to touch her and you didn't."

The grin faded around the edges. "Maybe." The grin flared back to life. "Or maybe I'm jealous that I didn't get to be in the middle."

I opened my robe, and the moment he saw me nude, his eye took on a look that I'd begun to know well. It was a look between pain and hunger, as if the wanting was so strong that it hurt him somehow. I'd assumed the look was because of the years of celibacy, but only Rhys looked at me like that. I liked it, and wondered about it, and knew it was something so personal that I'd never ask. If he didn't volunteer the story behind it, I would never know. If he ever lost the look, then, and only then, I might be able to ask.

Frost and Sage were arguing in the hallway behind us. Rhys, unfortunately, wasn't the only one in a teasing mood. Sage I couldn't control, but Rhys, that I could do something about.

I crawled naked onto the bed, and said, "Please, Rhys, don't tease Frost, not tonight."

He wasn't looking at my face, and I didn't think he'd heard me. I tried again. "Rhys, Rhys, up here, eye contact." I snapped my fingers to get his attention.

He blinked and took a long time to finally get to my face. "Did you say something?"

I hit him with a pillow, which he caught and wrapped his arms around. "I mean it, Rhys. If you make this difficult in any way, I'm going to be pissed." I picked up another pillow and hugged it. "I'm tired, Rhys, I mean really physically tired. I want sleep, not to wade through the emotional fallout from Frost sharing blood with Sage." I met his gaze and was happy to see the grin had faded. "Please, don't make this harder."

He was solemn now. "Asking me, or telling me?"

"Right now, I'm asking as a friend, a lover, not as princess."

He moved the pillow behind him so he was sitting up even

higher. "Okay, since you asked nicely." The grin crept back. "Besides, Frost isn't really my type."

I rolled my eyes. "If you make one homosexual joke, I will kick you out of this bed tonight. I swear it."

"Would I do a thing like that?"

"Yes, damn it, you would." I touched his arm, gripped it. "Rhys, please, don't."

Frost and Sage were almost in the room, and now I could hear what they were arguing about. Frost wanted Sage to take blood without using glamour, and Sage wanted to use glamour. It was more fun that way, the little demi-fey was saying.

Rhys's face went serious, and he sighed. "I like Frost, he's a good man in a fight, but he's been touchy as hell on a winter's day since he joined the courts as a sidhe."

I caught the odd phrasing, but I knew what Rhys meant. I'd seen Frost's first form. That form hadn't been sidhe. There'd been so much happening that I hadn't had time to think about the meaning of any of it. Frost hadn't always been sidhe, yet I'd been taught that you had to have sidhe blood in your veins to become sidhe. I remembered him dancing across the snow, child-like, beautiful, the way a rush of snow is beautiful when the wind lifts it up and throws it to the sky in a dance of shimmering silver. What I'd seen hadn't been sidhe. I wasn't sure what it had been, but if not sidhe, then what? If never sidhe before, then how was he sidhe now? Questions, and no time for answers, because Frost came through the door with Sage fluttering at his shoulder. I couldn't talk to Frost about what I'd seen in the vision in front of Sage. I wasn't sure that Frost would want it discussed even in front of Rhys, but I knew that Sage wouldn't be welcome in the discussion.

Sage entered fluttering at Frost's shoulder the way a taller fey would have walked at his side. "I will not do it without the glamour, and there's an end of it."

Frost was shaking his head, all that silver hair sparkling in the light. "I will not allow you to bespell me, Sage, and that is the true end of it."

"Gentlemen," I said.

They both turned with petulant anger plain on their faces. But Sage's face went from pouting to lust in the blink of an eye. He flew toward the bed with a laugh, fluttering above my head like a tiny helicopter trying to get a better view.

Frost stayed by the door, and the look on his face stayed petulant, angry, with just a hint of fear. It showed in his grey eyes for a few moments, real fear, then it was gone, lost behind his arrogance. I knew the arrogance was partly to hide whatever he was thinking. I knew he was more than that now, but the knowledge didn't really make him any easier to deal with because it meant he was unsure of the situation, or didn't like it. Never a good thing.

I held out my hand to him. "Come to me, Frost."

"To you I would gladly come, Meredith, but not to all of you."

I let my hand fall across the pillow that was still in my lap. Sage wasn't getting quite as good a show as he might have wanted, but he fluttered joyously above me because I tended to put on clothes or get under the covers before he took blood. He'd proven himself untrustworthy. I don't mind being groped when I've invited it, but unwanted attention I didn't need. I figured with Rhys and Frost, I'd be safe enough. Looking at Frost still standing by the door, I began to wonder.

"You agreed to this, Frost," I said.

"I agreed to give blood, but not to let the little fey work his glamour on me."

Sage turned in midair and fluttered back toward the bigger man. "A sidhe who fears the magic of a demi-fey, what riddle is this?"

"I do not fear you, little man, but I will not willingly allow any fey to use his magic upon me."

"Allowing Sage to use glamour when he takes blood is the compromise, since I won't give him sex."

"It is not my compromise," Frost said, and he seemed to look taller, broader of shoulder, more sure of himself. I'd learned that the more certain he seemed, the less certain he was, but he wouldn't have thanked me for knowing that, let alone for sharing it.

Rhys sat up from the pillows where he'd been reclining. "Princess, may I?"

I made a small motion, and sighed. "If you think you can help."

"Let Sage taste Frost"—he hurried with the next words, because of the look of outrage on Frost's face—"as he tasted me, a tiny lick, nothing else. Let's see if Frost really tastes like a god, or whether he just tastes sidhe."

It wasn't a bad idea. "Frost, will you allow Sage to lick you, that and nothing more?"

Frost opened his mouth, I think to refuse, but I added. "Frost, please, it's not that much to ask."

He hesitated a moment, then nodded, once. "I will allow it."

"Sage," I said, "a small lick like you gave Rhys in the other room, nothing else."

Sage flew close enough to the bed for me to see a truly evil smile, but he nodded. I didn't trust it, but he nodded again and fluttered toward Frost.

Frost started to take a step back, then seemed to realize what he was doing and stood his ground. Most sidhe seemed to believe that no one short of another sidhe could use glamour on them successfully. It wasn't true, but a lot of them believed it was. The fact that Frost didn't believe it made me wonder whose magic he'd fallen afoul of. He reacted as if he had reason to fear the demi-fey.

"Wait," I said. "Has Frost ever been given to the demi-fey for torture like Galen was given to them?"

"No," Frost and Rhys said in unison.

Sage shook his head. "We've never had the pleasure of the Killing Frost staked out for us." He licked his tiny lips, making enough of a show of it that we'd all see. "Yum."

Frost looked at me. "Don't make me do this."

"Do what? Let him lick your skin, see what you taste like? It's not a hardship, Frost. Did you fall afoul of some lesser fey's glamour? Is that why you're worried?" The moment I said it, I knew I'd been too bold.

"I have fallen afoul of no fey." His face was at its most beautiful, cold and arrogant, with the bone structure to make a plastic surgeon weep with envy. The grey of the silk robe seemed almost to blend with the glittering silver of his hair. He was like some sculpture too beautiful to touch, too proud to stoop to touching anyone else.

I wanted to ask him what was wrong, but didn't dare in front of the other men. I looked into that face, trailed my gaze down his chest, his waist, thought about everything that lay under the robe, and knew that even if we'd been alone, he might not have admitted that anything was wrong.

"Taste him, Sage." My voice sounded as tired and discouraged as I felt.

Sage moved forward, his wings barely moving, as if he should have fallen rather than floated. He hovered just over Frost's face, then darted in and out, a blur of yellow and blue and red. He was near the ceiling and out of reach before Frost could swat at his face, almost as if Sage had known he'd do it.

Sage was hissing, and at first I thought it was because Frost had swatted at him; then I heard the anger in his voice. "He tastes no different from the white knight."

"Then take my blood and let Frost out of it," Rhys said.

Sage flew near the bed. He crossed tiny arms across his chest and stamped his foot in midair, as if he were on solid ground. "No. I bargained for two sidhe warriors, and it's two I want."

"I'll give blood," Frost said, "but no glamour. I agreed to blood, not magic."

Rhys started to say something, but I touched his arm. "You'll have what we bargained for, Sage, all of it, but let Frost go back to his bed. He's no use to us tonight."

Frost flinched at my last words, a mere tightening around his eyes, but I'd made a study of him and knew what it meant.

"Who would you have in his place?" Sage asked, flying lower so that he and I were face to face. "Galen, perhaps?" His smile managed to be both evil and happy.

"You know better than to ask, Sage," I said.

He pouted, but he didn't mean it. "I will not share you with the goblin again. I want no drink from Darkness." He seemed to think about it for a moment, then alit upon the pillow in my lap. The purple satin sagged under his weight. He was always heavier than he looked, or even than I remembered. "Nicca, then, for he is all that remains."

I nodded. "Agreed."

"You have not asked Nicca if he will allow the demi-fey to take his blood," Frost said.

I looked at him, and he was still heart-stoppingly handsome. The question was, was beauty enough, and the answer, of course, was no. "I don't have to ask Nicca, Frost. If I send for him, he'll come, and he'll do what I tell him to do. Nicca won't argue about it, he'll just do what needs doing."

"And I won't," Frost said, tilting his chin upward, looking like something carved of arrogance and defiance.

I sighed. "I love you, Frost."

That softened his face, made the uncertainty rise to the surface for a moment.

"I love you in my bed, I love so much about you, but I will be queen. I will be absolute ruler of our court. You seem to keep forgetting what that means. No matter who is king, I will still rule. Do you understand that, Frost?"

"You would have a puppet as your king?"

"No, I would have a partner who knows that unpleasant things must be done, and doesn't argue about things that cannot be changed."

"I cannot be other than I am," he said, and his voice didn't match the steel calm of his face.

"I know that." My voice was soft.

For a second he looked woebegone, then the icy arrogance slid back into place. The mask that he'd worn for centuries at the court. He stared down at me, and there was nothing in his face that I could reason with. He was Frost, the Killing Frost. You do not reason with the cold of winter. You either take shelter from it, or you die.

His voice was as cold as I'd ever heard it when he said, "I

will send Nicca to you and I will tell him nothing but that you require him."

"Do that," I said, and couldn't keep my own voice from growing colder. I was angry with him, angry and frustrated, and I didn't know how to save the situation. I was a future queen, and I couldn't even handle my own personal life. That seemed a bad sign. I added, "Thank you, Frost."

"Don't thank me, Princess, I'm just doing my duty." He turned as if to go.

I called him back with my words. "Frost, don't do this."

He only half turned. "Do what?"

"Make this all about you and your hurt feelings. Some things aren't about you. Some things aren't personal at all, they are just necessary."

"May I go?"

I said a short silent prayer for patience with this impossible man, then said, "Yes, go, send Nicca to us."

He left without a backward glance, one hand rubbing the small of his back, which meant he'd had a weapon of some kind there. Frost seldom went completely unarmed. And when he felt insecure he touched his weapons, the way some women play with their jewelry.

"Well," Rhys said, "that went badly."

"Moody, even for the Killing Frost," Sage said, "and angrier."

"Fear," Rhys said, softly.

"What?" I asked.

"Fear," he repeated. "The haughtier Frost gets, the more nervous he is, and *nerves* is just another word for fear."

"What's he afraid of?" I asked.

"Me." Sage sprang into the air, twirling as if to show off his wings and his skill.

Rhys grinned. "You can be fearsome, but I don't think that's it."

"Then what?" I asked.

Rhys shrugged. "I don't know."

Nicca appeared in the doorway. His ankle-length hair was like a tousled cloak around his body, but he'd thrown on his robe of royal purple silk. The color suited him, bringing out the rich brown of his eyes, the reddish highlights in his nearly auburn hair. It made his skin seem darker, more chocolate. "Frost said you wanted me."

I explained what we needed, and he simply said yes. No fight, no pouting, no disagreement of any kind. It was more than refreshing. It was exactly what the night needed, something simple instead of difficult. Frost in my bed was a thing of great hunger, huge demands, and fierce pleasure. Tonight a little agreeable pleasure, some lesser demands, and a gentle hunger seemed just what the doctor ordered.

Chapter 12

I LAY BACK IN THE BEND OF RHYS'S ARM, NESTLED AGAINST THE curve of his shoulder, my head resting on the firm warmth of his chest. Nicca was propped up on his elbow, his body curved just behind mine. He kept a fraction of a distance between us, so that all I could feel against my skin was the humming vibration of his aura, his magic. I wanted to ask him to close the distance between us, to slide his body along the back of mine, but I didn't. I hadn't invited him here for sex. It was Rhys's night, and he'd stopped sharing me with Nicca after we'd defeated the Nameless and some of his powers returned. I'd assumed that with even more of his old power returned, he'd be even more reluctant to share me, so I hadn't asked. Feeling Nicca's warmth at my back made me want to ask.

I nuzzled along Rhys's chest, making a caress of moving my head enough to look at his face. "I want Nicca to stay with us tonight."

"I'll just bet you do," Rhys said, but the smile was starting to be replaced with that serious look in a man's eyes.

I stroked my hand up his stomach, gliding to his nipple and tracing lazy circles around the aureole until his nipple came to attention, and his breath came a little faster. He grabbed my wrist. "Stop that or I won't be able to think."

"That's the idea," I said, and smiled at him, but knew there was something more urgent than humor in my eyes.

"I notice you don't ask me to stay the night," Sage said. He landed on the hard, sculpted plain of Rhys's stomach.

"You are welcome to spend the night," I said, "but not in my bed, not in my body."

Sage stamped his foot on Rhys's solid flesh. "It is most unfair that I will use my glamour to make you feel such wondrous sensations, but I am denied the fruits of my labor. Especially since others will partake of that bounty."

"You're the one who wanted two sidhe men, Sage. You know the effect your glamour has on me, and on others."

He crossed his arms over his chest. "Yes, yes, only myself to blame." His face went instantly from a pout to a smile that was half lust and half joy. "I'll make you a wager."

I raised myself from Rhys's chest enough to shake my head. "No."

"What kind of wager?" Rhys asked.

"Don't do it, Rhys."

He looked down at me. "Why not?"

"You haven't felt Sage's glamour. I have."

A touch of sidhe arrogance mingled with Rhys's humor. It was our racial Achilles' heel, no mythological mixing intended. Our arrogance had been our undoing more than once.

"I think three sidhe should be proof against demi-fey magic."

I touched his face. "Rhys, you should know by now not to underestimate the fey just because they aren't sidhe."

He jerked away from my hand. I hadn't meant to touch his scars, hadn't meant to imply what his face said he'd taken as my meaning. He was angry now, as he always was when he was reminded of what the goblins had done to him. "I think it is you who forget what we are." The blue rings in his eye began to glow with a soft, pulsing color, robin egg blue, winter sky, all throbbing in time to his anger, and his power.

"If I am Cromm Cruach again, Merry, then Sage can't touch me."

I wanted to say, *What if you aren't?* but something in his face stopped me. What do you say to a man's pride? "I've never been a god, Rhys. I don't know what it means to be that untouchable."

"I do," he said, and there was a fierceness to him, almost a franticness that I'd never seen. I recognized fear when I saw it, though. Fear that he wouldn't be what he had been. Fear that he might never again regain what he'd lost. I'd seen the fear too many times, in too many other sidhe faces, not to know it. It was the fear of my people—that we were failing as a race, that we had already failed, and would all fade and die. It was a fear that we'd carried so long, it was almost a national phobia.

If I said no to his wager with Sage, then it was as much as saying he wasn't strong enough, wasn't good enough. It wasn't what I meant, but he was male, and no matter what their flavor, males all have some of the same failings; and I was female, and no matter what flavor we are, we share some of the same failings. His failing was the fragility of his ego; mine, that I was about to stroke his ego at the expense of nearly everything else. I knew it was a mistake when I opened my mouth and said, "Do what you want to do, but don't say I didn't warn you."

"So, white knight, do we have a wager?" Sage asked. "I use my glamour to bespell you all, and if I can work magic on three sidhe at once, then I gain my heart's desire."

"Rhys," Nicca said, "have a care."

"I'm not that stupid," Rhys said. "What is your heart's desire? I need to know that before I can agree to it."

"To fuck the princess," he said.

Rhys shook his head. "I can't bargain what I do not own, and it's her body, not mine."

"No intercourse," I said. "I will not let you have a bid for the throne, Sage."

He shrugged tiny shoulders. "Fine. If not the act itself, then what?"

I had to admit that weeks of feeling Sage's glamour pour over my mind, my body, had made me curious. His personal glamour for seduction was the best I'd ever felt. Just from a small bite on my hand, and his magic, he could bring me to the point of orgasm. It would be a lie to say I hadn't wondered if it would be even better if I allowed him to touch me.

But it wasn't that alone that suddenly made my body go still and quiet.

I had the most amazing lovers in the world, but there were things that they denied me, and themselves. We were trying to get me pregnant, which meant that all sex ended in one way, and one way only. If it couldn't get me with child, we didn't waste the seed. I had persuaded more than one of the men to let me take him in my mouth, but none of them would finish there, no matter how much I begged or how much they wanted to. It hadn't just been intercourse that they'd been forbidden for centuries, it had been any release, even by their own touch. There were so many things besides intercourse that they missed. They would talk about it, but not do it, because it was a wasted opportunity. A waste of seed to plant inside me. A waste of a chance to be king. I realized, suddenly, that I was beginning to feel like a brood mare. Something you mated only to beget a child, not because you wanted to be there. I knew they wanted me, but not truly that they would want me if there were anywhere else they could go. Would my handsome men still want me if there were no throne to win?

Galen would, and that was part of his appeal, but the others? I wasn't certain of the others. That made my chest tight, and not in a good way. Would the handsome sidhe want the short human-looking mortal if they could have chosen elsewhere? I didn't know, and they would never tell the truth. Of course they wanted me, what else could they say? But only Galen, and Rhys, had paid me any attention when I was just an unwanted thing, barely tolerated after my father's death.

The relentless pursuit of a baby had begun to make me feel as if that was all that held them to me. But of course, it was. Once I was pregnant and we knew who the father was, they'd evaporate, go back to that cold distance. I would not have them forever. I looked at Rhys, the shortest of the Queen's Ravens, but every inch of him was muscled, hard, firm, and so strong. I turned to Nicca, and he gazed at me through a tangle of his hair, his dark eyes seemed almost to burn out through the rich, rich chocolate of his hair. I had traced my mouth and hands down the winged pattern on his back, like the world's most vibrant tattoo. He was almost too gentle for me in bed, too submissive. But he was beautiful, and for this short time he was mine, mine to do with as I saw fit. Everyone else was worried about the fact that I wasn't pregnant. I was worried, too, but I also knew that it would close doors for me, shut me away from things I wanted. While I had them, I wanted to truly have them, not just play baby-making factory.

What did I miss most? That was easy. I missed the feel of a man in my mouth, where he started soft and small so I could take all of him in, even his balls, then feel the change in texture, in the sensation of it. I loved it, from beginning to end, and the last time I'd been able to do it, completely, had been with my last boyfriend. And he hadn't been sidhe, and he hadn't been capable of anything close to Sage's glamour. I wanted the feel of that hot release inside more than just my womb. It wasn't the thought of Sage that tightened things low in my body, but the thought of someone pouring himself down my throat.

"She's thought of something," Nicca said.

"What's put that look on your face, Merry?" Rhys asked.

"If Sage's glamour wins the night, I want him in my mouth. I want to feel one of you come inside my mouth."

"You know why we don't," Rhys said.

I'd sat up, pulling away from Rhys's body. "I know, I need to be pregnant, but there's more to sex than making babies." I took in a deep, shuddering breath. "I want to watch one of you bring yourself to orgasm while I watch. I want to feel you hard and firm against every inch of my body until you come. I want to be covered in it, not just one round of baby making after another." I felt strangely sad. "One night someone will get me pregnant, then once we know who the father is, everyone else is gone." I looked at all of them, even the tiny demi-fey standing on Rhys's stomach. "I want to make the most of all of you while I have the chance."

I touched both the larger men's thighs with my hands.

"You spent centuries being denied so many more things than just intercourse. Don't you want those things back?"

Rhys sat up, sending Sage fluttering into the air. Rhys hugged me. "Merry, I'm sorry. I'd love to oblige, but . . ."

I pushed away from him. "But we don't want to waste any seed. Yes, yes, it's all very important. I'm not even arguing. But for a night here or there, I want us to do whatever we want to do, and not worry about whether we're making babies or not."

"I don't think Doyle would allow that," Nicca said.

I turned on him and felt the anger rising through me like a hot wind. I felt it trip my magic, spread it in the beginning of a glow inside my skin. "Is Doyle here in this bed tonight?"

"No," Nicca whispered, and he looked worried. "I'm sorry, Merry, I didn't mean . . ."

"I am princess, and I will be queen." I shook my head. "I'm tired of everyone arguing with me. Fine, fine, for tonight intercourse with the two of you, but not with Sage."

I held my hand out to Sage, and he landed on it. He was strangely heavy, as if he weighed more than he should have. I'd held his Queen Niceven in my hand, and she weighed nothing, all air and gossamer, but there was meat to Sage.

"But you'll do what I want, won't you, Sage?"

"It would be my pleasure, Princess." He gave a sweeping bow, then fluttered up, gave me a quick kiss on my mouth, and rose laughing into the air. "You'd be surprised how many sidhe women won't suck a man's dick."

"You've been seducing too many Seelie sidhe," I said.

He looked down at me, hovering on his stained-glass wings. "Maybe, or maybe too many things in the Unseelie Court have sharp teeth. A man's got to be careful where he puts himself, or he'll lose more than his virtue."

"I don't bite," I said.

He pouted. "Oh, too bad."

I smiled at him. "Well, if you like it rough."

He looked serious for a moment. "Up to a point, yes."

"Show me the point."

"Merry doesn't get your point until you've bespelled all three of us. What do we get if you fail?" Rhys asked.

"I will never again try to put my point on, or in, the princess."

"Your word of honor?" Rhys said.

Sage put a hand over his heart and bowed in midair, a strangely graceful gesture. "My word of honor."

I wanted to call it off then, because I knew Sage too well. He'd have never offered that particular wager unless he was sure. But before I could say anything, Rhys said, "Done."

I sighed, then realized that, strangely, I was half hoping we lost. But whether we won or lost, I was going to talk to Doyle. Queen Andais had given me my guards to do with as I saw fit, but once I had a king, would she take them back? Would they lose the only opportunity they would have in the next millennium to touch themselves, to climb into a woman's mouth, to cover her body in seed? Taking them back, and cutting them off again, sounded like something Andais would do. She was a sadist, after all. If I put that as a possibility to Doyle, he might see things my way. If he didn't, I'd try it as an order. Though I didn't have much hope for that. Ordering the Darkness to do anything he didn't agree with usually meant he ignored me. Andais had said that the reason she never took Doyle to her bed was that if he got her pregnant, he wouldn't be content to be consort; he would have been king in more than just name, and she didn't share her power. I was beginning to see her point. Goddess help me, I was beginning to agree with my wicked aunt. That couldn't be good, could it?

Chapter 13

THE THREE OF US RECLINED ONTO THE PILLOWS, MY HEAD nestled in the curve of Rhys's shoulder; Nicca had scooted down low on the bed so he could rest his head on my stomach, his hair spilling out behind him like a cloak of brown silk.

Sage hovered above us like some tiny, lustful angel. "A bounty such as this is spread before few fey."

"From the look on your face," Rhys said, "I'm not sure whether you mean as food or sex."

"Both, oh, definitely both." He began to slowly float down to meet us.

Rhys put out a hand for him to land upon, but Sage glided to the side. I put a hand up automatically to keep him from landing on my bare breasts. I'd kept him far from such intimate parts.

"You're taking blood from us, not Merry," Rhys said.

"Never fear, gwynfor, you will not be passed over, but since I am a lover of women and to my knowledge you are as well, it will work better if I begin with the fair princess."

"I have not been called *gwynfor* in a very, very long time."

"You were the gwynfor, the white lord, and you will be again," Sage said.

"Maybe," Rhys said, "but flattery doesn't explain why you're on Merry's hand and not mine, or Nicca's."

Sage didn't weigh much, probably less than two pounds, but it was still awkward to hold him above my body. "It's his glamour, Rhys; let him work it the way he wants to. I want to actually get some sleep tonight. Unlike the immortal sidhe, I look tired when I've gone without."

Rhys looked at me. "Why do I think this has less to do with sleep, and more to do with the fact that you've changed sides on this wager?"

"It was never my wager," I said, "and the next time you make wagers with my body as prize, you should think long and hard before you do so without asking me first."

"You were here," Rhys said.

"But you never asked."

He thought about that for a second or two, then gave a small nod. "Damn, I'm sorry, Merry, you're right. I apologize."

"One day of being back to your godhead, and already you're falling into bad habits," I said.

"I am sorry."

"Don't apologize for that, Rhys, there are other things I'd rather have the apology for."

"Such as?" he asked.

"If I kicked you both out right now, Sage would do whatever I wanted. He's more interested in pleasure than in being king."

"What's that supposed to mean?" Rhys asked.

"It means that if any of you was here more for sex than for kingship, I'd have persuaded one of you to fall off the intercourse wagon by now."

"Merry, Cel will kill you if he wins this race. If he becomes king, he won't tolerate you alive. We're your royal guard, we're supposed to protect your safety above everything else, even our own desires, or yours."

Sage touched my finger with his hands, and that one small caress stopped my breath in my throat, sped my pulse in my neck. My hand floated downward almost of its own accord, until it rested between my breasts. Sage suddenly seemed heavier than I knew he was, and my arm was more tired than it should have been.

Rhys tried to stare down at us but seemed to be having trouble focusing. "What was that?"

"Sage," I breathed.

Nicca slid his face along my stomach, and that sensation

seemed as if his cheek were stroking things deep inside me. He gazed up my body at me and at Sage. "What did he do?" His voice was full of a soft wonderment.

"Touched my finger with his hands," I said.

"Shit," Rhys said, "shit."

Sage laughed, a high, delighted sound. "Oh, this will be fun."

Rhys started to say something, but Sage slid his arms around my three middle fingers, cupping the unbelievable softness of his skin against my whole hand. "Consort save us, I can feel the edge of what you're feeling. His skin is so soft, softer than anything I've ever felt."

Sage rubbed his hair along the tips of my fingers. His hair was like downy feathers; as if spider silk could be woven into hair, too soft to be real. The brush of that hair on my skin made Nicca shudder against me and brought Rhys's body hard against my hip. Eager, ready.

"I didn't understand," Rhys said in a voice gone both soft and deep.

"I tried to tell you," I said. "You wouldn't hear me."

"Why can we feel it when he touches you?" Nicca asked.

"I don't know."

"I know," Sage said, sliding his body down my hand until he sat straddling my wrist, "but I'm not telling."

He wrapped his legs around my wrist and I was suddenly aware that he wore nothing under his gossamer skirt. He was tiny, but the touch of that bit of sex felt more intimate than it should have, more important than it should ever have been.

I was suddenly aware of the pulse between his legs. The throb and ebb of the blood on either side of his thighs beat against the pulse in my wrist like a second heartbeat, as if the very beat of my blood would answer to the beat of his small body.

"Your hand, gwynfor, now I will take it."

It took Rhys a moment to focus, to understand. One of his hands was still half pinned under my body, and he held his free hand against his stomach, almost as if he was afraid of being hurt.

"A little blood, a little taste, nothing more, gwynfor, nothing more."

"Stop calling me that," Rhys said.

"But you are the white lord," Sage said, "and the white lord, the hand of ecstasy and death, feared nothing and no one."

Rhys reached out toward the tiny fey, slowly, reluctantly, his face already half-lost to the sensual call of the other's magic. The wager was lost before Sage ever touched him.

Sage stayed pressed to my wrist, like one of those old wooden carvings of the tiny fairies riding broomstraw, except my wrist was the whisk of a plant and his power did ride me, rode me like the wingless fey were supposed to ride the small flowering plants. Were the flowers as joyful to be ridden? Did it feel good to them to be torn away from their roots and plunged through the night sky?

Sage wrapped his tiny hands around Rhys's finger. He laid his small red mouth against the tip of his finger, like a tiny swollen rosebud. I felt Rhys's pulse like a distant line of music, a bass rhythm that you heard only through the walls at night, as you lay in your bed, and wondered where it was coming from. Sage opened his mouth, his lips still pressed against Rhys's skin.

Rhys actually said, "No, no."

Sage drew back enough to roll the glittering black of his eyes up to the much larger man. "Will you be forsworn, white lord? Will your courage fail you in the face of a mere demi-fey?"

I could see Rhys's pulse thundering against the skin of his throat, and his voice came rough around it. "I'd forgotten what you were."

"Forgotten what?" Sage asked, his mouth still hovering over Rhys's fingertip.

Rhys had to swallow to speak again. "Once, you were a court of your own, and size mattered not in power."

Sage gave a small laugh. "Do you remember what else we could do?"

"Your glamour could roll us, like a drunk on a Saturday night."

"Yes, white lord, it's what saved us from being destroyed by both courts." His mouth moved slowly back toward Rhys's finger, and the next words were spoken with his lips so close that they shivered along Rhys's skin: "The Nameless has given back a great deal, to all of us." He sank his teeth into Rhys's flesh.

Rhys's spine bowed, his head thrown back, eye closed. I felt that quick pain only lightly, a distant stab of pleasure.

Nicca writhed, climbing my body until his face almost touched Sage's leg. His arm convulsed around my waist, holding on as if he was afraid, or eager. I knew just from the press of his body that he was getting the hints of pleasure and pain, just as I was.

Sage began to suck at the wound, and distantly, I felt the pull. I'd had it often enough for myself to know that it felt as if that tiny mouth had a long, thin line directly from the tip of a finger to the groin. With every suck Sage pulled on things that shouldn't have been touchable from a small wound in a finger.

Sage's pulse between his legs beat against the pulse in my wrist, fast, faster, hard, harder, and I felt a third pulse. It was as if Sage had pulled Rhys's heart into his hand, and Sage was swallowing around the thick, meaty pulse of Rhys's heartbeat. I felt Rhys's heart beating down Sage's body, as if the smaller man were a tuning fork, a vibrating, trembling path from one throbbing heartbeat to another.

Rhys's body pressed tighter against the side of me. His groin was pressed against the curve of my hip, and almost against his will, it seemed, his body began to move against mine. I could feel him large and hard, rubbing against my hip. A rhythm began between the two of them. I felt Sage suck on Rhys, and with every suck Rhys pressed himself into my hip, buried the hard shaft of himself along my skin as if he were seeking another way inside me.

Rhys began to glow with that white light he held inside. His tricolored eye glowed like blue neon as he gazed down at me. His lips were half parted and he bent down to lay his mouth across mine, and the moment he kissed me, my power spilled upward, so that as he pulled back from my lips, magic trailed between us like the glow of stars. My body pulsed white as if I'd swallowed the moon, and it was spilling out through my skin.

Sage sat between us like a small golden doll, the veins in his wings shining like stained glass in a fall of sunlight. He wasn't sidhe, but power is power. For a moment I saw his red mouth pulse, as if he truly did hold Rhys's heartbeat in his mouth.

Nicca had begun to glow softly, the wing tattoo on his back pulsing faint traces of pink and blue and cream, and black. It was only the beginnings of his power, the first promise.

Rhys's hand under my shoulders convulsed, his fingers digging into my skin, and I felt him fight to close his other fist on Sage's fragile body. Rhys's breathing came fast, faster, until he threw his head back, his body arching against me. Something luminous and nearly liquid moved underneath his skin, like watching glowing clouds across the sky break apart, spilling like burning phosphorus. His white curls swirled around his face in the wind of his own power, and his hair ran shining with power, as if someone had traced a glowing wand in streaks through his curls. He opened his eye, and I had a moment to see its neon blue circles begin to swirl like a storm about to break over me, over all of us. Then he ground himself into my flesh, so hard that it hurt, and that brought me back to his body and chased back the power, just enough. He screamed, a second before he spilled over me in a scalding wave that flowed and dripped down my hip.

The feel of it bowed my back, flung my free hand skyward, writhed me over the bed, but I couldn't move, I was trapped between the thrust of Rhys's body and Nicca still wound around my waist and legs.

Rhys's heart beat inside my veins, faded, then was gone so abruptly that it scared me. I had to open my eyes and see that he was still there, still alive. It was strange because I could still feel him pressed along the length of my body, but it had been the taste of his pulse in my body that I had ridden. He lay collapsed beside me, hair scattered across his face, his neck bare and smooth, and his pulse thudded against the thin skin of his neck like something trapped. His power faded like the moon lost behind clouds.

I started to ask if he was all right, but the pulse of Sage's body froze the words in my mouth, and I turned to meet that tiny, glittering black gaze. His golden luminescence hadn't faded; if anything, he glowed brighter than ever, his wings like colored fire framing the central flame of his body. There was more of fierceness, of triumph, of power than lust on his face. "Whatever my lady wishes, so shall it be," he whispered.

Nicca held a shaking hand up and Sage laughed. "So eager, I like that."

"No gloating, Sage," I said, my voice still uncertain, as if I wasn't quite sure it was my voice.

"Oh, but Merry, I must. The donnan has paid me a high compliment."

"Donnan?" Nicca made it a question, then shook his head. "I was no one's chief, little, brown, or otherwise, Sage." His voice was shaky, but through the haze of glamour with Rhys and I beginning to fade like the moon sinking behind the trees, Nicca seemed determined not to be called what he had never been.

"As you will, then, Nicca," Sage said. He grabbed Nicca's fingers and pulled his hand across mine, so that Nicca's hand was cradled between Sage's body and my fingers. The back of his hand was hot gliding across my fingers and palm. That one simple touch brought the fading light in my skin back to a glow as if the moon had decided to rise twice that night.

Sage dragged Nicca's hand across his own lap until he bent his tiny, swollen mouth over the wrist. He laid that red kiss against Nicca's wrist, where the blue vein pulsed just under the skin, so close to the surface it was like an eager lover waiting to be taken.

Nicca crawled up my body so that he lay half upon me, using his free arm to support his weight; for a moment I looked down the length of his body to see him long and firm and full of a golden light that began to spread through his pale brown skin, as if the sun were rising inside his body. I felt his magic vibrate just above me like a trembling sheet of heat in the air. Sage's magic had caught Rhys unawares, but Nicca had learned from the other man's mistake, if it was a mistake, and he was using his own magic, trying to work through the glamour.

Sage bit into Nicca's wrist, and the pain distracted him, closed his eyes, shuddered his breath, but he held his body above mine in a sort of one-armed push-up. I couldn't taste Nicca's pulse as I had Rhys's. Nicca was fighting the glamour.

He managed to maneuver himself over my body, between my legs, and he began to lower himself down, pushing through the vibrating heat of his own magic, shoving it into me and over Sage. It made Sage hesitate and shiver himself.

I ran my free hand down Nicca's chest, stomach, and wrapped my hand around the long hardness of him. My touch bowed his back, lost him his concentration. Sage's glamour flooded over us both, and the blood that raced through my body spilled in white light out of my skin, danced my hair around my face. Nicca's skin was the color of deep golden amber, like dark honey if it could burn. For burn he did, with a golden light that I'd never seen from him before. It was as if Sage's glamour had stripped his skin away to reveal nothing but power.

I held him in my hand, firm and real, but he glowed so bright that I could not look upon him and had to close my eyes. It was like holding on to some vibrating, pulsing, piece of magic made solid. He was hot velvet against my palm, a gliding smoothness that throbbed down my hand to dance inside my veins, to spill heat through my body, like a searching hand that touched and glided over and through me, searching, searching, searching until his power found me, found my center, found that part that nothing should touch, and the power filled me from the inside out. His golden power raced with my magic, my body, my pleasure, so that his glow ran before mine, coaxed mine to shine bright and brighter, until the room was full of shadows from the shining of us, full of shadows that had no place in this room, as if our lights showed us hints of what lay around us, and it had nothing to do with this room, this bed, these bodies. The magic spilled out of us raw and wild, and Sage burned in the middle of it.

I fell back into my body screaming, bucking, fighting the bed, the men, everything, anything I could touch. I felt my nails slicing into flesh, and it wasn't enough. Three things brought me back to myself: blood in a hot rain across my face, Nicca shrieking, over and over again, and the feel of wings under my hands. Somewhere in all of it, I didn't want to tear Sage's wings, as he'd grown large under my hands.

Someone grabbed my wrists, held them over my head, pinned them to the pillows, and I didn't struggle. I couldn't see. Blood had landed across my closed lids, and the lashes were too thick with it. There was too much blood for a little rough sex. I blinked frantically, and I thought I was seeing double. Two pairs of wings rose above me like neon glass. One pair belonged to Sage—now nearly as tall as I was, his weight pinning me underneath him. But the others were larger, almost larger than I was, brown and cream, edges of pink, whirls of blue and red like huge eyes dotting the wings. They were only half unfurled, like a butterfly fresh from its chrysalis.

I stared up into Nicca's face. A face that was half pain, and half ecstasy, and all confusion. Blood glittered across us, glowing like liquid rubies, pulsing with the magic that still rode the air. The blood was Nicca's, from where his wings had burst from his skin.

It was Rhys who held my wrists, though he was as close to being off the bed as he could get. He was spattered with blood, but even as I watched, it was absorbed, as if his skin were drinking it. "I thought you were going to tear their wings," he said, and his voice held an edge of fear. I wondered how many of us had been screaming at the end. The blood seemed to like Rhys. He was drinking the power of this strange blood, this strange wound.

I was pinned under Sage and Nicca, though Sage was closer to center, and Nicca had spilled slightly off my body. I stared up at the wings, like stained glass with its own light. Nicca's wings were unfurling even as I watched, pumping larger with each beat of his heart.

Sage's mouth was smeared with liquid rubies. I'd never seen blood glow like that. He leaned down toward me, and I felt the power, not just of his glamour, or of Nicca, but of the blood itself. He kissed my lips, and the power burned against my skin, raised my face to his mouth, and we fed. He fed at my mouth like it was a flower, and I fed at his like it was a cup. We drank, sipped, and licked the power from each other's mouths.

When we raised back from the kiss, most of the blood was gone, as if it had been something else altogether. Rhys looked as if he were carved of white light, and his eye burned like some blue sun. He slid off the bed, shaking his head. "I've had enough, thanks. I'll just watch the rest of the show."

I don't know what I would have said, or if I had any words left, but one of the men still in the bed made some small movement and I turned back to them.

I lowered my hands to touch Sage's hair. In his small form it was soft, but here like this, the softness was almost overwhelming; just running my fingers through the silken brush of it caused me to writhe underneath them both.

Nicca cried out, and I gazed up at him, watched the fear leave his eyes, consumed with something darker and brighter. His eyes glowed as he lowered his mouth to mine. Sage moved just enough to let Nicca taste me. He licked the inside of my mouth as if it were a bowl, and he was trying to get the last drops from it.

I brought my hands down to glide along the sides of both

their bodies. Sage's skin was like warm silk. Nicca's skin was warmer, hotter. Sage writhed over me, impossibly soft and firm at the same time. But Nicca was like something carved of power, so that it was hard to feel anything but the throbbing beat of the magic inside him.

Sage dragged his body up mine, whispering against my skin. "Remember what you promised me, Princess?"

"Yes," I whispered, "yes."

I watched Sage move his body closer to mine, watched the thickness of him come closer to my face. Nicca had moved to one side, but he kept his hands gliding over my body so that he never lost contact with my skin. When Sage came to kneel in front of my face, I watched Nicca crawl between my legs, on his knees, so that the two of them echoed each other. I remembered the mirror on the bureau then, and I turned to see them. Sage's wings overlapped Nicca's body so that he was half hidden behind the gossamer colors. His own wings were almost full now, large and curved, luminous with color.

Sage touched my face, brought my attention back to him. I'd never seen him naked and full-sized before. He was bigger than I'd expected, not longer, but wider. I flicked my tongue across the tip of him, and it was as unbelievably soft as the rest of him. I ran my hands over him, the shaft of him as soft as most men's balls, and the skin of his testicles like something made of satin. I had no words for the fineness of the skin between his legs. It was softer than a dream, like a bag made to hold something magical.

He touched my hands, stopped them from moving along his skin. "Have a care, Merry, or you'll have me go before I've seen the inside of your mouth."

I pulled him between my lips, and it was like sucking on silk that happened to be warm and muscled, and alive. The sensation of the soft skin and the hardness of him made me cry out with him in my mouth. Which made him cry out, and arch above me.

I felt Nicca slide his hands under my thighs, felt him lift

me a little above the bed. "Say yes, Merry, say yes." His voice came hoarse with need, and I knew if I said no, he'd stop. But I didn't say no.

I drew Sage out of my mouth enough to say, "Yes, Nicca, yes."

I felt Nicca bump against me, his hands sliding farther underneath me, lifting me higher, holding me in the heat of his hands, my legs spreading wide.

I arched my neck so that Sage could slide into my mouth, down my throat, arched my neck so that I could take every thick, silken inch of him between my lips, my teeth, and deeper. Sage was as deep as I could take him when Nicca plunged between my legs.

I screamed, and it was muffled by the sweet flesh in my mouth. Nicca held me in front of his hips, helped the arch of my body, so that Sage slid more easily into and out of my mouth.

I caught a glimpse of a sea of wings above me, like the masts of faerie ships, then they seemed to catch a rhythm. Each plunged inside my body in time to the other, as if he could feel the other's body. Warm muscled silk in and out of my mouth, caressing my lips, my teeth, gliding along my tongue, bumping the back of my throat. Nicca was like something long and hot, almost burning between my legs, thrusting inside me until the head of him bumped into the deepest part of me. Then they both drew out of me, almost pulling free, then thrust inside me again, as if it were a dance, or a race to see who could thrust himself the deepest, the quickest, and they both found their depth at the same moment. Both of them hit me deep, then both withdrew, almost free of me, then back inside, faster and faster. Until they began to beat inside me, and I felt that heavy warmth grow inside me, filling up like a pool of water, one drop of pleasure at a time, one thrust at a time, one thick taste at a time.

Sage was like a shaft of sunlight, glowing in and out of me. I could only catch glimpses of Nicca's darker light, as if the sun had swallowed something brown and was determined to burn it away. They brought my skin to a white boil, and white flames began to dance across my skin, and I saw a green-gold light, and realized my eyes were glowing so brightly it was casting green shadows on the pillows.

I swallowed sunlight over and over; and the sun beat between my legs, and above all of it their wings shimmered, the colors dancing, fleeing through the air, until I saw that the room was full of butterflies carved of neon and power.

Nicca thrust between my legs and it was as if he grew impossibly long, impossibly warm, thrusting up through my body, as if he would touch where Sage was pulsing inside my mouth, as if the two suns would meet inside my body and I would be burned away, drowned in their twin powers, and that was the drop of pleasure that filled the pool, that spilled me over, that brought me writhing under their weight, that set me sucking at the sunlight in my mouth, made me grind my hips into the heat between my legs. Sage poured hot and thick down my throat, and I swallowed that salty power, felt the glow of it travel down my throat and through my body. Nicca came in a thrust that seemed to burn through my body in a long shaft of power as if it would rend me in two, bend me into something hot, and dripping, and liquid to run over the sheets, to spill along their bodies, as they spilled along mine.

When I came to myself, Sage was lying curled on his side, trapping one of my arms. Nicca was collapsed across my lower body, on his stomach, his wings curving over his back, his buttocks, his thighs, and one long graceful curve of winged tail ran off the bed and nearly touched the carpet.

I couldn't hear anything but the thundering of my own blood in my veins. My hearing came back slowly, and the first thing I heard was Sage's shaky laughter. I think he said, "How do you sidhe survive the sex? It would kill me in a month." He turned his head enough for me to see his face, and his eyes. There was a ring of glittering black on the outside of his pupils but inside that was a ring of charcoal grey, and inside that was a ring of palest white-grey. I stared into his tricolored eyes, and wondered what he'd say when he saw a mirror.

Chapter 14

SAGE STOOD ON TIPTOE, GAZING INTO THE BUREAU MIRROR, AS close to the glass as he could get. He was gazing at his new eyes, which seemed utterly fascinating to him. I seemed unduly fascinated with him. If he was in my line of sight, I stared at him. I couldn't seem to stop myself. The soft yellow of his skin looked as if his body had been drenched in a small piece of sunlight. His body was one long line from his feet—raised high on their toes—to his calves, his thighs, the curve of his buttocks, the smooth plain of his back, the swell of his shoulders, and over all of it his wings, held tight over his back. The broad band of golden yellow with its fusion of brilliant blue and splashes of red, and orangey red, was clearer than I'd ever seen it. The black veins that held the butter-yellow tissue of his wings together seemed thick and black as miniature roads, as if I could trace my way across his wings and find myself somewhere else. Some magical place where winged lovers came at my beck and call, and there were no responsibilities. No throne. No assassins.

I frowned and put my hands over my eyes to block the seemingly gorgeous view of Sage at the mirror. This wasn't what I really wanted, but of course, that wasn't entirely true. Wasn't my deepest desire to have a life where whoever came to my bed came out of lust, or true love, or at least friendship, and not because I was daughter of Essus and heir to a throne? The best glamour, the best enchantments feed off your own needs and desires. The more personal, the more secret, the harder it is to resist.

I concentrated on my breathing in the cool darkness of my

closed eyelids. Not being able to see Sage helped. I could think about something other than the sex we'd just had, wanting more of it, and wanting to touch his wings, wanting to see if the thick, black veins were truly paths that led to my heart's desire.

Stop it, Meredith, stop it. I tried not to think, but only to count my breaths. I took air deep into my body, and let it out slowly. When my pulse was calm, I started to count not the deep, even breaths, but just to count. When I reached sixty, I lowered my hands slowly.

I was staring into washboard abs so sculpted they looked artificial. I knew that stomach. I gazed up and found Rhys's chest, and finally his face. "Are you all right, Merry?"

I shook my head. "I don't know." My voice was only a whisper, as if I was afraid to talk louder. It wasn't until that moment that I realized I was afraid. But afraid of what?

I felt the bed move a moment before I felt Nicca's presence behind me. He wasn't a burning heat now, but it was as if he were the warmth of the earth itself. The warmth that lives down in the rich brown soil, and keeps all the seeds, and all the small creatures safe and warm through the winter. When his hands touched my shoulders, it was like being wrapped up in the warmest, softest blanket in the world. So safe, so warm, as if you could snuggle down and sleep for months, and wake refreshed, whole, and the earth would be made new again. The magic of spring itself was in the touch of his hands.

Something must have shown on my face, though whether it was fear, or longing, or something else, Goddess alone knew, because I surely didn't. Rhys asked again, "Are you all right, Merry?"

I whispered, "Get Doyle." It was all I had time to say before Nicca turned me in his arms, and planted a kiss on the bend of my neck. I was suddenly drowning in the scent of fresh-turned earth and the rich, green scent of growing things. His mouth tasted like fresh rain. My hands slid over his shoulders, and found the arch of his wings. It made me open my eyes and pull back from the kiss enough to gaze down his back at the newness of them.

When the wings had been only a pattern on his back, the details had been blurred. Now the sweep and color of them spread over his body like twin cathedrals. The main color was a pale buff tan, like the fur of some pale lion, and the tips of the forewings looked as if they'd been dipped in pink and violet-red. The deep violet-red wove down the edges in a scalloped pattern that mixed with white and purple, and was edged on one side with a reddish brown, like a braid of auburn hair laid across all that golden tan. That line of rainbow colors—violet-red, white, purple, and reddish brown—traced a second scallop on his lower wings, with a line of more golden tan on the other side of that run. There was an eyespot with a blue-green center larger than my hand in his front wings, edged with black, and a yellow that was almost an echo of his overall pale buff, then an edge of brilliant blue, and that violet-red repeated above that pool of eye color like some psychedelic eyebrow. The second eyespot on his hindwings was larger than my face, like a pool of blue-green iridescence, with that outline of black around every color as if to emphasize every shade. The pale yellow ring around the pool of sparkling blue-green, the thin gleaming line of blue and reddish violet arching over all that color. There was a heavier black ring around the larger eyespot, so that the thick velvet black that surrounded all that color sat in a pool of pinkish orange. The scalloped line of colors flowed down the edge of the rear wings as it did the front—red-violet, white, purple, and reddish brown tracing the edge of all his wings downward past the brilliance of pink and orange to spill on long curved tails so that that last grace of wing was thick with dark stripes of color.

The undersides of the wings were like dusty copies of the surface, with only the eyespots showing through with the same flashing brilliance of the surface. Thick brown hair like silken fur edged the base of the wings so that the line where the wings entered Nicca's back was hidden from me.

Nicca kissed the edge of my cheek, but all I could see were his wings. He kissed his way down my cheek, and when I never looked at his face, he bit me, gently, along the neck. It brought a gasp from my throat, but not my gaze to his face. He moved lower onto my neck, and bit harder. Hard enough that my eyes closed and when my eyes opened, his face was before me.

It was the same face as before, it was Nicca, yet it wasn't. There was a forcefulness to him, a demand in his eyes, his face, his lips. I stared into those brown eyes and saw that he wanted something. My pulse was frantic in my throat. I was afraid of the desire in his face. More than a want, though, it was need.

He made a sound low in his throat. "I want to sink my teeth into you. I want to feed." He gripped my arms hard enough that it bruised, and his fear flashed in his eyes. "What is happening to me? What am I becoming?"

"Is it food you want?" I heard myself ask the question, but didn't remember thinking of it. My pulse was slowing, and I felt calm, peaceful.

Nicca shook his head. "No, not food, not drink." He shook me, then seemed to remember himself, and stopped. I watched him fight to relax his grip on my arms, but he didn't let me go. "I want you, Merry, you."

"Sex?"

"Yes, no." He frowned, then he yelled, one wordless sound of frustration. "I don't know what I want." Then he looked at me, puzzled. "I want you, but it's like you are food and drink and sex."

I nodded and raised my hands until I cupped his arms. Even the skin of his elbows was soft. Had it been this soft before the wings came? I couldn't remember. It was as if I couldn't remember Nicca without the wings. As if he hadn't been real until they sprang from his back.

"She is the Goddess," Doyle said from the doorway. "We all crave the touch of the divine."

Through the unnatural calmness, I knew he was right. "I could make him into what the Goddess wants him to be, now, tonight."

"But she is a goddess and you are mortal, and you need

more sleep than she does," he said, striding into the room like some moving piece of the darkness itself. He walked to the far side of the bed and, after a moment's hesitation, bent down. He stayed kneeling by the bed, but a pressure I hadn't known was there eased. I could breathe again, and my pulse was back to its frantic dance. The fear returned with a flash of adrenaline that left me light-headed, but the fear faded almost as fast as it had come. Nicca blinked at me, looking confused. "What happened, just now? What happened?" He let go of my arms and moved back carefully onto the bed, having to move with care because of the wings.

Doyle was still kneeling by the far side of the bed. "It seems the chalice has a mind of its own."

"What do you mean?" I asked.

"It had unwrapped itself and fallen underneath the bed."

I walked around the bed to see that he had pulled the cup out from under the bed by the edge of the silk it still lay upon, but it was uncovered. "I wrapped it up, Doyle. Even if it had fallen over, it couldn't have unwrapped that neatly, not so that the silk was a perfect rectangle again."

He gazed up at me, still on one knee, his finger and thumb still holding the silk corner. "As I said, Merry, the chalice has a mind of its own, but I would move it farther from the bed if I were you. Otherwise you will have a busy night every time one of us comes to you."

I shivered. "What's happening, Doyle?"

"The Goddess has decided to become busy among us once more, so it would seem."

"Explain that," I said.

He looked up at me. "The chalice has returned, and on the day of its return Her grace pours upon us once more. Cromm Cruach walks among us once more, as does Conchenn. Those of us who were gods are returning to our former glory, and some who were never gods are being visited with such powers as they never dreamed to have."

"The Goddess is using Merry as a messenger," Rhys said. He frowned and shook his head. "No, Merry is like the flesh version of the chalice. It fills with grace and pours upon us."

"I had nothing to do with you coming back into your powers," I said, hands on hips.

Rhys smiled. "Maybe not."

"You were in the room," Doyle said.

I looked at him and shook my head. "No, Doyle, what happened with Maeve and Frost was different from what happened to Rhys."

Doyle stood up, brushing his hands down the front of his unbuttoned jeans, as if he were wiping the feel of something off his fingers. Wiping what away? Power, magic, the feel of the silk? I almost asked, then Sage spoke.

"Look at my eyes, Darkness. Look at my eyes, and see what our lovely Merry has done." Sage walked around the bed so Doyle could see the eyes up close.

"Rhys told me that your eyes are tricolored."

Sage's wings sagged a little, as if he were disappointed that his news had been spoiled. "I am sidhe now, Darkness, what do you think of that?"

A smile curled Doyle's lips, a smile I hadn't seen before. If it had been anyone else, I'd have said it was a cruel smile. "Have you tried to grow small since it happened?"

Sage frowned at him. "What does that matter?"

Doyle shrugged, and that smile deepened. "Have you tried to shift your form since your eyes changed? It is a simple question."

Sage went very still as he stood between Doyle and me, then I saw his wings shiver, like flowers caressed by a strong wind. He shivered once, twice, then he threw back his head and wailed. Wordless, speechless, a hopeless, wrenching sound.

It wasn't until the last echoes of that scream faded from the room that I could move. "What's wrong?" I reached around his wings to touch his shoulder.

He jerked away from me. "Do not touch me!" He was backing away, toward the door. Frost appeared in the door behind him, and Sage began to back away from him, too. It was as if he was afraid of all of us.

"What's wrong?" I asked again.

"Being sidhe comes with a price for those with wings," Doyle said, and there was a note of satisfaction in his voice. I'd always known there was some bitter history between the two of them, but I'd never realized just how bitter until that moment. I'd never seen Doyle be petty before.

Sage pointed at Nicca, who was still kneeling on the bed. "He knows nothing of wings. He has never flown above a spring meadow, or tasted how sweet and clean the wind can be." He pounded his fist into his bare chest. "But I know! I know!"

"I'm missing something," I said. "What difference does being sidhe mean for Sage?"

"You have stolen my wings from me, Merry," he said, and there was a look on his face, of such unbearable loss, that I moved toward him. I had to hold him. Had to touch him. Had to try to take that look from his eyes.

He held a pale yellow hand out toward me. "No, no more, Merry. I have had enough of the sidhe for one night."

Rhys cleared his throat, and the noise seemed to startle Sage. He turned to find Rhys almost behind him, having walked across the room to stand near the mirror. Sage looked wildly around the room as if we'd trapped him and he was seeking a way out. It was true that Frost was near the only door, but he wasn't trapped. Not in any way that I understood.

Sage pointed a finger at Nicca. "Do you know what we would call him if he had gotten his wings as a child?"

Everyone gave their version of blank face, though it looked like everything from humor to arrogance. It was Rhys who said, "I give up. What would you call Nicca if he'd gotten his wings as a kid?"

"Cursed." Sage spat the word as if it was the worst thing he could ever call anyone.

"Cursed, how?" I asked.

"He has wings but he cannot fly, Merry. He is too heavy for the wings of a moth to carry him aloft"—he smacked his fist into his chest—"as I am too heavy for mine now."

"What's happened?" Galen asked from the doorway. He

was rubbing sleep from his eyes. His bedroom was the farthest away from this room.

Before any of us could answer, Sage marched to him, brushing past Frost. "Look, look at what has become of me!"

Galen gaped at Sage. "What . . . your eyes."

Sage pushed past him, snarling one last phrase over his winged shoulder. "Wicked, wicked sidhe." And he was gone.

Chapter 15

"RHYS, GO WITH HIM," DOYLE SAID. "SEE THAT HE COMES TO NO harm."

Rhys went without a word. He was still nude, as was Sage. I had a moment to hope that there wasn't anyone outside the wall with a night-vision camera. Then I realized that bad publicity was the least of our worries. The fact that I'd thought of it at all proved that I'd been too long away from faerie, too long out among the humans.

"What harm could Sage come to?" I asked.

"His own," Doyle said.

"You mean he'll harm himself because he can't fly."

Doyle nodded. "I have known other winged fey to let themselves fade and die when they lost their wings."

"I meant him no harm."

"The sidhe are at their most dangerous when they mean us no harm," Frost said, and his voice held a bitterness that I'd never heard before.

"It's my night," Nicca said. He hadn't taken part in the conversation until now, and when I looked into his brown eyes what I saw tightened things low in my body. His need was so raw, and it wasn't the gentle need that he usually held, but something far more fierce.

"Look at you," Doyle said. "You are still power-besotted. I think the chalice is not done with you yet, Nicca, and I fear what that would do to our Merry."

Nicca shook his head, eyes still on me, as if nothing else were truly real. "My night."

Galen had come into the room and was gazing at Nicca's wings. "Wow, that's new."

"There are many things new tonight," Doyle said, and he sounded wary.

Nicca ignored them all. "My night." He held his hand out to me.

"No," Doyle said, and he took my hand and led me back away from the bed.

"She's mine tonight," Nicca said, and for a moment I thought we'd see a fight, or at least an argument.

"Technically, it was Rhys's night," Doyle said, "and you have both had your pleasure."

"If Rhys has had his night," Frost said, "then it is your night, Doyle."

Nicca balled his hands into fists. "No, we aren't finished." And his voice was like something that should call you from deep within the ground. He might have had wings, but his energy was all earth.

Doyle moved me behind him so that he formed a barrier between me and Nicca where he still knelt on the bed, those wings draped behind him like some magical cloak. "Listen to yourself, Nicca. I do not know what the Goddess has planned for you, but until we are sure it will not harm Merry, we will be cautious. Your godhead, or whatever, is not worth our Merry's life."

I peeked around Doyle's smooth dark arm and watched Nicca fight for control. It was as if something else wanted this, and that something else didn't necessarily care what Nicca wanted, or did not want.

He ended up on all fours, those wings flowing back along his body. His hair spilled across his face and over the foot of the bed like thick brown water. He took a breath that trembled along his back, shivered the rainbows of his wings. He raised his face up to the light with a look almost of pain, but he nodded. "Doyle's right, Doyle's right," he muttered over and over, as if to convince not just himself but whatever was riding him.

Doyle stepped forward and laid a gentle hand against Nicca's face. "I am sorry, my brother, but Merry's safety must come first."

Nicca nodded, almost as if he was unaware that Doyle had touched him. His eyes weren't focused on anything in the room.

Doyle moved back from the bed, using his body to move me backward, as if he still didn't trust Nicca. "No one who has not become a god can sleep with Merry until we understand what the chalice and the Goddess want."

"That means only Frost and Rhys," Galen said. He didn't sound happy.

"Only Frost until we know for certain how much power Rhys has recaptured," Doyle clarified.

"Not as much power as I'd hoped," Rhys said from the doorway. "Sage rolled me like a wino on Saturday night."

"Where is Sage?" I asked.

"It seems Conchenn was attracted by all the power. She's comforting our newest sidhe."

"I thought he'd had enough sidhe for one night," Galen said.

Rhys shrugged. "Conchenn can be very persuasive."

"How desperate she must be to take him into herself," Frost said.

"I don't know," I said. "She's made it pretty plain over the last two weeks that she'd love to have any of us in her bed."

"She's had us in her bed," Doyle said.

I looked at him with raised eyebrows. "Only to hold her while she cried herself to sleep, Doyle. That's not the kind of bed I mean."

Doyle gave a ghost of a smile. "When Maeve's grief began to abate she did make it . . . plain that she would have taken more active comfort."

I wondered at that smile. Perhaps Maeve had been more "active" in her attempts to seduce my Darkness than I'd known.

Rhys snorted. "Well, she's getting very active comfort right now."

"You don't understand," Frost said, "none of you."

"What don't we understand?" I asked, looking up into that coldly handsome face.

"How great her need must be to take Sage."

"He's sidhe now. Whether it's permanent, I don't know, but for tonight he's sidhe."

"It will be permanent," Frost said.

I frowned up at him. "No," I said, "you can be made sidhe for a night through magic, like Branwyn's Tears, but you're either born sidhe or you're not."

"That is not true," Frost said.

I had a sudden image of him as the beautiful child dancing across the snow. I had no problem with someone who had begun "life" as something other than flesh becoming sidhe. It seemed somehow right. But lesser fey, or humans, did not suddenly become sidhe. They just didn't.

"Once we brought sidhe to us like harvesting the fruits of the forest," Frost said. "They simply came to us."

"My father never spoke of such a thing." I didn't mean to imply that I didn't believe him, but doubt was in my voice.

"It was two thousand years, or more, ago," Doyle said. "We lost such abilities with the first weirding. Many of us refuse to speak of things that are truly lost."

"I think it is not so lost as we've been led to believe," Frost said.

"No one has deceived us," Doyle said.

Frost gave him a long look. "It was the Seelie Court that lost us the chalice, Doyle. They who stripped us of much of what we were."

Doyle shook his head. "I will not have this argument with you, or any of you," he said, looking at Rhys and Galen.

Galen held his hands out wide. "I've never had this argument with anyone."

"You're too young," Doyle said.

"Then can you explain it for those of us under five hundred?"

Doyle gave a small smile. "Most of the great relics that simply vanished were Seelie relics. The Unseelie relics remained, though lessened in power. Some believed that the Seelie court angered the Goddess, or the God, to lose such favor."

"We believed that they had done something so terrible that the face of deity turned from them," Frost said.

I looked at him. "I assume you believe that."

He nodded, and his face was like some beautiful sculpture, too handsome to be real, too arrogant to touch. He had retreated behind the cold mask he'd used for centuries in the Unseelie Court. I understood now that it was a form of protection, camouflage, if you will, to keep his pain hidden. I'd peeled back some of those layers and found what he'd hidden. Unfortunately, we seemed stuck at the moody, pain-exploration stage. I was looking forward to drilling through to another layer. There had to be more to him than mood. There had to be, didn't there?

"Many believe that," he said.

Doyle shrugged. "I know only that we diminished, and we came to the Western Lands. Beyond that, I know nothing for certain." He gave Frost a fierce look. "And neither do you."

Frost opened his mouth to speak, but Doyle cut him off with a gesture. "No, Frost, we will not reopen this wound. Not tonight. Is it not enough that you will share her body until we are sure the rest of us are safe?"

"I'm going back to bed," Rhys said, and it was abrupt enough that we all looked at him. "I want no part of this old argument, and after Sage's glamour took me so easily, I don't trust that I am truly Cromm Cruach. If I am not a god, then I'm too dangerous to be around Merry. If I am not a kiss. "Good night, sweet princess, we have to pack in the morning and catch a plane to St. Louis. So don't all of you stay up talking all night." He wagged a finger at us and left.

Galen looked at all of us. "I might as well go, too." He gave me a look of such pain. "Whatever is happening, I hope we clear it up soon."

I called after him, "Check on Kitto. This much noise should have woken him."

He nodded and left, carefully not looking back, as if he didn't want to see.

"To your room as well, Nicca," Doyle said.

"I am not a child to be sent to my room, Doyle."

We all blinked at him, because Nicca never spoke back to Doyle—really, to anyone. "It seems you have gained nerve with your wings," Doyle said.

Nicca gave him a very unfriendly look. "If you leave with me, then I will go."

"Are you implying that Doyle is trying to get rid of you so he can have me to himself?" I asked.

Nicca just kept that unfriendly look on Doyle.

Frost came out of his deep funk long enough to look at Nicca. "Nicca, it is I who ask Doyle to stay."

Nicca sent that dark look to Frost. "Why?"

"Because I trust him to keep Meredith safe."

Nicca crawled off the bed and stood before us, very straight, a slender, muscled brown vision framed with a fall of thick wild hair, and those wings. The wings seemed to fascinate me more than they should. It wasn't that they weren't lovely, but they drew my eye, my attention. Something wanted me to touch them, to roll myself along the brilliance of them, and cover my body in the brush of multicolored dust.

Doyle touched my arm, and it made me jump. My pulse was suddenly in my throat, and I didn't remember why. "You must leave tonight, Nicca. You fascinate her the way snakes fascinate small birds. I do not know what the cost would be to end this hold you seem to have on her, but I will not risk her life to find out."

Nicca closed his eyes, shoulders slumping, but that brushed the ends of his wings against the floor and he had to straighten his shoulders again. He used one slender hand to brush the fall of hair from his face, so that it fell like a deep auburn waterfall down one side of his body. "You are right, my captain." Something close to pain crossed his face. "I will see if there is another bed open for the night. If we keep ruining bedrooms, we're going to run out." When he was even with me, I reached out to brush his wings, and Doyle grabbed my hand, holding me back against his body, a hand on either of my wrists.

Nicca gazed back over his shoulder at me, then at Doyle. "We will speak of this later, Darkness." Again, it didn't seem like Nicca's voice, and even the look in his eyes was something I'd never seen.

Doyle actually took a step back, holding me against him. "Gladly, but not tonight."

Frost had moved up beside Doyle, his own problems forgotten in the wonder of seeing Nicca threaten Doyle. "Leave now, Nicca," Frost said.

Nicca turned his gaze on the other man. "I will speak to you, too, Killing Frost, if you wish it."

"Don't challenge them, Nicca, please don't," I said.

He turned that look on me, and his gaze went up and down my body. There was something in his look that was almost frightening, as if he wasn't thinking just about sex, but something more permanent. It was a look that held ownership.

"You beg me not to challenge them while you stand like that pressed against Doyle's half-naked body." His expression was one I'd never seen on him before, as if some stranger were inside Nicca's body using his face. He turned that stranger's face to Frost. "And you, who were never meant to be a god, would you now be king over us all? If you are the only man in her bed night after night, you will be." His voice was thick with a jealousy so harsh it was near hatred.

Frost moved a little in front of us. "I have not seen that look for many a long year, but I remember your envy, and what it cost us all."

It was Doyle who said, "Dian Cecht. Somehow you are in the power of Dian Cecht."

I didn't understand what was happening, but it wasn't good, that much even I knew. "Dian Cecht was one of the original Tuatha De Danaan, the healing god, but why do you name this power him?"

"Do you know the rest of his story?" Doyle asked.

"He slew his own son out of jealousy, because the son had surpassed the father in his healing skills."

Doyle nodded.

Nicca hissed at us, and his face, for a moment, was monstrous. Then he was handsome again, except for the hatred in his eyes.

"He's possessed," I said, and my voice was soft with the awfulness of it.

"You stopped the process before it finished," Frost said. "Has that caused this abomination?"

"I do not know," Doyle said, again, but I could feel his heart pounding against my hair. I knew he was afraid, but only the speeding of his pulse showed it.

Nicca slumped, almost swooned, then raised his face upward, and I saw terror there. "I was angry that you stopped us. I was jealous. The chalice brings to you what you bring to it. My anger has done this." He moaned. "I cannot fight this."

I prayed a prayer I'd spoken a thousand times before: "Mother help him." The moment the words left me, I felt the world tighten, as if the universe had caught its breath. There was a glow from across the room, as if the moon had risen beside our bed. We all turned and looked. The chalice sat against the wall where Doyle had dragged it, but there was light coming from it. I remembered my dream where the chalice had first appeared, remembered the taste of pure light, pure power, on my tongue.

"Let me go, Doyle," I said. His hands fell away from me. I don't know if it was to obey me, or because of the moonlit glow coming from that silver cup.

Nicca's face was his own again, but I knew, somehow, that the reprieve was temporary. That when the glow died away, Dian Cecht would return. We needed to be finished before that.

I started to take his hand, to lean into his body, but a hint of ugliness crossed his face. Dian Cecht was still in there, and Nicca's body was strong enough to tear through walls. "Kneel," I said, and because it was Nicca, he simply dropped to his knees without question. He had a moment where he had to settle the tips of his wings along the floor so they would not bend, then he gazed up at me, face patient, waiting.

"Someone hold his wrists."

"Why?" Frost asked, but it was Doyle who simply came to my side. It was Doyle who took Nicca's wrists in his dark hands and held them out in front of the other man.

I moved behind Nicca, stepping carefully over the delicate grace of his wings as they lay across the floor. I pushed my bare feet between his legs, and he widened his knees, so that I could stand between his legs, my body pressed against his buttocks, his waist, his shoulders, his head resting against my breasts. He fanned his wings and for a moment I was lost between them, and that velvet brush left a dazzling spray of color on my skin. I slid my hand up the back of his neck into his hair, plunged my hand through the warmth of it, dug my fingers in against his skin, so I could feel the heat of his body. I drew his head backward with a handful of his own hair like a handle to pry his face back, and to stretch his neck in a long perfect line. I gazed into his brown eyes, his mouth already slack when I bent toward him.

There was a moment when that other person tried to use his face, tried to spread hate and envy through those gentle eyes, but I held him by the hair, his face trapped for kissing, and Doyle held his wrists, like black rope. Dian Cecht struggled, but it was too late. I kissed that mouth, and felt power go from my lips to his. It was as if my breath itself were magic, and I breathed it into his mouth in a long, shuddering sigh.

Nicca's wings closed around me like a velvet shroud, soft and restricting, because I was afraid to fight against them, afraid I'd tear them to bits. His body trembled under my mouth, and his wings shuddered around me until I felt the tiny soft pieces of color fall like dry rain against my skin. The power began to end, and when it faded Nicca's mouth fed at mine. His wings squeezed around me, squeezed and released, squeezed and released, like being hugged by something more delicate than thought, and with every movement of the wings more and more of the color cascaded around me, glittering.

I fell into that kiss, those trembling wings, the velvet caress of the powder falling along my body, and I saw Nicca standing in a meadow, bright with summer flowers. It was night, but Nicca shone so bright that the flowers had opened before him as if he were the sun. The air was suddenly full of demi-fey, not the mere dozens that I knew, but hundreds. It was as if the very ground had opened up and spewed them into the sky. Then I realized that it was the flowers; the flowers had grown wings and filled the sky.

Nicca rose into the air as if he were walking on the tops of the grass, and I realized he was flying, flying upward through a cloud of demi-fey.

Then I was falling, almost as if I fell back into my body. I was still standing pressed against Nicca's body, one hand still entwined in his hair, but it was Doyle's face that I gazed into. His eyes widened and he opened his mouth as if to speak, but it was too late. He wasn't touching me, but he was touching Nicca, and so was I.

It was night in a forest that I had never seen before. A huge oak spread like a roof above my head, its great gnarled trunk big as a house. The branches were bare with late fall. Somehow I knew it wasn't dead, but only resting, preparing for winter's cold. As I watched, a thin line of light crossed the bark of the tree. The light widened, and I realized it was a door, a door in the trunk of the tree, swinging open. Music spilled out into the darkness in a wash of golden light. A black-cloaked figure appeared in the door, stepped out into the autumn night, and the door closed behind him. It seemed darker than it had before, as if my eyes had been dazzled by the light. He threw back his cloak, and I saw Doyle's face looking up through the branches, looking up at the cold light of the stars. The shadows under the trees on every side began to grow thicker, more solid, until things moved, and formed, and turned and looked at me with eyes that burned with red and green fire. They opened mouths full of dagger-like teeth, and one by one they set their great dark heads toward the sky and bayed. Doyle stood in the dark listening to that fearful music, and smiled.

I heard Frost's voice, distant as a dream. "Meredith, Meredith, can you hear me?"

I wanted to say yes, but I couldn't remember how to speak. Couldn't remember where I was. Was I in the summer meadow brushed by a thousand wings, or was I in the dark with the music of hounds belling around me? Was I still standing pressed to Nicca's body, still staring into Doyle's startled face? Where was I? Where did I want to be?

That was an easier question. I wanted to be in the bedroom. I wanted to answer Frost's frantic voice. The moment I thought it, I was there. I stepped back from Nicca, who was still kneeling on the floor. Doyle staggered back against the wall. Nicca fell forward onto all fours, as if he'd barely caught himself from falling.

Doyle gasped, "Merry," but it was as if what had happened had drained them both. With Maeve and Frost, I had been drained and weak, but not this time. I turned toward Frost, and he was staring at me with a mixture of fear and wonder.

"I don't feel tired this time," I told him. I moved toward him, leaving the other two men gasping on the floor behind me.

Frost backed away from me, and he must not have been thinking clearly, because he backed between the bed and the dresser, trapping himself. He was shaking his head over and over again. "Look at yourself, Meredith. Look at yourself." He pointed toward the mirror.

The first thing I saw was color. My skin was brushed with swaths of tan, pink, violet-red, purple, and a white that was almost lost against the shining white of my skin. Reddish brown like shining ribbons of dried blood traced down the sides of my body. A crush of vibrant blue-green touched each shoulder, and lower down along my legs. Black and yellow smeared around that iridescent blue-green, and a stroke of blue so bright it looked as if it should move glowed at shoulder and calf. With magic upon me, my skin shone like a pearl with a candle trapped inside it, but the color acted like prisms, so that my magic burned up through every drop of color, so that I was left a gleaming rainbow, as if Nicca's wings had exploded along my skin. My eyes burned with tricolored fire, molten gold, jade green, and an emerald to shame the brightest gem. But my eyes weren't just glowing.

Each individual line of color looked as if it were on fire, as if flame licked around my eyes. I remembered the gold and green shadows that my eyes had cast when I was making love with Sage and Nicca, and realized this must have been what my eyes looked like: The colored flames bled into one another so it was more like a true fire, first one color, then the next, ever moving. I peered into the mirror, stretching up on tiptoe to look closer, and realized I was standing as Sage had stood earlier. My hair was like rubies, but tonight it was as if every strand held ruby fire, so that my hair burned around my face, caressing my shoulders.

I'd seen myself with my magic naked for all to see, but never like this. It was as if I truly burned with power this night.

"You don't want me, Merry," Frost said. "I wasn't born sidhe. I'm not fit consort for a goddess."

I turned and gazed at him with my burning eyes. I half-expected the movement to change my vision, but it didn't. It seemed like it should. "I saw you dancing across the snow. You were like some beautiful child."

"I was never a child, Merry. I was never born. I was a thought, or a thing, a concept if you will. Yes, a concept given life by the gods. Given life by the very gods whose power now runs through my body. Their jealousy at watching me grow and become the Killing Frost was why I could not stay at the Seelie Court."

I moved away from the mirror, toward him. "Are they so much less than the queen's Killing Frost?"

"That's just it, Merry, they were my equal. I might best them at weapons, but they looked at me and remembered a time when I was less, and they were more, and it hurt them."

"So they turned you out," I said.

He nodded.

I stood in front of him now, so close that I ran my fingers across his robe, so lightly that all I felt was the silk and not the body underneath. But I wanted the body underneath. I had a sudden image in my head, bright and immediate, of pressing my body along Frost's pale skin until he was smeared with that glowing wash of color. It was so real that it closed my eyes, arched my back, flung my hands outward.

Frost's hands caught my arms. "Merry, are you all right?"

I opened my eyes, found his face worried. I looked down at his hands where they held my forearms. It was one of the few inches of skin that held no color, so that his hands were still just white. "I'm better than all right, Frost." My voice sounded strange, deeper, almost hollow, as if I had become an empty shell that my voice echoed out of. I drew my arms out of his hands and pulled on the sash of his robe. One firm tug and the sash unwound, the robe beginning to open.

Frost grabbed my hands this time. "I don't want to hurt you."

I laughed, and it had a wild sound to it. "You won't hurt me."

His grip on my hands tightened until it was almost painful. "You are power-ridden, Meredith, but that doesn't mean you aren't still mortal."

"You can only get godhead once, and you've had your turn," I said. "Now it's just extra magic that you have to learn to deal with. It's simply a matter of discipline, practice, and control." I pulled on my hands, and he loosened his grip, enough for me to pull free. I reached into that open edge of robe, found the smaller tie that still held it closed, and pulled on it. The robe fell open, revealing a thin line of pale flesh. "And I know you are disciplined, Frost, controlled"—I slid my hands inside that silk, touched the skin underneath—"and if practice makes perfect, that is certainly you."

He laughed then, abrupt and almost startling in its sudden joy. "Why is it that you can make me feel better? I almost killed you today."

I ran my hands up his body, traced the edge of his chest, ran fingers over his nipples, made him catch his breath. "We all got surprised today, Frost. But I seem to be getting better at bringing godhead to the sidhe." I spilled my hands to his shoulders, having to stand on tiptoe, to push the robe off his arms. He drew away from the wall enough for the robe to cascade to the floor, where it lay like a puddle of grey silk at his feet.

"I can see that," he said in a voice that grew ever deeper, ever more breathless.

I gazed upon him nude, and found him as beautiful as the first time I'd seen him. The joy of Frost unclothed never diminished. He was almost too beautiful to gaze upon, as if it hurt my heart to see him.

I laid a kiss on his chest, over his heart. I licked his skin, then gave his nipple a quick flick of movement that made him shudder and laugh at the same time. I gazed up into that laughing face, and thought, this, this was what I wanted from him. More than the sex, more than almost anything, his joy.

He gazed down at me, his grey eyes shining with the edge of his laughter. "I look in your eyes and there's no difference."

I began to kiss my way down his chest. "Difference?" I asked.

"You don't think less of me," he said.

I traced my tongue along the edge of his belly button, bit softly into the skin on either side, let my mouth work lower until I could go no farther without bumping into him, straight and firm, and perfect, pressed against his stomach. I slid my mouth over the velvet tip of him, as I dropped my body to my knees. I fought to swallow along his length, to the base of him. He was really too long for this angle, but I managed. He threw his head back, and closed his eyes. I pulled free of him, just enough to say, "Oh, I think more of you, now, much more."

I slid back over him, using my hands to guide him inside my mouth. I had closed my eyes, giving myself over to the thick, muscled feel of him in my mouth, concentrating on breathing, swallowing, when I felt his magic dance through his skin, jump inside my mouth. I knew without opening my eyes that his skin had begun to glow. I could feel it against my tongue, my lips.

He balled his hand into my hair and drew me back from him, forced me to gaze up and meet his eyes. "You don't think less of me for not being born sidhe."

I tried to kiss his body, but his hand tightened, and drew a small gasp from my lips. It sped my pulse more than taking him into my mouth had. "You were breathed to life by a god, Frost. If that's not special enough, I don't know what is."

He dragged me upward by my hair, pulling me to my feet so abruptly that it hurt, and almost scared me. Not real fear, but the fear that rides the edge of violent sex. He kissed me, and it was fierce, full of probing tongues, eager lips, and teeth; as if he couldn't decide whether to kiss me, or eat me. He pulled back from that kiss, and it left me breathless and dazed.

His eyes glinted like silver ice, and the tips of each strand of hair glittered like frost caught in sunlight. "I want you to cover me in this." He ran his free hand up my shoulder, came away smeared with iridescent blue, green, purple. He smeared it down my face, across my lips, then kissed me again, messy, hungry. He drew back with his mouth and one cheek covered in glittering color, like bits of neon smeared across his skin.

I threw my arms around his neck, and he wrapped his around my waist, lifting me up so that our bodies slid along each other. The movement smeared the neon colors along his skin, and just the sight of it brought a soft moan from me. We kissed, and I wrapped my legs around his waist, pressing the hard length of him against me. The feel of him there made me grind my hips against the hardness of him, rubbing the wetness of me against him. His knees went weak, and only a hand on the bed caught us. He eased us back against the bed, and the moment my hips were solid against the mattress, he pushed himself inside me.

I screamed, head back, eyes closed, and a second scream echoed mine. It wasn't until Frost stopped moving, frozen above me, that I realized it wasn't him who was screaming.

I opened my eyes and saw that his face was turned away from me, looking over the foot of the bed. The scream sounded again, and it was close, masculine, and wordless in its pain.

Frost pushed off me, rolling over the foot of the bed. I

scrambled onto all fours, crawling to the foot of the bed. Frost knelt near Doyle's head. Nicca knelt near his feet. Doyle's spine bowed, his hands scrambling at the air. It was as if every muscle in his body were straining at once in different directions. If he'd been human, I'd have thought poison, but you couldn't poison the sidhe, not with strychnine, at least.

Another shriek tore from his mouth, and his body rocked with the force of the spasms. "Help him!"

Frost shook his head. "I don't know what this is."

I spilled over the foot of the bed. Before I could touch him, his skin seemed to split, and his body ran like water, if water could scream, and writhe, and bleed.

Chapter 16

I REACHED OUT, AND FROST GRABBED MY HAND, PULLED ME back. "We don't know what this is." I didn't fight him, because he was right.

So I clung to his arms and didn't know what to do. I was supposed to be princess of faerie, and all I could do was kneel and stare while that strong body rolled itself into a mess of naked muscles and bone that glistened in the air, wet with blood.

When Doyle screamed again, I screamed with him. The others spilled into the room behind us with guns and swords, and none of it would help. I prayed, prayed as I had for Nicca, but there was no glow from the chalice this time. There was nothing but Doyle writhing on the floor, and the blood that crept outward like a widening dark pool on the carpet.

Frost walked backward on his knees, moving us away from that spreading wetness. He stumbled when he did it, and that one small movement freed one of my hands. It made no sense—in fact, it was the opposite of good sense—but I had to do it. I had to touch what was lying on the carpet, because it couldn't be Doyle. That writhing mass of muscle, bones, and tissue could not be my tall, handsome Darkness. It wasn't possible.

My fingertips found wet, warm flesh, no skin. Whatever I touched in the second before Frost jerked me back was something deep within Doyle's body, something never meant to be caressed by human hand.

Frost held my wrist and seemed horrified by the red blood on my fingertips. "Don't do that again, Merry."

"Is that fur?" Rhys asked the question, pointing a pale finger.

I looked back at what was left of Doyle, and at first I didn't see it. Then, among all the dark flesh, I saw an equally dark wash of fur, flowing like slow water to coat the naked meat that had once been a man. The bare glistening bones sank into that fur, and once hidden away they began to re-form with a sound like stones grinding together. A mouth formed out of that fur and bone, and it screamed, and it sounded human, but it wasn't.

When it was over, a huge black dog lay panting on its side amid the blood and fluids. My eyes tried to make sense of it, tried to see Doyle in that furred shape, but it was all dog. A huge black mastiff-type dog. I remembered the shadow dogs in my vision. What lay before us was a twin of the dogs that had formed from the shadows under the trees.

The great shaggy head tried to rise, but fell back as if exhausted. I tried to reach out to pet it, and Frost wouldn't let me. "Let me go, Frost," I said.

Rhys knelt on one knee near the dog's hind legs. "It's Doyle's dog form. I thought never to see it again." He reached out with the hand that wasn't holding a gun, and stroked down that furred side.

The dog raised its head and looked at him, then again fell back against the carpet, as if the effort had taken too much.

I stared at that furred form and was so happy that he was alive, not a disintegrating mass of flesh, that I didn't care if he was a dog. At that moment, it was so much better than what I'd feared. He wasn't dead. I'd learned long ago that with life, there is hope. With death, there is none. I believed sincerely in reincarnation. I knew that in another lifetime I might see the dead again, but it had been cold comfort at eighteen when my father died. It would have been very cold comfort if Doyle had turned into something that couldn't be healed, but only killed as a mercy. "Let go of me, Frost."

He released me reluctantly.

"Doyle, can you hear me?" I asked.

"It is still me, Merry." Doyle's voice was deeper, more growling, but it was definitely his voice.

I crawled to him, my knees sinking into the wet carpet. The blood was already cooling. I touched one of the long silken ears. Doyle nuzzled his great head against my hand.

Rhys stroked his hand down the furred side. "I always half envied you shape-shifters. Thought it must be cool to be an animal, some of the time." He laid his hand over Doyle's chest, over his heart, as if he could feel more than just the heavy thud of it. "But I've never seen a change that violent."

I brushed my hand down the warm and strangely dry fur, as if all that fur hadn't come through a wash of blood. Of course, maybe it hadn't. I didn't know that much about the mechanics of shifting form; no one really did. One of the first things to be lost when the fey left faerie in Europe was shape-shifting. Those of us who had fled to America, but kept to our hollow hills, had retained more of some abilities, but most of us were a backward lot and didn't trust or sometimes even believe in modern science. So there were no scientific studies of the phenomenon.

The fur was so soft, so thick under my hand. "Changes this violent only happen when one sidhe tries to force another into shifting against his will." My hand slid down the fur until it touched Rhys's fingertips. That one small touch thrilled along my arm up into my shoulder, my chest, a spasm of muscles and skin that was both pleasure and pain. It stole my breath, made me stare wide-eyed into Rhys's face.

Doyle's chest rose and fell under our hands, his heart like a great, thick drum.

"The magic isn't gone yet." Rhys's voice was hoarse.

Doyle rolled onto his back, his great muzzle opening wide, flashing a gleam of teeth like small white knives. Both Rhys and I pulled our hands back from him, just in case. He'd spoken only once. Some retained more of themselves in animal form than others. I'd never seen Doyle as anything but sidhe.

Doyle strained at the air with paws bigger than my hands. He growled, but there were words in it. "I can feel it, growing, growing inside me."

Then it was as if the dog's body split asunder, like a seed, and something huge, and black, and slicker-furred than dog sprang out of him. Rhys and I were left to scramble back. Frost grabbed me around the waist and ran us backward to the wall, giving room to the huge shape growing at the foot of the bed.

It spilled upward like a genie from a bottle, except that the bottle was Doyle's body. A great black horse shape flowed upward, as if something of flesh could be formed of water and smoke, because solid flesh did not push into the air like a fountain, or smoke rising from some great fire.

Maeve and Sage came through the door in time to see the horse become truly solid. The dog form was simply gone, like black smoke that faded around huge dark hooves.

The dog had been the size of a small pony, so the horse was even more massive. It tossed its black head and nearly scraped its nose on the ceiling. The neck was thicker than my waist. It stamped on the carpet with hooves the size of dinner plates. It moved uneasily on its huge legs, and even little movements made everyone back up. All the men were staring. Kitto seemed more frightened than the rest. He had moved back through the crowd so that he stood near the door, and I think only Maeve and Sage blocking the door kept him in the room. Another phobia to add to the list for the goblin.

It was Sage who broke the silence. "I'll be damned."

"Probably," the horse said. It was still Doyle's voice, but instead of the growl of the dog, it was higher-pitched and had lost that near-animal undertone. To say that the horse's voice sounded more human seemed wrong, but was still true.

Doyle shook out a mane as black as his own hair. "I have not been in this form since the first weirding."

Rhys came forward and passed a hand down the side of that smooth neck. The horse's body gleamed like some dark jewel.

I started forward, but Frost held me tighter, pressing the

back of my nude body against the front of his, but he wasn't
excited to be there. He whispered, "It's not over. Can't you
feel it?"

"What?"

"Magic," he breathed.

"Pressed this close to you, all I can feel is you. You all feel
like magic to me."

He looked down at me then, and I saw a thought in his
eyes, as if he hadn't known that before. "Then we make it
harder for you to sense other magic?"

I nodded. "Yes."

"That is not good," he said.

I rubbed my body against his, and felt him swell against me,
instantly. "I love it," I said, "I love being with you, all of you."

I don't know what he would have said, because the horse
tried to rear and found there was no room. It rose above us
like some black demon, hooves slicing the air. Rhys threw
himself backward, rolling across the floor to end up against
the others' legs.

The great form seemed to spread like a black coat, opening
down the middle. Black wings stretched out of that opening,
and the horse's form faded into smoke, or black mist. When
the mist cleared there was a huge black eagle standing on the
carpet. Its outspread wings must have been eight feet, maybe
more. One wing brushed the far wall and folded against it.
There simply wasn't room.

Standing, the bird was almost as tall as I was. I'd never
been that close to anything that large that was supposed to be
a bird. It cocked a head at me, and I saw those black-on-black
eyes, and strangely, the look was still Doyle.

Rhys had regained his feet. "An eagle, cool. I never knew
you were a bird."

The ebony beak opened, flashing paler colors. "I have never
been this." The words sounded even higher-pitched yet, as if
it were a voice meant for eagle screams, not human speech.

No one tried to get closer this time. No one tried to touch
him. He folded his wings in against his body for only a moment, then they spread wide again, and the thick breast

opened, like a coat, and Doyle stepped out in a swirl of darkness that moved like smoke but smelled like mist.

He stood naked before us for a second, then collapsed slowly to the floor. I would have rushed forward, but Frost still held me tight. It was Rhys and Nicca who reached his side first. Doyle managed to catch himself on one hand.

"Are you hurt, Captain?" Nicca asked.

Rhys was grinning. "That was a hell of a show."

I think Doyle tried to smile, but his arm began to tremble and slowly collapse, until he lay on the carpet on his side. Strangely, along with his clothes, the tie to his braid was gone, and that long plait of hair was starting to unwind across the floor.

"Let go of me, Frost, now!"

"You want to go to him," he said, and there was such sorrow in his voice.

I looked up at him. "Yes, as I'd want to go to any of you who was hurt."

He shook his head. "No, Doyle is special to you."

I frowned up at him. "Yes, as you are."

He shook his head again. He leaned over, whispered against my face. "Since he entered your bed, you have distanced yourself from me." He drew back and let me go. I watched him pull himself upright until he was the tall, handsome Frost. Imposing, impersonal, arrogant of face and bearing. But the look in his grey eyes was hurt, angry.

I shook my head. "I do not have time for this."

He just looked away as if I weren't there.

I turned to the others. "Rhys, is he going to be all right?"

"Yeah, he's just tired. I think from that first change. He fought like a son of a bitch."

Doyle's voice came tired but clear. "The less I fought, the easier it became."

"Good. Get him into the bed, so he can rest," I said, and turned back to Frost. I looked at him while I said, "Everybody out, except Doyle, Rhys, and Frost."

They all looked at one another. "Just do it, guys. Now." I was tired, too. A tired that went beyond the physical. And I'd had enough. Enough of my beautiful Frost. I'd decided to resort to brutal honesty, because I'd tried everything else.

There must have been something in my voice, because no one argued with me. How refreshing.

When the door closed behind them and Rhys was helping Doyle into the bed, I gave my full attention to Frost. "Normally, I would do this in private, but none of you believes me, most of the time, without one of the other guards to back me up. I don't want any misunderstandings, Frost."

Frost gave me a very cold look. "I understand that Doyle will be in your bed tonight."

I shook my head. "Frost, it is not Doyle being in my bed that's made me pull back from you. It's you who's made me pull back."

He looked away, as if he was at full attention but didn't see anything.

I slapped his chest, hard, because I couldn't reach his face. It startled him, made him look at me, and for a moment I saw something real in those eyes again, but only for a moment. Then he was all cold arrogance again.

"This pouting has got to stop."

He gave me cold eyes. "I do not pout."

"Yes, you do." I turned to the two men at the bed.

Rhys was tucking Doyle under the covers. He nodded. "You do pout."

Doyle lay heavily on the pillows, as if raising his head would have been an effort. "You do, my old friend, you do."

"I don't know what you mean," Frost said, "any of you."

"Something hurts your feelings, you pout. You perceive that something threatens your place in my affections, you pout. Things don't go your way in a debate, you pout."

"I do not pout."

"You're pouting, right now, this very second."

He opened his mouth, closed it, and a moment of puzzlement showed through. "I do not see this as pouting. Children pout, warriors do not."

"Then what do you call this?" I asked, hands on hips.

He seemed to think a moment, then said, "I merely react to

what you do. If you prefer Doyle to me, then there is nothing I can do. I have given you the best of me, and it is not good enough."

"Love isn't just about sex, Frost. I need you not to do this."

"Not to do what?" he asked.

"This"—I poked a finger against his chest—"this cold distant facade. I need you to be real, yourself."

"You do not like me when I am myself."

"That's not true. I love you when you are yourself, but you have to stop letting everything hurt your feelings. You have to stop pouting." I stepped back enough so I could look up into his face without straining my neck. "I spend so much energy worrying how you're going to take something. I don't have the energy to spare to tiptoe around your feelings, Frost."

He moved away from the wall. "I understand."

"What are you doing?" I asked.

"Leaving. That's what you want, isn't it?"

I turned to the two men. "Help me out here, please?"

"She doesn't want you to leave," Rhys said. "She loves you. She loves you more than she loves me." He didn't sound hurt; it was more a statement of fact. Since it was the truth, I didn't try to argue. "But every time you pull the cold, arrogant act, Merry pulls away. When you pout, she pulls away."

"The cold arrogant act, as you put it, is what saved my sanity with the queen."

"I am not the queen, Frost," I said. "I don't want a toy in my bed. I want a king at my side. I need you to be a grown-up." It should have been silly to tell someone hundreds of years my senior to grow up, but it was necessary. Sadly.

Doyle spoke from against the pillows, and his voice held the effort that speech cost him. "If you could curb your emotions, she would love you and no other. If you could but understand, there would be no contest."

I wasn't entirely sure of that, but saying so out loud would not help. So I let it go.

"And what matters who she loves, if there is no child," Frost said.

"It seems to matter to you a great deal." Doyle closed his eyes and seemed asleep.

Frost frowned. "I do not know how not to do this. It is a habit of centuries."

"Let's do this," I said. "Every time you start to pout, I just tell you to stop. You try to stop when it's brought to your attention."

"I don't know."

"Just try," I said, "that's all I'm asking. Just try."

A very solemn look passed over his face, then he nodded. "I will try. I still do not agree that I pout, but I will try not to do it."

I hugged him. When I pulled away, he was smiling. "For that look in your eyes, I would slay armies. What is a little emotion, to that?"

Anyone who thought that slaying armies was easier than fixing your own internal emotional mess hadn't had enough therapy. But I didn't say that out loud, either.

Chapter 17

IN THE MORNING THE GOLDEN GODDESS OF HOLLYWOOD WAS crying at our kitchen table. It might have been baby hormones, but then again, it might not. Maeve liked to pretend that it was Gordon who'd been the brains of the two, but the truth was that when she wanted to, she had a very good mind. A logical mind, a dangerous mind. She was trickier to deal with when she was thinking than when she was seducing. Crying meant either real emotion, or she was about to try to manipulate me. I didn't want her sad, but I sort of hoped she was, because I didn't want all her skills directed at me. She was the goddess Conchenn again, and there had been men and women greater than me over the centuries who hadn't been able to tell her no.

I stood in the doorway, debating a retreat, but I hesitated too long. She raised her head, and showed me tear-streaked, lightning-kissed eyes. Her hair was the yellow-blond of the glamour she usually wore, but her eyes were real. Of course, being Seelie sidhe, her skin was still flawless. She didn't have the decency to get blotchy or hollow-eyed. Though she was dabbing at her nose with a Kleenex, her nose wasn't the least bit red. If I sobbed my nose got red, and eventually my eyes would get red. Maeve could probably have cried for a hundred years and still have looked this perfect.

She dabbed at her eyes. "I see you're dressed to go." Her voice showed the tears that her skin did not. She sounded thick and snuffling, as if she had been crying for hours.

Somehow the voice sounding less than perfect made me feel better. Probably shallow of me, or maybe even insecure, but true.

She'd said I was dressed to go, not that I looked good. Which was a roundabout insult among us. If a fey has taken time with her wardrobe, then it was an insult not to compliment her, unless of course you thought she'd failed in her choices. I had taken care with my wardrobe today. I knew that not only would I be seeing my aunt, the queen, in the outfit, but there would be reporters as well. Every time we left Maeve's house there seemed to be reporters.

A black, ankle-length skirt hugged my hips and flared out as it flowed down my legs, in a material not found in nature so it wouldn't wrinkle on the plane. A black leather belt with a matching buckle was cinched tight at my waist. A green silk-and-spandex T-shirt was topped with a black bolero-cut jacket. Antique gold-and-emerald earrings picked up the green. Calf-high black boots showed under my skirt. They had three-inch heels, and the leather was shiny, and gleamed when the light caught it. I'd thought the emerald-green shirt brought out the green of my eyes, and the fit, along with the scoop neck, showed off my breasts. I'd normally have worn a shorter skirt, but it was January in St. Louis, and showing off my legs wasn't worth risking frostbite. But the skirt flowed as I moved, and the black overskirt gave an impression of floating, catching in the slightest wind, whether of my movement or air.

I'd thought I looked good, until Maeve had worded her sentence oh, so carefully.

"I take it you don't approve of the outfit," I said, and went for the teapot under its cozy. Galen had had to search Los Angeles over to find an honest-to-goddess tea cozy to keep our tea warm. Most of the men preferred a strong black tea for breakfast instead of coffee—Rhys being the exception. He just didn't think that hard-boiled detectives should drink tea, so he drank coffee. His loss. More tea for me.

She looked at me, almost startled. "I forget sometimes that

you were raised out among the humans in your formative years. Though, frankly, you can be blunt even by human standards." She dabbed at her eyes again, but there were no more fresh tears, just the tracks drying on her face. "You don't play the game."

I added cream to the sugar I'd put in my tea and stirred as I looked at her. "What game would that be?"

"I'm angry with you, so I imply that you don't look good. You're not supposed to ask me outright what I think of your outfit. You're supposed to simply worry that I think you look bad. It's supposed to eat at you, undermine your confidence."

I sipped my tea. "Why would you want to do that?"

"Because it's your fault what happened last night."

"What's my fault?"

A sound very close to a sob broke from her lips. "I had sex with that . . . that false sidhe."

I frowned, then finally realized what she meant. "You mean Sage?"

She nodded, and there were fresh tears. In fact she laid her head back on the pale pine of the table and sobbed. Sobbed as if her heart would break.

I set my tea down and went to her. I couldn't stand to hear that broken sound. I'd heard it often enough over the last few weeks since her husband had died, but lately, less. I was glad it was less. Most of the stories talk about what happens to the poor mortals who fall in love with the immortal, and how badly it goes for them, but Maeve was showing the other side. When the immortal truly fell in love with a mortal, eventually it ended badly for the immortal. We died, and they didn't. Simple, horrible, true. Watching Maeve mourn Gordon had made me worry about what I was getting myself into with a sidhe spouse. Eventually, whomever I married would be a widower. No way around it. Not a pretty thought.

I touched her shoulder, and she cried harder. "Did Sage hurt you?" I asked, and thought it was stupid even as I said it.

She raised her head enough to give me a tearful version of

her *how-dare-you* face. She said in a snuffly voice, "He could not hurt a princess of the Seelie Court."

I patted her shoulder. "Of course not, I apologize for saying it. But if he didn't hurt you, then why are you crying about it? The sex couldn't have been that bad."

She sobbed harder, covering her face with her hands. I think she said, "It was wonderful," but it was too muffled for me to be certain.

I still didn't understand why she was so upset, but the pain was real. I hugged her shoulders, laid my cheek against her hair. "If it was wonderful, then why are you crying?"

She said something, but it was lost in all the crying. "I'm sorry, Maeve, I couldn't understand you."

"It shouldn't have been wonderful."

I was glad she couldn't see my face because I probably looked as puzzled as I felt. "It was your first taste of sidhe flesh in a century. Of course it was wonderful."

She lowered her hands and turned to look at me, so that I had to stand back to give her room. "You don't understand," she said. "He isn't sidhe. It's a lie, an illusion, like the apple tree in my house. It was gone this morning."

"The tree?"

She nodded.

I frowned; I couldn't help it. "But I touched it, the leaves, the bark, the blossoms. I smelled the scent. It was real. Illusions can hide things, or make one thing look like another, but illusion can't bring something out of nothing. There has to be something real for the illusion to attach to."

"Normally, yes, but the sidhe once could build an illusion so solid that you could walk across it. Do you think that stories of castles in the air are fairy tales, Merry? Once the sidhe could do that. We could create something out of nothing. Things made of pure magic that were as real as anything in existence."

"So it was a real tree," I said slowly.

"Real while the magic lasted, yes. If there had been apples on the tree, you could have eaten them and they would have filled your belly. It was the way we had of making our few fey animals feed us again and again. They were magic, and that could be renewed."

"I know there is such a thing as illusion that is real, but my father said that such talents were lost long ago."

She nodded. "They were."

"So that is beginning to return to us, along with other magicks?"

"Yes." She smiled then, a watery version of the smile that had launched a thousand blockbuster movies, years before the term *blockbuster* meant anything. She took my hand in hers. "And you have brought that back to us, Merry, you and your magic."

I shook my head. "No, not me, the Goddess. I couldn't do any of this without divine help."

"You are too modest," she said.

"Maybe," I said, and I couldn't help myself, "though of course when you have such bad taste in clothes, it's hard not to be humble."

She wouldn't meet my eyes for a moment. "I am sorry, but I wanted to hurt you."

I squeezed her hand, then took my hand out of hers. "Why?"

"Because I blamed you for Sage seducing me last night."

"Rhys made it sound like you were doing more of the seducing," I said.

She actually blushed. "Truth. Hard, but the truth. I saw him shining in the dark. He glowed like a golden moon. I . . ." She turned so I couldn't see her face, put her back to me. "I knew that he was not one of your men. I thought he would not refuse me, and he didn't."

"You seduced him. It was wonderful. And now you're having morning-after regrets?" I said.

"Silly, isn't it."

"The fey don't regret sex, Maeve."

"You've never truly been Seelie Court, Merry. You don't know what the rules are there."

"I know that anyone who isn't pure-blooded is less, no matter her talents or magicks."

She turned in the chair enough to look at me again. "Yes, yes."

"I didn't think you held with that anymore."

"Neither did I."

I tried to reason it out. "You're upset because you enjoyed being with someone who wasn't pure sidhe?"

"I'm upset because Sage is not a prince of either court. He's a demi-fey whom your magic has brought into something more, but he is not sidhe, Merry. He will never be truly sidhe. A hundred years from now, even with his tricolored eyes, he will not be sidhe."

"You see how they are." It was Frost from the doorway. Neither of us had heard him come up, and we both jumped.

He wore a standard white dress shirt, tie, and dress slacks, but the tie was silver and only a shade less bright than the hair that shimmered around his shoulders. His slacks were dark grey, thick material, cut well so the pants managed to be roomy in the front and over the thighs but formfitting from behind. I'd admired the view earlier. A silver-and-diamond tie bar and matching cuff links glittered as he moved into the room. His usual loafers had given way to dark grey boots, mostly hidden by the generous cut of pant cuffs.

"How who are?" I asked.

"The Seelie." He said *Seelie* as if it was a dirty word. The way most Seelie said *Unseelie*.

Maeve stood up from the table. "How dare you."

"How dare I what?" he asked as he moved toward us.

"How dare you insult the Seelie."

"They would say the same of us," Frost said, and there was a level of anger in him that I wasn't sure of. I hoped this new anger wasn't his answer to the pouting. Trading one problem for another was not what I'd had in mind.

Maeve opened her shapely mouth, then closed it. She couldn't call him a liar, because it was true. She finally settled for, "I don't know what to say," in a much more subdued voice.

Frost turned to me. "She'd never have touched Sage if she was still part of the golden court."

"Oh, I don't know," I said. "I'm proof that more than one Seelie will sully her body with those not of her court."

He shook his head, and his hair caught the light more than the small diamonds he wore. No jewel could truly compete with his hair. "Uar the Cruel wed your grandmother to avoid a curse. Besaba went to your father as part of a treaty. Trust me, Merry, the shining ones do not come willingly to our beds."

"As you should know, Jackie Frost."

He winced but didn't back down. He turned to her and moved forward enough to invade her personal space by American standards. When she didn't move back, he invaded her space even by fey standards. They were almost touching, the entire lengths of their bodies. It managed to be threatening, not erotic. Frost was taller, but only by a few inches. They met each other's eyes, opponents, evenly matched.

She looked at him, but her words were meant for me. "He was not always sidhe. Did you know that?" Her voice was calm, but held malice the way the air can hold the beginnings of a storm.

"Yes," I said, "I know Frost's origins."

She glanced at me then, and surprise showed on her face. "He would not have told you willingly."

I shook my head. "He showed me willingly with his magic. I've seen him dancing over the snow. I know what he is, and what he was, and it changes nothing for me."

Her lovely face went from surprise to astonishment. She stepped away from him and took my arm. "Of course it changes how you feel. You thought you were bedding a sidhe, and you find he is merely the hoarfrost brought to life."

I looked down at her hand, and my face must have been as unfriendly as I was beginning to feel, because she dropped away from me.

"You mean it. You truly mean it. It makes no difference to you."

I shook my head. "None."

She looked puzzled then. "I don't understand that."

"You came back into your powers as Conchenn just last night. You slept with your first sidhe in a century. You wake up this morning, and you don't sound like Maeve Reed. You sound like just another Seelie noble. I've never understood why the Seelie embraced such a Victorian view of sex. It's so un-fey-like."

"You don't understand, Merry, how could you? Sleeping with a human would be forgiven, but not fucking a demi-fey. My need outrode my common sense last night. I was power-drunk. This morning, I'm sober."

"But you're exiled from the Seelie Court, Maeve, and the Unseelie Court doesn't care about origins, only about results. It's not where you come from, but what you can do for us."

She shook her head. "I can't shield my eyes. I can't make my glamour cover them this morning, and I don't know why. I've worn this glamour for decades. It feels almost more real than my true form, but I haven't been able to cover my eyes again. You gave me power, Merry, but you stripped me of things, too."

"So it's my fault that you fucked Sage?"

"Maybe," she said, but even in that one word there was doubt. She didn't really believe it.

"It doesn't really matter what the Seelie Court thinks of your actions, Maeve. If you ever go back there, the King of Light and Illusion will see you dead. You're welcome to join the Unseelie Court and come with us. You can be in the heart of faerie tonight." I watched her while I said it, and saw the hunger in her face before she hid it.

She gave me her publicity smile. "I am Seelie sidhe, Merry, not Unseelie."

"I was once a member of the golden court," Frost said.

"You were never a member of the court, Jackie Frost. Never!"

He gave her a cold smile. "Allow me to rephrase. I was

once barely tolerated at the court of beauty and illusion. Tolerated because as others faded in power, I grew. Not through some other sidhe's powers, but through the minds of the humans. They remembered me when they'd forgotten all of you beautiful, shining deities. Little Jakual Frosti, Jackie Frost, Jack Frost." He stepped in close to her again, and this time she shrank back from him, just a little. "But who still speaks of Conchenn? Where are your poems, your songs? Why did they remember me, and not you?"

Her voice was small. "I don't know."

"I don't know, either, but they did." He leaned in even closer, close enough almost to kiss. "Me they remembered, when so many they forgot. 'Tis a mystery."

He began to glow then as if the moon were trapped inside his body, and the light spilled out of his eyes, making them nearly as silver as his hair. The wind of his power filled the air around his body with a glowing halo of his own hair. He stood before her like some metallic vision, forged of liquid silver.

She couldn't stand so close to his power and not respond. She'd been without the touch of sidhe for too long for that. The need would not be quenched in one night's embrace, a few washes of power. Such hunger goes deeper than that.

His power brought hers in a golden rush, drained her hair to white-blond, and filled the air around her with the swaying of it. They were so close that their powers intermingled, yellow and silver merged in a line between them. This was not godhead, this was merely the power of the sidhe.

I watched them, and understood why my human ancestors had thought they were gods. Now they'd probably be mistaken for angels, or big men from Mars. I watched them glow at each other, and even through the light I could see the raw need on Maeve's face. Frost didn't look hungry, he looked satisfied.

He leaned in and pressed his shining lips to hers. The physicality of the kiss was chaste, but his power thrust into her like a spear of silver light. I saw that long shaft of power nearly bisect her golden-yellow light. For an instant her light darkened at its core, a flash of orange and red, like true flame. Then he drew back, stepped back until she glowed alone. "You would not turn me from your body, not even now with the memory of Sage's flesh like a raw wound in your mind."

His power folded away, leaving him pale, and still beautiful, but not a shining thing.

Maeve's power faded a little at a time as she spoke. "I could have taken lesser fey to my bed over the last hundred years. Other exiles like me. But I did not do it, because I hoped that someday the court would see Taranis's treachery, and when he was dead, I would be welcome back. They would forgive my human lovers, for the Seelie always did love human flesh in the dark. But you do not sully yourself with the lesser fey. You do not do that, and ever regain prominence in the high court of faerie."

"There is more than one high court of faerie," Frost said.

She shook her head. "No, there isn't. Not for me."

He shook his head. "This attitude will grow tiresome before we finish our visit to the Seelie."

"Frost, you just don't remember what they're like. You have not begun to see tiresome."

He sighed. "I remember all too well, Maeve." He looked sad for a moment. "I do not wish to return there and watch them treat us as lesser beings."

"Then stay here, with me." She turned to me. "Don't go back, Merry. Taranis wants you to visit him for a reason. He does nothing without a reason, and it will not be a reason that you will like."

"I know," I said.

She balled her hands into fists. "Then why go?"

"Because she will be queen of the Unseelie Court, and she cannot begin her reign by showing fear to Taranis," Doyle said from the doorway.

"But you are afraid of Taranis," Maeve said. "We all are."

Doyle shrugged. He was wearing black jeans tucked into knee-high black boots, a black T-shirt, black leather jacket. Even his belt buckle was black. The only color showing was the silver earrings that graced the pointed curve of his ears. There was even a diamond stud in one earlobe. "Afraid or not, we must show a brave face."

"Is it worth dying for? Is it worth getting Merry killed?" She pointed at me, rather dramatically, but she was an actress. Besides, the sidhe could be a dramatic lot, even without training.

"If he kills Merry, Queen Andais will kill him."

"He released the Nameless to try to kill me so that I wouldn't reveal his secret. Do you really think he'd hesitate at full-out war between the courts?"

"I didn't say war, Maeve."

"You said the queen would kill Taranis; that means war."

Doyle shook his head. "For slaying the heir to her throne, I think Andais would do one of two things. Either challenge him to a personal duel, which Taranis will not want; or have him assassinated, discreetly."

"You mean you would kill Taranis," Maeve said.

"I am no longer the Queen's Darkness." He came to stand next to me. "I have heard that she has a new captain of her guard now."

"Who?" Frost asked.

"Mistral," Doyle said.

"The Bringer of Storms. But he has been long out of favor."

Doyle nodded. "Nonetheless, that is her new champion."

"He is no assassin, and he is never discreet. He comes like his namesake with much wind and noise." Frost was openly disdainful.

"But Whisper is quiet enough to make up for it," Doyle said.

Frost looked startled. Maeve was frowning. "I don't know these names."

"They have all but faded into their names," Doyle said. "What you once knew them by is no more."

"Whisper," Frost said. "I thought he'd gone mad."

"I'd heard that rumor, too."

I remembered Mistral. He was everything the queen abhorred, loud, bragging, quick to anger, unforgiving. He was almost the epitome of a bully, but he was too powerful to be refused entrance to the dark court once he'd gotten himself kicked out of the golden. Queen Andais made sure we accepted all who were powerful, but she didn't have to like them, or use them much. She could make sure they were always seated far away from her and given duties that kept them from her sight.

Mistral had been so out of favor during my lifetime that I barely remembered his face, and could not truly recall ever having spoken with him. My father had thought him a fool.

"I don't remember anyone among the guard called Whisper," I said.

"He displeased the queen once, long ago," Doyle said, "and she had him punished. He was given to Ezekiel in the Hallway of Mortality for"—he frowned, looked at Frost—"for seven years, wasn't it?"

Frost nodded. "I believe so."

I swallowed before I could speak. "He was given over to be tortured for seven years." My voice was breathy with the horror of it. I'd been in the Hallway of Mortality. I knew exactly how good at his craft Ezekiel was, and I could not imagine seven years of such attention.

They were both nodding.

Even Maeve looked pale. The Seelie Court did not condone torture, at least not the overt kind that Ezekiel dished out. They had more subtle ways of doing it, magical ways, that were less messy, less personal. You could cause someone excruciating pain without getting your hands dirty. Queen Andais liked calling a spade a spade. Torture was supposed to be messy, or what good was it?

"I have heard tales of your Hallway of Hell."

"See, Taranis even lets his court adopt the words of a faith that tormented and tortured our followers," Frost said. "He has allowed his court to become an ape of the humans."

"If your century begins with seventeen, or earlier," I said.

Frost shrugged, as if a few hundred years made no difference.

"Call it what you will, but that your queen would mete out such punishment is proof that I do not want to be a part of your court."

"What did he do to earn seven years with Ezekiel?" I asked.

"I don't think anyone knows but Whisper and the queen," Frost said.

I looked at Doyle. "You've been her left-hand man for a millennium, or more. You'd never left her side until she sent you here to Los Angeles to fetch. You know, don't you?"

He let out a small breath. "If she wanted others to know, Merry, she would have told them. I will not endanger anyone by sharing that particular bit of truth."

I let it go. I didn't want Andais to have an excuse to send any of us to the Hallway of Mortality. I could live the rest of my days without knowing what Whisper had done to merit seven years, as long as I never had to endure another minute with Ezekiel's voice in my face.

Frost turned to Maeve. "You've refused to go to the Unseelie Court with us, even though you know that Taranis may try to kill you while we're gone."

"You will be turning me over to new bodyguards at the airport."

"The same human bodyguards who nearly got themselves killed trying to save you from the Nameless. The same bodyguards who, if we hadn't come along, would have died to a man, and you with them."

"We will take another plane to another country, far from the king and his powers."

"She will probably be safer than we will, Frost. For we will beard him in his den, the very heart of his power."

"But she would be safer still at the Unseelie Court, under the queen's protection," Frost said.

"We have had this discussion," Doyle said. "It is done."

Frost looked at her. "It isn't that you loathe the Unseelie

Court, or even that you're afraid of them, of us. It's that you're afraid that once you enter the darkling throng and are surrounded by faerie once more, you will never leave."

"She could make me a prisoner, for my own protection, and you would not be able to break me free," Maeve said.

"You wouldn't be a prisoner, Conchenn, you'd simply embrace the dark, because the light won't have you. Many a Seelie lord and lady has found that the dark is not half so ugly as they thought, or half so terrible as they were taught." He took a step toward her, and she took a step back.

"They embraced the dark because they had no choice," she said in a voice that was almost choked. "It was the darkness or be exiled from faerie forever."

"Exactly," Frost said. "There are no prisoners among us. Whisper could have fled the Unseelie Court. The queen would not have pursued him, for she knows that for a sidhe to leave the Unseelie Court is to have no place to go. No home in faerie. We take the queen's laws, not because we have no choice, but because even seven years of torment is better than being cast out, as you were, by your king."

I saw tears shine in her eyes as she rushed past us all and out the far door.

"Did you have to do that?" Doyle said.

Frost nodded. "Yes, I think I did. She's endangering herself by refusing to go to the Unseelie Court. It's foolish."

"Not half so foolish as entering the Seelie Court of our own free will," Doyle said.

The two men looked at each other, and something passed between them. Frost's shoulders slumped just a little before he straightened and said, "I do not like either plan."

"You've made that clear," Doyle said.

Frost looked at me. "I will go with Merry, but I will not like it." He smiled, but it was wistful, so full of old sorrow that it made my chest tight. "And I fear, my sweet, sweet, princess, neither will you."

I would have argued with him if I could, but since I agreed with him, it seemed silly. "We visit the Unseelie Court first,

Frost, and the goblin court after that, and only then the Seelie Court."

He shook his head, and the smile became bitter. "I hope that the sights we see at the goblin court are the worst we will have, but I fear that no horror will compare to the bright beauty that awaits us at our last stop."

Sadly, no one argued with him.

Chapter 18

IT WASN'T THAT MAEVE REED'S PERSONAL JET WASN'T COM-
fortable, because it was. The only one of us who hated to fly
was Doyle. He had chosen his seat early, buckled himself in,
and kept a death grip on the arms of the nice swively seat.
He closed his eyes tight, hugged the seat, and it was just acknowledged that if we were ever attacked inside an airplane,
Doyle would not be that helpful, at least not at first. When
I'd discovered his phobia over flying in planes, I'd actually
been pleased. It had made him seem less perfect, less the
Queen's Darkness and assassin. It seemed like a long time
ago that I'd needed that. I looked at him across the narrow
aisle. The tension in his body sang in the air around him, almost like a kind of power. Of course, fear can be fuel for
magic.

"I would ask what you are thinking," Frost said from beside me, "but it seems obvious."

I turned my head against the padded seat back so I could
meet his eyes. "What am I thinking?"

"You're thinking about Doyle." He wasn't angry, and he
wasn't pouting. Maybe his voice wasn't happy, but he wasn't
pouting. It was progress.

"I was thinking that once his fear of flying made him seem
less the queen's perfect assassin."

His face started to close down, that cold mask building up.
"That is not all."

I touched his arm. "Don't pout about this, Frost. I was just
thinking that if we are ever attacked on an airplane, it's the
one place Doyle won't be at his best. That's all."

I watched him struggle to swallow all that sullenness. It looked like it might choke him, but he was trying. He was trying so obviously that I didn't say what else I was thinking: that if I had been sitting there having some wild fantasy about Doyle, it was none of Frost's concern. I was supposed to enjoy all of them, but I kept it to myself. Frost was trying, and chastising him for being possessive, a very un-fey-like emotion, wouldn't have helped.

I squeezed his arm and let it go. Good for me.

Rhys knelt in front of me. He was wearing his white eye patch with the tiny seed pearls on it. It went with the white silk trench coat, white fedora, and pale cream-colored suit. The only color he wore was an icy pink tie. He looked like a cross between an ice cream man and the ghost of some 1940s detective. He'd even piled all that white curly hair up under the hat. He looked younger without the hair, all soft lines and kissable lips. He was hundreds of years older than I would ever be, but kneeling there, he looked like he'd never seen the wrong side of thirty.

He smiled up at me. "Doyle gave me something to give to you." He glanced behind at their leader, still sitting with his eyes tight shut. He turned back to me with a chuckle. "He knew he'd be indisposed." He pulled a white ring box out of his coat pocket.

The smile that I'd given him faded. "Do I have to?"

"Yes, you do." He suddenly looked a decade older, not a bit less handsome, but the boyishness was gone as if I'd imagined it.

Frost leaned in to add, "It is the queen's ring, Merry, given to you from her. It is one of the symbols that you are her heir. You must wear it."

"I don't mind the ring," I said, "but with the chalice on the plane, I'm a little worried that it might up the magic on the ring as it's done on other things."

The two men looked at each other, and I could tell it was the first time they'd thought of it.

"Damn," Rhys said, "that could be a problem."

Frost looked very serious. "A problem, or a salvation.

Once the ring was a great relic of power, not merely a chooser of the queen's fertile lovers."

"Funny," I said, "I keep hearing that the ring is a great relic, but no one, not even my father, would tell me what it did once upon a time." I looked from one to the other of them, and they exchanged one of those glances that said neither wanted to tell me.

"What?" I demanded.

They sighed in unison. Rhys sat back on his knees, the ring box still unopened in his hands. "Once, the ring made Andais irresistible to any man whom the ring reacted to."

"That doesn't sound bad enough for the looks on your faces. What else?"

They exchanged another glance.

"Drop the other shoe, okay."

"Shoe?" Frost asked.

"She means, just tell her," Rhys explained. He was one of the few guards who hadn't spent the last fifty years hiding in the hollow hills. Rhys owned a house outside the faerie mounds. A house with electricity, a television, and everything. He was probably one of the only sidhe who knew who Humphrey Bogart had been, or who Madonna was.

"You know that moment in all the Cinderella movies where she's at the top of the stairs, and the prince looks up, stunned?" Rhys asked.

"Yes," I said.

"Then he walks toward her like he has no choice."

I nodded. "Yes."

"That irresistible," he said.

"You mean once the ring's reacted to you, you're like some besotted schoolboy?"

He sighed. "Not exactly."

"It isn't just the men," Frost said.

I looked from one to the other. "What do you mean?"

Sage tromped up the aisle to us. He was wearing a pair of Kitto's dress slacks and a T-shirt that had had to be ripped up the back to accommodate his wings. His waist was tinier than Kitto's, so he had a belt cinched tight. He wore a pair of

Kitto's jogging shoes laced as tight as they would go, because his foot was narrower than the goblin's. He had a blanket wrapped around his upper body, because the jacket ripped up the back wouldn't keep him warm. He needed one of the heavy woolen cloaks that the courts had designed centuries ago for the human-sized, or bigger, winged fey. Nicca was also going to be a very cold boy once we landed. But we'd alerted the guards who would meet us at the airport, and they'd have cloaks. Until then, Sage huddled in his blanket as if he could already feel the cold. At his new size he had no clothes that fit him.

"What they are so delicately trying to tell you, Princess, is that once that ring was a matchmaker."

I frowned up at him from my seat.

He sighed. "Oh, to be young again," but he made it sound like a bad thing. "The ring can tell a fertile match, not just from touching bare skin, but from across a room, at first sight. Both the man and woman fell hopelessly in love and lived happily ever after."

"Queen Andais has never struck me as the happily-ever-after type."

"She had control of the ring, Merry, like any good weapon, or tool. She would throw a great ball and invite all the eligible sidhe, and a few of us lesser beings to serve at table or entertain. Then she'd stand near the door, and as each woman came through, she'd touch her with the ring, and almost always someone would step forward. They would fall upon each other like lustful rams, be huge with child within a few months, marry, and be a perfect match. Once upon a time, the ring didn't just pick out which sidhe were fertile. Oh, no, it was the happy-ever-after ring. That's what we used to call it. Where do you think the humans got all that crap from?"

I raised eyebrows at him. "I hadn't really thought about it. I know for a fact that most fairy tales are just that, stories."

"But the elements of them"—he drew a pale yellow hand out of his blanket far enough to shake a finger at me—"the essentials, they got from us, from true stories." He frowned. "Not all of us are Irish, Scottish, or anything that is part of what they call the British Isles. We hold survivors from nearly every part of Europe."

"I'm aware of that," I said.

"Then act like you know. Surely Prince Essus told you that some fairy tales were passed-on true stories."

"My father told me most were simply made up."

"Most," Sage conceded, "but not all." He waved his finger at me again. "If the chalice has brought back the complete power to that ring"—he pointed at the box—"then if you have your perfect match on this plane, you'll know it, and if you don't, you'll know that, too."

I looked at the little box, and suddenly it seemed more important than it had even a moment ago.

"That's not how the queen used it," Rhys said, "not for herself."

"No," Nicca said softly, from behind us. "Once her own true love was killed in battle, she used the power of the ring to fill her bed. She was able with its help to make another sidhe elf-struck."

I turned and looked at him. He wore slacks that were so dark brown, they were nearly black, and boots that matched underneath. His hair spilled over his naked upper body, because his wings were even larger than Sage's, and though we'd tried to get a silk-and-spandex tee over them, in the end we'd been defeated. They were too huge, and too oddly shaped, all swirls and tail.

"I thought she would go mad when Owain died." Doyle's eyes were still shut tight, his hands gripping the chair arms, but his voice sounded normal enough.

"What no one had realized was that the ring had an added power," he continued in his calm voice. "Apparently, it acted as a kind of protective magic around the couples of its choosing. It guaranteed a happy ending, by making sure no tragedy befell them."

Rhys nodded. "The ring had begun to fade in power—we knew that because the great matchmaking ball had failed some decades before. A sidhe would come to the door of the ballroom, and no one would step forward. But we didn't understand that the ring had kept us safe, not just happy and fertile."

"Until the battle of Rhodan," Frost said, "where we lost two hundred sidhe warriors. Most of them had been wed to their love matches."

"It was the first time in our history that a single couple that the ring had brought together had not had a happy ending," Doyle said.

"It wasn't just one couple," Rhys said, "it was dozens." He shook his head. "I'd never heard such keening."

"Some of those left behind chose to fade," Doyle said.

"Suicide, you mean," Rhys said.

Doyle opened his eyes enough to glance at Rhys, then closed them again. "If you prefer."

"I don't prefer, it's just the truth," Rhys said.

Doyle shrugged. "Fine."

Galen had drifted up behind everyone. "Did the ring ever pick more than one person for anyone?" He was dressed all in pale spring green.

"You mean once someone was widowed, did the ring ever find them someone else?" Doyle asked.

"That, or literally pick more than one person for someone. I mean, you may get a child from every match the ring made, but to be truly happy, not just magically in love, did the ring ever have trouble choosing just one person for someone?"

Doyle opened his eyes again and actually turned to look full at Galen. "Do you not believe in soul mates, one perfect love for each person?" It would have seemed an almost silly question from anyone else.

Galen glanced at me, then forced himself to look away to meet Doyle's dark gaze. "I don't believe in love at first sight. I believe true love takes time to build, like friendship. I believe in instant lust."

He moved directly behind my seat. I could feel him like

some warming fire. I wanted him to put his hands on the back of the seat, to be closer to that warmth. As if he'd heard me, he put his hands where I wanted them, and it was all I could do not to touch my head against his fingers. But somehow with the ring box sitting there, I wasn't sure I wanted to be touching him when I put it on. I was pretty certain that touching no one was the best idea, until we knew if the ring had been affected by the chalice.

"Could we get the queen's permission not to wear it until we're at the faerie mound?" I asked.

"No," Doyle said, "she was most insistent."

I sighed. We did not want Andais angry with us. We so didn't want that. "Fine, give me the box, and everybody stand back."

"It's not a bomb," Rhys said, "just a ring."

I frowned at him. "After what I've just heard, I'd almost prefer a bomb." *Almost,* I added in my head.

I didn't want my choices limited here and now. I was afraid of whom the ring would pick, and why. I didn't trust magic in matters of the heart. Hell's bells, I didn't trust matters of the heart at all. Love was an unreliable sort of thing, sometimes.

Rhys handed me the box, and after I repeated my need for privacy, all of them got up and walked away from me. Kitto remained at the back of the plane with a blanket over his entire body, hiding. Hiding from his fear of metal, and modern technology. He was afraid of so many things that it seemed less remarkable for him to be afraid of airplanes than for Doyle, who feared almost nothing.

The rest of the men divided themselves into two groups. One stood around Doyle, who was still in his seat, though watching everything now. The other stood near the back of the plane.

"Open it," Rhys said, from near Doyle.

"She's scared," Galen said, and his voice held an edge of the nerves that were scrambling around my stomach.

"Scared of what?" Sage said. "Finding her perfect match?

What a stupid thing to fear. Most would give their lives to have such a problem."

"Be quiet," Nicca said.

Sage opened his mouth to complain, then closed it, looking puzzled, as if he wasn't sure himself why he listened to Nicca.

I stared at the box in my hands, licked my lipsticked mouth that was suddenly dry, and couldn't for the life of me understand why I was so afraid. Why be afraid of finding out if my perfect match was here, among these men? No, that wasn't the fear, I realized. What if the ring didn't find my perfect match here and now? What if my perfect match wasn't any of them? What if that was why I hadn't become pregnant?

I looked up and scanned the faces around me. I realized that in a strange way, I loved them all. I certainly valued them all. I also wasn't sure how Frost or Galen would take it if the ring chose someone other than him. Both had shown a very un-fey-like tendency to be jealous. If Frost wasn't the chosen one, well, I doubt I'd seen pouting like that from him.

I looked up at Galen, and knew that he loved me, truly loved me, and had loved me when I had no chance of being queen. He was the only one, except Rhys, who had made it clear he wanted to be my lover when it would gain him nothing but my body, and maybe my love. Galen was such a romantic. I think he'd come to terms with not being my husband, not being king to my queen, if I got pregnant by someone else. But I think in his heart of hearts he believed that I was his soul mate. He could give me up, as long as he got to keep the ideal of what could have been.

I stared back down at the box. If the ring chose someone else, Galen would have to find a new dream, a new love, a new everything.

"Open it," Rhys said.

I took a deep breath, let it out slowly, and opened it.

Chapter 19

THE RING WAS A HEAVY SILVER OCTAGONAL, NOT PERFECTLY round, as if it molded to all the fingers it had encircled. It was actually a very plain, almost mannish-looking ring. Inside there were words carved, in an ancient form of Gaelic, too old for me to read, but I knew translated to read, "For if my loves come not to me, dark and dismal my life will be."

There was nothing threatening about it. And yet ... I touched its cool silver with a fingertip, and nothing happened. But then nothing ever did until it was on your finger. It was picky that way.

"You must put it on, Meredith," Doyle said. I'd almost broken them all of calling me anything but Merry. It was the beginning of the return to court formality. I hated it.

"I know, Doyle."

"Then hesitating is foolish. We must know what problem it represents before we land. There will be human police to hold back the press, but there will still be cameras and reporters to catch whatever befalls. Best that it befall us now, and here in private." He turned in his seat to face me more fully, forcing him to let go of one of the seat arms. I had some idea what that cost him. "Put it on, Meredith, Merry, please."

I nodded, and took it from its box. It was warm to the touch, but nothing more. I took a deep breath, and wasn't sure whether to pray before I slipped it on, or not. Prayers had taken on an entirely new meaning in the last twenty-four hours.

I slipped the ring on my finger. It was too big for me, but

almost instantly I felt that first spark of magic. It would be exactly my size now. A small magic. I looked up at all of them. "I don't feel any difference in it."

"You stopped wearing it because it was giving us all shocks when we had sex," Rhys said. "It never did do much from a distance."

"Not on my finger," I said.

He grinned. "Can we try touching it to bare skin and see if that's changed?"

"I think that would be wise," Doyle said.

Rhys shrugged. "My idea. If no one objects I'll be the first guinea pig." He started forward, but Frost spoke.

"I object."

Rhys hesitated. He glanced at me, then at Doyle, and shrugged again. "Be my guest. We'll still have to try more than one of us with the ring, just to see."

"Agreed," Frost said, "but I want to be first."

No one argued with him, but Galen's face said plainly that he wanted to. It was a tribute to how much more grown-up he was than Frost himself that he let it go.

Frost came to stand in front of me and gazed down at the ring on my hand. He held his own hand down toward me, and I raised my hand up to meet his. His hand closed over mine, his fingers brushing the ring.

It was as if some huge invisible hand caressed the front of my body, as if there were no clothes, nothing but my skin, for the magic to stroke. Frost collapsed to his knees, his eyes wide, lips half open in a movement caught between desire and surprise. His hand convulsed around mine, pressing his flesh harder into the ring. The magic responded in a second wave of desire more powerful than the first. It ended low in my body, throwing me back against the seat, bringing a cry from my lips. My body spasmed and my hands jerked against Frost's, breaking the ring's contact with him.

He half fell onto the floor, barely room for his broad shoulders between the seats. He was panting and weak, and I wasn't much better.

"I know Merry just had an orgasm," Rhys said, "a small one, but a real one. Did you, Frost?"

He shook his head, as if speech was too much. He finally managed a breathy, "Almost."

"The magic of the ring was distracting before," Doyle said, "but not this distracting."

"Is it just Frost?" Galen managed to sound neutral and worried at the same time.

Rhys grinned and climbed over the seats to wedge himself between the seats and my legs. "I don't think Frost can stand yet."

"Help him up," Doyle said.

Nicca came forward, but his wings got in the way so badly that he gave it up and stepped back. Galen helped Frost into one of the nearby seats, clearing the aisle and giving Rhys room to drop to one knee beside me.

"Not so far to fall," he said, grinning.

"You never have far to fall," Galen said.

Rhys gave him a look but didn't rise to the bait. "You're just jealous because I get to go next."

Galen tried to make another joke, but finally just stepped back and said, "Yeah, I am."

Rhys touched my shoulder, bringing my attention from Galen's somber face back to him. "I like to know a girl's at least looking at me during sex."

I gave him a look. "You know how it is, Rhys, a man gets as much attention during sex as his skills deserve."

"Oooh," he said, holding a hand over his heart, "that one hurt." But his tri-blue eye sparkled with more than humor. "If I didn't think I'd knock out a tooth, I'd kiss your hand instead of just holding it."

It made me laugh, and I was still laughing when his hand closed over mine, where it lay in my lap. All laughter ceased, all breathing ceased, and for one frozen moment there was nothing but a wash of sensations, as if one sensual pulse built into the next, and the next. It wasn't until someone's voice said, "Breathe, Merry, breathe," that I realized I hadn't been.

My breath came back in a harsh gasp, and my eyes flew open. Only when I opened them did I realize I'd closed them.

Rhys was half collapsed against the seat in front of me, with a near-drunken grin upon his face. "Oh yeah, that was a lot of fun."

"It's not just Frost," Nicca said.

"No." Doyle didn't look entirely happy about that, though I wasn't sure why. "Galen, next," he said.

There were some protests, but Doyle waved them away. "No, we must know if this reaction is only to those who have godhead, or if it's going to be everyone. If everyone, then Merry cannot touch the guards on the ground in St. Louis, not in front of the reporters or the police."

"Tell me again why we have human policemen waiting for us in St. Louis," Rhys said. His eyes were still unfocused, but his voice was almost normal.

"One of the tabloids ran a picture of all of us rushing into the main house last night, with guns drawn and very few clothes. The ambassador to the courts did not believe the queen's assurances that it was not an assassination attempt on the princess, but simply a misunderstanding. I believe, and the queen believes, that the rulers of St. Louis do not wish to be seen as being careless of the princess's safety. If something goes wrong, they want to be able to say they did their best."

Rulers of St. Louis. Sometimes I forgot for days at a time how old Doyle and the rest were. Then they'd say something like that, and you knew their thoughts and vocabulary were formed in a time before mayors, or Congress, or anything remotely modern.

"The humans are no longer content with some of the queen's stories," Doyle continued. "The ambassador to the courts is most unhappy that they will not show him Prince Cel. He doesn't believe that Cel is merely away."

The tabloids had been the first to speculate why Prince Cel, who had been fairly visible in St. Louis and Chicago attending hot nightspots, had suddenly decided to stay home. Where was the prince? Why had he vanished now that

Princess Meredith was back in the land of faerie? That last headline had been a little too close to the truth, but there was nothing we could do about it. Because the truth—that Prince Cel was being tortured for six months as an alternative to a death sentence—could not be shared with the human press, or even the politicians.

Among other crimes, Cel had set himself up as a deity to a human cult in California. I think he'd thought it was far enough from home that he wouldn't get caught. Unfortunately for him, I was in Los Angeles and working as a private detective. If Cel had known that, he would have put his scheme somewhere else, and he'd have tried to kill me sooner. One of the rules that President Thomas Jefferson's government insisted on was that if the sidhe ever set themselves up as gods in the United States, we would all be expelled from American soil. For that reason alone, any other sidhe would have been executed. But Cel also gave the human wizards the ability to magically ensnare, magically rape fey women. Mostly to humans with fey blood in their ancestry, but you do not give the power of faerie to humans to be used expressly to harm the fey. It isn't done. He was also sucking the magical energy of the women in question. He shared some of the power with his human followers, but he ate most of it. Magical vampirism is a crime among us. A crime punishable by death, and a nasty death at that. The only exception to the law is a duel. During a duel, or a war, you can do whatever you can get away with, as long as it doesn't breach your honor. Though some of the fey have an interesting view of honor. Cel should have died for all that, but he was the queen's only child, coheir to the throne. Most of the court had no clue as to the extent of Cel's treachery. They thought he was being punished for trying to kill me. Nope. The queen didn't like me that much.

So instead of death, he'd had the magic he'd given to the humans turned against him. A magic that made your skin crawl with desire and drove you nearly mad to be touched, to be fucked. I'd had it turned on me, so I could speak with some authority. He had been covered with Branwyn's Tears,

one of our last great magicks, and chained in the dark with
his need and no way to relieve it. It was a horrible thing to do
to anyone. But he wasn't enduring anything he hadn't allowed to happen to others, except for the length of the punishment. Six months is a very long time in the dark. He'd
endured three months of his punishment, and still had three
to go. People were taking bets at the court that his sanity
would not survive. They were also taking bets that he'd kill
me before I could kill him.

"If the humans do not believe us, there is nothing we can
do," Frost said.

"True, but we can give them less to talk about, not more."
Doyle turned his head to look at Galen. "Touch the ring and
see what happens."

Galen stepped up between the seats. There was heat in his
eyes, and a look on his face that brought heat in a rush across
my cheeks.

He dropped to his knees beside my chair, and cupped both
his hands over mine without touching the ring. He leaned in
toward me. "I want the ring to react to my touch." He spoke
the last word with his breath against my mouth. "I want it to
sing through me, and bring us both to our knees." His lips
touched mine, and his hands closed tight over mine, in the
same moment.

The ring flared between us, jerking things low in my body,
tingling along my lips, as if I'd tried to kiss something that
held electrical current. Galen's lips were soft and willing, but
no matter how hard he pressed his hand into the ring, it did
not become the near-overwhelming thing it had been with
Rhys and Frost. The ring did continue to beat against us like
waves of electricity. I wasn't fond of electricity on my skin,
and I pulled back from the kiss, tried to draw my hand out of
his. He wouldn't let me go.

"Let go, Galen, it's hurting me."

He released me slowly, reluctantly.

I sat in the seat, taking deep even breaths, trying to work
past the last vestiges of the power. "That hurt. I mean that really hurt."

"You just don't like electricity," Rhys said.

"I like it just fine in lamps, or computers, but not on my skin, thank you."

"You're just no fun," he said.

I frowned at him, but looked back at Galen, still kneeling before me and looking disappointed. I knew part of his look was from the ring not working for him as it had for the others, but that might not have been all of it. "How about you?" I asked him gently. "Do you like electricity, too?"

He looked puzzled, but said, "I've never tried it in anything but small appliances."

"Did what the ring did just now feel good to you?"

"Yes."

I made a mental note. Even if I didn't like electricity as foreplay, if some of the men did, then things could be worked out. I was willing to use it on them for their pleasure, as long as I didn't have to experience it more than to check the strength of it. You never hook anything up to anyone else that you haven't let bite your own skin. Just a rule. You don't have to enjoy it yourself, but you do have to know what it's doing to the person who does.

"It would seem," Doyle said, "that the ring has grown in strength in every way."

I nodded. "I don't remember it ever giving that strong of a power surge before."

"But it didn't do between us what it did with Rhys and Frost," Galen said, sounding as unhappy as he looked. Whatever emotion flowed through Galen, you always knew it. It filled his face, his eyes. He'd begun to have moments when he could hide his feelings. I'd both been happy to see it and mourned the necessity of it. Galen with every thought clear in his eyes for all to read was damn near a political liability in the courts. He needed to master his outward emotions, but I had not enjoyed watching the process. It felt like we were stealing some of the innocent joy that made Galen, Galen.

I touched his face with my left hand, the hand I didn't wear the ring on. The queen had always worn the ring on her left hand, and I had first put it on the same hand, out of habit, and found the ring preferred being on my right hand. So it got to be on my right hand. I did not argue with relics of power any more than I could help it.

I pressed my hand against his cheek. He raised sad green eyes to me. "Rhys and Frost have come into their godhead. I think that's all the extra sensation between us meant."

"I'd love to argue," Rhys said, "but I agree with Merry."

"You really think so?" Galen asked, the way a child would, trusting that if you said a thing, then it would be true.

I stroked my fingers down the side of his face, from the soft warmth of his temple to the curve of his chin. "I don't just think it, Galen, I believe it."

"I believe it as well," Doyle said. "So as long as Meredith touches the other guards only briefly, it should not be a problem. All of the Unseelie Court knows that the ring is alive once more on her hand. Though perhaps not how very alive it has become."

"It was growing stronger even before the chalice returned," I said.

He nodded. "That is why we put it away in a drawer, so it would not discomfort our lovemaking."

Rhys did an exaggerated pout. "And I was having such fun."

My hand was still touching Galen, but I said to Rhys, "Do you want to be strapped down and have me run electricity along your skin?"

Rhys reacted as if I'd slapped him. The reaction of just thinking about it shuddering through his body. Watching him respond that strongly to the idea of it made me want to do it. Made me want to give him that much pleasure. "That was a big yes," I said.

He managed a breathy, "Oh, yes."

Galen was laughing softly.

Rhys frowned at him. "What's so funny, green man?"

Galen was laughing so hard that it took him two tries to say, "You're a death god."

"Yeah, so what?" Rhys asked.

Galen sat flat on the floor, his knees tucked up in the

smaller space, but turned so he could see Rhys. "I have this image in my head of you hooked up like Frankenstein's monster."

Rhys started to get angry, then he couldn't manage it. He smiled, a little, and the smile just got bigger until he was laughing with Galen.

"Who is Frankenstein's monster?" Frost asked.

That got them laughing even harder, and spread the laughter through the plane to those who knew the answer. Only Doyle and Frost were left out of the joke. The others had embraced television and all it could offer while in California. Even Kitto was laughing from under his blanket in the back. I don't know if the joke was that good, or you just had to be there, or if it was tension. I was betting on tension, because when the pilot told us we'd be landing in fifteen minutes, it just didn't seem that funny anymore.

Chapter 20

IT SEEMED EVEN LESS FUNNY HALF AN HOUR LATER. OF COURSE, when you're about to walk into a major press conference, and you're certain they're going to ask questions you can't answer truthfully, nothing seems very funny.

More St. Louis city policemen than I'd seen in a while met us on the tarmac and closed ranks around us. With the guards around me, and the police around them, I felt like a very short flower inside some very tall walls. Next time I'd have to wear higher heels.

We entered the lounge that is just for private planes and there met the rest of my guards. The only one I knew well was Barinthus. I saw him when the police parted like a curtain, just a glimpse between Doyle's dark back and Galen's brown leather. Frost was behind me in a silver fox coat that nearly trailed on the ground. When I'd pointed out how many animals had died for the coat, he'd informed me that he'd owned the coat for more than fifty years, long before anyone thought badly of owning fur. He'd also touched my long leather coat and said, "Please don't complain to me when you're wearing half a cow."

"But I eat cow, so wearing leather uses the entire animal; it's not wasteful. You don't eat fox."

He'd gotten a strange look on his face. "You have no idea what I've eaten."

I didn't know what to say after that, so I gave up. Besides, the January cold had hit us like a hammer when we stepped out of the plane. Coming from Los Angeles to St. Louis in the middle of winter was almost a physical wrenching. It made me stumble on the steps. Frost steadied me, toasty in his immoral fur coat. Fur was warmer than leather, even if it was lined. But I huddled in my long leather coat, hands in leather gloves, and walked down the steps with Frost's bare hand on my elbow the whole way. When I was on flat ground he let me go, and everyone fell back into a bodyguard circle. Sage and Nicca brought up the rear. If we were attacked, no one was expecting much of Nicca. One, he wasn't used to having huge wings to deal with when he moved. Two, he was huddled in a cotton blanket over a bare chest. The sidhe can't freeze to death, but some of them can still be cold. Nicca was spring energy; he could be cold. His wings were held tight together, drooping like a frostbitten flower behind him.

Rhys cursed softly. "I should have gone shopping for a heavier coat."

"Told you so," Galen said, though he wasn't much better in his leather jacket. It was too damn cold for something that left your ass and legs bare.

Kitto was probably the warmest of us non-fur-bearing sidhe in a bulky down coat that was nearly a Day-Glo blue. It wasn't attractive, but he was warm.

The private lounge was warm enough that the difference between cold and hot fogged my dark glasses. When I took them off, Barinthus's hair gleamed through the forest of bodies around me. His hair isn't as shiny as Frost's, though few sidhe could boast that, but Barinthus has some of the most unusual hair in either court.

His hair was the color of ocean water. The heartrending turquoise of the Mediterranean; the many deeper blues of the Pacific; the bluish grey of the sea before a storm, melting into a blue that was nearly black. The color of water when it is deep and cold, and the currents run thick and heavy like movement of some great ocean beast. The colors moved, and flowed into each other, with every trick of the light, every turn of his head, so that it didn't seem like hair at all. But it was hair, hair like a cloak to the ankles of his nearly seven-foot frame. It took me a blink or two to realize that he was wearing a long leather coat dyed a deep sky blue like a robin's egg. His hair seemed to blend into the soft leather. He came toward us with his hands extended and a smile on his face.

Once he'd been a sea god, and he was still one of the most powerful of all the sidhe, for he seemed to have lost less of what he was. He'd been my father's best friend and chief adviser. He and Galen had been the most frequent visitors to my father's home after we left the court when I was six. We left because by that late age I'd shown no magical talents, unheard of in a sidhe, however mixed her genetics. My aunt, the queen, had tried to drown me like a purebred puppy that didn't meet standards. My father had packed me and his entourage and gone to live among the humans. Aunt Andais had been shocked that he'd left faerie over a small misunderstanding. *Small misunderstanding,* her exact words.

Barinthus's blue eyes with their slits of pupils were warm with true joy at seeing me. There were others who were looking forward to seeing me for political reasons, sexual reasons, so many reasons, but he was one of the few who wanted to see me just because he was my friend. He'd been my father's friend, now he was mine, and I knew that if I had children, he would be their friend, too.

"Meredith, it is good to see you once more." He reached to take my hands in his, as was his wont in public, but another guard pushed between us. He reached for me as if to steal a hug, but he never finished the movement. Barinthus pulled him back by the shoulder. Doyle moved in front of me to block him, and I stepped back so abruptly that I slammed into Frost. The fur of his coat tickled along my cheek. His hands found my shoulders as if he were ready to swing me around behind him, farther away from the upstart guard.

The guard in question was within an inch or two of Doyle's height, which made him nearly six feet tall, but not quite. The first thing I noticed about him was his coat, not usually the first thing I noticed about the guards of the sidhe. The fur coat seemed to be made of alternating broad stripes of black and white mink. Bad enough the animals had to die, but for a striped coat—that was just sad. It did match the hair tied back from his face to trail down over one shoulder to the bottom of his thighs. His hair was a series of narrow stripes—black, pale grey, dark grey, and white—all perfectly uniform so there was no mistaking his hair for someone who had gone grey. It was either an elaborate and well-done dye job, or he wasn't human. His charcoal-grey eyes were a shade darker than most, but they could have been human eyes.

"Just wanted a little squeeze," he said in a voice that sounded less than sober.

"You are drunk, Abloec," Barinthus said in a disgusted voice. His grip on the man's shoulder tightened so that his white skin seemed to be melting into the striped fur.

"Just happy, Barinthus, just happy," Abloec said, with a slightly lopsided smile.

"What is he doing here?" Doyle asked, and his normally low voice held an edge of rumbling growl to it.

"The queen wished the princess to have six guards. I was allowed to choose two, but she chose the other three."

"But why him?" Doyle said, with emphasis on the word *him*.

"Is there some problem here?" one of the human police officers asked. I would have said he was tall, except I had Barinthus to compare him to, and few looked tall beside the sea god. His grey hair was cut very short, very severely, and it left his face stranded and bare looking. He would have looked better with more hair around his face to soften the features, but there was a look in his eyes, a set to his shoulders, that said he couldn't have cared less if his hairdo flattered his bone structure.

Madeline Phelps, publicist to the Unseelie Court, stepped up beside the officer. "No problem, Major, no problem at all." She smiled when she said it, showing very white, very straight teeth, framed by a deep burgundy, almost purple lipstick. The color matched her short, pleated skirt and bodyfitting double-breasted suit jacket. Purple was probably the new in-color for the year. Madeline kept track of things like that. She'd cut her hair since last I saw her. It was very close to her head, but left long in thin lines around her face and down her neck, so though the hair was shorter than anyone's except the major's, it managed to touch the collar of her royal purple jacket. When she moved her head to smile up at the policeman, the light caught purple highlights in her brown hair, as if she'd given it a wash of color rather than a true dye. Her artful makeup complemented a slender face, and though she was a few inches taller than me, she was small for a full-blooded human.

"It looks like a problem," the major said.

I wondered what I'd done to deserve someone with the rank of major being in charge of my police security. Was the queen keeping as many secrets from us as we were from her? Looking up into the major's serious face, I thought, *Maybe*.

Madeline smiled and tried to win him over, even putting a hand on his forearm. His eyes didn't thaw; in fact, he stared at her hand until she took it away. "Do you know the old saying about the duck?" he asked in a voice that was still utterly serious.

She looked puzzled for a second, regained her smile, and shook her head. "Sorry, can't say that I do."

"If it looks like a duck, quacks like a duck, and walks like a duck, it's a duck," he said.

Madeline looked puzzled again, which didn't mean she was. She capitalized on being small and cute, and only at odd moments did you realize just how shrewd and businesslike she really was.

I'd never had much patience with women who hid their intelligence. I thought it set a bad precedent for the rest of us. "He means if it looks like a problem, sounds like a problem, and acts like a problem, then it's a problem," I said.

The major, whose nameplate said WALTERS, turned his cold grey eyes on me. It wasn't just the normal unreadable cop eyes, either; he was mad about something. But what? His eyes thawed a little, as if he liked that I'd stopped playing games, or as if he wasn't mad at me. "Princess Meredith, I'm Major Walters, and I'm in charge of this detail until we cross over onto sidhe territory."

"Now, Major," Madeline said, "you and Captain Barinthus are both in charge, that's what the queen agreed to."

"You can't have two leaders," the major said, "not and get anything done." He glanced at Abloec, then at Barinthus, and the look said he didn't like the way Barinthus was running his men. What Major Walters couldn't know, and none of us would ever admit outside the sidhe, was that if things weren't running smoothly, it was almost always Queen Andais's fault, or her son's. But since Prince Cel was still locked safely away, it had to be something that the queen had done.

For the life of me I couldn't think why she'd have allowed Abloec to be seen in front of as much media presence as was likely to be in the press conference. He was addicted to everything, drink, cigarettes, drugs. You name it, Abe liked it. Once he'd been the greatest libertine of the Seelie Court, a lover and seducer par excellence. He was cast out of the Seelie Court for seducing the wrong woman, and Andais would only allow him into the Unseelie Court on one condition. He had to join her guard, which meant that Abe went from being one of the busiest lovers of the sidhe to being celibate. He'd taken to drink, and when stronger drugs were invented he took those. Unfortunately for him it was almost impossible for a sidhe to become completely impaired by alcohol or drugs. You could get drunk, but never to the point where you passed out. Never to the point where true oblivion could ease your pain. The best Abe could do was take the edge off and become addicted to damn near everything. My father had kept him far from me, and my aunt despised him, thought him weak. So he'd been hidden away on small duties for centuries, an embarrassment to us all. So why was he here, now, in such a public forum? It made no sense. Not that everything Andais did made sense, but in public she always came off as the perfect queen. A drunken guard was not good press. A drunken guard entrusted with the life of a princess and heir to a throne was worse than simply bad press, it was careless. Andais was many things, but careless was not one of them.

"I earned the right to be here, Darkness, trust me on that,"

Abe said. His smile was gone, and there was something very sober in his charcoal-grey eyes.

"What's that supposed to mean?" Walters asked.

Neither the guards nor I had to ask. If he'd earned it, then he'd done something that he'd hated but had pleased the queen. It usually involved sex, or sadism, or both. The guards kept their secrets about what humiliations the queen demanded of them. There's an old saying that you'd crawl over broken glass for someone, or something. Apparently that wasn't just a saying with the queen. What would a person do to end hundreds of years of celibacy? What wouldn't he do?

It must have shown on at least some of our faces, because Walters looked even grumpier and said, "What aren't you telling me?"

Barinthus and Doyle gave him their empty faces, honed to unreadability by centuries of court politics. I turned in against Frost's body so that my face was hidden from the major. I just didn't give good blank face anymore.

Frost slid one arm across my shoulders, but opened his coat so that I was snuggled inside it. Most people would have thought that he was trying to get me closer to his body, but I knew better: He was opening his coat so he could go for his gun, or knives if he needed to. Hugging was fine, but for the guards, duty had to come first.

Since it was my life they were protecting, I never got my feelings hurt about it.

"To my knowledge, Major," Barinthus said, "we are not concealing anything from you that will impact your ability to perform your job."

Walters almost smiled. "You're not going to deny that you're withholding information from me, from the police?"

"Why should I deny it? You would have to be a fool to believe that we have shared all we know with you, and I don't think you a fool, Major Walters."

He looked at Barinthus, and it wasn't an entirely unfriendly look. "Well, that's good to know. You don't want Abe here, do you?"

"Obviously not," Barinthus said.

"Then why is he here?"

Madeline tried to intervene. "Major, we really must get them all ready for the press conference."

He ignored her. "Why is he here?"

Barinthus blinked at him, and his second eyelid flicked down and up. The clear membrane allowed him to see underwater. When it showed on dry land, it meant he was nervous.

"You heard me say that Abloec was not my choice, but the queen's."

"Why would she send a drunk?"

"I resent that," Abloec said, leaning in toward the major.

Walters wrinkled his nose. "Your breath smells lethal."

"Just good scotch," Abloec said.

Barinthus grabbed him by both shoulders. "We need some privacy, Major Walters, to discuss things."

Walters gave Barinthus a sharp nod and called his men out. He tried to leave two, but Barinthus asked him not to. "You are welcome to put officers at both doors, as long as they are outside and do not try to eavesdrop."

"Unless you yell, they won't hear you."

Barinthus smiled. "We will try not to yell."

Walters herded his men out, and Doyle called, "Please, hold the door for Ms. Phelps."

The publicist looked at him, her eyes wide, mouth in a little O of surprise. It was an act, because she recovered too quickly. "Now, Doyle." She put her well-manicured hand on his arm in its black leather jacket. "I have to get you all presentable for the press conference."

He looked at her much the way Walters had, except meaner. She let go of his arm and took a step back. For a moment the real Madeline stared out; ruthless, determined. She played her trump card with a face that was harsh with her anger. "The queen's orders are for me to make sure you are all lovely for the press conference. When she asks why I didn't do that, do you want me to tell her that you contradicted her orders?" She, more than most of the humans who dealt with the court, knew what the queen was capable of, and she used that knowledge well.

I turned in Frost's arms so that my face was framed by the fur of his coat. "None of us is contradicting my aunt's orders," I said.

The look she gave me was just this side of insolence. Madeline had enjoyed the queen's favor for seven years now. Seven years of basking in the absolute power the queen had over beings who could have snapped Madeline in half with their bare hands. She felt safe behind the shield of Andais's power. Up to a point, she was right. Beyond that point— well, I was about to remind her of what that point was.

"We have a major press conference, Meredith." She didn't even bother to use my title now that no other humans were around to listen. Her glance flicked from Galen's much loved, old brown leather jacket to Doyle's short black one, and finally to Kitto's Day-Glo parka. Her lip curled just a bit. "Some of the coats, some of the hair, and you are seriously not wearing enough makeup for this kind of photo opportunity. I have makeup and wardrobe outside." She turned toward the door as if she'd fetch them.

I said, "No."

She turned back, and the arrogance on her face would make any sidhe proud. "I can call the queen on my cell, but I promise you, Meredith, that I am following her orders." She actually slipped a small phone out of the inner pocket of her blazer. A phone so tiny it hadn't disturbed the line of her jacket.

"You are not following her orders, not to the letter," I said. I knew I looked small, near child-like, peeking from amid the ticklish fur of Frost's coat. And for the first time it didn't matter, not to people like Madeline. I could hide my power until we needed it. I didn't have to be forceful to win this one.

She hesitated with the phone open in her hand. "Of course I am."

"Did my aunt tell you to dress us, and primp us, as soon as we came in out of the cold? Were those her express orders?"

She narrowed her carefully lined and shaded eyes. "Not in so many words, no." She sounded uncertain, then gained her businessy tone as she continued, "But we have the press conference, and then you'll have to change again before the big party. We have a timetable here, and the queen doesn't like to be kept waiting." She hit a button on her phone, put it to her ear.

I stepped out from the warmth of Frost's body and whispered in her other ear, "I am heir to the throne, Madeline, and you've always been nasty to me. I'd start trying to make nice if I were you and I liked my job."

I was leaning so close that I heard my aunt's secretary answer the phone, but not what he said. Madeline said, "Sorry, hit the wrong button. Yes, they're here. We've got some challenges, but nothing we can't handle. Okay, okay, great." She hung up and stepped back from me the way I'd seen people step back from Andais and Cel over the years, as if she was afraid.

"I'll wait out in the hall." She licked her lips, glanced at me, but couldn't completely meet my eyes. She wasn't as good at court politics as some. There were those who had tried to kill me before, who would smile and nod to my face, acting as if we'd always been best friends. Madeline wasn't up to that level of duplicity. It made me think better of her.

She hesitated at the door. "But please, hurry. We really do have a rather tight schedule, and the queen did say, exactly, that she had outfits for everyone for the party tonight. She'll want everyone changed before the festivities begin." She didn't look at me as she left, as if she didn't want me to see what was in her eyes.

When the door clicked firmly behind her, Galen asked, "What did you say to her?"

I shrugged and cuddled back against Frost. "I reminded her that as heir to the throne, I might have some say in who gets hired or fired."

Galen shook his head. "She went pale. That wasn't just from the threat of being unemployed."

I looked at him. "Exiled from faerie, Galen, not just unemployed."

He frowned. "She's not elf-struck."

"She's not addicted to us, no, but her reaction tells me that she doesn't want to lose her special place among us. She doesn't want to lose the chance of touching sidhe flesh even if it's only in passing."

"Why does knowing that matter?" he asked.

"It means that we have leverage with Madeline that we didn't before, simple as that."

"That's not simple," he said.

I looked into his so-honest face, and the near pain it caused him to watch me outthink him, outmaneuver him. I might never need the knowledge that Madeline valued her job enough to be nice to me; but then again, I might. Every bit of knowledge, every bit of weakness and strength, pettiness, cruelty, or kindness, of everyone, could be the very piece of information you needed to survive. I had learned not to undervalue anyone's allegiance, even if it was allegiance simply from the need to cover all bets. It wasn't that Madeline would be cruel to Cel when he was freed, but she'd be nice to both of us now, and that was a start.

Chapter 21

"WELL HANDLED," BARINTHUS SAID WITH A SMILE, "BUT THE publicist is right about one thing. Time grows short." He motioned another guard forward.

He was tall, slender, and looked tanned to a lovely brown, but it wasn't a tan. Carrow always looked like a summer-browned hunter with his brown hair streaked with summer gold like any human who'd been outdoors day after day. His hair was cut short and simply. He looked very human until you reached his eyes. They were both brown and green, but not hazel, no. They were green like a forest stirred by the wind, so that one breeze turned the world to sparkling green and another deep and dark.

With most of the sidhe I'd had to ask what kind of deity they'd been, but like Barinthus, Carrow screamed what he had been. I looked up into the face of one of the great hunters.

Carrow's smile brought one of my own. He had been the guard whom my father entrusted to teach me the ways of bird and beast. When I'd entered college for my biology degree, Carrow had actually visited me and sat in on some of my classes. He'd wanted to know if they'd learned anything new since last he checked. In most classes, no, but he'd been fascinated by microbiology, parasitology, and Introduction to Genetics. He was also the only sidhe to ask me what I'd do with my degree if I hadn't been Princess Meredith.

No one else had cared, or rather they couldn't conceive of

anything but court politics. When you can be a princess, why would you want to do anything else?

Carrow started to drop to one knee, but I caught his arm and drew him into a hug.

He gave his easy laugh and hugged me tight.

"I was surprised to hear you were a detective in a big city." He drew back enough to see my face. "I thought you'd run away to the wilderness and play with the animals, or at the very least a zoo."

"I'd need at least a master's degree for wildlife biology, and most zoos, too."

"But a detective?"

I shrugged. "I thought the queen would check anyplace I could use my degree. I didn't even tell anyone I had a biology degree at the detective agency."

"I hate to interrupt old home week," a new voice said, "but has the ring reacted to Carrow, or not?"

I turned and found a guard I was not pleased to see. "Amatheon," I said and I couldn't hide, even in that one word, how unhappy I was to see him.

"Don't worry, Princess, I'm just as unhappy to see you as you are to see me." He turned his head, and the winter sunlight drew copper and gold highlights from his red hair. The shoulder-length waves bounced as he strode toward me.

"Then why are you here?" I asked.

"The queen ordered it," he said, as if that explained everything.

"Why?" I asked, because it explained nothing.

He moved gracefully in the tailored leather coat. It fit his upper body like a glove but flared out around his hips and legs so it was like a leather robe. The black leather made his hair richer, brighter, like copper flame. When he was close enough for me to see his eyes, I had that moment of dizziness that his eyes always gave me. His pupils were petaled layers of red, blue, yellow, and green, like a multicolored flower.

"You're lovely to look at, Amatheon. To say anything else would be lying."

His handsome face smirked at me.

"But pretty is as pretty does, and you are Cel's friend, last I knew. I don't think he'd take kindly to you protecting me, let alone anything else."

Doyle had moved in front of me, just enough to keep Amatheon from closing the distance between us. Frost had moved up on the other side of me, as if there were any question of Amatheon getting past Doyle. Amatheon ignored them both, all his attention meant for me. "Prince Cel does not rule the Unseelie Court, not yet. Queen Andais has made that clear to me." The smirk was gone when he said that, and the arrogance slipped a bit. I wondered how Andais had chosen to make her point so terribly clear to him. I trusted Aunt Andais to choose a painful method, and for once I was glad at the thought of one of the guards suffering. Petty, but then Amatheon had been one of the sidhe who'd made my childhood unpleasant.

"Good of you to remember that," Doyle said.

Amatheon's eyes flicked to him, but came back to rest on me. "Trust me, Princess, I wouldn't be here if I had a choice."

"Then go," I said.

He shook his head, sending his hair sliding over the leather of his shoulders. The last time I'd seen him, the hair had been to his knees. Most sidhe took it as a point of pride to have hair that had never known a blade. In fact, fey who were not sidhe were forbidden from having hair to their ankles.

I gazed up at him. "You've cut your hair since last I saw you."

"As you've cut yours," he said, but his face was sullen.

"I sacrificed my hair to hide the fact that I was sidhe. Why did you cut yours?"

"You know why," he said, and he fought to keep his face behind its arrogant mask.

"No, I don't."

Anger broke through his mask, tore it away, and I watched something close to rage in his flower-petal eyes. He balled his hands into his shoulder-length hair. "I refused to come here today. I refused to be one of your men. The queen reminded me that refusing her anything is not wise." He forced himself to relax, and the effort was visible and near painful to behold.

"Why is it that important that you get a chance in my bed?" I asked.

He shook his head, and the movement of his newly shortened hair seemed to bother him. He ran his hands through the thick waves, shook his head again, and said, "I don't know. That is the truth of it. I asked, and she told me I didn't need to know. I just needed to do what I was told." The anger was mere sullenness now, showing the edge of fear that had been there all along.

He looked at me, and he wasn't angry with me; he just seemed tired and beaten. "So here I am, and the queen wishes me to touch the ring. If it does not react to my skin, then after we deliver you safely to the court, I am free to leave this guard detail, but if it sings to my touch . . ." He looked down at the floor, and his hair spilled around his face. He looked up abruptly, combing his fingers through the hair to keep it back. "I must touch the ring. I must see what happens. I have no choice, and neither do you." He sounded so unhappy that it made me like him better than I ever had before. Not like him enough to take him to my bed, but I always had trouble hating people if they showed me something that wasn't hateable inside them. Andais had seen that as a weakness; my father had seen it as a strength. I still hadn't decided.

Without taking his gaze from Amatheon, Doyle asked, "Do you wish to allow it?"

Frost moved closer to me so that his coat enveloped me like a cloud.

"Allowing him to touch the ring means nothing, costs us nothing," I said. "When I speak to the queen about him, I would rather have done everything she wished, up to that point."

"She will not allow either of us to pass on this, Princess."

His hand went to his hair, and he stopped himself with a visible effort. "She will have us bed, if the ring knows me."

I wanted badly to ask him again, why, but believed he knew no more of Andais's logic than did I. "What happens after will be a problem for another day." I stepped up to touch Doyle's arm. "Let him pass."

Doyle glanced at me, as if he wanted to argue, but he didn't. He simply stepped aside, allowing me to step forward, but Frost did not move back. He stayed so close that the line of his body touched mine.

"Frost," I said, "we need a little more space."

He glanced down at me, then at Amatheon, then he took a small step to the side, his face its best arrogant mask. Neither he nor Doyle liked Amatheon. Maybe it was something personal, or maybe, like me, they didn't like the idea of someone who was Cel's man being near me.

"Frost," I said again, "what if the ring picks up on you, and not Amatheon? Give us enough room so we know that the reaction is for him alone."

"I will give half an arm's length of room, but no more. He has been Cel's cat for far too long."

Amatheon gazed up at the slightly taller man. "The princess is under the queen's protection, magically given. If I raised a hand to her, then my life would be forfeit, and the queen would make me beg for death long before she gave it." His eyes looked haunted. "No, Frost, I would not go back under the queen's tender care, not even to keep this half-human mongrel off our throne."

"Oh, nice," I said.

Amatheon sighed. "You know how I feel, Princess Meredith. How I've always felt about you and your being in line to the throne. If I suddenly said you were wonderful and a perfect future queen, would you believe me?"

I just shook my head.

"The queen has . . . persuaded me that my beliefs are not so precious as my flesh and my blood." His face seemed to crumble for a moment, almost as if he would cry. He regained himself, but the eyes that turned to me were raw with emotion. What had Andais done to him?

"You should have just agreed, like I did." The other guard I could have done without seeing was Onilwyn. He was handsome, but there was a roughness to his face, an almost unfinished quality, so that although he was handsome by human standards, by sidhe standards he was coarse. He was broad of shoulder, and muscular; even just a glimpse of his clothed body framed by the long fur coat, and you had a sense of the power of him. He was so thick through the shoulders and chest that he seemed shorter than the others, but it was illusion. Onilwyn's thick wavy hair was tied back in a ponytail. The hair was a green so dark it held black highlights when the light touched it just so. His eyes were the color of green grass with a starburst of liquid gold dancing around the pupils. His skin was a pale green, but it wasn't a white-green like Galen's, where you were not sure whether it was white or green. No, Onilwyn's skin was a pale solid green in the same way Carrow's skin was brown.

"You would agree to anything that saved your hide," Amatheon said.

"Of course I would," Onilwyn said, as he glided toward us. I'd never understood how such a bulky man managed to glide, but he always did. "So would anyone with any sense."

Amatheon turned to look at the other man. "Why are you Cel's man? Do you believe he should be king? Do you care?"

Onilwyn shrugged thick shoulders. "I prefer Cel king because he likes me, and I like him. He's promised me many things once he's on the throne."

"He promises many things," Amatheon said, "but that is not why I have been his follower."

"Then why?" Doyle asked.

He answered without looking away from Onilwyn. "Cel is the last true sidhe prince we have. The last true heir to the bloodline that has ruled us for nearly three thousand years. The day that someone who is part human, and part brownie, and part Seelie takes our crown is the day we die as a people. We will be no better than the mongrels in Europe."

Onilwyn smiled, and it was so full of spite that it hurt to see it. "But here you are, lover of the pure Unseelie blood, here you are." He stood in front of the taller man, gazing at him with that cruel, satisfied smile. "Forced to bed one of the mongrel horde. Knowing that if you get her with child you, personally, will be responsible for placing her on the throne. Such delicious, thick, spreadable irony."

"You're enjoying this," Amatheon said in a strangled voice.

Onilwyn nodded. "If the ring is alive to our touch, we are free of our celibacy."

"But only with her," Amatheon said.

The other man shook his head. "What does it matter? She's a woman, and she's sidhe. This is a gift, not a curse."

"She is not sidhe."

"Grow up, Amatheon, grow up, before this naïveté gets you killed." He looked at me for the first time. "May I touch the ring, Princess?"

"What happens if I say no?"

Onilwyn smiled, and it was only a little less pleasant than the smile he'd given Amatheon. "The queen knew you wouldn't like it, or rather like me. Let me see if I can remember the message."

"I remember it," Amatheon said in a dull voice. "She made me repeat it over and over while she—" He stopped abruptly, as if he'd almost said too much.

"Then by all means, give the princess the queen's message," Onilwyn said.

Amatheon closed his eyes as if he were reading something inside his head. "I have chosen these two with care. If the ring does not react to them then so be it, but if it does react, then I want no arguments from you. Fuck them." He opened his eyes, and he looked pale, as if the recitation had cost him something. "I do not wish to touch the ring, but I will not go against the queen's orders."

"Not again, you mean," Onilwyn said, and he looked at me. "May I touch the ring?"

I glanced at Doyle. He gave a small nod. "I think you must, Meredith."

Frost started forward.

"Frost," Doyle said, and that one word held a warning.

Frost looked at him, and he looked horrified. "Are we helpless to protect her from this?"

"Yes," Doyle said, "we are helpless to go against the queen's orders."

I touched Frost's arm. "It's okay."

He shook his head. "No, it is not."

"I don't blame you, Frost," Onilwyn said. "I wouldn't want to share, either." He looked around the room at the other men. "Of course, you are sharing, aren't you?" He pouted out his lower lip, but his eyes stayed malicious. "Such a small piece to share among all of you, and now here we come to take even more of it away."

"Oh, for Goddess's sake, Onilwyn, stop being such an ass." The last guard in the room had been so quiet in his corner that I hadn't seen him, but that was Usna's way. He could be unseen in a crowd, and only when he spoke would your mind register that he had been there all along. Your eyes would see him, but your mind just kept forgetting to tell you about it. It was a type of glamour, and it was a type that worked on other sidhe, or at least it always worked on me.

Neither Doyle, Frost, nor Rhys seemed surprised, but Galen said, "I wish you wouldn't do that. It's always so damn unnerving."

"Sorry, little green man, I'll try and make more noise when I sneak up on you." But it was said with a smile.

Galen grinned at him. "All cats should wear bells."

Usna pushed himself away from the wall and the chair he had been perched on. Usna rarely sat in a chair. He reclined, he curled, he slumped, but he rarely sat. Usna moved across the floor like wind, like shadow, like something more air than flesh. In a race of men who were known for their grace, Usna put them all to shame. To watch him truly dance upon the floor at a gathering of the sidhe was to watch him the way you watched flowers in a wind, or the sway of branches in spring. The flowers could not be anything but artlessly beautiful. The tree in full blossom did not know it was beautiful, but it was, and so was Usna. Oh, there were others more handsome, Frost to name just one. Both Rhys and Galen had lovelier mouths. In fact Usna's mouth was a little wide for my tastes, the lips a trifle thinner than I preferred. His nose was perhaps too small for his face. His eyes were large and lustrous, but they were a nondescript shade of grey, neither as dark as Abloec's, nor as pale as Frost's. They were just . . . grey. Usna was slender to the point that he seemed almost effeminate. His hair had stubbornly never grown beyond his hips, no matter how hard he'd tried; only its color set it apart. Patches of copper red, patent-leather black, snow white, as if his hair were a patchwork quilt. Though of course, it wasn't a patchwork, more a calico. Usna's mother had been made pregnant by another sidhe's husband. The scorned wife had said that her outside should match her inside, and changed her into a cat. The magical cat gave birth to a child, Usna. When he grew to manhood, which was years younger than nowadays, he returned his mother to her true form, avenged them both on the sidhe who had cursed her, and lived happily ever after. Or would have, if killing the sidhe who'd cursed his mother hadn't gotten him kicked out of the Seelie Court. Apparently the enchantress in question had been the king's current mistress. Oops.

Usna never seemed to mind. His mother was still a member of the shining court, and though he was not, they still met and talked, and had picnics in the forest. His mother drew the line at meeting him inside the hollow hill that made up the border of the Unseelie Court, and no Unseelie noble was welcome in the Seelie Court. But they had the forest and the fields, and seemed content.

He glided to the edge of the growing circle around me and said, "May I touch the ring?"

I said the only thing that came to mind: "Yes."

Chapter 22

USNA'S FINGERS SLID OVER MINE IN A DELICATE, ALMOST dainty movement until he came to the ring, and there he hesitated. He met my gaze with grey eyes that were neither dark, nor light, but terribly medium. The eyes should have looked ordinary, but the force of his personality burned out of them, so that it wasn't the color or shape of his eyes that made you stare, but just him. If he'd had beautiful eyes to match all that, it would have been totally unfair. He was charming enough without it.

"Cut the foreplay short, Usna," Onilwyn said, "the rest of us are waiting."

Usna moved those eyes to the other man, and the heat that had a moment ago been sensual was suddenly almost rage. The change had been instantaneous, as if sex and rage were but a blink away from each other inside Usna's head. The thought should have given me pause, but instead it tightened things low in my body, brought a small sound from my lips.

Usna's eyes flicked back to me, drawn by that small sound. The heat in his eyes slid into something between anger and sex—hunger. I didn't know if he was still thinking of killing and eating Onilwyn or of having me. It wasn't Usna's fault, but sometimes he thought more like an animal than anything human. It was there in his eyes now.

And that was the moment he chose to slide his fingertips across the ring.

It pulsed to life in a breath-stealing, skin-dancing wash that drew a cry of delight from Usna and nearly buckled my knees. I swayed, and he caught me automatically, which took his bare skin away from the ring. We held each other in a loose embrace, trying to learn how to breathe again. He laughed, and it was a joyous low chuckle, as if he was very pleased with himself, and me.

"The reaction wasn't that strong when the ring first went on her hand," Barinthus said. "It was just a flash of warmth."

"It's gotten stronger," Doyle said.

"My turn," Abloec said, and his voice was still clear even though he swayed ever so slightly.

Usna turned me in his arms, as if we were dancing, but that one graceful movement put me on the other side of him away from Abloec. Usna looked to Barinthus, and only after he had gotten a small nod from him did he turn me back toward Abloec.

He reached out a hand that was as steady as his voice, but Rhys interrupted, "You need to let her go first, Usna. You wouldn't want your fertility to reflect on Abloec, would you?"

Usna nodded, and spun me, as if he heard music I did not, passing me to Abloec, as if it were indeed a dance. Abloec fumbled, trying to catch me, and failing. He was too drunk for dancing. Too drunk for so many things.

I stepped far enough away that my hand barely reached him. I wanted my distance for several reasons: one, he smelled like he'd gargled with whiskey; two, he was drunk enough that I wasn't sure what his body would do when he touched the ring. If he fell, I didn't want him dragging me down with him.

He grabbed my hand, awkwardly as if he was seeing double, and wasn't sure which hand was mine. But it didn't matter that he couldn't see straight; once he touched the ring, it flared to life. It was like a wave of heat that rushed over my skin, and flung Abloec to his knees. Only the fact that I'd braced for it kept me on my feet.

I pulled my hand free of his, easily, because the magic had finished what the drinking had begun. He stayed on his knees in the fantastically striped mink coat because he couldn't have stood.

"Was the queen angry when he showed up drunk today?" Doyle asked.

"Yes," Barinthus said.

"He will be worse than useless in a fight."

"Yes," Barinthus said, again.

They stared down at the kneeling guard, and both their faces showed what they wanted to do with him. If the queen had not chosen him, he'd have been sent back to the court in disgrace, and never seen the press conference. But sadly, that wasn't an option.

Onilwyn stepped around the kneeling guard the way you'd step around garbage in the street. He held out his hand, wordlessly, and I didn't try to argue. The queen had sent him, and that was that. Besides, letting the ring touch him didn't put him in my bed. I was still hoping to talk the queen out of Abloec and Onilwyn. I'd have to keep at least one of the three of her choice, and strangely the best of the bunch was Amatheon. That he was the best of the three made me wonder what the queen was basing her decisions on. If I could think of a way to ask her that wouldn't be insulting, I'd ask.

I gave Onilwyn my hand, and the moment his fingers touched the ring, it flashed through me like a knife, a cut of pleasure so sharp, it hurt. Onilwyn actually jerked back from me and said, "That hurt. That actually hurt."

I rubbed a hand across my stomach, fighting an urge to touch lower, because it felt almost like a wound, and it wasn't my stomach that was hurt. "I've never had the ring hurt like that, not at first touch. Not ever."

Onilwyn's eyes were wide enough to flash the whites, like a frightened horse. "Why did it do that?"

"It seems to be acting differently with each man." Barinthus turned to Doyle. "Is that also something new?"

Doyle nodded.

Onilwyn backed away from me, cradling his hand. I wondered if it was only his hand that hurt, or if he, too, was fighting an urge to hold lower things.

"Carrow," Barinthus said, and motioned the other man forward.

Carrow didn't hesitate, coming to me with the same smile he'd been giving me since I could remember. He, like Galen, never had a hidden agenda, but unlike Galen, the only thing that showed on his face was a polite good humor. It was his version of Frost's arrogance, or Doyle's blankness.

"May I?" he asked.

"Yes." I held my hand out to him, and he took it.

His hand slid over the ring, and there was nothing. Nothing but the warm brush of his skin against mine. His hand was warm in mine, but that was all. The ring lay cold between us.

For just a second a disappointment showed through that smile, so bitter that it filled his eyes with a brown so dark it was as if night had fallen in his eyes. Then he recovered himself, closed long lashes over his eyes, and bowed, giving my hand a kiss. He made light of it all as he stepped back, but I had some idea what that casual act must have cost him.

All eyes turned to Amatheon, for he was the only one left. The look on his face was painful to see. The conflict inside him was painted across those handsome features. One thing was clear: He did not want to touch the ring. I don't think he wanted to know. He was male, and he had needs, and this was his only way out of the trap the queen had all of her guard mired in. But Onilwyn had said it best: For Amatheon to have his needs met with me, who represented almost everything he thought was wrong with the sidhe, was almost worse than forced abstinence.

"This is not the choice that either of us would make, Amatheon, but we must make the best of it." I walked toward him, and panic carved his face into harsh lines. He looked as if he wanted to run, but there was nowhere to go. Nowhere that the queen wouldn't find him. She was the Queen of Air and Darkness, and unless there was a land where night never fell, she would find him. Eventually, she found everyone.

I stopped out of arm's length, almost afraid to close the distance. The fear on his face, in the set of his shoulders, was horrible to see. It was as if even standing here was a sort of torture. "I would not force this on you, Amatheon, not if either of us had a choice."

His voice squeezed out from between clenched teeth. "But we have no choices."

I shook my head. "No, none."

It was as if he rebuilt himself before my eyes. He shoved the fear and conflicts down inside somewhere. He worked at it, until his face was smooth and arrogantly handsome once more. His hands clenched tight at his sides were the last thing he brought under control. He uncurled them one painful knuckle at a time, as if the effort were a mighty thing. And maybe it was. There are times when I think that it is harder to master yourself than any other thing on earth.

He let out a breath that shook only a little. "I am ready."

I held my hand out to him, as if I expected a kiss. He hesitated only a moment, then he took my hand in his, and the moment his finger brushed the metal, magic pushed across my skin like a warm wind.

Amatheon jerked back as if it had burned him. His eyes were wide and frightened, but it wasn't from pain. It had felt as good to him as it had to me. I'd have bet money on it.

"The ring has been satisfied," Barinthus said. "Let us have the woman back, and let her fuss with us. The queen wishes us to be perfect for the interviews."

"What of him?" Doyle asked, nodding at Abloec, who was still on his knees, smiling happily, if a little lopsided.

"We will put him to the far side away from the princess. Now, we have cloaks for those with wings." He watched both Sage and Nicca come forward and shrug out of their blankets as Usna brought the folded cloaks. "I look forward to hearing this explained in the queen's presence."

"Has the queen forbidden you from asking such questions?" Doyle asked.

"No, but she has decreed that all such explanations must wait for her ears." The corner of his mouth twitched, as if he were fighting not to smile. "Queen Andais seems to think we are keeping things from her."

"Who is we?" I asked.

"All the court, apparently," he said, and the clear membrane over his eyes flicked into place again. Something had happened in the court, or was happening, that was making Barinthus very nervous.

I wanted to ask what, but couldn't. With Onilwyn and Amatheon there, it was the same as having Cel's ears on the walls. All that we said in front of them would find its way back to Cel's network of allies. Hell's bells, Onilwyn and Amatheon were his allies. What was the queen's purpose sending them to my bed? Was there a plan in her mind, or had her special brand of madness reached some new level? I didn't know, and I couldn't ask while we had people who would report back to her, or back to Cel's people. I could not afford for either side to hear me accuse the queen of being mad. Everyone knew she was, but no one talked of it. No one ever said it out loud. Not unless he was very, very sure he stood among friends.

I looked around the room at the new guards, and at my own men. Sage was being fitted into a golden wool cloak that made him look as if he'd been carved of thick yellow honey. His wings sprang from the back like a stained glass surprise. Sage was not mine. Sidhe, or not, he still owed allegiance to Queen Niceven, and she was not my friend. She was my ally, as long as I could keep her happy, but she was not my friend.

Amatheon would not meet my gaze. Onilwyn did, but only for a moment, before he hid his frightened eyes. He hadn't liked the bite of the ring, and truthfully, neither had I. Usna was helping fit Nicca into a rich violet-red cloak, setting it with a silver and opal brooch. He was too busy joking with Nicca about the wings to notice my glance. Carrow had drawn apart from the others, because he would not be permanent among us. The queen would not waste a guard who wasn't fertile on me.

With only Sage as a question, we could order him out of a room, but if Andais insisted on saddling me with more and more people I did not trust, we'd soon run into someone who would not go meekly from the room so we could plot. Or maybe that was her idea. She'd once tried to send a spy to me, a spy who was acknowledged as her spy. But he'd tried to assassinate me, and she hadn't picked anyone to replace him after he died. Maybe that was it. I looked at the three new guards whom Barinthus hadn't wanted to be here, and thought, yes, that was it. They were her spies. One or all of them were her spies. She'd sent three because she wanted to make certain at least one of them was chosen by the ring. How she would laugh when she found out that all her spies had passed the test.

Chapter 23

HALF AN HOUR LATER WE WERE STANDING ON A DAIS WITH three microphones standing in the middle of it. Madeline had rallied and gone back to her normal pleasure in being able to boss around some of the most powerful beings left on the planet. Of course, if Madeline Phelps were intimidated by the powerful, or even the scary, she'd never have survived seven years working for Queen Andais. Doyle and Barinthus had finally reminded her that we were on a tight schedule, and allowed her to exchange Galen's much-loved leather jacket for a tailored suit jacket. I'd known Kitto's Day-Glo coat would have to go, but I hadn't realized that jeans and a polo shirt were not acceptable. The problem in Los Angeles was that Kitto was too broad-shouldered for most boys' fashions, but not tall enough for most men's, so his shopping choices were limited. Apparently the queen had thought of that, and to complement the black slacks that we had been able to find, she supplied a jewel-tone long-sleeved silk shirt, but the black jacket she had sent did not fit. It was too broad through the shoulders and long in the arm. Madeline had finally admitted that the jacket looked worse than the shirt by itself. The other men, she had to admit, grudgingly, looked fine. Actually, there wasn't a man among them who ever just looked fine. Fabulous, handsome, amazing, but not fine.

I, on the other hand, needed a shorter skirt. She supplied one that was a fringe of black pleats that barely covered my upper thighs. My penchant for wearing thigh-high hose under any skirt meant that when I moved, the lacy tops flashed. If I wasn't careful how I walked on the raised dais, I'd flash a hell of a lot more than the tops of my hose. I was glad that I'd worn nice black underwear, with no peekaboo lace or holes. If I flashed, at least all they'd see would be solid black satin. Of course with a different skirt, I needed different shoes. Madeline had brought a pair of four-inch spike patent-leather heels. I'm good at it, walking in heels, but I made her promise that I could change before I went out into the snow. Spike heels are not made for snow, unless you want to break an ankle.

I stood on the dais against the wall with Frost on one side and Doyle on the other. The rest of my guards ranged on either side. It was a little like standing in line before a firing squad—though the police stood in a semicircle at the base of the dais, to make sure that it didn't become a real firing squad. Truthfully, unless the queen was keeping big secrets from us, I think the police were there mainly to keep the reporters from rushing the stage. Or maybe that was just my level of discomfort with this many media in one room. It was a near-claustrophobic sensation, as if they were breathing too much of my air.

I'd been doing events like this since I could remember, but ever since my father's death, and the press coverage of his assassination, I'd not been as comfortable with the media. During the most painful event of my life, they had kept asking me, *How do you feel, Princess Meredith?* My father, whom I adored, had been slaughtered by unknown assassins. How the hell did they think I felt? But the queen didn't allow me to say that to anyone. Not the truth. No, Queen Andais, with her own brother dead, had made me face the media and be royal. I don't think I'd ever hated the fact that I was a princess more than during that year. If you're royal, you aren't allowed to mourn in private. Your pain is paraded across the evening news, the tabloids, the daily papers. Everywhere I looked I saw my father's picture. Everywhere I looked I saw his dead body. In Europe they'd published pictures that the American papers wouldn't touch, and it had been bloody. My father's tall, strong body, reduced to a red ruin. His hair spilled out across the grass like a black cloak, the rest of him nearly unrecognizable.

I must have made some sound, because Doyle touched my arm. He leaned in and whispered, "Are you well?"

I nodded, licked my freshly lipsticked mouth, and nodded again. "Just remembering the first press conference I ever saw this full."

He did something in public that he had never done as the Queen's Darkness: He hugged me, albeit one-armed, so he still had some chance of getting to his weapons. I leaned in against his leather jacket and the solid warmth of him underneath. I ignored the burst of flashbulbs, tried not to think that the image was being captured in every medium known to man, or woman. I needed the hug, so I took it, and tried to let go of my gloom. We were here to discuss my search for a husband, a prince, a future king. It was a happy occasion, and the queen would want us smiling.

Madeline took the first question while I was still leaning against Doyle. It was for me, of course.

Doyle gave me a last squeeze, and I sashayed, smiling, on my four-inch spike heels. The question was one I'd had before; most of them would be. "Princess Meredith, have you chosen a husband?"

"No," I said.

The next reporter stood up to ask his question. "Then why this visit home? What have you come to announce?"

The queen had told me how much truth I could tell. "My uncle, the King of Light and Illusion, is throwing a ball in my honor."

"Will you be taking your guards?"

That was a tricky question. If I just said yes, then they could print that I didn't feel safe in the Seelie Court without bodyguards. Which was actually the truth, but we couldn't let them know that. "My guards go everywhere with me—" I hesitated, and Madeline came in close enough to whisper, "Steve," to me. I finished, "—Steve. It is a dance, after all, and I wouldn't leave my best partners home twiddling their thumbs, would I?" Smile, smile, and move on.

A woman asked, "Queen Andais announced that there will

be a dance tonight in your honor at her court. When will you be going to the Seelie Court?"

"It's planned for two nights hence," I'd added *planned for* in case something awful happened and we decided it was too dangerous to go. The *hence* was because the media liked it if we put in an archaic word now and then, or even just a word that they thought was archaic. I was a faerie princess, and some people were disappointed that I talked like a Midwestern native. So occasionally, I tried to sound the way people wanted us to sound. Most of the men still held at least an edge of their original accent. It was just me who sounded like the American girl next door. Well, me and Galen.

"Are the courts going to reconcile?"

"To my knowledge the courts aren't feuding, unless you know something I don't, Maury." I actually remembered his name on my own. Smile, cock my head to one side, give them a glimpse of how young I can still look when I need to. It was my version of Bambi eyes: *See how harmless and cute I am, don't hurt me.*

I got laughter for the cute act, and more flashbulbs, until I was nearly dazzled blind by them. I answered the next question with spots dancing through my vision. I'd have worn sunglasses if my aunt hadn't sent word that I couldn't. Sunglasses weren't friendly. We wanted to look friendly. She'd allowed the guards who had brought sunglasses to wear them. Nearly a first. It meant that she was worried, more worried than the last time I'd been home. And still none of us knew why.

I had to admit with most of them in dark glasses, they did look like backup singers. *Merry and her Merry men.* That's what the media had coined for us. Not quite the name of a rock group, but I'd heard worse.

"Which of your guards is the best in bed?" This from a female reporter.

I shook my head enough to make my hair swing, and the emerald earrings catch the light. "Oh, now—" Madeline whispered the woman's name in my ear. "—Stephanie, a lady doesn't kiss and tell."

"But you're not a lady," a man's voice piped up from the back of the room. I knew the voice. He'd spoken loud enough that the room had gone quiet, so that his next shout was very clear: "Just another faerie slut. Royal blood doesn't change that."

I leaned into the microphone and made my voice low and rich. "You're just jealous, Barry."

A number of the policemen in the circle were already working their way toward the back of the room. Barry Jenkins was always on the do-not-let-him-in list. I had a restraining order against him dating back to my father's death. He'd gotten better, or worse, photos than anyone of my father's body, and me weeping over him. The courts had agreed that what he'd done subsequently had infringed on the rights of a minor—me. They'd ruled that he could not profit by the exploitation of a minor child. That meant that all his photos that he hadn't used yet were useless. He couldn't sell them. He had to give the money he'd already received for photos and articles to charity. He'd gone from maybe winning a Pulitzer to nothing. For that and an incident on a lonely country road, where I took my own revenge, he'd never forgiven me.

He'd had his own revenge, in a way. When my once-upon-a-time fiancé, Griffin, had sold intimate pictures to the tabloids, it had been with Jenkins's byline. I wasn't a minor anymore, and Griffin had gone to him, so he hadn't even had to come within fifty feet of me to write the story.

My aunt, the Queen of Air and Darkness, had declared a death sentence on Griffin. Not for hurting me, but for betraying our intimate secrets to the humans. That was not allowed. To my knowledge they were still hunting for him. I think if she could have sent Doyle after him, he'd have been dead by now, but her Darkness had better things to do than revenge. Keeping me alive, and getting me pregnant, were more important to her than Griffin's punishment. Hell's bells, they were more important to me.

I didn't want Griffin dead. His death wouldn't change

what he'd done. It wouldn't change that he'd been my fiancé for seven years, and that he'd betrayed me with anything he could sleep with. We'd been broken up for more than three years before he betrayed me in the press. Griffin seemed to believe that he was so good that I'd take him back. His delusions weren't my problem. So he'd gone back to the queen's guards, and because I refused him, she'd declared him celibate again. If he didn't sleep with me, he slept with no one. Part of me had enjoyed the irony of it. Part of me had enjoyed the revenge. The next day the tabloids had carried the pictures, and his interview with Jenkins.

The policemen stationed at the doors closed off Jenkins's escape so he could only stand there and wait for the other policemen to come get him. "What's the matter, Meredith, afraid of the truth?"

"The restraining order says that you must stay at least fifty feet away from me, Jenkins. This room isn't that big."

He was unpleasant enough that Major Walters sent another three men to help control the situation. I think it was more to keep the cameras back, and see that Jenkins's struggles didn't break any expensive equipment, than any thought that Jenkins was a danger to me or anyone else.

The remaining police tried to cover the front of the podium, but there weren't enough of them. If the press rushed us now, we were finished, but of course they were more interested in the scene with Jenkins. It'd make some headlines tomorrow. So far the disruption was the most interesting thing to happen, and they'd lead with Jenkins and the old feud, unless we gave them something juicy.

Doyle and Frost both moved forward to flank me. Doyle actually touched my arm to lead me back against the wall, closer to them all. I shook my head, and finally whispered, "I don't want my father's death to make front-page news again. I can't live through it twice."

He looked puzzled even behind the dark glasses.

"They'll dredge it all up, Doyle. They'll dredge it all up to explain Jenkins."

Frost touched his shoulder. "She may be right."

Doyle shook his head. "Your safety comes before anything else."

"There are different kinds of safety," Frost said. There was no trace of the petulant child I'd come to dread. Frost was acting like a grown-up, and I was so happy to see it that I hugged him around the waist. It felt incredibly good to hold him that close. I hadn't realized until that moment how anxious I was.

"What do you want us to do?" Doyle said, and his voice was gentler.

Magic prickled across my skin. The three of us looked up, and all the other sidhe were searching the room. It was a spell, but from where, and for what?

One of the policemen in front of the dais stumbled, as if he'd tripped over nothing. I saw the man turn toward us, saw the wide surprise in his eyes.

Frost turned, giving his back to the man, and beginning to move me away. I'd see the pictures later, but when it was actually happening I saw nothing but Frost's shirt, felt nothing but him picking me up, starting to run. A gunshot exploded behind us, and another so close behind that it was almost one shot. Frost threw himself on the floor. I felt his body pushing us down, but could see nothing but the white of his shirt, the flare of his grey jacket. I could smell the shots like a burning in the air.

There was no sound. The roar of the guns so close in such a small place with such good acoustics had robbed me of my hearing, temporarily, I hoped. I saw feet I thought were Galen's before I felt the heavier weight as he threw himself on top of Frost, and formed a living shield around me. More weight, but I couldn't see who, not even to guess.

The first thing that let me know I wasn't deaf was the thick beat of Frost's heart against my ear. After that my hearing came back in stages, like a broken video, bits of shouting. So much shouting. Screams.

I only know what happened because of the video later, and the pictures. The video that we would see over and over again on every newscast. The officer with his gun pointed at Frost's back, trying to kill me, as if he couldn't see that Doyle had a gun pointed at his chest from less than two feet away. The police officers on either side with their guns out, looking around, not understanding that one of their own was the problem. One had his gun pointed at Doyle. The be-spelled officer fired, as another officer finally understood that something had gone terribly wrong, and smashed into the first one's shoulder. But Doyle had fired before the first bullet had gone wide and pierced the wall behind us. The police officers rode the bespelled cop to the ground, where he was already wounded by Doyle's shot. There would be pictures of Rhys and Nicca behind Doyle with guns in one hand and swords in the other, and Barinthus and the others forming a wall around us.

While it was happening, I was crushed under the white and grey of Frost's body while my hearing returned—and what I heard mostly was screams. Something warm dropped onto my forehead, something liquid and heavier than sweat. I couldn't move my head enough to look up, but another drop joined the first to trickle down my skin, and I caught that whiff of metallic sweetness that was blood.

I tried to push him off me, tried to ask how badly he was hurt, but it was like trying to move a mountain. I managed to say, "Frost, Frost, you're hurt."

If he heard me, he ignored me. Everyone ignored me. It was as if I were strangely nonessential to the events. The man had tried to kill me, but now it was the police and the bodyguards who were onstage, not me.

I heard Major Walters bellow, "Get her out of here." The cry was taken up, like a battle cry. "Get her out of here, get her out of here," so many voices yelling, so many male voices yelling it.

The weight above me lifted, and I saw the lights of the room again. More voices, "My God, she's hurt!" The cry was taken up again, "She's hurt, she's hurt, the princess is hurt." There would be a picture of me later with blood running down my face, but it wasn't my blood. I think I was the only one who knew that at first.

Kitto was still kneeling close to me, and I knew that he had been one of the bodies in my living shield. Barinthus held down his hand to me. "Merry-girl." He hadn't called me that in years. I took his hand while Galen tried to look at Frost's shoulder, and the bigger man shrugged him off. It never occurred to me that Barinthus hadn't touched the ring in the other room.

His hand met the ring as he pulled me up, and he froze in midmotion, a look of startlement on his face. The guards who were new looked around for another threat, because they felt the magic. My guards felt it, but they knew it wasn't another attempt on my life. I heard Frost say, "Consort save us," and Rhys say, "Shit." Then the room was gone, swallowed in a blink of magic. The water was warm as a bath, warm as blood. Barinthus was beside me, helping me tread water. The nearly invisible webbing between his fingers had flared to life, one strong arm stroking the water, while the other held me against his body. We were both nude, and it had been the warmth of the water that had kept me from noticing. Which meant the water was the exact temperature of my body. I could feel his legs moving, keeping us afloat, keeping us in the middle of a vastness of water that was as blue as his hair, as green as his hair, as grey as his hair. His hair streamed down his shoulders into the water, and where it touched, it was as if each strand became a current, like a melting of color that swam away from us, until I couldn't tell what was hair and what was water, and still his body was solid against mine. Part of his body grew more solid as our bodies bumped against each other in the warm, warm water.

"Merry," he said, "what have you done?"

I opened my mouth but it wasn't my words that came out: "I bring you back your ocean, Manannan Mac Lir, come take it from me."

He touched my mouth with his hands, and for a moment only his strong legs kept us afloat. "Do not say that name, for

I am not he. I have not been that for long years." He looked stricken, as if hearing the name had hurt him somehow.

I realized in a distant way that I wasn't entirely alone in my body, nor entirely in control of it. The thought should have frightened me, but it didn't. The power was so so soothing, so safe. It was like being wrapped in peace.

"Come, drink of me, and hold me to your lips." My body entwined around his, wrapping us together in the warm water. It was as if I'd known that he would try to push me away, but there was no way to break free now. My small, rounded arms were like gentle chains, my legs around his waist solid as the mountain's root. Strangely, I knew that he could not free himself of me. He could deny me, but he could not cast me aside. My body's weight forced him to glide onto his back, his head only barely above the quiet waves.

His eyes flashed white. "You are not Merry."

"I am Merry," and I knew it was true.

"But not Merry alone." His arms and legs fanned the water, pressing parts of him against me in a way that we had never been.

"No, not Merry, alone."

"Danu," he said, and his voice was the rushing whisper of waves on some distant shore.

I slid my hands behind his neck and raised my body along his, until my mouth hovered over his, and the tip of him caressed against the opening of my body. The feel of him touching the edge of me brought me back into myself, chased her soothing presence back, just enough. I said, "Barinthus."

"Merry, do you agree to this? The Goddess and God mean well, but I have seen them use people, and I no longer believe that the end justifies the means."

I raised back enough to gaze down at him. He floated underneath me, his hair flowing out in a halo of blue, green, grey, navy, turquoise, and his face caught like a flower in the center of all that color, all that movement. Everything around us was water, moving, flowing, slapping in tiny waves. His body was the only solid thing in all that moving vastness. But I did not cling to him, I rode him, and he held me, but there was no fear. I felt in him the same sense of peace that I held within myself. They say the ocean is a treacherous place, but sitting there staring into his blue eyes as the sea rocked us, feeling the press of him against my body, long and solid, where only the flexing of his hips or mine would close that last distance, I saw nothing but gentleness in his eyes. He would pass this by, all this, give it up, yet again, if I but said no.

I put my face next to his so that a hard breath would have made us kiss, and said, "Drink of my lips." My lips touched his, and the next words were mouth against his own mouth, as if I ate the words and gave them back to him. "Let me feel the strength of you inside me."

He drew back just enough to speak. "It will not be all it could be, for you are mortal, and might drown." With that warning, his mouth came up to meet mine, and as our lips touched, he thrust into my body. Power poured out of my mouth and spilled into his as his body pushed into mine, and it was as if the magic flowed both from me and into me. We became a circle of mouth and body, of magic given and received, of life and small death, of his strength holding us above the waves, of my softness bearing us down. It was almost as if one magic were trying to keep us afloat, and the other sought to drown us. In the midst of life, death; in the midst of joy, danger; in the midst of ocean, land. The earth itself called to me, leagues and leagues below us. The land rolled underneath its blanket of ocean, and I felt it. I felt the earth turning under us, spiraling around, and it was as if the earth felt my thoughts, and stirred in her bed.

I felt the wave of power coming up from underneath us, like some huge, dark creature, swimming up fast and faster, sleek and dark and deadly. It hit us in a wave of power that threw the sea into towering waves, and boiled the land underneath us so that steam filled the air. The water was no longer warm but hot, hot enough that I cried out and jerked my mouth free of his. I saw his face, felt his hands on my hips, felt his body thrusting up into mine, and it wasn't just the hard length of him. It was as if the miles and miles of ocean underneath me were rushing between my legs, spilling into me, through me, over me, and we were pushed into the air on a column of water that glistened like crystal, and glittered with bits of burning rock, like melting fire. I understood now why he'd asked my permission, because I wasn't a goddess, I was only Merry, and I could not hold all that he offered. I screamed, half in pleasure, as he brought me, and half in fear, because I could feel no end to it.

Over the sound of the ocean boiling underneath us, I heard him say, "Enough!"

I was on the floor on the dais with Barinthus half collapsed on top of me. We blinked up into each other's faces, and I watched my own confusion chase across his eyes. I knew where I was, and I knew what had happened, but the change was—abrupt.

I saw my Doyle and the others who were mine standing around us, facing inward, hands spread, touching one to the other so they formed a circle around us. I could see the power in that circle that they had thrown up so desperately to contain what had happened. The guards who had come with Barinthus were staring in at us, and the police were screaming, "Get her out of here!" Seconds had passed, no more.

Barinthus got to his knees and reached for the hand that did not hold the ring, to help me sit up.

That seemed to be signal enough, because they all lowered their hands in unison. The circle went down, and water surged outward, a miniature flood that soaked the dais, and the chairs nearest us, and all the policemen. Frost's pale grey slacks were soaked to charcoal; Rhys's white silk trench coat, ruined. Only two people stood in the center of that spray of water and stayed dry—Barinthus and me.

Major Walters came up brushing water out of his eyes. "What the fuck was that?"

Doyle started to say something, but Walters waved it away. "Fuck it, get her out of here before something else goes wrong." When they all looked at each other instead of moving, Walters leaned into Doyle and said in a voice that would have done any drill sergeant proud, *"Move!"*

We moved.

Chapter 24

I STUMBLED ON THE WAY OUT, AND IT WAS GALEN WHO LIFTED me in his arms and crawled into the middle limo on his knees. There'd be a picture the next day of me with blood on my face, looking very frail in Galen's arms. Which meant that some bravely stupid reporter, instead of taking cover when the guns and magic came out, had trailed us to take more pictures. I guess you don't win Pulitzers by playing it safe.

I was actually in the limo, still in Galen's lap with the other guards piling in, when I realized it wasn't my aunt's personal car. It was just an ordinary stretch limo. Which meant it was actually bigger inside than the Black Coach, but not half so scary.

The door shut, someone slapped the roof twice, and we were moving. Doyle walked over everyone's feet and made Galen scoot down so he could sit on the other side of us, against the far door. No one argued with him. Rhys and Kitto were on the half seat across from us. Barinthus was on the swiveling seat that faced us. The seat left a sort of short hall-way for others to reach more seats even deeper into the limo. When they said *stretch*, they meant it.

Sage and Nicca were there in the next open space, on the last two swivel seats so they could sit sort of sideways with their wings. Usna was curled on the far side, with his legs tucked under him, trying to squeeze water from his calico hair. He looked disgusted with the whole arrangement. Maybe he just didn't like being wet.

I realized dimly that Galen's pants were wet and it was

soaking into my panties. I pushed off his lap, and I could almost stand normally, one of the pluses of being short. "You're getting me wet."

"Everyone is wet except for you and Barinthus," Usna said from the front.

Galen caught my arm, touching my face and the blood that had already gotten tacky to the touch. "Is any of this yours?"

"No."

Barinthus was looking at him. "I saw blood on Frost's jacket, even after the water. If it doesn't wash off after that much water, then it is fresh."

"I noticed it, too." Doyle leaned around Galen, water glistening on his face in the overhead lights. "How badly are you hurt?"

Frost shook his head. "Not badly."

I touched the dark stain on his left shoulder. "Take off your jacket."

He pushed my hand away. "I am not badly hurt."

"Let me see for myself," I said.

He looked up at me with eyes gone as dark a grey as they could go, like clouds before a storm. He was angry, but I didn't think it was at me; maybe about the situation. "Frost, please."

He pulled off his jacket too quickly, and winced with the movement. He turned those dark storm eyes to Doyle. "It is inexcusable that that human got a shot off."

I knelt on the seat beside Frost to see the bloodstain on his shirt. "I can't see through the shirt."

He grabbed the sleeve near the seam and pulled, ripping the sleeve away.

"If I had shot him before he fired, then the police might never believe that he would have shot at all."

"You deliberately allowed him to fire." Frost said it as if he didn't believe it.

He wasn't the only one who was surprised. It didn't seem like good reasoning to me. My hand must have squeezed his arm, because he hissed. I mumbled, "Sorry," and inspected the wound. The bullet had gone in one side and out the other. It looked clean enough, and the bleeding was already slowed, nearly stopped.

"Bullets will not kill us, Frost, and Meredith was lost behind you. He couldn't have hit her."

"So you let Frost take a bullet," I said. For the first time in all of this, my skin ran cold. It was as if the fear had been waiting for me. Waiting until I got somewhere more secure.

Doyle thought about that for a second, then nodded. "I allowed the policeman to get one shot off, yes."

"The bullet went through me, Doyle, and lodged in the wall. If it had been lower, it would have gone through Merry."

Doyle frowned. "It does not seem like good reasoning, now that you say it like that."

Barinthus leaned forward and passed a hand just in front of Doyle's body. He pulled back, rubbing his fingers together as if he'd touched something. "A spell of reluctance, very subtle, but it clings to you like the remnants of some cobweb."

Doyle nodded. "I can sense it." He closed his eyes for a moment, and I felt the small flare of magic as he burned off the last pieces of the spell. He took a deep, shuddering breath, and opened his eyes. "There are few who could work such upon me."

"How is Frost's shoulder, Meredith?" Barinthus asked.

"I'm no healer, but it looks clean enough."

"None of us is a healer," Barinthus said, "and such a lack could mean the difference between life and death someday. I will speak to the queen about assigning you a healer."

The limo went around a corner, and I nearly fell. "You need to sit down," Galen said. "If you don't want to get wet, then sit on Barinthus's lap."

"I do not think so," Barinthus said, and his voice held a tone I'd never heard before.

"Why not?" Galen said.

Barinthus spilled his long leather coat off his lap where he had folded it shut. His pale blue pants were dark and stained just over the groin. "I am not exactly dry."

There was one of those moments of awkward silence, but Galen knew just what to say. "Is that what I think it is?"

Barinthus closed his coat over his lap again. "It is."

"What will you tell the queen?" Doyle asked.

I went to kneel between Barinthus's chair and the arm of Rhys's and Kitto's seat. "The queen can't hold him to the rule."

"The queen can do as she pleases," Barinthus said.

"Now, wait, she sent the guards to me to be lovers, right?" They all turned solemn faces to me. "Well, we had sex. It was partly metaphysical, but isn't her rule that anyone the ring reacts to, whom she sends to me, is fair game?"

You could see the tension begin to leave them, much like the water that was dripping down from their hair and into their faces. Everyone's hair was plastered to his head, even Galen's and Rhys's curls. It takes a lot of water to make curls lie straight. Everyone who hadn't worn black had water stains on his clothes. How much water had been in that last burst of power?

"So I am now one of your men?" Barinthus asked, voice soft, almost joking.

"If it will save you from being put to death, yes."

"Only for that reason, and no other?" His face was very serious as he gazed down at me. I had to look away.

I'd always thought of Barinthus as my father's friend, our adviser, a sort of uncle. Even when the ring had recognized him months ago, it had never occurred to me to include him in my lovers. And he had not asked.

"The queen will be royally pissed," Usna said from the front. "She has been meeting with you for weeks, discussing which men to send to the princess. Which men would the ring recognize?" He'd given up trying to get his hair dry and was starting to unbutton his shirt, though he'd have to take his shoulder holster off first if he wanted to lose the shirt. "How could you not have told her that the ring knew you?"

"How do you know this wasn't my first taste of the ring?"

Usna gave him a withering look. "Please, Barinthus, the queen sent you with the other guards to try the ring when the princess first returned to court. Because you did not mention it, we all assumed the ring did not know you." He struggled out of his shoulder rig so that it flapped around his waist, and he began to peel the shirt from his skin, revealing that the red and black in his hair trailed down his body, in places. "The ring certainly knew you tonight."

"I never lied to anyone about the ring," Barinthus said.

"No, we never lie to one another," Usna said, "but we'll omit so much that it would be more sporting to simply lie." He let the wet shirt fall to the floor of the limo and stood up enough to start working at his belt.

"Are you actually going to strip in the car?" I asked.

"I am wet through and through, Princess. If I can get the clothes off, I will begin to dry. The clothes will stay wet longer than my skin will."

"It is true that the ring sparked for me when Meredith first returned to the courts, but I thought then that I could be of more use to her if I remained at the courts, as her ally. Sadly, I still think so."

"The queen will give you no choice," Usna said, "except to see the Hallway of Mortality before you bed the princess. That choice you may have."

I looked at Barinthus. I wanted to ask him if he would claim his true name before the entire court, or at least the queen. But I couldn't ask without giving away that there was more secret to tell. It was his secret, not mine.

If he understood my look, he ignored it. "When I touched the ring many months ago, it was nothing like today. Nothing."

"The ring has grown stronger," Doyle said.

"That alone may not be it," Rhys said.

We looked at him.

He moved aside his soaking-wet trench coat and held up

the chalice. Those of us who knew it was back were shocked. Barinthus, who hadn't known, was beyond shocked.

"Where did you get that?" Barinthus finally managed in a voice that was barely a whisper.

"I rescued it from the dais, where it had fallen. It was hidden underneath a flap of your coat. I don't think anyone got a picture of it. When Barinthus stood, I palmed it, as discreetly as I could."

"It was locked in the makeup case, wrapped in cloth," I said.

Nicca held up the small case from where it had been sitting by his feet. "I fetched it with us, as Doyle directed. I had not held it before, so I did not notice the change in weight."

"How did it get out of the box?" I asked.

Doyle motioned, and Nicca opened the box. The black silk covering lay folded in the bottom of the case. I started to pull the silk out, to help put the chalice inside again, but Doyle said, "No, Merry, do not touch it and any one of us at the same time. We are not equipped to do another emergency circle of power. I am not entirely certain that it would be successful inside the metal of the car while it was moving."

"Do you think we contained the energy?" Rhys asked.

"I do not know," he said.

"I do not mean," said Barinthus, "where did you get it just now. I mean how did it come to you?"

"I dreamed of it, and when I woke it was in bed with me."

"I thought this was a secret," Sage said.

"Barinthus needs to know," Rhys said, "and all cats love to keep secrets."

"Princess and Darkness have no problem with that?" Sage asked.

Doyle and I exchanged glances, then both of us shook our heads. "No," we said together.

Usna had managed to wiggle out of all his clothing. He crawled toward us with his shoulder holster flapping loose over his bare shoulders and his sheathed sword in one hand. Crawling on all fours, even with the sword in one hand, seemed strangely suited to him. His right shoulder and most of his upper arm were black, and, if I remembered, his back was red and black. A flash of red decorated what I could see of his right hip, and the calf of his left leg.

He spoke to them, but he stared at me. "What came in a dream?" His voice was lightly curious, and held none of the heat of his gaze.

"This," Rhys said.

When Usna saw what Rhys held, he raised up on his knees and cursed long and soundly in Gaelic. "The chalice, the real chalice?"

"It would seem so," Barinthus said.

I was inches away from Usna where he knelt. Perhaps I had been too much among the humans, but it struck me as odd that he could be this close to me nude and not be aroused. Something in me felt slighted by that. Childish? Maybe. But I had the almost irresistible urge to cup him in my hand and make him notice me. I must have made some small movement because Barinthus touched my shoulder, stopped my arm from finishing the motion.

"Do you feel compelled to touch him?"

I thought about that. "Maybe, sort of."

"Then do not do it here with the chalice so close. As Doyle has said, we are in a moving car. The water at the press conference would have been enough to flood the interior of this car."

I leaned back on my knees, resting on my heels. It wasn't entirely comfortable because of the spike high heels. The patent leather just didn't have as much give as regular leather.

"You're right," I said, and crawled away from Usna and the chalice. I didn't stop until my back hit Galen's damp legs and the puddle of water that was collecting under the three men on the seat. I stayed in the water. My hose, skirt, and panties were all black. It was uncomfortable, but it wouldn't ruin anything I was wearing. At that moment it was more important to be as far away from the chalice as I could get. Stretch limo or not, there just wasn't room to run.

"What would have happened if the princess touched me?" Usna asked.

"Perhaps nothing," Barinthus said, "or perhaps much." He turned toward Doyle. "The chalice always had a mind and agenda of its own. Has that changed?"

Doyle shook his head. "On the contrary, it seems to have grown worse."

"Consort help us," Barinthus whispered.

The driver spoke over the intercom. "The bridge is blocked off, police lights everywhere."

Doyle hit the button. "What's happened?"

Silence, then the driver's voice again. "The river is over the bridge. I haven't seen the river that high since the big flood of 'ninety-four. Strange, we haven't had any rain."

In the silence that followed, we all looked at one another. "It looks as if we did not contain all the power from Barinthus's return to godhead," Doyle said.

I remembered the earthquake that had happened after I brought Kitto into his power. A thought occurred to me. "Was there an earthquake in California after we left today?"

Barinthus shook his head. "I checked the weather to see if your plane would be delayed; there was no earthquake." He looked suddenly thoughtful. "There was a freak windstorm, almost a tornado, which they do not have there, but it was not close to the airport."

We all exchanged glances, those of us who knew.

"What is it?" Barinthus asked.

"When I brought Kitto into his power, there was an earthquake later that night."

"What has that to do with the windstorm?"

"Nicca's wings came at the same moment that . . ." I shook my head. "Sage, just show him."

Sage turned to Barinthus and the now staring Usna. Sage was smiling, enjoying the hell out of all of it. He lowered his sunglasses enough for them to see the tricolor of his eyes.

Usna hissed. "Goddess, he's sidhe."

Barinthus touched Sage's face, put the newly colored eyes toward the light. "He is not sidhe, no part of him." He let go of Sage and turned to stare at me. "You did this?"

I nodded.

"How?"

"Sex."

Barinthus frowned. "You said Nicca's wings came at the same time."

I nodded. "Yes."

He seemed to think about that for a moment. "You had sex with both of them at the same time."

The fey did not have a problem with multiple partners, and it was rude of him to remark upon it. "What does that matter?" Doyle said, coming to my defense.

"The queen is convinced that Meredith must take more than one lover at a time, to conceive."

"Why?" I asked.

He shrugged. "I am not sure, but she has been very clear on her plans in this area." By wording it that way, he implied that she had been unclear about her plans in other areas.

"I have taken multiple lovers before this, Barinthus."

"Who?"

Rhys was wrapping the chalice in its silk robe, tucking it into the case once more, as he answered, "Me and Nicca."

Nicca closed the lid of the makeup case and tested the latch, though I think we all knew that that wasn't the problem.

"The queen seems quite taken with the idea that Meredith must take more than one lover at the same time. When she finds out that this has already been done and no baby has come . . ." He shook his head, and looked at me. "The queen seems calmer of late, Meredith, but in some ways more determined. Once set upon a course of action, she is no longer distractible by putting an attractive man in her way, or an opportunity to torture. Her hobbies do not seem to interest her as they once did."

That sex and torture were my aunt's hobbies had always made her difficult to deal with, or so I'd thought. Barinthus was saying the opposite.

"Are you saying that you used sex and pain to distract her over the years?" I asked.

He nodded. "It was like offering a child candy. They take their sweets and forget what they were angry about. But in the last few weeks, no amount of painful candy derails her thoughts. She will take the diversion, use it up, and then come right back to where you wanted her not to go." He was frowning. "On the one hand, it is good to see her thinking with her head instead of her groin. On the other hand, we at court had become accustomed to dealing with her groin. The head is not so easily distracted."

"If she's thinking with her head and not lower, then why is she fixated on me with multiple lovers?"

"She seems determined that that is the only way you will become pregnant. That, and she is choosing plant and agricultural deities for you. She seems equally fixated on that."

"And you have no idea why?" Doyle asked.

He shook his head. "I know that something has happened. She tortured Conri, tortured him personally."

"Didn't he just get tortured for trying to kill me last time I was here?"

"Yes, but he had done nothing wrong. He seemed as shocked as the rest of us when she took him. She paraded his broken body in the great room, made everyone walk by him and see what had been done to him, but he was gagged the entire time, so he could not speak. He lies isolated in a cell, seen only by Fflur, the queen's healer."

"Conri was one of Cel's staunchest supporters among the guards," Doyle said.

Barinthus nodded. "Yes, and what a scrambling there was among Cel's people, who had persisted in making it clear that they considered Meredith unfit for the throne. They toadied, and did everything and anything they could dream up to win the queen's favor."

"Was Conri the only one she tortured?" I asked.

"As of now, but the rest of Cel's allies are frightened."

"You made mention of him not being able to speak," Doyle said. "Do you think he told the queen something, something she doesn't want others to know?"

Barinthus nodded. "I do."

"Do you have any idea what it is?"

"Only that it was after Conri's torture that the queen began to fixate on multiple lovers for Meredith and that most of them should be plant or agricultural deities." He shrugged. "You now know what I know. If you can make more sense of it than I, I will be happy to hear it."

Doyle shook his head. "I will think upon it."

"We all will," Rhys said.

The others nodded.

The driver's voice came back on the intercom. "They're starting to let cars through. The river just went back down. Weird."

Someone gave a nervous laugh. I said, "Well, it could have been worse."

They all looked at me. "We may have flooded every river and stream around St. Louis," Doyle said. "How much worse could it be?"

"St. Louis used to be part of a great inland sea, about a million years ago, give or take a millennium," I said softly.

The silence in the car was suddenly thicker than before, heavy with a sort of shared horror. "Kitto got a small earth tremor. Nicca and Sage got a windstorm," Galen said. "I don't think bringing Barinthus back into his godhead would rate sinking most of a continent."

I knew exactly which of us knew that Barinthus was Manannan Mac Lir by who looked at him, and then away. Galen didn't know. But I did, and the thought of raising that much power without a formal circle of protection made my blood run cold. Though that could have been the puddle of water I was sitting in, too.

Chapter 25

IT WAS A LONG, COLD WALK FROM THE PARKING AREA TO THE faerie mounds. The snow was knee-deep on me, and there was no way for my mortal body to wade through it in four-inch spike heels and a miniskirt. Not without breaking an ankle or getting frostbite. So I was carried, and the only one who wasn't wet through was Barinthus. Everyone else's clothes began to freeze in the icy wind, and those who had no magical protection against the elements shivered as we waded through the snow.

Barinthus carried me easily. What would have had me floundering in the powdery depths was nothing to his height. I'd always known he was two feet taller than me, but as he carried me in his arms pressed against his broad chest, I was aware as I had never been before how physically imposing he was.

It was both comforting to ride in his strong arms, and unnerving. Curled up in his arms, I felt quite the child. He had carried me many times as a child, but now I had memories of him that did not match being childlike in his arms. I lay against his body and felt not embarrassed, but not comfortable, either.

I looked up at him from the nest he'd made of his coat for me. If he was cold without it, I could not tell. He looked out before him, and not at me, at all, as if I were indeed a child that filled his arms. Maybe I was to him. Maybe what had happened at the press conference hadn't changed how he saw me. The magic had meant something to him, that I knew, but as for the rest, perhaps I was no more than his old friend's daughter. He had always been more of a true uncle to me than any to whom I was related by genetics.

If it had been almost any other guard whom I had had such an intimate moment with and he'd ignored me like this, I would have done something to make certain he could not ignore me. But it wasn't anyone else, it was Barinthus, and somehow it seemed beneath both our dignities for me to grope him.

I must have sighed heavier than I meant to, because my breath came out in a cold white cloud. "Are you warm enough, Princess?"

The moment he asked, I realized that I shouldn't have been. I was coatless with almost nothing on my legs and lower extremities. "I'm warm enough, and why is that?" Then I realized what he'd called me. "You called me *Princess*. You never use my title."

He looked down at me, his clear eyelid flickering into sight, then vanishing again. "Do you not wish to be warm?"

"That is an evasion, old friend, not an answer."

He gave that deep chuckle that passed for a laugh. Held this close to his chest, the sound of it reverberated through my body, caressed me in places nothing should have touched me, save magic.

I shivered under that touch.

"My apologies, Princess, it has been long since I felt this much power. It will take me time to control all of it as finely as I once did."

"You're keeping me warm."

"Yes," he said, "can you not feel it?"

I was safe behind the shields I wore every day, every night. Shields that kept me from moving through a world of wonderment and magic. Some fey simply existed in the raw magic that surrounded everything, but I had found it confusing, frightening, as a child. My father had taught me how to shield out the noise of the everyday magic. But I should have been able to feel a spell done next to my skin. Even through the everyday shields.

I didn't lower my shields, because we were too close to

faerie. I wasn't sure if it was being mortal, or merely not as powerful, but I found that without my shields to hide behind, the power of faerie was near overwhelming. Of course if it were either of those things, the humans who occasionally lived among us wouldn't have survived long. Madeline Phelps had no magic, no psychic gifts. How did she survive? How did she keep from being driven mad by the singing of the sithen?

I sent a tiny tendril of my own power through my shields. Many would have had to drop shields to do magic, but they were sidhe who did not have to weave their protection so close to their skin, as I did. With every loss there is some gain; with every gain, some loss.

I could feel his magic close above us, like an invisible pressure around us. We moved in a circle of his magic. I tested that magic, and it felt warm and vaguely liquid. I closed my eyes and tried to see his shield inside my head. I had an image of water rolling turquoise and lovely, warm as blood from a shore that was far from here, and always warm.

I could have done something similar by calling the heat of the sun, or the memory of warm bodies under blankets, but I would have had to fight to maintain the spell while I moved. Standing still, I was good at all kinds of shielding; moving, not so good.

"The water is very warm," I said.

He said, "Yes," without looking at me.

Galen came up to stride beside us. He was shivering in his wet clothes. Ice had formed in strands of his shorter hair, and there was a tiny cut on his cheek. His hair was just long enough to touch his face with the frozen strands. "If I hop on your back, will you keep me warm, too?"

"The sidhe are impervious to the cold," Barinthus said.

"Speak for yourself," Galen said, teeth nearly chattering.

Nicca waded through the snow on our other side. He was shivering, too. "I have never felt the cold as I do this day." His wings were held tightly together, rimmed with frost, like a stained-glass window in the snow.

"It is the wings," Sage called from behind us. Rhys had actually allowed the smaller man to ride on his back. Rhys seemed totally unaffected by the cold. But Sage huddled against Rhys, and I wondered why Rhys didn't help the demi-fey keep warm, as Barinthus helped me. "We are butterflies, and that is not a creature meant for winter snow."

"I am sidhe," Nicca said.

"As, apparently, am I," Sage called, "but I am still freezing my nuts off."

Galen laughed and nearly stumbled in the snow.

Doyle called back from the front of our little group. "If you will stop gossiping, we can all get inside more quickly, and all will be warm."

"Why aren't you shivering?" Galen asked.

Amatheon answered over to the far right, shivering with his own newly shortened hair icy and cutting his cheeks every time the wind blew it against his skin. "The Darkness is never cold."

Onilwyn called from the far left. He was shivering, too, but at least his long hair kept the ice in his hair from lashing his face. "And you cannot freeze the Killing Frost."

The mention of him made me glance back to see him bringing up the rear. It wasn't that he couldn't have walked faster, because he could have—the cold truly meant nothing to him—but Doyle had ordered him to be our rear guard. There had been one attempt on my life; they were taking no chances.

I realized we were missing one of our number. I had to raise up to find Kitto struggling behind us in the drifts. I think I would have asked someone to help him, but Frost fished him out of the snow and tossed him up on his shoulders. He did it without asking. He did it without a word of any kind.

Kitto didn't say thank you, for both Frost and he were old, and among the oldest of us, thank you was an insult. You had to be younger than three hundred to be comfortable with modern niceties. Which meant that only Galen and I would have thanked someone for a thank you. Everyone else was too old.

I settled back into Barinthus's arms and magic. "Why am I

suddenly *Princess* to you, Barinthus, and not Meredith? You've called me *Meredith* or *Merry-girl* since I was a child."

"You are no longer a child." He stared studiously ahead as if the way were treacherous, and he had to be careful. I did not think it was the snow that he feared.

"You're trying to distance yourself from me?"

"No." Then a small smile curled his lips. "Well, perhaps, but not a-purpose."

"Then why?" I asked.

He glanced down at me again, and that flicker of eyelid came and went again. "Because you are princess, and heir to the throne. And I have too many enemies among the sidhe to be allowed in your bed."

"Once they learn you have come back into your god-head . . ."

"No, Meredith, if they discover that, then they will try to slay me before I have returned to my full powers."

I started to say, *They will not dare,* but I knew better. "How much danger have you been in, staying here and trying to drum up support for my claim to the throne?"

He would not look at me again. "Some," he said.

"Barinthus," I said, "truth between us."

"I do not lie, Princess. *Some* is an honest answer."

"Is it a complete answer?" I asked.

That made him smile again. "No."

"Would you give me a complete answer?"

"No," he said.

"Why not?"

"Because it would make you worry when you leave again, and I remain behind."

"Everyone else the ring has recognized my aunt has sent to Los Angeles with me."

"You know what they call me behind my back."

"Kingmaker," I said.

"Queenmaker now." He shook his head, that long blue hair trailing like a cloak behind him in the sudden rise of wind.

"They have feared me as a power behind the throne for millennia. Do you believe they would tolerate me as your consort, knowing that I might become king?" He shook his head again. "No, Meredith, no, the queen herself understands this. It is why she did not send me the last time you came home. I have too many enemies, and too much power, to be allowed so near the throne."

"And if you got me pregnant?"

He stared off into the distance. "We have had our moment, Meredith. The queen cannot allow us more."

"This isn't what you said in the car, when Usna suggested it."

"We had many ears in the car, and not all of them our friends," he said.

"Barinthus—" He hushed me with a small shake of his head.

I glanced up and found both Amatheon and Onilwyn closer than they had been. Close enough perhaps, to hear our words. I knew almost with a certainty that they were spies for Queen Andais. The question was, who else would they spy for? Did Queen Andais really believe that either man would tell secrets only to her? No, it wasn't their loyalty she counted upon. It was their fear. Andais counted on all the sidhe fearing her more than anyone else.

Yet someone had tried to kill me. Someone had risked the queen's anger. Either they did not fear her as they once had, or fear alone is not enough to rule a people. She was still the Queen of Air and Darkness, and that was plenty scary enough for me. But I'd never believed that fear alone was enough to rule the sidhe. Of course, neither had my father, and his lack of ruthlessness had gotten him killed. If I survived to come to the throne, I knew I could not be Andais; I didn't have the stomach for it. But I also knew I could not be my father, because the sidhe already saw me as weak. If I were as compassionate as my father, it would be my death. If you cannot rule by fear, or by love, what is left? To that, I had no answer. As the faerie mounds rose out of the winter twilight, I realized that I didn't truly believe there was an answer. Two words came into my mind as if someone had whispered them: *ruthless* and *fair*.

Could you be ruthless and be fair, at the same time? Isn't to be ruthless to be unfair? I'd always thought so, and my father had taught me so, but maybe there was a middle ground between the two. And if there was, could I find it? And if I did, did I have enough power, enough allies, to walk that middle road? To that last question, I truly had no answer, because I knew enough of court politics to understand that no one really knows how much power she has, how good her friends are, how stout her allies, until it's too late, and she's either won, or lost; lived or died.

Chapter 26

THE FAERIE MOUNDS LOOKED LIKE SOFT SNOW-COVERED HILLS, and if you did not know the way in, that's all they would be. Of course, the mounds, like almost everything else in faerie, were never quite what they seemed.

There were two things you needed to go inside the sithen. One, to know where the door was; two, to have enough magic to open that door. If the sithen was feeling playful, the door would move repeatedly. You could spend an hour chasing the door around a hill the size of a small mountain. Or perhaps it only played with me, because when Carrow laid his tanned hand against the white of the snow, there was a sound of music. I could never tell you what the tune was, or if it was singing or merely instruments. But it was beautiful music, and the closest thing we had to a doorbell. Though it was more to let you know that you'd found the door than to announce you to everyone inside. No music meant you hadn't touched the right spot. Carrow laid that small flare of magic against it, and the door was suddenly there. Or rather the opening was there, for there was never truly a door to the Unseelie sithen. There was just suddenly an opening big enough for us all to walk inside, four or more abreast. The opening always seemed to know exactly how big it needed to be. It could grow large enough for a semi to pass through, or small enough for a butterfly.

The twilight had deepened to near darkness, so that the pale white light from the opening seemed brighter than it was. Barinthus carried me into that light. We stood in a grey stone hallway, big enough for the semi to have kept on driving, at least to the first bend of the hallway. The size of the door didn't change the size of the first hallway. It was one of the few things that never changed about the sithen. Everything else could change on the sithens', or the queen's, whim. It was like a fun house made of stone, so that entire floors could move up and down. Doors that led one place would suddenly lead somewhere else altogether. It could be irritating, or amazing; or both.

The opening vanished as Frost, the last of us, stepped through. It was just another grey stone wall. The door could be just as invisible from this side as the other. The white light came from everywhere and nowhere. It was steadier than firelight, but softer than electric light. I'd asked what the light was once, and been told it was the light of the sithen. When I'd protested that that told me nothing, the reply was, it told me what I needed to know. A circular argument at best, but in truth I think it's the only answer we have. I don't think anyone alive today remembers what the light truly is.

"Well, Barinthus, are you going to carry the princess all the way to the queen?"

The sound of swords clearing sheaths made a soft metallic hiss, like rain on a very hot surface. Guns are quieter when you draw them. But guns and swords pointed down the hall toward that voice, and some weapons pointed back toward the now invisible door, just in case. Barinthus and I were suddenly standing in the center of a well-armed circle.

The sidhe who'd spoken was smiling. The sidhe standing next to him was not. Ivi's smile was insolent, mocking. He made himself the butt of his own jokes more often than anyone else. He was tall, as tall as Frost or Doyle, but he was slender as a reed, and as graceful as a bed of reeds when the wind makes them dance. I'd have liked him better with shoulders a little wider, but the lack of them made him seem even taller, willowy. His hair fell straight and fine to his ankles. The hair was his most outstanding feature, medium to dark green, with a pattern of white veins running throughout. It was only when he got closer that you realized that his hair bore the mark of leaves as if the hair had been tattooed with ivy. As he moved down the hall, it was as if wind blew the leaves apart, and they re-formed only as his companion grabbed his arm and held him back. I think Ivi would have kept on in the face of all those weapons; walked down that hallway with a smile on his face and laughter like darkness in his eyes. Once I'd thought him careless, but as I grew older I tasted the sorrow in him. I began to realize that it wasn't carelessness, but despair. Whatever had prompted him to become one of the Queen's Ravens, I don't think he enjoyed the bargain as much as he'd hoped.

The cautious hand on his arm belonged to Hawthorne. His black hair fell in thick waves past his knees. When he turned his head, the light gleamed rich green from those black waves. He wore a silver circlet that held that heavy mass back from his face. The rest of him, from broad shoulders to feet. was covered in a cloak the color of pine needles, a rich deep green, which was held closed over his shoulder by a silver brooch.

"What is wrong, Darkness?" he called to us. "We have done nothing."

"Why are you here?" Doyle called back.

"The queen has sent us to meet the princess," Hawthorne said.

"Why only the two of you?"

Hawthorne blinked, and even from this far away I could see that strange pink shade that his inner circle of eye had. Pink, green, and red were Hawthorne's tricolored eyes. "What do you mean, only the two of us? What has happened?"

"They don't know," Barinthus said, quietly.

"How long have you been standing here, waiting?" Doyle asked. But he'd already relaxed his pose, the gun in his hand beginning to lower to point at the floor.

"Hours," Ivi said, and swirled the edge of his own pale green cloak out like a skirt at a dance.

Hawthorne nodded. "Two hours, or more. Time moves oddly in the sithen."

Doyle put up his gun, and as if that were a signal, swords were sheathed, guns holstered, until they all stood at ease, or as easy as they got.

"I ask again, Darkness, what has happened?" But no one had to explain, because some shifting among the guards had let him see me. I'd forgotten about the blood on my face. I'd wiped some of it off with a bit of wet cloth from one of the men, but not all of it. Only soap would get it all off. "Lord and Lady protect us, she's hurt!"

"It is not her blood," Doyle said.

"Then whose?"

"Mine," Frost said, and he moved up through the crowd of guards, and again, as if that were a signal, they all began to move down the hallway toward the other two guards.

Ivi wasn't smiling when he said, "What happened?"

Doyle told him, the brief outline, leaving out what happened when Barinthus touched the ring.

Ivi was shaking his head. "Who would dare? Princess Meredith bears the queen's mark. To harm her is to risk the queen's mercy. None of her Ravens would risk that." There was absolutely none of Ivi's banter in those words. It was as if the news of the assassination attempt had frightened him out of his jokes and into something more real.

Hawthorne's tricolored eyes were wide. "Who indeed would dare?"

Barinthus was still holding me in his arms, but there was no snow now, no cold. I touched his shoulder. "I can walk now."

He looked at me as if he'd forgotten he was holding me, and maybe he had. He had to bend over to put me safely on the stone floor. I shook the back of my skirt in place, smoothed it with my hands, and knew that the pleats in back simply would not be perfect until the skirt was ironed. There was nothing I could do about it. I just hoped that the news of my near death would distract her from my less-than-perfect clothing. You never knew with Andais; sometimes she would direct her anger at small things if she couldn't deal with the large.

Ivi went to one knee before me, and when he did, the cloak caught on his leg and pulled to one side, baring his shoulder, part of his chest, and the edge of his hips. He was nude under the cloak.

"Princess Meredith, greetings from the Queen of Air and Darkness. She sends us as gifts." That lilt of mockery was back in his voice.

Hawthorne had also dropped to his knees, but the way he held the cloak tight with only his hands showing made me wonder if he was wearing anything more under his cloak than Ivi was.

"We are gifts for your stay if the ring doth know us," Hawthorne said, and he sounded as if he would have been angry if he dared.

"Surely this can wait," Onilwyn said. "If the queen truly does not know of what has happened, then she must be told."

It was Usna who answered that. "If you want to hurry off and give the queen bad news, by all means run along. I, for one, do not want to be the first person to tell her." He was still nude, carrying his sheathed sword in his hand. The queen had been known to shoot the messenger, as it were.

Onilwyn looked a little pale. "You may have a point."

"But so do you," Barinthus said. "The queen needs to know. I cannot believe that no one has contacted her."

"She did not know near three hours hence," Hawthorne said.

"If she knew now, there would be more men," Doyle said, and no one argued with him.

"She was entertaining herself," Ivi said, his voice rich with that self-loathing humor, as if every word meant more, "and gave word that only the princess's arrival would be good enough to disturb her."

"Surely someone would have interrupted her fun and games for this," Barinthus said.

Hawthorne looked up at him. "You are one of us, Lord Barinthus, but she does not treat you as she treats most. She respects your power. The rest of us are not so lucky. If we interrupt her game, then we are to take the place of the one she plays with." He looked down and a shudder passed through him. "I would not interrupt her for an attempted assassination."

"If I'd died, then one of you would have told her?" I

asked, and my own voice held an edge of what Ivi usually sounded like.

"You have stripped us of all who were powerful enough to beard her in her den, Princess," Hawthorne said.

"Darkness, Frost, Barinthus," Ivi said, "teacher's pets compared to the rest of us."

"Mistral is still here," Doyle said.

Hawthorne shook his head. "He fears her, Darkness, as do we all."

"She has gotten better in the last few months," Barinthus said, "easier to talk to."

"Again, Lord Barinthus, perhaps for you," Hawthorne said.

"Let us finish our speech," Ivi said. "Then you can all draw straws for who gets to be the bearer of such evil tidings."

"You say that as if you don't get to draw a straw," Rhys said.

"We don't," Ivi said.

"Hawthorne, explain," Doyle said.

"We are gifts for the princess, if the ring doth know us."

"You said that already," Rhys said.

Doyle gave him a look, and Rhys shrugged. "He did."

"And if the ring knows you," Frost said.

"Then we are to invite the princess to bed us." Hawthorne was careful to look only at Doyle, as if I weren't standing there.

Ivi snorted, as if trying not to laugh.

"What is funny in that?" Doyle asked him.

"That's not what the queen said."

"It is the meat of what she meant," Hawthorne said, and there was an air of offended dignity in his tone.

Ivi laughed out loud.

"What did the queen say, Ivi?" Doyle's tone was resigned, as if he really didn't want to know, but understood that there was no choice.

"If the ring knows us"—and he finished the rest in an imitation of the queen's voice good enough to raise the hair at the back of my neck—"then fuck Meredith, fuck her as soon as you see her. If she gets picky then you may go to her room, or yours. I don't care, just get the job done."

"Well," Galen said, "that's . . ."

"A little less than poetic even for the queen," Rhys said.

"That'll do." Galen looked a little shocked.

"Do I get a say in this?" I asked.

Hawthorne bowed until his forehead nearly touched the stone. "I am sorry, Princess."

"What he won't tell you," Ivi said, "is that he asked what we were to do if Princess Meredith did not wish to bed us as soon as she entered the sithen." He imitated the rhythm of Hawthorne's speech.

"And what did my aunt say?" I asked.

Ivi smiled up at me, and his dark green eyes held a fierce triumph that I didn't understand.

Hawthorne answered with his face still bowed toward the stones, his voice holding sorrow the way Ivi's usually held mockery. *"Are you Unseelie sidhe or not? Persuade her."*

Ivi kept his darkly joyful face turned up toward me. "He asked, and if she will not be persuaded?" And again he echoed the queen's voice so well that it raised chills upon my skin, *"Persuade her, or take her, or tell her what I have said, and let that be your persuasion. If Meredith will not take the pleasure I offer her, then perhaps she will take pain instead. For there is both to be had here among the Unseelie. Remind her of that if her sensibilities are too delicate for fucking."*

"I would change what she has sent us for, if I could," Hawthorne said, and he prostrated himself against the stone, his forehead pressed to the floor.

I turned from Ivi's gloating face to Barinthus. "I thought you said she'd gotten better over the last few months."

"She has, she had," he said, and he had the grace to look embarrassed.

"Come on, Princess," Ivi said, "put that pretty hand out and see what happens. If the ring doesn't know us, then we're all free."

"He's right," Doyle said, "let them touch the ring, and if it is cold to them, then we can go to the queen and give our news."

"And if it is not cold?" Frost asked.

"Then we can fuck up against the wall," Ivi said.

"Over my dead body," Galen said.

"If you want it that way," Ivi said.

"Boys," I said.

Galen looked at me. Ivi continued to look at Galen.

"No killing each other unless I tell you to."

Ivi looked at me then, and that fierceness held a note of puzzlement. "What does that mean?"

"It means that if you annoy me enough, Ivi, I have more than half a dozen of the best warriors the sidhe ever produced, and if I asked nicely, they'd slice you into pieces for me."

"Ah, but that would not be obeying the queen's directive."

I bent down just the little bit I needed to be face-to-face with him, and I felt an unpleasant smile cross my face. "Oh, but it would be. Corpses routinely have one last orgasm just as they die. The queen's exact orders are not to come before her without your seed upon my body. She didn't specify where or how that happens, now, did she?"

The triumph was gone, the mockery faded as I watched, until the only thing left in those dark green eyes was fear. It didn't make me happy to see him fear me, but it did give a certain satisfaction.

He licked his lips as if they'd suddenly gone dry, and said, "You are your aunt's bloodline."

"Yes, Ivi, I am, and it would be best if you did not forget that"—I leaned in close above his lips—"ever again." I laid a gentle kiss upon his mouth, and he flinched.

As I raised my hand to cup Ivi's face, Barinthus grabbed my wrist and pulled my hand away from the other man's flesh. "Perhaps the queen should know of other events before we use the ring again."

We all had a moment of exchanging glances. Hawthorne said, "What else has happened?"

"Let us say that the ring has risen in power," Barinthus said, "and I am no longer certain what will happen when the princess presses it to anyone's flesh."

Ivi gave a dark laugh. "I see what happened when she touched you, Lord Barinthus." He was staring at the other man's groin, and the stain that had set into the front of the leather pants.

Abloec pushed to the front, to stand near Ivi. He knelt down beside the other man. It was the steadiest I'd seen him, as if the cold had sobered him. "I am soaking wet, freezing, and sober. I don't want to be any of those three things. You are going to shut up, and we are all going to go to the queen." He looked up at the rest of us. "When she hears about the flooding, she'll want to make sure that the princess is in a se-cure area before the ring is used."

"Flooding?" Hawthorne said.

"Every river in the area," Abloec said.

Hawthorne glanced up at Barinthus. "You mean touching Lord Barinthus flooded the area?"

Doyle and Barinthus said in unison, "We believe so."

Galen and Rhys said in unison, "Yes."

Usna pushed through us all, still nude, and getting angry. "We're going to see the queen now, because I want to be warm again."

"Would you risk your life for a little comfort?" Frost said.

Usna gave him a wide grin. "What else is there to risk one's life for these days? Haven't you heard, Killing Frost, the days of myth and magic are gone. The days when there was anything worth fighting for are over." He looked at Barinthus as he finished, then his grey eyes found me, and he gave me a lingering look. It wasn't sexual, or food, or any-thing that I would have expected from Usna. It was a consid-ering look. A look that held far too many guesses that were far too close to the truth.

The moment passed and his eyes were simply full of good cheer. He clapped Abloec on the shoulder. "Let us go forth and beard the queen in her den of iniquities."

Abloec got to his feet frowning. "You would help bear such news, knowing what she may do?"

"She'll hate the assassination attempt, someone will bleed for that one, but the rest"—Usna threw his arm across the other's shoulders—"the Queen will love the other news." He started moving Abloec down the hallway, and the rest of us began to trail after. Usna called back over his shoulder at me, "If I were you, Princess, I'd be worried that she does not put you in a magical circle like an animal in the zoo, and just send one of us after another to see how many of us you can bring back to . . ." He put his sword pommel over his lips as you'd place a finger to say, *Shhhh*. "Save that for the queen's ears, eh." And he glided down the hallway ahead of us, his nude body in its calico colors leading the way, with Abloec still pressed to his side.

Chapter 27

THE ONLY DOORS IN THE ENTIRE SITHEN THAT WERE BLACK were the doors leading to my aunt's chambers. They were a shining improbable black stone that stood taller than the tallest guard, and wider than that semi the first hallway could hold.

The doors were their usual ominous selves, but the two men who stood at attention before the doors were not usual. One, there were rarely guards on this side of the doors. The queen enjoyed an audience, especially if that audience could not participate, no matter how much they wanted to. Sometimes you'd find guards outside if they were waiting to escort people away once the queen was finished speaking with them. But somehow I didn't think that was it. Call it a hunch, but I was betting the guards were there waiting for me. What was my first clue? They were nude except for enough leather belts and straps to hold swords and daggers, and boots that came to their knees.

"I'm sensing a theme," Rhys said.

So was I. Because not only were they more nude even than Hawthorne and Ivi had been, but they were also vegetative deities. Adair still bore the name of what he had been once, for *adair* means "oak grove." His skin was the color of sunlight through leaves, that color more common among the Seelie than the Unseelie, the color we call *sun-kissed*. His ankle-length brown hair had been butchered short, shorter than Amatheon's by nearly half a foot. Someone had shorn him, so that there was almost nothing left to remind the eye what beauty once framed that golden body.

Amatheon spoke as if I'd asked, "I was not the only one who was reluctant, Princess. She began her . . . example with Adair."

Adair's eyes were three circles of gold and yellow, like staring into the sun. Those eyes held nothing as he watched us come toward the doors. He had been cast out of the Seelie Court for speaking too strongly against their king, and to avoid exile from faerie he had joined the Unseelie. But he had never truly taken to the dark court's way of life. He existed among us, and tried to be invisible.

I spoke low: "I know why you do not want my bed, but Adair and I have no quarrel."

"He wants to be left alone, Princess. He wants to not be involved in this fight."

"Unless you're Switzerland, there is no neutrality," I said.

"So he learned."

The other guard still stood in a cloak of his own pale yellow hair. That hair framed a body that was a pale whitish-grey, not moonlight skin like mine, but a soft, almost dusty color. His eyes gleamed out of a narrow, high-cheekboned face, eyes the color of dark green leaves, with an inner star of paler green like some sort of starred jewel. His lips were the reddest, ripest, prettiest in the courts, either court, if you asked me. The ladies envied him that mouth, and only the brightest, most crimson of lipsticks came close to producing it. His name was Briac, though he preferred to be called Brii. *Briac* was just another form of the name *Brian*, and had nothing to do with plants or agriculture. I knew that Brii was some sort of plant deity, or had been, but beyond that his name kept its secrets.

He smiled as we came nearer—those red, red lips, distracting from the jewels of his eyes, the curtain of his hair, and even the long naked lines of his body. As if he felt me looking, his body began to respond, as if my approach was enough to whet his anticipation and bring him partially erect.

Adair's body was as empty of reaction to my approach as his eyes. He was lucky I was not my aunt, for she sometimes took lack of response on an involuntary level as a personal insult. I did not. Adair had, at the very least, had his pride cut away with his hair. I had no idea what other pains my aunt had put him through to make him willing to stand at this door and await me. He was angry, on that I would have bet a great deal. Anger and embarrassment are not always the best aphrodisiac. My aunt has never truly understood that.

Brii's head went to one side like a bird. His smile slipped a little. "You have not done your duty by the princess."

"There was an assassination attempt on the princess," Doyle said.

The last of his smile was gone. "The blood."

"What else did you think it was from?" I asked.

He shrugged and gave a rueful smile. "Someone else's blood smeared on the queen's face would mean she had had a very, very good time. My apologies for assuming the same of you." He gave a bow that swept his hair out and around one arm like a cloak, then stood up smiling again, with that look in his eyes that was all male, and said plainly that no amount of unpleasantness could take all the pleasure from this duty, at least not for him.

Adair stood on the other side of the doors, wooden-faced and limp-bodied. He wouldn't even look at me.

"We must tell the queen of the attack." Doyle moved up as if to touch the doors.

Adair moved first, but Brii followed, and their arms crossed in front of the door handles. "Our orders were very specific," Adair said. His voice tried to be as empty as the rest of him, but failed. There was a razor-thin edge of rage in those simple words. So much so, that it danced a line of magic down the hall, across our skins like tiny bites. He was fighting very, very hard to control himself.

I rubbed my arm where the edge of his power had touched me, had hurt me, totally by accident, and cursed my aunt. She'd made it so that Adair would obey her orders and bed me, but she'd made certain that neither one of us would enjoy it.

"And what were those orders?" Doyle said, his dark voice, lower even than normal, sounding as if it would crawl down your spine and hunt for vital organs.

Brii answered, trying to make his voice upbeat, concilia-
tory. I didn't blame him; I wouldn't have wanted to be standing between Doyle and Adair when the flags went up, either.
"If the ring knows both Hawthorne and Ivi, then they are to
service the princess as soon as possible. If the ring does not
know both of them, then one of us is to take the place of the
one the ring did not recognize." He smiled at Doyle, as if trying to ease some of the tension. It didn't work.

"Open the door, Brii. We have much to tell the queen, and
much of it is not only dangerous but also not something to be
discussed in the hallway, where more ears may hear us than
the queen would like."

Brii actually moved back, but Adair did not. Somehow I'd
known he wouldn't. "The queen has been at great pains to be
certain that I follow all her orders. I will do as she has . . . bid
me, and follow those orders to the absolute letter. I will not
give her cause to abuse me again this day." The anger had
quieted and didn't bite down the hall now, but Doyle moved
like a horse when a fly settles on it. Perhaps all that stinging
anger had gone only on his skin.

"I am captain here, Adair, not you."

"It is good to have you back, *Captain*"—Adair made that
last word an insult—"but whatever your rank, it is not greater
than the queen's. She is our master, not you. She made this
very clear to me, Darkness, very clear."

They were almost touching, so terribly close, almost too
close to fight. "You refuse my direct order?"

"I refuse to disobey the queen's direct order, yes."

"I ask you one last time, Adair, will you step aside?"

"No, Darkness, I will not."

Magic breathed through the hallway. That first hot breath
that it draws sometimes, like the tensing of a muscle before a
blow. It wasn't that I didn't think Doyle would win. He was
the Queen's Darkness. It was that it seemed a waste to fight
among ourselves when we had enemies to fight. I didn't
know who those enemies were, not yet, but they'd tried to
kill me earlier today. We needed to save our energy for them,
not spend it in senseless bickering.

"Stand down, Doyle," I said, soft but clear.

The magic grew in the hallway, as if the very air were drawing a breath.

"I said, stand down, Darkness," and this time my voice was not soft.

The power that was growing all around us hesitated, flickered. Doyle did not turn from the man he faced, he merely growled, "He stands in our way, and we must needs see the queen."

"We will see the queen," I said, and began to work my way up through the men. I looked at both Abloec and Usna. "Do you both stand by what you said, that you will tell the queen what needs telling?"

"I forgot how wretched it is to be sober, so let this wretchedness end. I will tell the queen of what I saw; you have what word is left me." He even began a bow, but it seemed to hurt his head, so he stopped in midmotion.

"Usna," I said.

He gave me that cat-that-ate-the-canary smile and said, "Of course, Princess, I am always a man of my word."

"I will allow no one past me until we have obeyed everything the queen instructed," Adair said.

"Do you really think that you can withstand the might of this many of your fellow Ravens?" Barinthus asked, though he did not move up closer to the door. I think he was afraid of what might happen if he used his power to fight. I know I was.

I stepped past Frost's back and got a glimpse of Adair's determined face before Frost moved in front of me. "You are too close, Meredith," he said.

I shook my head. "Not close enough, Frost."

He frowned down at me. "I did not save you from a human assassin to have you hurt by your own guards."

"I will not be hurt, not in that way, at least."

Puzzlement filled his grey eyes, and he frowned harder. "I do not understand."

There was no time to explain it. Power was building on the very air again. A glance showed that Adair's skin was beginning to glow.

"It wasn't a human who tried to assassinate me today, Frost." I made sure my voice carried. "It was sidhe magic that bespelled that human. Sidhe magic that put a spell on Doyle that made him slow to defend me. Only a sidhe could have put such a spell on the Darkness himself."

Brii spoke up as I'd hoped he would, "Who could bespell Darkness, except for the queen herself?"

"There are those who can, but none that stood with us today," Doyle growled, his eyes still on the softly glowing Adair. "But someone powerful enough to send a spell from a distance and for none of us to notice it until too late."

"I don't believe you," Adair said.

"May the sluagh eat my bones if I lie," Doyle said, his voice still a threatening growl. It was like listening to a dog speak, too low for a human throat.

Adair's glow faded around the edges so that the center of his face glowed like a candle in the middle of him. "Even if I believe you, even if I agree that the princess should see the queen immediately, if I allow you to pass without a fight, I will be at the queen's mercy." He raised a hand as if to touch his hair, then stopped, as if he could not stand to touch the near-bare scalp. "I have been at her mercy, and I do not care for it."

"Let me pass, Frost."

He moved. Reluctantly, but he moved.

I touched Doyle's arm. "I will tell you this for a third and a last time, Doyle, stand down."

His dark eyes flicked to me, then he took a breath so deep that it ended with his body shuddering like a dog ruffling its fur after a nap. He took one small step back from Adair. "As my princess commands, so shall it be." His voice was still deeper than normal, and perhaps only I could hear the question in that growl. But he trusted me enough to do as I said. Trusted me enough to let me take his place in front of Adair.

I looked up at Adair, and I could not keep a moment of sorrow out of my eyes when I beheld his short hair up close.

Adair turned his face from me, mistaking my sorrow for pity, I think.

"I will let you taste the ring, Adair, as the queen wishes."

His gold-and-yellow eyes slid back to look at me, though his head was still turned away. "Has the ring not known Hawthorne and Ivi?"

I ignored the question, which was not a lie. I stared into his eyes, concentrated on their beauty. Their inner circles were gold, like metal melted down; the next circles were yellow, the yellow of pale sunlight; and the last and widest circles were almost an orange-yellow like the petals of a marigold. I gave to my eyes the wonder that I saw before me, so that Adair turned his face full to me, and his coldness thawed a moment before anger returned. "Do you think to win with seduction what Doyle could not win with magic?"

"I thought we were supposed to be seducing each other. Isn't that what the queen wants?"

Adair frowned at me, clearly puzzled. It wasn't that he was stupid, but more that he wasn't accustomed to people simply agreeing with his arguments. Most people weren't.

"I . . . yes . . . The queen wishes two of the four of us to bed you before you come before her."

"Then don't we need for the ring to recognize at least two of you?" I kept my voice very matter-of-fact, but I stepped in closer to him, so close that a hard thought would have closed the distance. I could feel his body now, not the flesh of it, but the vibrating energy of it, like a line of warmth just above my own. Even through my clothes, even through my shields, and his, I felt his magic like a trembling thing. It nearly took my breath, and it puzzled me. With most of the sidhe, they had to be manifesting power on purpose to feel like this against my skin. Then I realized that vegetative deities were often fertility deities as well. I could boast, or complain, of five different fertility deities in my lineage, but I'd never lain with anyone who had once been worshiped as one.

His body reacted to the power that shivered between us even as he closed his eyes and fought to not react. But it was like, well, a force of nature. There were precious few fertility deities, fallen or otherwise, among the Unseelie; that was a Seelie court power for the most part. My father, Essus, had been an exception, but even he was not a fertility of sex and love but more of sacrifice and crops.

I found enough air to speak, but it was on a whisper that I said, "When the time comes, make sure we do not bring down the walls."

Doyle's voice came from behind me like molasses, slow and dark: "What are you going to do?"

"What Adair wants me to do."

Adair looked at me then, and his eyes held pain, but it was a pain born of desire. He wanted to unleash the power that vibrated between us, to unleash it and let it spill between us, over us. Like me, he had not felt the rush of another's magic that so mirrored his own in a very long time.

I was not such a fool as to believe it was the sight of me that filled his eyes with such need. It was the power that trembled and beat like a third pulse between us. I'd been near Adair before and never felt so much as a twinge of such things. Only two things, perhaps three, had changed. One, he was nude, and he was one of the guards who did not participate in the casual nudity of the court or the casual teasing. He seemed to believe, as had Doyle and Frost once, that if there was no release then they did not wish to play. I stood there, wanting to close that last inch of distance between us and near afraid to. So much power already, what would it be like to touch his skin, to let my body sink in against that power, and the power that lay in the muscles and meat of him.

I put my hands out to either side of his waist, against the slick black stone of the door. Even that cold touch could not cool the rising power between us. His body was no longer ignoring me, but standing firm and solid, tight against his own stomach, though he lay a little to one side, a graceful, thick curve instead of the straightness I'd become accustomed to.

I raised my gaze back up until I found his eyes again. With every other tricolored iris each individual shade burned brighter, but as Adair's power spilled through his eyes, it was as if the colors became one, the golden yellow of sunshine. His eyes were simply yellow light, as if two tiny, perfect suns had come to rise in his face.

It took him two attempts to whisper, "Princess."

The power breathed and writhed between us, as if our two magicks were a line of air, one hot, one cold, so that as they mixed, storms would rise. I steadied myself, against the stones and slowly, slowly, began to lean into that warmth.

It was like bathing in power, and I mourned that I wore clothes and could not feel what this was like on my bare skin. But I would not have stopped now, not even to undress. I would not lose an inch of closeness to the trembling heat. A second before my body touched his, Adair said, "The ring . . ."

Our bodies touched, and the magic thrust through us both, tearing a cry from our throats, stripping us of our shields and most of our control. We filled the hallway with shadows. My skin glowed like the moon on the brightest of nights. Adair glowed as if the sun in his eyes had spilled over his skin. It wasn't that he was formed of light, but as if his skin lay just over the light, like a film of water over a fire.

But it wasn't hot, this fire, it was warm. A warmth to keep you safe on a winter's night. A warmth to bring your fields back to life after the long cold. A warmth to drive desire through your body, and all other thoughts from your mind. It was the only excuse I had for forgetting that I had not touched him with the ring. All that had gone before was without the touch of that magic.

I raised my hands to caress the sides of his body, and the ring brushed against him, the lightest of touches, and the world trembled around us, as if the air itself had drawn a breath. Adair began to fall backward. He put one arm around my waist, and the other had a sword naked in it, before his back hit something solid.

We were half standing, half leaning inside a stone alcove. Adair shoved me behind him, so that his tall body blocked most of the opening, and hid me from sight. I stumbled in a small hole and fell back against the limbs of a small dead tree that covered the back of the alcove. The light in our skins had not died away, so that it bounced shadows on the crumbling stone and the rock-strewn hole at my feet. I knew this alcove, but it was floors lower, and had never been near my aunt's rooms.

Doyle's voice came: "You are safe. This is no attack."

"Then what is it?" Adair said, and his voice held a tension that was only a little reassured by Doyle's words.

"The queen's doors moved through the stone as if the stones were water," Barinthus said, "and the alcove appeared behind you."

"You know that the sithen rearranges itself," Doyle said.

"Not this suddenly," Adair said.

Now that I knew I wasn't in imminent danger, I moved my feet, carefully, out of the empty pool. Once it had been a bubbling spring. The story was that the spring had a fruit tree behind it, so that from the outside the tree was small like an apple tree espaliered against the stones, but if you knelt at the spring to drink or lay offerings, then the tree rose above you and there was a glimpse of meadows behind it. Once there had been entire worlds belowground for the fey to live in. Our hollow hills had hidden other suns and moons, and meadows, and pools, and lakes, from the sight of the humans. But all that had been long gone before I was born. I had seen a few rooms full of dead trees, dead grass, long dead and covered with the dust of centuries.

I touched the tree at my back, for the wall ended within my arm's length. The tree was small and pinned against it. The wood was dry and felt lifeless, but a few crumbling leaves clung here and there, and the trunk seemed thick for a tree that was barely taller than I.

There was hardly room for me to stand with a foot on either side of the dry pebbled basin. Adair's back took up almost all the opening, save for a small space above his head. Barinthus would have been too tall to stand inside the stone arch.

The light was pulling back from Adair's body, leaving a wash of red, as if the sun were setting across his lower back and buttocks. The white in my own skin was fading as well, but it was merely the dying of the light. Adair's body held a wash of colors, like the sky itself.

Adair moved out of the alcove, only a step. He was still

close enough for me to touch his lower back. The moment I did, the color flushed deep crimson under his skin, and he let out a strangled cry. That one touch seemed to stagger him, because he groped for the stone wall.

He looked back at me, his eyes swimming down to three golden circles of color, still brighter than they had begun, but they no longer shone like small individual suns. He managed to gasp out, "What did you do to me?"

I could feel his power on my fingertips where I'd traced his skin. Could feel it, heavy and thick upon my fingers, like the heavy blood of trees, but there was nothing to see on my hand, only that sensation of thick liquid. I didn't know what I'd done to him, so what could I say?

I started to reach out to him, to offer the power on my fingers back to him, but something stopped me. Suddenly I knew what I needed to do. I moved to the front of the alcove and knelt inside it, in front of the dry spring bed. There, to the side, hidden in the dry leaves, was a small wooden cup. It was cracked on one side. Cracked with age and disuse.

"Come, Meredith, let us see the queen." It was Barinthus's voice.

Doyle said, "Not yet, Barinthus, wait a moment."

"You opened the door while I was distracted," Adair said, and his voice held anger again. "It was a trick!"

I held the dirty cup in my two hands, for it had no handle, and my hands were too small to hold it comfortably one-handed. I held it toward the place in the rock where the water had once bubbled forth. I knew exactly where the water should have flowed from. I knew it even though I had never seen it. I touched the cup to the rock, just below the opening.

"There is no water to be had from this place, Princess," Adair said.

I ignored him and held the cup against the rock. I sent the power on my fingers into that small dark opening, spread it on the crack like invisible jam, so thick, so rich. I knew in that instant that it had been meant for another more real liquid to be spread upon it. But this would do; this, too, was part of Adair's essence. Part of his power, his maleness. Male en-

ergy to touch the opening in the rock, like the opening of a
woman. Male and female to bring forth life.

I called my power, let my skin dance with silver and white
light, and the moment my power touched his where it lay
against the rock, water trickled from the opening, filling the
cracked cup.

Someone said, "The queen is coming."

Adair touched my arm, grabbed it. "You have tricked me!"
He jerked me to my feet, spun me around to face him, and as
he did water spilled out of the cup, into his surprised face,
across his naked chest. The water dripped down his body in
clear, shining lines. He let go of me, eyes wide.

The cup in my hands was formed of white wood, polished
until it gleamed. Images of fruit and flowers covered the
wood, and peeking out of that lovely tangle of vines and
leaves were the faces of men. Not just one green man, but
many, like hidden images in a children's puzzle. A woman's
image graced the other side of the cup, hair flowing like a
cloak down her body. There was a dog on one side of her,
and a tree heavy with fruit on the other. She smiled at me
from the wooden cup. It was a knowing smile, as if she knew
everything I would ever want to know.

Doyle said, voice uncertain, "The queen awaits us inside,
Meredith. Are you ready?"

I knelt back at the alcove and found the water trickling
clear and sweet into the basin. The dried leaves and debris of
years that had filled it were gone. The basin was a roughly
round depression full of water-smoothed pebbles and rocks.
I held the cup underneath the water, and it gave a small gur-
gle, flowing faster, as if eager to fill the cup. When the water
overflowed the cup, running down my hands, in cool fingers,
only then did I stand.

I stood with the cup filled to the brim, more water over-
flowing down my arms, trailing underneath the sleeves of
my jacket. There was energy in the water, a quiet, humming
power. With that inner eye, I could see the glow of power in
that water, and the wooden cup was like a white star inside
my head.

"Who is the cup for?" Doyle asked.

"One who needs healing, though she knows it not." My voice held an echo of the glow in the cup.

"I ask you again, who is the cup for?"

I didn't answer him, because he knew. They all knew. The cup was meant for the Queen of Air and Darkness. The cup would cleanse her, heal her, change her. I knew the cup was meant for her, but I did not know if she would drink it.

Chapter 28

ANDAIS STOOD IN THE CENTER OF THE CHAMBER CARVED OF moonlight and darkness. Her white skin shone as if she'd captured the full moon inside her skin and all its soft radiance spilled out of her. Her hair was a fall of blackest night, except that if I looked at her from the corner of my eye there were pale points of light in her hair, like scattered stars, but when I turned to face her directly, there was only a shimmering blackness, unrelieved by any light, the heart of deepest, emptiest space. The kind of empty darkness that held no warmth, no life.

The triple grey of her eyes glowed, but it was subdued as if lit only by reflected light. Her eyes were light grey storm clouds lit by distant lightning, with no light of their own. That last thick ring of charcoal was like the sky before it fell upon the earth and poured its rage upon us all.

The look in her eyes alone would have stopped me at the door. Her power filled her like some stroke of fate waiting for its victim, making me want to turn around and run. I was still touched by the magic that had revived the spring. The magic that Adair and I, merely touching, had awoken. But that bright, healing spell faded to ashes in my heart with a look from Andais's power-mad eyes. There was nothing sane in them.

I stood barely inside the door, afraid to move, afraid to attract her attention. All the new power, all the new self-discovery, all the newfound joy and love; and I was suddenly back to being a child again. A frightened rabbit huddling in the grass hoping the fox will pass me by. When I swallowed, it hurt, as if my fear meant to choke me. But I wasn't the rabbit that this particular fox was hunting.

Eamon stood on the small platform at the end of the room, the one that was usually curtained off. He was tall and pale, with his fall of ankle-length black hair the only thing that shielded his body from our view. Eamon was one of those who did casual nudity around the court. I'd seen him nude before and, if he survived the night, would again. No, it wasn't Eamon's beauty that sped my pulse. It wasn't even the implements of torture and death that hung on the wall behind him, framing his body like a collage. It was the queen's words, and his answer to them.

"Do you defy me, Eamon, my consort?" Her voice was calm when she asked it, too calm. It matched nothing in the room, not even the expression on her face.

"I do not defy you, my queen, my love, but I beg you. You will kill him if you do not stop this."

A voice called from behind Eamon, "Don't stop, please, don't stop."

"He does not wish to stop," Andais said, and she moved one hand, negligently, bringing my attention to the whip in it. It had been lost against the blackness of her long skirt, so that until she moved it, I had seen nothing. It was like some well-camouflaged snake, hidden until it would strike. The whip made a heavy slithering sound against the floor, as she moved it back and forth. An idle gesture that raised the hair on the back of my neck.

"You told me once that you valued him because he could take so much pain. If you kill him, you will not have him to play with, my queen." I realized that Eamon was standing in front of the alcove in the center of the wall. He was blocking the view of the place where I knew there were chains bolted into the wall. Whoever it was, he was shorter than Eamon's six feet, and could be killed by a mere whip. Most of the fey could be decapitated, pick up their heads under one arm, and strike back at their enemy. They were not easily killed or injured. Who would need to be shielded like this? Who would Eamon risk himself for? No name came to my mind.

There were other guards in the room. They were all nude.
Clothes, armor, weapons lay in a heap at the foot of her bed,
as if she'd lain among the silk and fur, and ordered them all
to strip. Which she may have done, but seeing a dozen of the
sidhe, kneeling, heads bowed, their hair loose and covering
their nudity like robes of many colors, was both a lovely
sight and a disturbing one.

What had happened? What had changed since Barinthus
and the others left the mound and came to fetch me?
Barinthus had said she was getting better; this was as bad as
I'd ever seen her.

I was afraid to speak, afraid to make any noise, for fear
that all that anger would turn in my direction. I wasn't the
only one perplexed about how to proceed, for Doyle stood in
front of me, and a little to one side, as motionless as I was, as
motionless as we all were. Our entrance through the door had
turned her eyes to us, but now that we'd stopped moving, she
had turned all that attention back to Eamon. None of us
seemed willing to risk sharing that attention with him.

She drew the whip out behind her, and there was room
among the kneeling men, room, as if this wasn't the first time
the whip had come snaking back along the floor. Not the first
time that night, nor the twelfth, nor the twentieth. The men
stayed like a strange garden of beautiful statues, so very still,
as the whip whispered back along the floor. The queen sent
the whip forward, using her whole arm, shoulder, back, and
finally lower body. She threw the whip the way you throw a
good punch. Her wrist flicked at the last moment and gave it
that added curl that would make it crack.

It made the sound of a tornado rushing past, and I knew
from hard experience that on the receiving end of that lash,
the sound was even more overwhelming, like standing on the
railroad tracks while the train thunders down toward you,
and you can't move out of the way. Not because you don't
want to, but because you're chained in place.

Eamon could have moved, but he did not. He stood there,
and used that tall, commanding body as a shield for whoever
lay behind him. The bullwhip struck him full across the chest

with a near-explosive crack that overwhelmed the sound of it hitting his flesh. With a small whip you'd have heard the meaty slap of it. But this was her largest whip, the one that looked like a melanistic anaconda, something long enough and thick enough to crush your life out. I feared that particular whip, because I was mortal, and though Eamon's flesh reddened, it did not bleed. I would have bled.

I like rough play, but not the way the queen did it. She played over the edge and down into the abyss. She went places that my body didn't want to go, and couldn't have survived even if I had. I realized in that moment not who was chained to the wall behind Eamon, but what. There were a few humans who lived at our court. Most were not like Madeline Phelps, the publicist. It wasn't a job. They had been chosen hundreds of years ago, and taken to faerie, some willingly, some not. But they stayed willingly now, because if they stepped but one foot outside faerie, they would age and wither and die. It was a sacred trust, the humans you captured. Some were servants, but usually it was something that attracted sidhe attention. Some were stolen for their beauty or musical talent; in Ezekiel's case the queen had admired his ability at torture. You prized them enough to steal them away from the human world. It was illegal now, but once when we had been a law unto ourselves, both courts had done it. But for whatever reason, once they were given a home here, it was considered bad form, a breach of contract, a sin, to take their lives. They were offered a life of immortality without aging, so you could abuse them, but not to the point of killing them. You couldn't steal from them the very thing that had made them willing to come to faerie in the first place.

Once I realized she had a human against the wall, I was almost certain who it was. Tyler was her current human lover. Last time I'd seen him, he'd been a blond with a skater's cut and a real tan. He was barely old enough to be legal. He was also, according to current rumor, a pain slut. If he was enjoying what the queen was doing to him, he'd passed from pain slut to suicidal.

The great black whip came whispering and slithering back along the stone floor. She sent it out behind her among her silent, immobile guards, and it was roaring through the air, cutting like lightning, against Eamon's flesh. The force of it moved his body as if he'd been shoved, but other than a reddish mark, there was no sign it had hurt him.

Andais made a sound low in her throat, almost a growl, as if that did not satisfy her. She let the whip fall to the ground, like some discarded skin, suddenly empty of life.

She raised her pale hand with its carefully painted nails and gestured toward Eamon. He stumbled back and had to catch himself on the rim of the alcove, or he would have fallen in on top of the one he sought to protect. His fingers grew mottled with the effort to keep himself from falling that last inch backward. Her power filled the room like the pressure before a storm, when the air feels solid and hard to swallow. The pressure grew, and grew, until it was hard to breathe, as if my chest could barely lift against her magic. I knew in that one moment that if she wanted to, she could make the air so heavy that you would suffocate, or at least I would; you could not kill the sidhe by mere suffocation.

She squeezed her hand into a tight fist, and Eamon's arms began to shake with the effort of holding himself against the push of her magic. He spoke between gritted teeth: "Do not do this, my queen." His fingertips moved, his grip beginning to break. He dug into the very stone with the strength that had allowed the sidhe to conquer nearly all of Europe. The stone cracked under his fingertips, but he was able to dig himself fingerholds in it. Blood filled those holes, and began to trickle down the rock. He'd sliced open his fingers, but he held his ground.

I struggled to force my chest to rise and fall, but it was as if I were pushing against some great weight. I could not catch my breath. The cup spilled from my hand, and only Galen's hand on my arm kept me upright. I'd never felt her magic like this. Not like this.

She began to walk toward Eamon, slowly, pushing her power before her like some huge invisible hand. I knew from my own experience that the closer she was to you physically, the stronger this particular magic could be.

Eamon began to tremble, and the blood flowed faster, pooling out of the rock, running down in scarlet rivulets. The effort to hold against the force of her magic made his heart race, his pulse beat harder, and that forced his blood to run faster, made it spill out of him.

My vision ran in streamers of grey and white and star-like patterns. Someone else grabbed my other arm, I couldn't see who. My knees buckled, and I sagged in his arms as darkness ate the light. The air was solid, and I could not breathe it. The light went grey, and then I gasped. My breath came in a long ragged cough that doubled me nearly in two, and only other hands kept me from falling to the floor. When the coughing fit passed, the light came back, and I realized the air was cool against my face. I could breathe again. Galen had a double grip on my right arm, and Adair had my left, a hand around my waist, while my legs remembered how to stand.

I thought the queen had left the room, but she hadn't. She was merely standing in front of Eamon, narrowing her magic down upon him. She had concentrated it on a smaller and smaller point until the rest of the room had emptied of her power.

Eamon had kept his grip on the wall, his mouth open wide, but he wasn't gasping, because gasping implies breathing, and I didn't think he was doing that. It was as if she could bring the pressures of atmospheres to bear upon you. She could use the very air as a weapon. I'd always known everyone was afraid of her, but I'd never seen her use her power like this, and for the first time I realized it wasn't just her absolute ruthlessness that kept her in power for over a thousand years. I looked at the faces of the guards, the greatest warriors the sidhe had to offer, and I saw fear on their faces.

They were afraid of her. Truly afraid of her.

Andais laughed, and it was a wild, unnerving sound that promised pain or death.

She'd picked up a blade while I was mostly unconscious. Now she used that blade on Eamon's chest. She sliced at him as if he were a piece of shrubbery that she wanted to clear away. I expected to see blood spraying, but the air was so heavy that it held the blood close. Made it drip slowly, so that she'd made half a dozen wounds before the first began to bleed.

"Lady help us," Doyle said, and his voice sounded so sad, so empty. He was standing almost directly in front of me. I realized that somewhere in her walk toward Eamon, he had moved to block me from her sight. He sighed, and glanced back at the others. There was a look on his face that I'd never seen before.

Rhys sighed back at him. "I hate having to do this."

"As don't we all," Frost answered from my other side.

I found that I had enough breath to speak. "What are you going to do?"

Doyle shook his head. "There is no time to explain." His black eyes were turned away from me, looking at Eamon and the queen. Eamon's chest and stomach were decorated in blood, shallow cuts dripping down his body. There were deeper wounds on his chest that looked like wide scarlet mouths. She'd opened him up on one side of his body so that the white bones of his ribs glittered through the blood.

He repeated, "There is no time," then he was striding toward the queen. Frost followed him, and Rhys followed them both, giving me a backward glance. "It will look worse than it is. Remember, we'll heal."

My pulse was suddenly faster. What were they planning to do? I started forward, but Galen and Adair held my arms. What had been comforting, and supportive, was suddenly a trap. They held me, not so I wouldn't fall, but so I would not follow.

"Let me go, Galen," I said.

"No, Merry, no." But he wasn't looking at me as he said it; his eyes were all for Eamon. Tall, handsome Eamon, being turned into so much raw meat. "They'll be all right." His voice didn't sound as certain as his words.

I looked at Adair. "Let me go."

Adair shook his head. "I will not, Princess. I will stand and I will hold you, so you do not interfere."

Brii said, "You'll stand and hold her, because then you don't have to help." He moved past us in a swirl of yellow hair.

"Help do what?" I asked, and looked from Galen's serious face, his attention all for what was happening against the wall, to Adair, who would not meet my eyes or look at the queen butchering Eamon.

Doyle was close enough to touch the queen now. His deep voice carried. "My queen, we have returned."

It was as if she didn't hear him, as if the world had narrowed down to the blood-soaked blade in her hand, and the body she was cutting.

"My queen." This time Doyle reached out and laid his dark hand on the whiteness of her arm, just above where the blood had begun to run and stain her skin.

She turned on him in a movement almost too fast for the eye to follow. The blade flashed silver, and fresh blood flew in an arc from Doyle's arm.

I said his name before I could think. The queen turned puzzled eyes out into the room, as if seeking my voice, but Doyle stepped into her line of vision, and she slashed at him again. She hit him once more before Rhys moved up a little ahead of him. I couldn't hear what he said, but whatever it was, it was enough. She struck him. Only the twitch of his shoulders showed that it hurt, but he moved backward as if trying to escape the blow. She didn't like that. She came for him in a wild, slashing attack, and Amatheon was suddenly in her way. She opened his arm from shoulder to hand. The blow made him stumble and turn to protect the arm. She drove the knife into his back, and he fell, dropping to his knees. His eyes were wide with pain, and something else: resignation.

"Welcome to the world of the guards, Princess," Adair said. "Welcome to how we keep each other alive. None but the queen and her Ravens have ever witnessed this. You are most privileged." That last held an irony, a bitterness that seemed to cut the very air, as if there were power in it.

A small sound brought my gaze to the guards still kneeling on the floor in a host of bare skin and silken hair. Hair the

color of new-mown hay, hair the color of oak leaves, hair the
color of dragonfly wings in the sun, hair the color of purple
Easter grass, skin that glistened in the light like white metal,
skin that shimmered as if sprinkled with gold dust, skin that
held the richness of fur on its surface like some elaborate tattoo, skin as red as flame, as pink as bubble gum. Even
stripped of their armor, their clothes, their weapons, they
were all different, all so terribly unique. They were the Unseelie sidhe, and stripping them could not make them less.

I wasn't sure who had made the noise, but one pair of eyes
glared up at me through a fall of grey hair—not the grey of
age, but the grey of clouds before a rain. The eyes that stared
up through that long, pooling hair were a swimming green
color, that greenish-yellowish, near gold, that the world
looks just before the might of heaven roars down on your
head. His eyes were the color of the world before it drowns
in a storm. Because that was who he was, Mistral, the master
of winds, bringer of storms. His eyes were as changeable as
the weather, and this swimming green was a sign of high
anxiety. I'd been told that once upon a time, the sky darkened
when Mistral's eyes looked like that.

He caught my gaze, and held it. He told me with his eyes,
his face, that I was just another useless royal. That I stood
there guarded and well while they bled. Perhaps it was just
my own guilt that I read in his eyes. My father had raised me
to believe that being royal meant more than just having
power over people. It meant in a way that people had power
over you, too, because you were supposed to take care of
them. I was in line to be queen, to have the power of life and
death over these men, but here I was hiding. Hiding, and so
afraid I could barely think. The feel of Galen's and Adair's
hands on my arms had gone from an insult to a comfort. I
wanted them to hold on to me. I wanted an excuse not to have
to do anything. I was hiding behind the very people whom I
was supposed to keep safe. I felt the look in Mistral's eyes
like a blow. He knelt on the floor, knelt where the queen had
told him to kneel, probably with the promise that if he moved
he could be chained against the wall, too. That was her usual

threat. I'd once knelt on this same floor until I passed out. I was after all only mortal, and could not kneel for a day and a night. They could. And if she willed it, they would.

I could still hear the sounds from across the room, but I stared at Mistral as if his face were the only thing in the world because if I looked away, I would have to see what was happening. I didn't want to see. I was tired of seeing horrors. But no matter how hard I tried, I could still hear.

Small gasps, the sound of ripping cloth, and that thick, meaty sound that is flesh parting under a blade. It has to be a truly deep wound for that sound, a wound to the heaviest, most vital parts of the body. Finally a sound like spraying water, as if someone had turned on a hose, made me look.

I turned toward that noise, slowly, the way you turn in nightmares. Galen tried to move in front of me. But it was as if he, too, were moving too slowly. I saw Onilwyn's face wide-eyed with surprise. Blood fountained from his neck, spraying out and around like crimson rain. I caught a glimpse of pale spine before Galen's broad shoulders blocked my view.

I looked up at him, saw the pain in those pale green eyes. My voice was a hoarse whisper: "Move, Galen, let me see."

He shook his head, his hair drying into haphazard curls as the ice had melted. "You don't want to see."

"If I am princess here, then you must move. If I am not princess here, then what in the name of all that grows and lives are we doing here?"

It was enough. He moved and I could see what the queen had done to her Ravens, to her men, and to mine.

Chapter 29

SHE WAS HACKING AT FROST. HIS DOVE-GREY SHIRT WAS BLACK with blood. He turned as he fell, and the lower half of his long silver hair clung to his body, scarlet with blood. He fell to all fours, head down. She raised the knife for a two-handed heart strike, and Doyle's arm was there, sweeping her arms away from Frost's exposed back, bringing her murderous attention to himself. His skin and clothing were so dark that it was harder to see the blood that was already on him, but bone glinted white and red on his side, where she'd nearly cleaved him to the heart.

I spoke his name, soft, a whisper. "Doyle."

Andais began to slash at him, and he guarded his body with his arms. Blood flew from him as her blade tried to find bone, tried to find something to kill. It was as if by not allowing her to slash at the main meat of his body, he offended her. Even in her madness, this was not allowed. You did not fight the queen and live. In truth, she could not kill him, but she drove him to his knees with the fury of her blows. The knife was red with blood, the hilt slick with it, so Andais had to change her grip as she drove the point downward. It looked as if all her force was committed to plunging the knife into his chest. He moved his hands to block it, and she moved, like dark lightning, a blur of black and red, and plunged the blade into his face.

The force of the blow spun him around, and I watched his face split from chin to the top of his cheekbone. She could not kill him with the knife she wielded, but she could maim him.

Something inside me changed in that moment. I was still

afraid, so afraid that it sat like something stale and metal on my tongue, but they say that hatred grows out of fear. Well, sometimes so does rage. The fear that had been a small, cringing thing rose inside me, and found it had wings, and teeth, and claws. Hatred, not of Andais, but of the terrible waste of it all. This was wrong. Even if I had not loved these men, it would still have been wrong.

Rhys darted in, took a blow that spurted blood from his arm, but it was as if she had grown tired of playing. These were the best warriors the sidhe could boast, but I watched her move like something liquid, faster than Rhys could follow, as she'd been too fast for Doyle. I realized in that moment that they weren't entirely playing; she was simply better than they were. She was the Queen of Air and Darkness, the dark goddess of battle.

If the Ravens could not stand against her, then what could I do? The men were all faster, stronger, better than I was. There was no weapon here that would aid me, except in getting myself killed. But I could not stand and watch, and do nothing. The anger translated into power, and I could not stop my skin from beginning to glow. The beginnings of power that would be as nothing to Andais.

Galen and Adair looked at me. Galen shook his head, "There is nothing you can do, Merry." His grip tightened almost painfully on my arm. "They won't die."

"No," Adair said in his bitter voice, "we will heal, as we have healed before."

"Not this bad," and it was Mistral's voice, soft, but purring with thunder, so that it called goose bumps up and down my body, and something about it made my skin glow brighter. His strange, drowning deep eyes met mine, and he said, "She's never slaughtered us like this. Something's wrong."

I looked back at Adair and Galen. "Is he right?"

"They'll heal," Galen said, but even he didn't seem sure.

"Mistral speaks truly." Adair looked away from the slaughter, and the face he turned back to me held such pain, and shame. The Ravens came of a tradition in which not to willingly take a death blow meant for your leader was the worst of shames. But that loyalty was bought by being worthy of loyalty. We were not always hereditary rulers; in fact, that was a human idea that we embraced, but once the best of us had ruled, regardless of bloodline, so long as they were sidhe.

Mistral turned his face from me, as if he could see my hesitation written across my face, but he whispered, "Mother help us, for no one else will."

Andais's bare arms were slathered with blood, and as those smoothly muscled arms wove through the air, drops of blood followed them. Not the blood of her victims, but hers. She was bleeding. Bleeding from small wounds at her shoulder, chest, and neck. The Queen of Air and Darkness had wounded her own flesh in her battle frenzy. She feinted at Rhys's body, almost the same move she'd used on Doyle. Her arm flew out in an arc that I both knew was coming and could never have avoided. It was like watching fate strike, no way to stop it.

I screamed his name, "Rhys!" as the blade plunged into his eye, his only eye. She ground the knife into his face as if she'd cut that last blue orb from his flesh.

Amatheon tried to lure her out, but it was as if she didn't see him. She saw nothing but the ruin she was making of Rhys's face, heard nothing but the screams she finally had torn from his throat.

My power came upon me like an invisible dagger spilling into my left hand. The hand of blood, my second hand of power. Always before it had been a thing that caused me pain to use, a pain so intense it doubled my vision, but not this time. This time it came quietly, suddenly, and more completely than I'd ever felt it. I'd used my hands of power, but until that moment I hadn't embraced them. I was human enough to want pretty powers, not some of the most frightening among us. But that was a child's wish, and it fell away from me. I had one of those moments of clear sight when it is as if you can see through to the heart of everything around you.

I didn't have to conjure the smell and taste of blood; the

room stank of it. As if someone had poured raw hamburger on the floor, and we had all stepped in it. The taste not just of blood but of meat clung to the back of my throat.

Barinthus had thrown himself across Rhys, used his back as shield, while she screamed and hacked at him. Rhys had thrown his head back, and his good eye was a red ruin. He was still screaming, wordless, hopeless.

I looked at the wounds in her shoulders, and with Galen and Adair still holding my arms, I simply thought, *Bleed*. Blood trickled out of the wounds on her arms, faster than before, but no one seemed to notice that the queen was bleeding, least of all her. She was too lost in battle lust to notice. I had no hope of slaying her. She was truly immortal. What I hoped was to weaken her, distract her. I could no longer watch and do nothing. I called the blood from her body, and she ignored me. She cut at Barinthus as if she planned on hacking a hole through him; as if she'd crawl inside him and drag Rhys back out the other side.

I had meant to distract her, but that had been a fool's thought. She, who had been a goddess of battle, would not be slowed by a little blood loss. My father's words came back to me: *If you ever stand against my sister, kill her, Meredith, kill her or never lift a hand against her.*

I extended my left hand, palm out, and I let my magic go like letting a bird, long trapped, wing skyward. It felt so good to let it out, to let go, to stop trying to be something I wasn't. This was a part of me, too, this blood. Blood spurted from her arms, and still she did not notice, but some of the men did.

Adair had already let me go and stepped back. I think he didn't want to be too close when Andais awoke from her lust. I think Adair didn't want her to think he'd had anything to do with it.

"Merry, Merry don't." Galen pulled on my right arm, reached across as if he'd take both my arms. I thought, *Bleed*. He jerked back from me with the tiny ice wound on his hand gaping as if I'd cut him with a blade. His eyes were wide, and I saw fear there. Fear of me, or for me, I couldn't tell.

Blood poured down her arms like crimson water, and still she carved at Barinthus's back. I thought at her what I'd thought at Galen, *Bleed,* and the small wound across the front of her body widened as if an invisible knife had cut across her skin. She slowed, hesitated between one blow and another.

I looked at the pure white line of her throat with that tiny bloody point, a bare nick in the skin, but somehow across the room it loomed large in my vision. I could see it so clearly, smell her blood just under that pure skin. I made a fist of my hand, and pictured what I wanted that small wound to do. Her white throat opened like a second mouth, a red ruin of a mouth. I think she would have screamed, but she couldn't. Blood gushed from her body, and she forgot Barinthus. Forgot Rhys. Forgot everything, but turned those tri-grey eyes to me. I saw recognition in those eyes. The air around me grew heavy like the weight of a storm. I screamed, "Bleed for me!"

Blood gushed from her throat, pouring out as if some giant pump were spewing it out of her. If she'd been human, she'd have fallen and died, but she wasn't human. She raised a hand toward me.

Galen threw himself in front of me, and went to his knees, hands at his throat; his mouth opened and closed, but no sound came out. I didn't have time to be horrified, or wonder what she'd done. He'd sacrificed himself so that I could kill her, because in that moment I forgot she was queen, or sidhe, or anything, I simply wanted her to stop. Dead is stop.

My voice came out in a hiss, a sound like a knife being drawn from a sheath, and the only word was *"Blood!"* The power lashed outward from me, and it hit the men along the way, glancing blows, as if an unseen blade sliced along their wounds, spurting blood as the spell passed them.

The queen saw it coming, saw her peril. She clenched her fist and suddenly it was as if the air were solid, and my chest could not rise to breathe. I began to fall, but not before the spell hit her, not before I saw blood pour from her mouth, her nose, her ears, her eyes. I fell to my knees beside Galen's writhing body, but even as my vision clouded grey, dancing with white stars for lack of air, I saw Andais fall to her knees. She stared at me with her blood-rimmed eyes, and I think she said something, but it was lost. My ears were ringing with the silent scream of my body, fighting to breathe. I fell onto my stomach. Even as I died, I fought to watch her.

Andais collapsed like a broken, blood-soaked doll, face-down on the floor. She made no effort to catch herself. She just fell, and blood welled out of her like a scarlet lake spreading out and out.

Darkness ate my vision, and my body fought on the floor against her magic, fought to breathe, and couldn't. I lay on the floor pressed to death by her last spell, and though my body panicked for me, scrambling for air, I wasn't afraid. My last thought before darkness ate my vision blind was, *Good, as long as she can't hurt them anymore, it's good.* Then my body stopped fighting to breathe, and there was nothing but darkness and the absence of pain.

Chapter 30

I STOOD ON A MOUNTAIN LOOKING OUT OVER THE LAND. I could see the land spreading green and rich until it merged with the misty blue of the horizon, like looking out at an emerald ocean of land. I stood for a glorious moment alone on the crest of that great hill, and then I knew that I wasn't alone. Not a sound, or a movement, just the certain knowledge that when I next looked behind me, someone would be there. I expected it to be the Goddess, but it was not. A man stood in the bright sunlight. He wore a cloak that covered his face in shadows and swirled in the sweet wind, hiding his body. One moment I thought I saw broad shoulders, the next not so broad, but slender of waist. It was as if the body the cloak covered changed even as I watched.

The wind streamed my hair back from my face and billowed his cloak around him. It brought with it a scent of forest and field. He smelled of wilderness untamed and of fresh-tilled earth; but overall the rich scent of him was a perfume that was impossible to describe. It smelled, for lack of a better term, masculine. But it was more than that. It was the way a man's neck smells when you are deeply in love and lust. That sweet scent that makes your body tighten and your heart fill. If the cologne manufacturers could have bottled it, they'd have made a fortune, because he smelled like being in love.

He held out his hand to me, and like his body the hand changed even as I walked toward him. The tone of the skin, the size of the hand; it was as if his form swam through many forms, until the hand that took mine was Doyle's dark skin, but when I looked up it was not Doyle's face that I saw in the hood. It was shadows and glimpses of all my men. All who had known my body flew across the face of the God, but the arms that pulled me close were very solid, very real. He pulled me in tight to his body, the cloak streaming around both of us, almost like wings. I laid my face against His chest, wrapped my arms around his waist, and felt utterly safe, as if nothing else would ever hurt me again. It was like being home, the way home is supposed to be but never really is. Peaceful, content, exactly what you need, and everything you ever wanted. It was a moment of perfect peace. Perfect happiness, as if this feeling could go on forever.

The moment I thought it, I knew it could. I could stay here, held in the arms of the God, and I could move on to a place where it was perfectly peaceful, perfectly happy. I could move forward into the waiting peace, but I thought about Doyle, and Frost, and Galen, Nicca, Kitto, Rhys, oh, Goddess save us, Rhys. Had the queen taken his eye and left him blind? That perfect peace hit the shoals of my tears, and could not stand against them.

The arms that held me were just as strong, the chest with its strong heartbeat just as steady, and that pulsing joyfulness still sang through Him. He had not changed, but I had. If I died, what would become of my people? Andais wasn't dead, she couldn't be, and when she woke her wrath would be a terrible thing.

I hugged the feel of this peace and joy to me, I clung to it the way a child clings to a parent when she fears the dark, but I was not a child. I was Princess Meredith NicEssus, wielder of the hands of flesh and blood, and I could not rest yet. I could not leave my people to face the queen's anger without me.

I leaned back enough to look into the face of the God. And I could still not see it. Some say that God has no face, some say He is the face of whomever you love the most, some say He is the face of whoever you need Him to be. I do not know, only that for me, in that moment, He was shadows and a smile. For He kissed me, and His lips tasted of honey and apples. A voice sounded in my head, and it held both the rumbling deep of Doyle and Galen's laughter: "Share this with them."

I woke, gasping, my chest on fire. I tried to sit up, and the pain threw me back to the floor, to writhe, and the writhing hurt so badly I tried to scream, and there wasn't enough air for it.

Kitto's face loomed over me. He whispered, "Mother of God." He was thick with blood from the waist down, and more of it covered his upper body. I didn't remember the queen hurting him. I tried to ask, but just breathing hurt so badly that I couldn't. Every breath felt as if knives were stabbing into me from both sides. It hurt so badly, I wanted to writhe again, but I knew that moving hurt worse, so I fought, my hands scrambling against the floor, fighting to hold myself as still as I could.

The floor was wet, and I knew it was blood. But I didn't remember being this close to all the blood. It was almost as if Kitto read my mind, because he leaned in close and said, "I dragged you into the sidhe blood. The hand of blood can feed on blood." He had to lean in close because there was so much shouting. Men's voices raised. I could only catch fragments from the noise, "Mortal Dread is here . . . She will kill us all . . . madness . . ."

Kitto leaned in close. "Merry, can you hear me?"

I managed the barest of whispers, "Yes." I didn't understand what the fight was about, but I thought I understood what Kitto had meant about the blood. He'd dragged me into the blood to try to heal me. Maybe it had helped, but something was very wrong inside me. It hurt to breathe; it was obscene when I tried to move. The God had given me back my life, but I wasn't healed. Even as I thought it, though, I felt the kiss upon my lips. It tingled as if He'd only that second drawn away. I smelled fresh apples, and when I licked my lips, I could still taste honey.

Galen pulled himself into view, using his hands and arms to drag himself forward so he could look down into my face. He smiled, though his eyes held a shadow of the pain he was feeling. I remembered him writhing beside me, because he'd taken the first rush of Andais's spell. I think she'd broken most of my ribs, and probably done the same to him. I tried to raise a hand to touch him, and found I did have breath enough to scream. My scream cut through the fighting better than any sword. When the echoes of my scream died, a silence as thick and heavy as any I'd ever heard filled the room. Kitto tried to push Galen away, but I fought the pain and reached out enough for Galen to put his hand in mine, and that one touch flowed through me like a soothing balm. Helped me settle back against the floor. Helped me relearn how to breathe, carefully around the pain.

My lips tingled, and it was as if I'd just bitten into an apple. The crisp, mellow sweetness was melting on my tongue. Apples dipped in honey; the taste of it filled my mouth. There was an echo in my head of that voice: *Share it with them.*

"Kiss me," I said.

A look of such pain came into Galen's face. He thought this was a good-bye kiss. I was hoping it wasn't.

He made small sounds as he wormed his way closer to me. I knew that the broken bones were stabbing into him every time he moved, but he never hesitated. He crawled those last few inches to put his face above mine. He laid his lips against mine, so gently, but as my breath eased out into his mouth it wasn't apples and honey I tasted. Galen tasted like the scent of aromatic herbs. I could taste dew, and feel the soft edge of a basil leaf. He tasted of basil, rich and thick and warm. Basil still growing in the earth, leaves flung wide to the sun, and dew upon the leaves.

He drew back just enough to whisper, "You taste like apples."

I smiled up at him. "You taste like fresh herbs."

He laughed, and I saw his face tighten, as if it hurt, then he said, "That didn't hurt." He'd tightened in anticipation of the hurt. He took a deep breath, making his chest rise and fall. "It doesn't hurt." His smile was everything I needed it to be when he said, "I'm healed." He managed to make it both a statement, and nearly a question.

Frost dropped to his knees beside us, one of his hands tucked in tight against his stomach. I thought at first it was his arm that was injured, then I saw something red and bulging pushing around the edge of his hand. Andais had gutted him.

I managed to whisper his name, "Frost."

Galen moved away so that he could be closer to me. Frost touched my mouth with his fingertips. "Save your strength."

I could taste apples again, as if I'd just bitten into one, and dipped it into something thick and sweet and golden. I didn't need a voice this time to know what to do.

Frost moved his fingers back from my mouth, reluctantly, as if he didn't want to stop touching me. I whispered, "Kiss me."

A silver tear spilled from one eye, but he bent over me. The movement was slow and painful, and brought a sound low in his throat. He finally laid himself beside me, one hand still holding in what the queen's knife had spilled, but the other hand touched my hair. The look on his face was so raw, if I'd ever doubted he loved me, the doubt was gone; in that one look, I knew.

He kissed me, delicate as a snowflake, melting on my tongue. It was as if winter had a taste. Not just the crispness of the air with snow on the ground, but as if my tongue licked along some smooth, cold icicle, and snow filled my mouth, and melted down my throat like the sweetest of snow cones. He melted down my throat, and when his mouth moved back from mine, our breaths fogged in the air between us. I realized I could breathe and the sharpest of the pain was gone.

Frost sat up and drew his hand away from his stomach. That frightening red bulge was gone. He smoothed his hand down his stomach and gave me wide surprised eyes.

Doyle was there, kneeling by him. He spread the cloth wide, touching that smooth white flesh. Only when he turned to look full at me did I see the ruin Andais had made of one side of his face. The cheek down to his beautiful lips flapped loose. It was a wound that even a sidhe would need stitches for. Without some guidance, the cheek would heal as it wished, not as you might wish it.

I reached out for him, to share the power of the God, but he moved away, and motioned to someone behind him. I tried to raise up from the ground, to touch him, and the pain lanced through me, forced me onto my back, drove the breath from my body again. I was better, but unlike Frost and Galen, I was not healed.

Two of the guards brought Rhys forward. He sagged between them, and the sight of his face made me cry out. Not in horror, but in pain. Andais hadn't cut out the eye, as the goblins had so long ago, but she had burst it. I could see nothing of that beautiful blue, lost in the blood and the fluid that had rushed down his face. The skin around the eye socket was ringed on both sides with deep, jagged wounds that showed the bone of both skull and cheek. It looked as if she'd tried to cut away the skin from around his eye. Rhys's scar was just a part of him, and I loved every inch of him, but this . . . This was a ruin of him. He was well and truly blind. The queen had made sure he would not heal this, not with his own body's abilities. Not with any magic we had left to us.

I looked up into his face, and felt rage such as I had seldom known. Rage at the waste of it. So useless, so pointless. I didn't ask why, because there was no answer. The why was simply because, which was no answer at all.

I understood now why Doyle had drawn away and motioned for Rhys to come forward. I'd never before been able to heal with my kiss. If the ability did not last, Rhys needed it more. Doyle would scar, but he would still be Doyle. Rhys's injury was the sort to unmake a man, or remake him into someone else.

Andais's untouched guards were on either side of him, and I had a moment of anger that they had done nothing to stop this.

They helped Rhys kneel, but when he felt my hand, he recoiled. "Don't touch me, Merry, don't look."

It was Kitto, still kneeling in the cooling blood, who said,

"She has returned from the Summerlands with the kiss of birds inside her."

Rhys moved that blind face, as if he'd look at Kitto. "I do not believe you."

I actually did not know the term *kiss of birds*, but I'd ask questions later. "Come to me, Rhys, and let me prove it."

Doyle pushed the others back, and it was he and Frost who guided Rhys to me. His face was covered in blood, but I did not shrink from it or try to brush it away. It was just another part of Rhys. His lips were salty with it. His lips touched mine, but he did not kiss me. I had to put my hand at the back of his neck, and the movement made me gasp.

He drew back, or tried to; only Doyle and Frost's hands kept him from moving away. "She is injured, too," Frost said, "raising her hand to the back of your head caused her pain. It was not a gasp at your appearance." And Frost had said exactly what needed saying. Because Rhys stopped trying to pull back.

"How badly is she hurt?"

"Kiss me, Rhys, and I'll feel better."

This time he came to me, and didn't make me move more than necessary. This time when our lips met, he kissed me back, and it seemed to need both of us to be willing. For that one shared kiss was as if home had a single taste, as if the smell of fresh bread, clean laundry, wood smoke, laughter, and something warm and thick bubbled on that fire. Rhys didn't taste like any particular food, but his lips held the essence of all that was good and made you feel content, sated, happy.

I raised my hands up to hold him, without thinking, but the pain it caused rode away and vanished on the sensation of him. He drew back at last, and I clung to him, for I wanted more of that taste. I opened my eyes.

Rhys blinked down at me. That circle of robin egg blue, winter sky, cornflower blue, looked down at me. I was lost between laughter and tears, staring up at him in silent wonder.

"Goddess be praised." He whispered it so low, I don't think anyone else heard.

"Consort be praised," I said, in a whisper back to only him.

He smiled then, and something inside me loosened at the sight of it; a tightness I hadn't known was there went away. If Rhys could smile like that, everything would be all right.

Rhys moved away, and I took Doyle's wrist. I intended him to be next, for I did not know how long this blessing would last. He shook his head. I opened my mouth to insist, but Mistral appeared, carrying Onilwyn in his arms. I knew that Mistral and Onilwyn were not friends, but in this moment the guards seemed united in a way that was beyond friendship, or whom you like and whom you hate. Onilwyn's head lay backward at an odd angle, the muscles holding it in place severed. His spine was a glistening whiteness in the fearsome wound that had once been his neck. The front of his clothing was blue-violet with his own blood. His pale skin the color of wheat, green and fresh from the earth, had been bleached to a sickly greenish white. Only the wide staring of his green-and-gold eyes let me know he was indeed still alive. Andais had slit his throat so completely that his breath whished and hissed, and gurgled wetly through the top of his severed windpipe. If he'd been human his throat would have collapsed under the damage, but he wasn't human, so he still breathed, still lived, but whether he could heal from such a terrible wound depended on how much personal magic he still had left. There was a time when the gods themselves blessed all of us, made of us saints able to withstand a decapitation, but that had been centuries ago. Not all of us could heal such damage now.

There was the very real possibility that Onilwyn would linger for days, but in the end, he would die. He was not a man whom I would have wasted such blessing from the God upon, but I also didn't have it in me to turn away from him. He was still one of my people. He had risked all to help save the others.

I met Doyle's gaze, and I let go of his wrist, slowly, reluctantly, but he was right. He could live and heal his wounds. Onilwyn could not.

Mistral knelt carefully, on the blood-slick floor, and started to lay Onilwyn down beside me. But too much blood had gone down his windpipe and he was choking, and trying to clear it, using nothing but the muscles of his stomach and chest. He made a horrible wet rattling sound, then blood spat out of the end of his neck, and he took the faintest of breaths, as if afraid that more blood would flow back down.

Goddess help us.

"I don't think he'll do well on his back," Mistral said, and his voice tried for neutrality, but failed. He was angry, and I couldn't blame him.

"No." I tried to sit up, but the pain took my breath and laid me back on the bloody floor. I waited until the pain had subsided, then said, "Kitto, help me lean up."

He looked to Doyle before he did it, and when Doyle nodded, Kitto moved in behind me, but Galen was already there. "Let me, Kitto, she healed me, let me help her."

Kitto nodded and moved back.

Galen lifted me, gently, into his lap, so that my head and shoulders were cradled against his body. It didn't hurt too badly. "A little more," I said.

He did what I asked without looking at Doyle first. I was almost sitting up, fully supported by his body, before the pain came, like a knife, but it was a duller blade than last time. I could bear it. "There, just there." Galen went very still behind me.

"Wait." It was a woman's voice, so it must have been the queen, but it did not sound like her. "Wait," the voice said again, and the one word was pain-filled.

After what she had done to them, to all of us, a body would think none of us would have listened to her, but we did. We should have cursed her, but we didn't. We froze, waiting for her to make a slow progress across the room.

Mistral had moved back, just enough to let me see across the room. The floor was marked by a wide red path as if a heavily bleeding body had been dragged across it. That bloody path ended at the queen. She sat, propped against the wall. She had pulled Eamon into her lap, and I had never been so aware of what a large man he was, or perhaps she seemed smaller. His broad shoulders seemed to overwhelm her. She was a tall woman, and she always filled more space than just the physical, but now she sat with Eamon in her arms, and one arm wrapped around Tyler's naked, blood-soaked leg, and she seemed small.

But she had healed. Her neck wound had been almost as severe as Onilwyn's, but where he was still a broken thing, she had only a hand-sized gash in her white throat. The wound seemed to be growing smaller, even as we watched. Not visibly, not like we could actually see the wound closing, but like trying to watch flowers bloom. You knew it was happening, but you just couldn't catch it actually happening before your eyes. She was our queen and that meant that the power of the sidhe ran stronger through her than through any of us.

I looked back at Onilwyn, who lay in Mistral's arms like some huge broken doll, then back to our queen with her nearly healed throat. Anger warmed me. If what Adair had said at the beginning of all this was accurate, then she had been abusing the guards for centuries. How could she treat such a gift so badly?

"Wait," she said, again, and I saw something that I never thought I'd see, tears. The queen was crying.

"Heal Eamon first, and Tyler."

We all looked at her. I'd really thought she'd ask for her own injuries first. The queen did not share magic, she hoarded it. Taranis, the king of the Seelie Court, was the same way. It was almost as if they both feared that someday the magic would run out, and they knew that to rule here, you needed magic.

I wanted to say no, but Amatheon spoke before anyone else. "Yes, my queen." His voice was tired, and thick with something like grief. He walked, stiffly, to a point between the two groups of us, the queen with her injured lovers, and me with mine. Technically, Onilwyn and Mistral weren't mine, but somehow it felt very much as if everyone on this side of the room was not on her side.

Amatheon was still cradling the arm she'd cut open. The back of his coat was so blood-soaked it had glued itself to the back of his body like a second skin. "Bring the princess," he said.

"She is too injured to move," Galen said.

"As the queen bids," Amatheon said, "so we must do. Bring the princess." Perhaps he was too tired and in too much pain to control his face, because a fine, deep rage sparkled in those flower-petal eyes. But after the show Andais had just put on, it wasn't merely fear of losing his beautiful sidhe hair that made him willing to simply obey her.

Galen repeated, "Merry is too hurt to move."

"We can bring Eamon to the princess." Frost's voice was neutral, his face an arrogant mask.

"No," the queen said.

Galen bowed his head over me. He whispered, "No, no more."

Rhys looked at her with his renewed eye. "Merry needs a healer before she is moved."

"I know that," the queen said, and there were the first stirrings of anger in her voice. Old times, rearing their ugly head.

Galen leaned over me enough to hide my view. "I won't let her hurt you again."

He was too close for me to look in his eyes; I had to be content with the smoothness of his cheek, the fall of his hair. "Don't do anything foolish, Galen, please."

"My queen, do you need help?" This from Mistral.

Galen drew back enough so I could see. The queen who had looked small and dwarfed beside Eamon was standing with the larger man in her arms. Even hurt, she carried him easily, although he had to be almost twice her body weight. She was tall enough, long enough of arm, to cradle him. She was sidhe, and that meant she could have picked up a small car. It was that she was willing to carry him that made us all stare.

She spoke to no one and everyone. "Take Tyler down, gently, and bring him, too." She carried Eamon toward me, and cried as she came. If it had been anyone else I would have said, *She grieved.*

She knelt beside me and stumbled as she did it, managing

a wry smile. "You sliced me up, niece, and you did a good job of it."

I took it as the compliment I thought it was meant to be. "Thank you."

She knelt beside me, cradling Eamon in her arms. "Heal him for me, Meredith."

Eamon's body was a mass of bloody stab wounds, so many that his chest looked like tenderized steak. His heart had to have been pierced multiple times, but he was sidhe, and his poor heart kept beating, even cut up. There didn't seem to be an inch of his chest undamaged, as if he wore a shirt of blood and meat.

She made a small sound, almost a sob. "Nuline came, and we shared wine, and she left, and I went mad."

I fought to keep my face blank, because Nuline was one of Cel's royal guards. To accuse the prince's guard was almost the same as accusing Cel himself of the poisoning. They did nothing without his orders, for fear of what he would do to them. If Andais was a sadist, then you needed a new word for Cel. None of them would dare risk Cel's displeasure. None of them would poison the queen without Cel's permission, or at least believing they had it. Had he given the order from his dark prison?

Doyle spoke carefully with his ruined mouth. "I smell no poison."

"There are other ways to use your nose, Darkness," she said.

He leaned in toward her face, slowly, painfully. When he was an inch or less from her face, he sniffed the air. "Magic," he whispered. He very carefully licked her cheek, but the movement seemed to hurt him. He drew back. "Bloodlust."

She nodded.

"If it was in the wine, then why isn't Nuline here, butchered or butchering?" Amatheon asked.

"She is a thing of spring and light. There is no bloodlust to call in her," Andais said. The queen looked at me, and those tri-grey eyes were full of a sorrow that I hadn't known Andais was capable of. "They were very clever." She said, *they*. Would she make that logic jump to Cel? Or would she do what she had always done, and find a way for it not to be his fault?

"I had not felt such a rush of battle madness for centuries. It felt so good. Every wound, every harm I caused made the bloodlust grow. I'd forgotten how amazingly good it felt to slaughter, not for effect, or information, or to invoke fear, but simply for the love of it. Whoever did the spell knew my powers, intimately." Andais reached out a bloodstained hand toward me. "Heal my Ravens, and I will slay Nuline."

"Only Nuline," I said.

"I will slay the one who did this to me." Her voice was firm, but there was a wariness in her eyes. She knew what I meant. "Heal my Ravens, Meredith." Her hand touched my arm, and that one touch echoed through me. Made the magic that the God had placed inside me ring like a great bell. Andais must have felt it, for she looked wide-eyed at me.

Galen whispered, "What was that?"

Doyle spoke carefully through his ruined mouth. "The God's call."

I heard the voice in my head: *All power comes from the head.* I understood then, or hoped I did. The reason that the Unseelie couldn't have children was that Andais couldn't have children. The reason our magic was fading was that Andais's magic had begun to fade. She was our queen, our head.

I looked up into her startled face, and said the words I had to say: "Come, Aunt, let us embrace."

She leaned over me, and the look on her face was almost unwilling, as if she was as caught up in the magic as I. She was my aunt, my father's sister, and had known me since birth, but in all those years she had never kissed me.

The press of her lips was like touching the skin of some delectable fruit, where the skin lies thin and ripe against your mouth. The scent of ripe plums filled my senses as if I could drink it out of the very air, or sip it from her lips. My mouth was pressed to hers, and I opened to it as if I would take a bite from the ripeness of her mouth.

The sweet taste of her stirred the magic, woke it like heat

to rise up, up inside me, to spill shimmering and burning along my skin. The heat melded into the honeyed sweetness of the fruit, and I could feel the summer sun caressing the thick, glowing skins of the plums as they hung heavy on the tree. The heavy summer heat clung to our skin, filled the world with the drowning scent of fruit, so ripe, so heavy that it was ready to burst its thick silken skin, ready to give up its meat to the sun's caress and the drowsy hum of bees. The fruit held itself in a perfect moment of readiness, the breath of absolute perfection. One second more and it would fall from the tree, ruined; one second less and it would not be the sweetest thing to ever touch mortal mouth.

I came back to myself in the blink of an eye. I opened my eyes and found Andais like some silver dream, shining so bright that she made nests of shadows around everything in the room. And I realized that it wasn't just her who made shadows quiver through the room. I'd seen my skin glow like moonlight, but never like this. It was as if my skin were filled with a white, almost silver fire of burning magnesium. A flame so clear and pure that it would blind if you gazed too long.

Andais and I were like two entwined stars, one white and one silver, both bright enough to blind. But I wasn't blinded. The glow didn't hurt my eyes. I could see her face like a floating thing, eyes closed. I had to pull back to see her lips like carved garnets lost in the cool, silver fire.

Her eyes blinked open, slowly, as if she had been asleep. The moment she opened those eyes the swirling grey in them eased out, like the breath of a dragon, soft and clinging as mist. There were things in that mist, things I didn't want to see. The hair on my body raised with the nearness of half-seen images, my skin crawling, shivering with those fleeing shadows. Fear tightened my throat, and I realized in that moment that we were both kneeling beside each other. I couldn't see anyone else through the mist of her eyes. I held her in my arms while her eyes bled mist into the twin glows of our power.

The mist smelled damp, dank, but over it all I could still smell the scent of fruit, perfect, waiting. Waiting to yield its sweetness in that one perfect moment when the world held its breath and waited for the hand that would touch this perfect woman, this perfect offering, and give her the glory she was due. Even as I thought, I knew I was God-ridden. But with the God's power filling me, she was beautiful. Hair of raven's wings, eyes of mist and shadow, skin formed of starlight and moon's brightness, lips the color of heart blood. It was a terrible beauty, something that would call to your body and make your heart cry. I knew also that if my magic had been different, there would have been different fruit upon this tree, and I was glad that I could call the Seelie Court to my blood.

The God rode over me, and I was back to the perfect moment when even a breath would spoil all, and there was only one thing to do. You honored the gift.

I kissed those crimson garnet lips, and found my own lips were like deep, red rubies, like melding two separate jewels. I felt my hands cupping the sides of her face, and found the bones of her face delicate, fragile under my hands. My hands were smaller than hers, they had to be, but for this moment they were large enough to cup her face and hold it, gently. I became for that moment the sun, all that was male, all that was the best of what it meant to be male, at his height of prowess, the Summer King, Lord of the Greenwood. I kissed her as she was meant to be kissed, gentle, firm, held in hands larger than my own, held in a strength greater than her own, and the more tender for that, the more careful for it. I kissed her as if she would break. Then she pressed into the kiss, her power spilling through my mouth, and the kiss grew into something less cautious, more sure of itself. At the invitation of her lips, her eager hands on my body, the power of the greenwood rode through her, pierced her. She tore her mouth from mine and cried out.

Our powers fell into each other, and for a few shining moments the glow of silver and white merged until there was but one glow, one fire. It wasn't her face I saw. This face was young, with thick brown hair and laughing eyes: the next face was red-haired and green-eyed; then hair like clean white cotton and skin almost as pale. Woman after woman slid before my eyes, and I felt myself change, too. Taller, shorter, broader, bearded, dark of hair, pale of skin, dark of skin. I was many men, all men, no man. I was the Lord of Summer, and I had been always. And the woman before me was my bride, and always had been. It was the eternal dance.

The first thing I noticed that was of this world and not the next was that my knees hurt. I was kneeling on stones. The second was the woman who was holding me, stroking my hair. She held me so close that I could feel her smaller breasts pressed against mine.

Andais smiled down at me, and she looked younger, though I knew that wasn't exactly it. Her eyes were bright, and her dark red lips smiled down at me, because kneeling she was still taller.

"Are you healed?" she asked.

The moment she asked, I realized that I'd forgotten I was hurt, but I took a deep breath and felt . . . fine. No, better than fine. "Yes," I said.

Her smiled brightened into something close to a grin. Andais did not grin. "Look at what our magic has wrought." She gestured out at the room. Onilwyn knelt, eyes a little dazed, but his throat was white and perfect once more. Eamon was sitting up, and there were no more holes in his chest. Doyle turned a perfect face to me, and gave a nod, almost a bow.

"They're all healed."

Tyler, the human whom she had nearly killed, was laughing and crying beside Mistral. I think he spoke for us all when he giggled and said, "That was absolutely the most amazing feeling. It was like being light."

I looked back at Andais. There was a look in her eyes that was disquieting, calculating, and something else, something new. I realized she was still holding me very close. I tried to move back, and her arms tightened, kept our bodies pressed together. I was no longer God-ridden. I was no longer a match for her in strength, or anything else.

The smile she gave me was one I'd only had from lovers, and it prickled down my skin to see it on her face.

"If you were a man I would take you to my bed for this night's work."

I wasn't sure what to say, but knew I had to say something. "Thank you for such a compliment, Aunt Andais."

She cocked her head to one side like a hawk that's spied a mouse. "Reminding me that you are my niece will not keep you out of my bed, Meredith. We are like most deities, we often intermarry, or interfuck." She laughed then, and it was a better, more purely amused sound than any I'd ever heard from her. "The look on your face." She laughed again, and let me go.

She stood, and stretched, and even that small movement prickled power along my skin. "I feel so very much better." She looked down at me and offered me her hand.

I took it and let her help me to my feet. She kept my hand in hers, giving me very serious eyes. "Come, Meredith, let us go kill the traitor who tried to bespell her queen. Doyle tells me we have an assassin to find as well."

I wondered then how long I'd been insensible. All I said out loud was "As my queen wills it."

She pulled me suddenly and roughly against her, putting my arm behind my back with her hand still holding it. "I am grateful, Meredith, very grateful for this gift of magic, but do not misunderstand. If I think that by bringing you into my bed I can recall that magic, I will. If I think that by sending you to anyone's arms, that level of magic can be reborn, I will send you. Is that clear?"

I swallowed and took a deep breath before I answered, "Yes, Aunt Andais, it is clear."

"Then give your auntie a kiss."

What else could I do? I put a light kiss upon those lips, and she slipped her arm through mine, patting my hand as if we were the best of friends. "Come, Meredith, let us go slay our enemies."

I'd have been a lot happier to accompany her to the throne room if she hadn't kept touching me. It wasn't so much a lover's touch, but almost like you'd pet a dog. Something you stroke for comfort, and because it can't say no.

Chapter 31

WE GOT ONLY AS FAR AS THE SPRING. IT BUBBLED AND SANG among the stones. The queen dropped to her knees before it. "I have not seen this water flowing in nearly three hundred years." She gazed up from her knees. "How did it come to be here?"

The men turned and looked at me. The look was more eloquent than any words.

"This is your doing, is it?" she asked, and her voice held an unfriendly purr, as if we were no longer best friends.

Eamon, who had stayed close to her side since his miraculous healing, laid a hand on her shoulder. I expected her to toss his gesture away, but she didn't. Her shoulders rounded under his touch, her head almost bowing. When she raised her head, there was a smile on her face more tender than any I'd ever seen before.

She asked her question again, in a voice that matched that smile, but all the attention of her face was for Eamon. "Did you bring the spring to life, niece?"

It was a trickier question than she meant it to be. If I said yes, then I was claiming more credit than was my due. "I and Adair."

The gentle look left her face as she turned to me. "You must truly be a wondrous piece of ass. One quick fuck and he risks his life for yours."

I was puzzled by most of what she'd said, but concentrated on the latter part. "If he fucked me, it was on your orders. The punishment of death for breaking his celibacy no longer applies. The guards were always allowed to fuck if the queen wills it."

Some of her anger faded to a look I couldn't decipher, as if she was thinking. I remembered Barinthus's words that her mind was harder to keep distracted than her groin had been. "You did not see Adair's heroics, then?"

I looked at her, fighting to keep my face neutral. "I don't know what you mean, Aunt."

"When you bled me, after Galen had taken some of my sting, Adair threw himself in my path as well." She didn't look pleased. "As I said, you must fuck like a courtesan. Bloody fertility goddesses, always think they're so wonderful."

I wasn't sure if admitting Adair and I hadn't had sex would please her or enrage her. So I said nothing. Apparently, Adair and all the others who had witnessed thought the same thing, because no one spoke up.

Eamon's hand squeezed gently on her shoulder. She patted his hand, but said, "Adair, come to me."

The guards parted and Adair came to the front to stand beside me. He risked a glance at my face, then dropped to one knee before the queen. His head was bowed so his face was hidden from her. It was the proper thing to do, but I'd seen the anger in his eyes before he knelt. He had to master his face better than that or he would not last at court, any court.

I looked down at where he knelt, golden and perfect except for the lack of hair. He was immortal, and had once been a god, and had risked all that to help me. The queen had promised me that all the Ravens I took to my bed would be mine. My guards, and no longer hers. Technically, she couldn't harm him, not if she believed we'd had sex. Of course, the same was true of Doyle, Galen, Rhys, Frost, Nicca, and, though she did not know it, Barinthus. But her promise had not kept my true guards safe. In fact, crazy or not, bespelled or not, that she had harmed them meant she was forsworn. I'd promised to keep them safe, and by dying to prove it, my promise stood. Hers was broken. She was an oathbreaker. Sidhe had been cast out of faerie for such things. The problem was that the only person who could hold her to that level of faith, was her.

"Galen and Adair took blows meant for the princess. The princess's own guard took blows meant for Eamon and Tyler." A look like pain crossed her face, and she held on to Eamon's hand where it lay on her shoulder. "I am grateful that Merry's men saved me from destroying that which I hold dear. But none of the Ravens threw themselves in Merry's way. No guard of mine tried to help me, once battle was joined, even though it was not a declared duel. Only a declared duel would have freed my guard from protecting me."

Mistral dropped to his knees on the other side of her, though I noticed that he was just out of reach. Not that that would truly help if things went badly. "You ordered us to kneel, and not to move, my queen. On pain of joining your human against the wall." He gave her a look that was a mixture of appeal and anger. "None of us would risk your anger."

"But that is not all, Mistral. That, I could forgive. I heard others talk of slaying me. Of taking my own sword Mortal Dread and killing me before I awoke. I heard the treacherous talk."

I remembered snatches of conversation myself. This line of reasoning could end nowhere that I wanted us to go. But how to distract her? Doyle's deep voice fell into that nervous silence. "Should we not attend to Nuline, who is truly traitor to the courts, before we place blame for loose talk?"

"I say who and what we attend to first," she said.

Eamon knelt beside her, and even kneeling he was bigger than she. I'd never appreciated before how broad his shoulders were, how physical his presence was. He whispered something against the side of her face.

She shook her head. "No, Eamon, if they will not protect me, and would rather see me dead, then they may turn and join our enemies. We will be besieged on two fronts. You must never leave an enemy behind you."

"Is it not better to fight a war on one front, rather than two?" I asked.

She looked up at me, befuddled. I didn't know if it was the aftereffects of the spell, or something else, but she wasn't herself.

"It is always better to fight a war on a single front, instead of two," she said, at last. "That is why the traitors before me must die first."

"The spell was meant to make you butcher your guards," I said, the way you'd talk to a slow child. "If you execute them now, you will be doing exactly what your enemies wish."

She frowned at me. "There is logic in what you say. But talk of murdering your queen cannot go unpunished."

"And what is the penalty for being forsworn among us?" I asked.

"An oathbreaker," she said.

"Yes."

"Death or banishment from faerie," she said, and her voice was very sure, but her eyes held something. Either she saw the trap or she was worried about something else.

"You swore to me that all the men who came to my body would be my guards, the princess's bodyguards, no longer Queen's Ravens."

She frowned at me. "I remember."

"You also promised that no harm would come to them without my permission, just as no harm can come to your guards without your permission."

She frowned harder. "Did I promise you that?"

"Yes, Aunt Andais, you did."

She looked down at the bubbling spring. "Eamon, did you witness this promise?"

Eamon looked up at me, and something in his eyes let me know he was about to lie. "Yes, my queen, I did." Eamon had not been in the room when Andais made the promise. He had lied for me. No, not for me, for all of us.

Andais sighed. "The queen's promise must be inviolate." She stood and looked down at me. "I am forsworn, Princess Meredith, but I am also queen here. We have a quandary upon our hands."

"Since the promise was made to me, then the wrong was done to me."

"So you may forgive it," she said, "but I assume that this forgiveness comes at a price." The eyes were watchful, and there was a warning in them that I could not read. There was something she was afraid I would ask, and she did not wish to give it.

"I am blood of your blood, Aunt. How could it be otherwise?"

"And what is your price, niece of mine?"

"A price for each of my men that you injured."

"Blood price then," she said.

"It is my right."

Her face was as closed and guarded as I'd ever seen it. "And what blood would you demand?"

"Blood price can be paid in other coin," I said.

A look slid through her eyes, almost of relief, then she nodded. "Ask."

"Any guards who spoke of Mortal Dread are to be forgiven. All are allowed to arm themselves before we go to the throne room. And we show a united front before the rest of the court until the would-be assassins are caught and executed."

She nodded. "Agreed."

The guards put back on their armor, some of which looked like the pelts of animals or the hard shiny coats of insects, and some of the more knightly-looking armor came in colors that no human-wrought steel could have achieved. The queen went to the wall and touched the stones. A piece of the wall vanished, and there was nothing but darkness in its place. The queen reached into that darkness and drew out a short sword whose hilt was formed of three ravens with their beaks holding a ruby nearly the size of my fist, and their wings flung outward in silver to form the guard. The sword's name was Mortal Dread, and it was one of the last great treasures left to the Unseelie Court. This weapon of all our weapons could bring true death to the sidhe. A mortal wound with its blade was mortal for all. It could also pierce the skin of any fey, no matter its magic, or what substance it called flesh.

She turned to me with the sword in her hand, and I did not fear, for she had no need of such magic if she meant to slay me. She stared down at the blade, letting it catch the light. "I am still not myself, Meredith. My mind is half besotted with the effects of the spell. I have not allowed myself such a surrender to slaughter in centuries. Such should only be used against one's enemies." She looked up, and there was sorrow in her eyes. A heavy knowledge. She knew that none of Cel's guard would have dared such a thing without his knowledge, if not his approval. He had not said, *Kill my mother,* from his jail. No, it would be more along the lines of, *Will no one rid me of this inconvenient woman?* Something where, if questioned, he could truthfully deny the order. Deny knowing that they would take his words of anger and make them real. But it was a game of words, and half-truths, and lies of omission. The look in her eyes was of someone who could no longer afford half-truths.

"I feared for my son's sanity, Meredith." Her voice held a note of apology. "I allowed one of his guard to go to him and slack the lust of Branwyn's Tears before he went mad."

I just looked at her and my face showed nothing, because I didn't know what I felt in that moment.

"You allowed one of his guard to slack his lust, to save his mind, and that very night another of his guard gave you a spell that would drive you to slaughter your most powerful protection."

Her eyes were frightened. "He is my son."

"I know," I said.

"He is my only child."

I nodded. "I understand."

"No, you do not. You will not understand until you have children of your own. Everything before that is pretense of sympathy, a dream of understanding, a nightmare of things you think you believe."

"You're right, I have no children, and I don't understand."

She held Mortal Dread up to the light, as if she could see more in its slender surface than was there for me to see. "I am still not sane. I can feel the madness inside me now, can feel what I've become. I've felt this feeling before, but now I wonder if my love for seeing the blood of others has had help. Help for years, perhaps."

I didn't know what to say to that, so I said nothing. Silence was good when anything you said could be taken so wrong.

"I will see Nuline dead, and the ones who are behind the attack on you, my niece."

"And if they are the same people?" I asked.

Her eyes flicked to me. "And what if they are?"

"You decreed that if any of Cel's people tried to kill me while he was still imprisoned, his life would be forfeit."

She closed her eyes and leaned her forehead against the flat of the blade. "Do not ask me for the life of my only child, Meredith."

"I have not asked."

She let me see that famous anger in her eyes. "Haven't you?"

"I have merely given the queen's words back to her."

"I have never liked you, niece of mine, but nor have I hated you. If you force me to kill Cel, I will hate you."

"It is not me who will force your hand, Queen Andais, it is him."

"They could have acted without his knowledge." Even as she said it, her eyes showed that she didn't believe it. She wasn't crazy enough to believe it anymore.

She looked at me, and something passed through her tri-grey eyes with their rings of black that left each grey darker and richer because of it, as if she had used eyeliner on her own irises.

"Far be it from me to complain if we're talking about killing Cel," Galen said, "but everyone knows that any attempt on Merry while Cel is still imprisoned means a death sentence for him."

"If we can prove his people were responsible," Mistral said.

"But don't you see, Nuline is part of his guard. If Nuline brought the spell, then it must be Cel who sent her—but what if it wasn't?"

"I am listening," Andais said.

"Nuline is like me, she's not good at court politics. She's

not good at deception. What did she say when she brought the wine to you?"

"That she knew it was one of my favorites and hoped its sweet taste would remind me of just how sweet my son could be." Andais was frowning now. "The words do sound like a speech given to her by someone else." She shook her head. "I am the Queen of Air and Darkness, I do not fear assassination attempts. Perhaps such arrogance has made me careless." She said it slowly, as if she didn't really believe it.

"People often give her gifts," Mistral said. "It is a way of currying favor."

"One more offering in a wealth of offerings will go unnoticed," Doyle said.

"We need to know where Nuline got the wine," Galen said.

Andais nodded. "Yes, yes, we do." There was something in her voice that I didn't like. It was a purr of hatred. Hatred will blind you to the truth, especially if you want to be blinded. She said, "Bring me my Darkness."

Doyle came at her call, but he stayed by my side. "I am, by your own words, the princess's Darkness now."

She waved it away, as if it meant nothing. "Call whomever you like master, Darkness. I ask only if you can track this spell back to its owner."

"I could not track it off your skin, but the bottle is still here. It is too powerful a spell not to leave a taint, a signature as it were, of the one who made it. If I can smell their skin, taste their sweat, then yes, I can track this to its owner."

"Then do it," she said, and she looked at me as she said the last: "Wherever this trail leads, we will follow, and punishment will be swift."

I looked at her, afraid to believe that she meant what I hoped she meant.

"Heard and witnessed," Barinthus said.

The queen did not look at him, but only at me. "There, Meredith, another oath to hold over my head."

"What do you want me to say, Aunt?"

She took in a deep breath and let it out slowly. Her gaze fled from my face and found a piece of wall to look at, as if she didn't want anyone to read her eyes in that moment. "What would you do, if you were me, niece?"

I opened my mouth, closed it, and thought. What would I do? "I would send for the sluagh."

She looked up then, her eyes very hard, as if she were trying to see through me. "Why?"

"The sluagh are the most feared of all the Unseelie. The sidhe themselves fear them, and they fear little. With the sluagh at your back, as well as your Ravens, no one will try a direct attack."

"You believe someone would dare attack me, us"—she motioned at the waiting knights—"head-on?"

"If the spell had gone its course, Aunt Andais, you would have slaughtered all your guards, and then with no one left to kill in this room, where would you have gone? What would you have done?"

"I would have found others to kill, any others."

"You would have ended in the banquet hall where there are sidhe who would not stand idle while you sliced them open," I said.

"They would have looked for a reason for my behavior," she said.

"I don't think they would. You have slaughtered and terrorized this court for a very long time. What you did here tonight is not that far from things I have seen you do before."

"Before, most of the slaughter had a purpose," she said. "My enemies fear me."

"Slaughter done coldly, and slaughter done in the heat of madness, look much the same when you are on the wrong end," I said.

"Have I been such a tyrant that the entire court would believe this of me?"

The silence in the room was thick enough to wrap around us all. To wrap us and choke us, because none of us knew how to answer the question without either lying, or angering her.

She gave a bitter laugh. "There is answer enough in your

silence." She rubbed at her head as if it ached. "It is good to be feared by your enemies."

"But not by your friends," I said, softly.

She looked at me, then. "Oh, niece of mine, have you not learned, yet, that a ruler has no friends? There are enemies and allies, but not friends."

"My father had friends."

"Yes, my dear brother did have friends, and it's most likely what got him killed."

I fought back that flare of anger in me. Anger was a luxury that I could not afford. "If I had not been here today with the hand of blood, to bleed the magical poison out of your body, you would be dead, too."

"Be careful, Meredith."

"I have been careful all my life, but if we are not bold tonight, then our enemies will see us both dead. Perhaps Cel was even meant to die tonight. To be executed for killing me, and you. It would clear the way to the throne for other bloodlines."

"No one would be so foolish," she said.

"No one at court knows that I have the hand of blood. But for a quirk of magic, this would have worked exactly as they planned it."

"Fine, call the sluagh, and then what?"

"If I were you, or if I were me?" I asked.

"Either, both." Again she was studying me, trying to understand me.

"I would contact Kurag, Goblin King, and warn him, and have him bring more goblins than he is usually allowed into our sithen."

"You think he will throw his lot in with you against the entire Unseelie sidhe?"

"If I gave him a choice, no, but he has no choice. He is my sworn ally, and to deny me aid is to be forsworn. The goblins will kill a king for that."

She nodded. "Three months from now, he will not be your ally."

"Actually, four," I said.

"It was only six months, and they are half gone," she said.

"True, but Kitto is now sidhe, and for every sidhe-sided goblin I bring into their power, I gain a month of Kurag's aid."

"Will you fuck them all?" It was said with no offense, as if it was the only way she knew how to ask the question.

"There are other ways to bring someone into his power."

"You would not survive hand-to-hand combat with a goblin, Meredith."

"Kurag has agreed that we may help the princess bring over his people," Doyle said. He touched my arm, and in anyone else I would have said it was nerves. But it was the Queen's Darkness; Doyle didn't get nervous.

"Most will not agree to fighting you, Darkness, or the Killing Frost. They will pick on those among Meredith's guard whom they believe they can defeat. They will try to kill your men." She turned back to me. "How will you prevent that once the fight is joined?"

"I will choose champions," I said. "They fight the warriors of my choice, not theirs."

"I assume you will choose Darkness and Frost."

"Probably," I said.

"Many will refuse to fight them, so I ask again, are you willing to bed all the goblins who will line up for a taste of your shining flesh?"

"I will do what I said I would do."

She laughed. "Even I have not stooped so low as to bed a goblin. I would have thought it was beyond the pale for you."

"I think you'd like goblin sex. They like it rough."

She looked past me, and I realized she was looking at Kitto, who was trying to stay close to me and be as invisible as possible at the same time. "He looks a little fragile for my idea of rough."

Kitto pulled back even farther behind me and Doyle, and Galen. I moved just enough to bring her attention more firmly to me. "When you have to lay ground rules that your lover is not allowed to bite off pieces of your body, I think that qualifies as rough."

She looked past me again at the sliver of face that Kitto had left in view. She jumped, and said, "Boo." He scrambled behind me, and then pushed back into the other guards, putting distance between himself and the queen.

Andais laughed. "Fierce indeed."

"Fierce enough," I said.

"I will call the sluagh. You call the goblins." She put her head to one side like a bird that had spied a worm. "I can call the sluagh from a distance, for I am their queen, but how will you call the goblins?"

"I will try the mirror first."

"And if that fails you?" she asked.

"I will use blade and blood, and magic to call him."

"An old method," she said.

"But effective."

She nodded, then closed her eyes for a moment. "The sluagh come to my call. I grant you the use of my own mirror to try for Kurag's attention."

"You sound doubtful that I will gain his attention."

"He is a crafty one, for a goblin. He will not wish to be drawn into the royal squabbles of the Unseelie Court."

"The goblins are the foot soldiers of the Unseelie Court. Kurag can pretend that our infighting means nothing to him, but so long as he calls himself a part of the Unseelie Court, then he must pay attention to our squabbles."

"He will not see it that way," she said.

"Let me worry about Kurag."

"You sound confident. You cannot bed him, for you cannot help him commit adultery."

"Sometimes you gain more from the promise of a thing than from the thing itself."

"You cannot offer what our laws forbid," she said.

"Kurag knows our laws as well as we do, never believe otherwise. He forgets them only when it is convenient for him. He will know that it is not sex I am offering."

"Then what?"

"A chance to help me clean myself up."

She frowned. "I do not understand."

And she didn't, because though Kurag knew the laws of the sidhe, the same could not be said of our queen about the laws of the goblins. I knew that the fluids of the body were more precious to the goblins than almost anything. Flesh, blood, sex; somewhere in that combination was a goblin's idea of perfection. I was going to offer the goblins two out of three, and the touch, though not the taste, of sidhe flesh. I would have said that I was going to offer them all three, but knew better. The goblins' idea of flesh is a piece they get to keep in their stomachs or in a jar on a shelf.

Chapter 32

THE RUMOR MILL OF THE COURT HAD ME DEAD. SOME OF THE sidhe had access to television, and they'd spent a good part of the afternoon watching the tapes from the press conference. The shooting, the downed policeman, and finally Galen carrying me out with blood running down my face. The human media reported only that I'd vanished into the back of a limo, and there were no reports of me at any hospital. We hadn't had time to tell anyone anything, and our very own little press agent, Madeline Phelps, didn't know anything to tell. We had been met at the door to the sithen by guards and taken straight to the queen. No one else had seen us. No one else knew we had actually arrived, safe or otherwise.

The queen and her men were cleaning the blood off and getting dressed for the banquet. She and her entourage would go into the great hall as if nothing were wrong. She would take her throne. Eamon would take the consort's throne. They would leave the prince's throne and that side of the dais empty, as it had been since I left and Cel was imprisoned.

Doyle would enter with the queen, but not at her side. He would be one of the guards at the doors, so that he could scent all the nobles as they came in. He would search for the magic that the wine held. If he had appeared in his old place at the queen's back, there would have been questions, but no one would question him wishing to return to her service and no longer be exiled from faerie. No one would question that she would punish him by keeping him farther from her royal person.

The queen and her men would answer no questions. In fact, the plan was for her to be totally silent. To ignore all questions, until someone was finally bold enough to go to the throne and ask permission to speak. That would be my cue to come through the door with my entourage. I would still be covered nearly head to foot in blood, blood not my own, making the point, better than anything we could have planned, that I was a fit heir to Andais. Some of the men were leaving the blood on them, and some were cleaning themselves free of it. It depended on who wanted to be part of the floor show.

We waited in the outer room before the big doors that led to the great hall. The silence was filled with a thick slithering of some giant snake, but what moved on the ceiling and against the walls wasn't reptilian. Roses filled the room. They'd been dying for centuries, until they were only dried vines and naked thorns, but they had awakened to my blood, my magic. Now months later the walls were lost in the deep green of leaves and fresh canes. Huge scarlet roses bloomed everywhere, their scent so heavy on the air that it was like swallowing perfume, almost overwhelming in its sweetness. The roses moved in the dimness of the chamber. It was the sound of vines and stems and leaves sliding over each other that filled the waiting room. A blossom would get pulled too far into the writhing mass, and a shower of scarlet petals would rain down upon us. I knew that some of the thorns near the ceiling were the size of daggers. The roses were not ordinary in any way. They were meant as a last-ditch defense if any enemy managed to get this far. The fact that most of our enemies were welcome here made the roses more a symbol than an actual threat.

Our plan to find Nuline and ask her where the wine had come from had failed. Sholto's sluagh had found Nuline, but she'd been beyond questions. Her head was still missing. Her death meant either that the would-be assassin was taking no chances, or that he, or she, or they, already knew they'd failed to kill the queen. It changed nothing about our plans, but it did make a person wonder.

Sage stood just behind Rhys and Frost at my back. We'd had to introduce his new form, along with its tricolored eyes, to his Queen Niceven. She was furious that he couldn't change back, but intrigued with his being newly sidhe. Intrigued enough to help us. The demi-fey were the ultimate spies—so tiny, so inoffensive. The sidhe ignored them as if they were truly the insects that they mimicked. They were not considered a power in the courts, and thus they could be anywhere, everywhere. Queen Niceven had scattered her people among the court. They would listen and report back. They would spy for me and for Queen Andais.

King Kurag, with his many-armed queen on his arm, was behind us in the waiting room. He and his entourage of goblins would enter as part of my entourage. He would take his throne at the end of the hall, closest to the doors, farthest from the throne, but we would enter together, and some of his warriors would stay with me as we walked the length of the hall.

In person Ash and Holly looked both more sidhe and less. Handsome and arrogant as any the court could boast with that flawless golden sunlit skin, but the eyes, vibrant green and burning red, respectively, were pure goblin, huge and oblong, taking up more of the face than sidhe or human eyes. It gave the goblins superior night vision, but marked them as *other*. Physically, they were bulkier, seeming to have more muscles under that lovely skin than they should have. I was betting they were stronger than a pure sidhe.

Ash had been more than happy to take part in our show of unity. Holly had not wanted to help. It was beneath him to sit at a woman's feet, especially a sidhe woman. I had had to let Holly have a little preview, and once he licked the blood along my skin, he hadn't argued again. They were goblin enough to value the sidhe blood that covered me. For tonight that was good; for later, when they came to my bed, it was a little unnerving. But one problem at a time; tonight had enough without borrowing.

Sage said, "Queen Niceven says that one of the royals has knelt on the floor before the queen." He took in a breath, then said in an excited voice, "Now!"

Barinthus and Galen pushed the doors open, and the stronger light of the great hall spilled around us. We were moving as the doors opened. I walked a little in front of Rhys and Frost; then came Nicca and Sage, and beyond that everyone just picked a partner and followed me two by two, with Galen and Barinthus coming at our backs just ahead of the goblins.

Doyle stayed by the door, as planned, and we gave no acknowledgment of him, as if he'd angered us. The plan, as it were, was rolling along.

Gasps, furious whispers, and even one muffled scream met me at the door. I think for a moment the herald at the door didn't recognize me. The only part of me that wasn't pasted with blood were my eyes, and even the lashes of one eye were stiff with it. I'd spent my life being treated as lesser, as someone not of importance, and certainly not dangerous. I admit that a large part of me enjoyed that first moment when they watched me cross into the hall. I enjoyed their fear, their surprise, their worry. What had happened? What had changed? What did this mean? They were some of the best court politicians in the world, but now all their plans were thrown into the air simply because I walked into the throne room covered in blood.

Queen Andais sat on her throne, her white skin clean and pure where she'd scrubbed the blood away. Her dress was black and bared her shoulders and arms. Diamonds gleamed in her hair, hiding the metal of the tiara behind the dazzle of their light. A line of diamonds graced her neck and spilled across her chest as if the necklace were a rope, or a serpent, caught in midmotion. The diamonds were the only color to her simple black dress and the long gloves that covered her arms and hands. Though perhaps *color* wasn't the right word for the effect. It was more as if the jewels bent the light around her head and neck like a halo sliding down her body.

Mistral stood behind and to one side of her throne in his armor, with his spear resting against the dais. Mistral as her new captain did not surprise me, but her new second in command did. Silence was hidden behind his armor; only his long braid of pale brown hair showed from underneath his helmet. He was called Silence because he never spoke except to whisper in the queen's ear, or Doyle's. How can you command if you will not speak?

Tyler curled at her feet on the end of a bejeweled chain, his only clothing the shining of the collar. Eamon sat in the smaller throne just below hers, the consort's throne. He was dressed all in black except for a silver circlet at his pale brow.

We passed the empty table and throne where the sluagh sat, because the sluagh were behind the queen. Nightflyers like a cross among giant bats, tentacled horrors, and airborne manta rays clung to the stones at her back, going up and up like a living curtain of dark flesh. Things with more tentacles than flesh stood behind the throne. The hags, Black Agnes and Segna the Gold, were cloaked and waiting behind the queen, taller than the guards at her back. The hags normally stood at their own king's back, but Sholto had a new place to sit.

An empty throne that had once been reserved for the heir, but had become known as the prince's throne, awaited me. Sholto's throne had been placed on the dais, just below mine. For tonight, it was to be a consort's throne as well. My consorts, though, not the queen's. For me, it would be whomever I was going to sleep with that night.

Sholto, King of the Sluagh, Lord of That Which Passes Between, Lord of Shadows, sat on the dais for the first time, tall and pale, with moonlit skin to make any Unseelie sidhe proud. His hair was white as snow, long and silken, and, as was his wont, tied back in a loose ponytail. His eyes were tricolored; a circle of metallic gold like mine, then a circle of amber, and last a line the color of leaves in the autumn. He was as fair of face and body as any sidhe who graced the court, sitting there in black-and-gold tunic, black pants tucked into knee-high boots of softest black leather, with more gold edging the turned-down tops. His cloak was fastened with a gold brooch carved with the device of his house.

He looked every inch the sidhe prince, but I knew, better than most, that looks could be deceiving. Sholto was wasting magic to hide what lay under his clothes. Almost all his stomach, down to his lower abdomen, was a mass of tentacles. Without his glamour, it would have bulged under even the generous cloth of a tunic. Modern clothing was nearly unwearable without his magic to make everything lie smoothly. His mother had been Seelie sidhe. His father had been a nightflyer.

As King of the Sluagh he could have any female of his court in his bed. As a member of the queen's guard, no one at Andais's court could sleep with him but the queen herself. I don't think it would ever have occurred to her to take him to her bed. She called him *my perverse creature*, or sometimes simply *my creature*. Sholto hated the nickname, but you didn't complain to Queen Andais about nicknames, not even if you were the king of another court. If Sholto had been content with the females of his court, then I would have had nothing to bargain with, but he was not content. He wanted sidhe skin against his body. So our bargain was struck, and if not tonight, then tomorrow I would find out if I could stomach all the extra pieces he had growing from his body. I hoped I could, because like it or not, I would have to bed him for tonight's help.

Afagdu stood to one side of the dais. He'd been on his knees before the throne when the doors opened. He, too, was dressed in black, as most of the court was. Courtiers often dressed in their sovereign's favorite color, and black had been Andais's signature color for centuries. Afagdu's hair was so black it seemed to melt into his cloak, and the beard on his face made it seem as if his tricolored eyes floated in his face, lost in all that blackness. His voice carried through the hall, cutting across the whispers and gasps. "Princess Meredith, is that your blood, or someone else's?"

I ignored him and went to stand before the dais, directly below the queen. I bowed, but only from the neck. "Queen Andais, Queen of Air and Darkness, I come before you covered in the blood of my enemies, and my friends."

"Meredith, Princess of Flesh and Blood, join us."

There were more gasps at the new title. Doyle had wanted to keep my new power secret so we could surprise my enemies, but Andais had overruled. She wanted the court to fear me, as they feared her. She could not be persuaded from it, and she was queen.

Sholto stood and came down the two steps left him. He smiled and offered me his hand. I took it, and found his palm sweaty. Why would the King of the Sluagh be nervous?

I gave him a smile, and wondered if the effect was friendly, or frightening, from my mask of blood.

He led me to my throne, and once I was seated went back to his own. The others crowded around. Kitto took his place at my feet, and all we needed was a jeweled collar to mimic Tyler at the queen's. Rhys and Frost took their places on either side of my throne. The men whom I had taken to my bed spread out behind me and to either side. Barinthus had included himself in this list, and I could not protest. The queen had been both puzzled and intrigued, but left it for later. The others, hers and mine, filled out around the room. Andais wanted it clear that the guards were there not to protect us, but to be a threat to the rest of the Unseelie.

The nobles did not like the guards scattering throughout the room. They did not like it at all. Afagdu went back to his own throne to the left side, smiling, outwardly at ease. He was not one of Cel's toadies; nor was he a fan of the queen. He kept his own counsel, and made sure the nobles attached to his house did as well.

Two Red Caps strode forward. If the goblins were the foot troops of the Unseelie, than the Red Caps were the shock troops—stronger, bigger, more uniformly vicious than the goblins themselves. The Red Caps were eight and near ten feet tall, respectively. Small giants, even among the fey. You would expect creatures so tall, so wide, so muscular to move like a lumbering bull, but they didn't. They moved like huge hunting cats, eerily graceful. One was the yellow of old paper, and the other the dirty grey of dust. Their eyes were huge oblongs of red, as if they looked out at the world through fresh blood.

On their heads were the round scarlet caps that gave their people their name, but the cap of the tallest one was not merely scarlet cloth. Thin lines of blood ran from his cap down his face, to trail down shoulders as broad as I was tall. Blood ran from his cap in near-continuous rivulets, never quite reaching the floor, almost as if his body absorbed it, though there were dark lines in his clothes. Perhaps the cloth soaked it up?

I was betting that this one's hat had begun life as pure white wool. Once all Red Caps had had to dip their hats in blood to get that crimson color. The blood dried up, and you would have to have another battle to dip your hat in the blood of your enemies. The custom had made the Red Caps some of the most feared warriors among us; for sheer bloodthirstiness, it was hard to beat them.

Either the big grey one had dipped his hat freshly for the banquet, or he had that rarest of natural abilities: He could keep the blood fresh and flowing. Once, when the Red Caps had been a nation of their own and not part of the goblin empire, it was a prerequisite to be war leader among them.

The smaller one did not argue when the larger pushed his way in front and knelt first. Kneeling, he was as tall as I was sitting in the big chair, on steps above him. A very big boy indeed.

His voice was like rocks sliding against each other, a sound so deep that it made me want to clear my throat. "I am

Jonty, and Kurag, Goblin King, has ordered me to protect your white flesh. The goblins honor the alliance between Princess Meredith and Kurag, Goblin King." Having said that, he leaned that great face toward me. His face was nearly as wide as my chest. I'd spent too much of my life around such giants to be afraid, but when he grinned and flashed teeth like jagged fangs, it did take a certain amount of trust to let him lower that mouth over the hand I held out for him.

"I, Princess Meredith, Wielder of Flesh and Blood, greet you, Jonty, and return the honor of the goblins by sharing the blood that I have spilt with them."

He did not touch me with his hands, as that was not necessary for this show of solidarity. He merely put his nearly lipless mouth against my skin, and touched the tip of his tongue against my hand. His tongue was sandpaper-rough, like some great cat. As that rough surface scraped the dried blood from my hand, the palm of my left hand pulsed. I'd had the hand of blood hurt, ache, fill me with so much pain that I screamed for release, but I'd never felt it just give a small pulse.

The goblin kept his mouth pressed to the palm of my hand, but he rolled his eyes up to look at me. It was a strangely intimate look, like the way a man looks up when his tongue caresses much more intimate things than the palm of a woman's hand. My palm felt warm, and wet. That warmth ran up my arm, spilled over my body in a wave of heat that left me gasping, and wet. Wet with blood, as if I'd just that moment rolled in it. The blood ran from my hair into my face. I raised a hand to keep the drips out of my eyes, but the other Red Cap was suddenly there. He ran his rough tongue over my forehead, making a sound low in his chest. I half expected Jonty to push him away, but he stayed kneeling over my hand, staring up at me with that intimate look in his eyes.

A voice came from behind them, "Kongar, away from her, now!"

The Red Cap grabbed my half-raised hand and licked it

while he held it in his big hands. It was an insult to touch me. It implied sexual favors among the goblins. Hands closed on him and jerked him backward. Ash and Holly sent the much larger man spinning across the floor, sliding backward just in front of the doors.

"He lacks control, Kurag," Holly said, "I don't trust him around sidhe flesh."

Kurag's rumbling voice filled the hall: "Agreed." He motioned, and two other Red Caps went to fetch the fallen one from the floor. Kongar got to his feet before they reached him. Blood ran down his face. For a moment I thought Ash and Holly had injured him; then I realized his hat was bleeding. His hat, covered in dried blood, was bleeding like the blood on my body.

He raised a hand to touch the blood, put it to his tongue, and looked at me the way I'd look at a good steak. One of the other Red Caps tried to touch the blood, but Kongar pushed his hands away. He allowed the other two to lead him back to stand with the other goblin guards, but he wouldn't let them touch the fresh blood.

Ash said, "You've had your fill, Jonty."

Jonty gave me those strangely intimate eyes again, then rose smiling with blood smeared around his mouth. He licked his lips as he went to stand behind me, to join my guards. I heard him mumble to Ash as he passed, "Queen's blood."

Ash had dressed in a green that matched his eyes and looked good with his blond hair and golden skin. He dropped to his knees at my right hand, and if his blond hair had been longer, he could have passed for sidhe. Holly dropped to his knees at my other hand. The red that he wore did bring out his eyes, but as he lowered his face to my hand, rolling his eyes upward in anger, I was reminded forcibly of the Red Cap's scarlet eyes. I wondered if that was what his father had been.

The feel of Ash's mouth on my skin turned me to look at him. He licked the blood from my hand in a long, sure stroke. Holly echoed him on my other arm. Their tongues were soft and strangely gentle as they licked the blood from my skin. They each took one of my hands in theirs, at the same time, as if it were choreography that they had practiced together. I tried to move my hands, and both of them squeezed down at the same time, pinning my hands to the arms of the throne. The sensation made me close my eyes, catch my breath. When I opened my eyes, the fresh blood had leaked down, and I tried to raise my hands to wipe my eyes, but they wouldn't let me. They pressed down harder, and moved like two shadows, so that both of their mouths reached my face at the same time. They licked just above my eyes, drinking the blood from my forehead as if I were a plate covered in something too good to lose.

They licked over my eyes, pressing just a little too hard, and it wasn't exciting in that moment. I was very glad I'd negotiated for no injuries. They could lick the blood off the surface, but no biting. They couldn't make more blood once this was gone, not unless we renegotiated. With both of them licking, nearly feeding at my face, I didn't think I'd be in a hurry to renegotiate. There was something unnerving about the two of them—exciting, but unnerving.

They leaned back enough so that I could blink and open my eyes. They loomed above me with the look on their faces . . . Sex was in that look, but there was a hunger that had less to do with sex and more to do with meat. They may have looked more sidhe than Kitto, but the look in their eyes made it clear that looks could be deceiving.

I'd been waiting for the queen to speak, or for some of the nobles to speak to her, while the goblins and I shared blood. I turned my head just enough to see the queen. She watched us with hungry, eager eyes, and I knew it was not just me, but the goblins. They moved like body and shadow, so synchronized that it would be nearly impossible not to wonder. Queen Andais was not accustomed to wondering about a man without some chance of having that curiosity satisfied. But if the queen tasted goblin it would be in secret, the way most of the sidhe treated them, and the sluagh, and others.

Good for a dark night, but not good enough for daylight. That attitude was one of the reasons that Holly and Ash had been intrigued by my very public offer.

I understood why no one had interrupted the show. If the queen was enjoying herself, you interfered at your peril. If you spoiled her fun, she was apt to make you do something equally entertaining.

Movement made me look upward, and I found a cloud of demi-fey like huge butterflies dancing above my head. I knew what they wanted. Most things in the Unseelie Court liked a bit of blood. But the demi-fey, unlike the goblins, have fewer rules. I gazed up into those hungry little faces and realized that I could give what I'd promised their Queen Niceven now, instead of later. Fresh blood, sidhe blood, royal blood. I was covered in it.

"My goblin lords," I said, "I have coin for other allies."

They stared down at me, as if they would not give up their prize. I felt Rhys and Frost move behind me. "No," I said, "no interference from my guards, not when I do not need it." I looked up into the goblins' faces, and they gave a small bow, just from the neck, and both moved to take the places we'd bargained for, at my feet. This had been the thing that Holly fought against the most, but with his mouth smeared with blood, his hands covered with it, he didn't seem to mind. They both settled at my feet and began to lick the blood off their faces and hands, like cats cleaning cream from their whiskers.

I raised my arms into the air as if I expected birds to alight. "Come, little fey, you may take the blood that is on my skin, but no bite of my flesh are you allowed."

One of them hissed, and the tiny doll-like face was transformed into something frightening, but only for a moment. Then the black doll eyes were as blank and innocuous as the tiny body and lovely wings tried to be. I knew that left unchecked they'd have gladly eaten the flesh from my bones. But they weren't unchecked, and there was too much at stake for me to be squeamish.

They looked so dainty, but they were heavier, meatier than the insects they mimicked. It was more like being covered in small monkeys with graceful wings, grabbing hands, and feet that slid in the blood on my skin. Tiny tongues lapped at the blood, tickled along my skin. One grazed me with needle-like teeth, and I fought not to jerk away. I spoke softly, clearly: "Only the blood that lies on my skin is allowed, little ones."

One female swung forward in my bloody hair, as if my hair were a vine, so she could see my face and I could see her little white dress spattered with blood, her perfectly carved face smeared with it. She spoke in a sound like the tinkling of bells. "We remember what our queen said, Princess. We remember the rules." Then she stayed where I could see her, wrapped her hands in the strands, and rolled her body like a dog on a rug, until her pale beauty was covered in crimson.

I could feel another Barbie-sized figure wrap its tiny body in the back of my hair. I could not see if it was male or female, but it made little difference. None of them was thinking sex; all of them were thinking food. Food and power, for the blood of the sidhe is power. We can pretend that it is not so, that blood has no magic, but it is lies. Pretty lies. Tonight, I wanted truth.

I was hidden under a blanket of slowly fanning wings when a voice came from the waiting nobility. "Queen Andais, if we are to have a show, should not the princess come down to the middle of the floor so we can all get a better view?" The voice was male, drawling, in a cultured sort of way. Maelgwn always sounded as if he were mocking someone. Most often himself.

"We will have a show, wolf lord," Andais said, "but this is not it."

"If what we have seen so far is not the show, I am breathless with anticipation."

I turned my head to look toward him. Wings flickered against my face as the demi-fey beat their wings fast and faster in their eagerness at the feeding. So many wings, so much movement, that it was like being touched by dozens of tiny breezes, tickling and dancing across my body. If I hadn't been afraid they'd take a bite out of me, it would have been interesting.

Maelgwn sat in his throne, and though he sat upright as any, he still managed to give the impression he was lounging. The look on his face was indulgent, as if he only humored us all. As if at any moment, he would simply get up and lead his people out to do something more important than attend silly banquets. The nobles at his table dressed as nearly everyone did in styles ranging from pre-Roman to the seventeenth century, though many people seemed to have stopped around the fourteenth century, and to modern designer fashions to nothing but the skin they were born with. The difference for Maelgwn's house was that almost every single one of them wore an animal skin somewhere. Maelgwn had a hood of wolf skin with the ears framing his face, and the rest of the huge grey-white fur trailing around his shoulders. His upper body showed muscular and nude under that fur. Whatever covered his lower body was lost to view behind the table. There were men and women at his table with boar's heads and bear's heads atop their faces. A woman with a swath of mink, another with fox, and some who boasted feathered cloaks, or merely small badges of feathers. But no one at Maelgwn's table wore the fur and feathers as a fashion accessory. They wore them because once it had held magic, or been a badge of what they could become. Maelgwn was called the wolf lord because he could still change shape to a great shaggy wolf. But most of the shape-shifters, like Doyle, had lost their ability to leave their human forms.

Not all shape-shifters were part of Maelgwn's house, but no one who called him master had not at some time been able to call animal form. Few could still do it. Another magic lost like so many others.

The thought made me look for Doyle. He was still at the far doors. Had he sniffed out the would-be killer? Did he know whose magic had nearly destroyed Andais and her guard? I wanted him to come to me, to tell me, but we were all playing our parts. We were letting the court believe he'd begged to return to Andais, and he was being punished by being put on door duty, far from the throne. Farther from the throne meant farther from royal favor, and that was never good. It was the only way to get him near the doors, close to everyone who had entered, without arousing suspicion. But how long did we have to pretend before the queen gestured for him to come forward?

I fought not to tense under the fanning wings, the tiny hands and feet. I wanted to brush them all away and call Doyle to me. I wanted to end this. But Andais had always liked to draw out her vengeance. I was more the kill-them-and-get-it-over-with type. Andais liked to play.

The tiny white fey, now scarlet from head to foot, leaned in toward my face and said in her bell-like voice, "Why so tense, Princess? Still afraid we'll take a bite?" She laughed, and most of the others laughed with her; some like the ringing of bells, some hissing like snakes, and others strangely human in tone. They rose in a laughing cloud, all stained-glass wings and blood-covered bodies, as if carrion birds had mated with butterflies.

Andais's voice resounded through the room, not in a ringing tone like an actor's but just conversationally, as if it was no effort at all for her voice to fill every corner. "And what would you give, Maelgwn, for your house to regain its abilities?"

"What do you mean, O Queen?" he said, and his voice still chided, but his eyes held something more cautious.

She looked down the center of the room until her gaze found Doyle. She called out, "Darkness, show him what I mean."

The queen's nerves were better than mine. I'd have made Doyle come and give me his news, his accusation, but instead she'd make a show of his traveling the length of the hall. Or perhaps it was that she was more fey than I was. Most fey are not a practical people. They will make a joke or play a game on the way to the gallows. It is their way, and one thing I lack. I wanted to scream at her to just get down to business. But I kept my seat, and my mouth, and let her unfold the events as she wished. In that moment, I wished I had not told her that some of the men's powers had returned. If she had not known about Doyle's return to power, this particular display would have waited.

Doyle pushed away from the doors, gliding down the center of the room, but he did not change. He simply walked to us while the court watched, at first in silence, then in a growing murmur of half-heard comments and laughter. By the time Doyle reached the dais, the queen was scowling at him.

He knelt in front of the dais, more in front of her throne than mine. Which was fine: It was her court.

Maelgwn said, "I think my house already has the power to walk the length of the throne room, my queen." He did not laugh outright, but it was there in the edge of his voice.

Doyle spoke. "I ask permission to give my weapons for safekeeping."

"Why should I give you permission for anything, Darkness? You have failed me once already tonight."

"Many of the enchanted objects that were lost years ago, went during a shifting of form." He undid his belt that held both his twin daggers, as well as his black-hilted sword. The daggers were nicknamed Snick and Snack. Once they'd had other names, but I'd never heard them. They hit whatever target they were thrown at. The sword was Black Madness, Bainidhe Dub. If any hand but Doyle's tried to wield it, they would be struck permanently mad. Or at least that was the legend. I'd seen the weapons used only once before, against the Nameless. I had not gotten to see all their powers in one battle. He slid the belt out from the loops of his shoulder holster with its very modern nonmagic gun. He left the gun in place, the shoulder holster flapping a little loose without the belt to hold it down.

He knelt with the weapons belt in his lap. "In the Western Lands I was wearing no weapons when the change came upon me. All that I was wearing vanished, and did not return with my human form. I would not risk the loss of these blades." He spoke low, and only those closest to the dais would have heard him.

The queen's anger faded under Doyle's caution. "Wise, as always, my Darkness. Do as you see fit."

He rose to his feet and walked up the steps with the belt and its precious weight held in his hands. Then he did what he had never done in my memory. He laid a kiss upon her cheek, and I was close enough and at an angle to see him whisper in her ear. The only reaction Andais gave was a knowing smile. It left the impression that Doyle had whispered something nefarious in her ear.

He moved to me then, and laid the same gentle kiss against my cheek. I had only moments to decide what my face would show, for I was not the actress that my aunt was. I'd already decided that if I could not control my face, I would hide it.

He whispered against my ear, "Nerys reeks of the spell."

I turned my head in against his so that my face was nestled in the bend of his neck. I drew in the rich scent of his skin, the warmth of him, and hid my shock. Of all the ones it could have been, Nerys was not on my list.

She was simply Nerys—it meant "lord" or "lady"—and though head of her own house, she had lost enough magic that she had given up her true name and adopted something that was more title than name. But she was not a creature of politics. She and her house were as close to neutral as any of the sixteen houses of the Unseelie Court. Nerys and her people were not fond of Cel, or of anyone. They gave the queen her due, but no more. They were cautious, and kept to themselves, and were powerful enough to get away with it. The attack on the queen had been rash, so unlike Nerys. If it had been anyone but Doyle telling me this, I might have doubted him, but I could not doubt Doyle. I was glad that my face was buried against his neck, though, because I could not have fought off the surprise.

He seemed to understand that, because he leaned into me until I touched his shoulder, gently, let him know that I had my face politically correct. I would not look at Nerys and her people. I would not give it away before it was time.

He leaned back from me, and his dark eyes asked, without words, if I was up to this. I gave a small nod and a smile. I was his lover, but I could not make my smile as lascivious as the queen had made hers. He laid his blades in my lap, giving up the pretense that he had come back to Andais. Of course, I don't believe that any of them, except perhaps Eamon, would have put their most precious weapon in the hands of the queen. For some of them, it had been years since she'd let them even hold the last of their own magic. They would not have given the weapons back to her, for fear she would keep them. In that moment, Doyle showed not just his trust but also that I could be trusted to share, and not merely to take.

He took his gun out of its holster and handed it to Frost. "It's a good gun," he said.

Frost actually smiled.

Rhys said, "And hard to come by in faerie."

Doyle nodded.

I had a moment to wonder if Doyle was up to this demonstration, but then he strode to the farthest edge of the dais, took a running start, and launched himself out into the air. He was obscured for a moment by a black mist that folded in upon itself, and he was flying out over the court with huge feathered wings, as black as his skin.

There were gasps and sounds of pleasure, as if some of the court were enjoying the show. The black eagle circled once, then came to the center of the room and began to flap its way to the floor, but before those great talons landed, the wings seemed to dissolve into mist, and it was great black hooves that struck the stones and pranced a few steps among the tables. The great black stallion walked to Maelgwn's table and looked at the wolf lord with Doyle's dark eyes. Either the mist rose up again, or the horse became the black mist, and it dissolved into the black mastiff that I had seen before. The huge dog panted at Maelgwn. Even sitting, the dog was tall enough to see over the table and meet Maelgwn's gaze.

The wolf lord gave a motion somewhere between a nod and a bow. It seemed to satisfy the dog, because it charged toward the dais. The great paws hit the steps and bounded up to sit next to me. The dog sat beside the arm of my throne, and I reached out to stroke that soft fur without thinking about it.

The mist rose up, and it felt as cool as it smelled, like breathing in rain deep in the forest. My hand tingled with magic as Doyle's body grew and shifted. There was no sliding of bones and flesh as there had been in California. Even with my hand lost in the black mist, it felt light and effervescent, like bubbles or electricity against my skin. Doyle was just kneeling beside my throne in human form, nude, with his long black hair lying in a dark pool at his feet.

My hand was still on his face, stroking his human cheek as I'd been stroking the dog's seconds before.

I wanted to compliment him, but I didn't dare let the court know that I'd never seen such an effortless performance.

"Most impressive," Maelgwn said, and there was nothing but seriousness left in his voice. "I don't remember you being a bird."

"I was not," Doyle said.

"So you have gained what was lost, and added to your powers besides."

Doyle nodded, my hand still playing in the thick fall of his hair.

"How has this miracle come to pass?" Maelgwn asked.

"A kiss," Doyle said.

"A kiss," Maelgwn repeated. "What does that mean?"

"You know a kiss," Rhys said from behind me, "you just pucker up your lips . . ."

"I know what a kiss is," Maelgwn interrupted. "What I don't know is how a kiss has brought about this change in the Darkness."

"Tell him whose kiss brought you back into your powers," Andais said.

"Princess Meredith's kiss," Doyle said, still kneeling by my chair, still with my hand playing in the thick warmth of his hair, tickling along the back of his neck.

"Lies." This from Miniver; she was head of her own house. She was tall and blond, and could have passed for Seelie Court, because once she had been. She had come to the Unseelie and fought her way to a position of power, until the tall commanding beauty was the head of her own house in the dark court. That she had preferred to rule in the Unseelie Court, rather than accept exile to the human world, meant that the Seelie Court would never accept her back. Her exile from the shining throng would be eternal. They sometimes took back those who had wandered among the humans, but once you went to the dark court, you were considered unclean.

She stood in front of her throne, a shining thing with her yellow braids sliding over a dress of shimmering gold cloth. A golden circlet graced her brow, over the perfect arch of dark eyebrows and the tri-blue of her eyes. She had never adopted the darker colors favored by Andais and her court. Miniver dressed as if she expected to walk into a different court.

"Did you say something, Miniver?" Andais said, and by merely leaving off any title she had insulted the golden figure. It was a warning. A warning to sit down and shut up.

"I said, and I say again, that it is a lie. No mortal could bring anyone into his power."

"She is a princess of the sidhe, and that makes her a little more than a mere mortal," Andais said.

Miniver shook her head, sending those heavy yellow braids sliding along the gold of her dress. "She is mortal, and you should have drowned her when she was six, as you tried to. It was weakness for your brother that stopped your hand."

She spoke as if I could not hear her, as if I were not sitting there alive in the same room with her now.

"My brother, Essus, once told me that Meredith would

make a better queen than my own son, Cel, would make a
king. I did not believe it then."

"At least Cel is not mortal," Miniver said.

"But Cel has not brought back a single drop of the power
we have lost. Nor have I," Andais said, and there was no teasing to her now. There was no showmanship.

"And you would have us believe that this half-breed mortal has done what pure sidhe blood has not?" Miniver pointed
at me in what I thought was an overly dramatic gesture, but it
did show the sleeve of her dress to perfection, flashing the
slits of cloth open so that the blue cloth of the underdress
showed through. Sometimes if you've lived nearly forever,
you think overly long about how things appear. "This abomination cannot be allowed on the throne, Queen Andais."

I thought *abomination* was a little harsh, but I said nothing,
for in a way it wasn't me she'd challenged, it was the queen.

"I say who will and who will not sit on the throne of this
court, Miniver."

"Your obsession with a hereditary monarchy of your own
bloodline will be the death of us all. We have all seen what
happens on the dueling ground when one of us shares blood
with that thing. They become mortal through the disease that
her blood carries."

"Mortality is not a disease," Andais said quietly.

"But it kills like one." Miniver looked out over the court,
and there were a lot of faces turned to her. Many showed by
either silence or nodding that they agreed with at least this
much. They, too, had worried about my blood. "If this mortal becomes queen, then we are honor-bound to take blood
oath from her, to bind us to her. To take blood oath, very
much as we take on the dueling ground." Miniver looked up
at Andais, and there was something close to pleading on her
face. "Don't you see, my queen, if we take her blood into us
and bind ourselves to her mortal peril, then we could lose our
own immortality? We would cease to be sidhe."

It was Nerys who stood up and said, "We would cease to
be anything."

Three, then four others of the noble houses of the Unseelie stood. They stood and showed their support for what Miniver had said. Six houses out of sixteen stood against me. That was something we had not foreseen. Or I had not.

Doyle had gone very still under my hand. All my men had gone very still, except the goblins at my feet and the Red Cap at my back. Either immortality didn't mean the same thing to them as it did to the sidhe, or other things were happening with the goblins. Things I had not quite grasped.

"I say who will be my heir," Andais said, "unless you wish to challenge me to personal combat, Miniver, Nerys, all of you. I will gladly fight you each in turn, and this arguing will cease."

Miniver shook her head. "Your answer to everything is death and violence, Andais. It has led us to be childless and near powerless, but our immortality, you cannot have that."

"Then challenge me, Miniver. Make yourself queen, if you can."

If Miniver's anger could have flown across the room and struck Andais, the queen would have died where she sat, but Miniver's anger did not have that kind of power. The day when the fey, any fey, could have killed with simply an angry thought was centuries past.

Andais looked at Nerys. "You, Nerys, do you wish to be queen? Do you wish it enough to challenge me to a duel? Defeat me and you can be queen."

Nerys just stood there, staring at her with tri-grey eyes that nearly mirrored the queen's own. Nerys's long black hair was done in a series of complicated braids that hung like a heavy cloak at her back. Her dress was white with touches of black in the trim, the belt, the lace at her wrists. She looked cool and collected. There was no sense of outrage that Miniver vibrated with.

"I would never presume to challenge the Queen of Air and Darkness to a duel. It would be suicide." Her voice was quiet, and somehow dark. But there was no anger in it, nothing that could give true offense.

"But attacking me from secret, an assassination attempt,

that would not be suicide, would it?" Andais's smile was not pleasant. "Not if you didn't get caught."

Nerys just stood there, looking up at the throne, with no hint of fear, no panic, no anything. If Andais thought she could frighten Nerys into a confession, she was wrong. Nerys was going to force Andais to produce proof. Did she not understand that we had proof? Did she think that with Nuline's death, she was safe?

"Assassination is a pretty business, so long as you are not discovered." Andais looked down the line of standing nobles, I think so that she did not single Nerys out, but it was like many things tonight, in trying to do one thing, another thing was accomplished.

Miniver began to move through her people to the space between her table and the next. Some of her people touched her arm; she shook her head, and they let her go. She walked out from between the tables, her back ramrod-straight, like something carved of gold and amber.

"Do you have something to say, Miniver?" Andais asked.

"I challenge the princess Meredith to a duel." For someone who had seemed so angry, she was strangely calm as she said it.

People at her table cried, *No, do not do this.* She ignored them, and kept her Seelie face pointed toward the dais. She never looked at me, only at Andais. She asked for my life, but it was not me she asked it of.

"No, Miniver, it will not be so easy as all that. The princess has had one assassination attempt tonight. We do not need two."

"I would have preferred my spells to work earlier tonight, but if she will not die from a distance, then I will do it here, now."

My face gave nothing away, because it took a few seconds for me to realize what she'd said. Andais looked amused, her eyes glittering.

Doyle had stood, putting himself more in front of me. My other guards moved to shield me from her sight, and whatever she might do. I had to peer between them to see that more of the armored guards spilled around her to form a half circle. She was as tall as any of them, and there was nothing fragile or fearful about that shining figure. She seemed very sure of herself.

"Are you admitting, before the entire court, that you tried to assassinate Princess Meredith earlier tonight?" Andais asked.

"I am," Miniver said, and her voice rang through the room, matter-of-fact, as if now that the worst was happening she didn't need her anger anymore.

"Take her to the Hallway of Mortality, and leave extra guards."

They began to close around her, but Miniver's voice carried: "I have given challenge. That challenge must be answered before my punishment begins. That is our law." I think the guards might have managed to take her away, but there were other voices.

"Regrettable as it is to agree with such an undeniable criminal," Afagdu said, "Lady Miniver is correct. She has challenged the princess, and that challenge must be answered before any action may be taken about her crime."

Galen spoke from behind me. "So she tries to kill Merry earlier, fails, and now she gets another try. I don't think so."

"It is our law." Doyle's hand had reached out, and I took it, resting my face against the nude line of his hip. Nervous touching.

"No," Andais said, "the young knight is right. To allow her to go forward with this challenge is to reward her for trying to assassinate a royal heir. Such treachery will not be rewarded."

"When it was Cel and his allies who challenged the princess over and over, you did not intercede," Nerys said. "You were more than willing that Meredith take the field when it was your son behind the duels. We all knew that Cel meant her death. Meredith did her best to give no offense to anyone, yet sidhe after sidhe found an excuse to challenge her. When you challenge a mortal being to duel after duel against the immortal sidhe, what is it but an assassination plot by another name?"

Andais shook her head, not as if she did not agree but as if she didn't want to hear. "Take Miniver away, now!"

"No one is above the law, except the queen herself, and the princess is not yet queen." This from another of the lords who had stood when Miniver gave her rant against my mortality.

"Have you turned against me, too, Ruarc?" Andais asked.

"I speak the law, nothing more," he said.

"You did not stop the duels before," Nerys said.

"I stop it now," Andais said.

"Are you saying that Meredith is too weak to defend her claim to the throne?" Afagdu asked.

"If that is true," Nerys said, "then let her take the throne, for once she is queen we can challenge her and if she refuses, she will be forced to relinquish her crown."

Maelgwn spoke, and he, like Afagdu, had not been one of the nobles who stood. "Princess Meredith fights now, or later, my queen. Too many of the houses have lost faith in her. She must regain that faith or she will never be queen."

"We have not lost faith," Miniver said from behind her wall of guards, "for you cannot lose what you have never had."

Doyle's hand tightened on mine, and I slid my arm around his waist. I'd been trapped by our laws before. I probably knew the laws concerning dueling better than most, because I had looked for a loophole three years ago, before I'd been forced to flee the court before I was dueled to death. And everyone had known that Cel was behind it all. If someone else hadn't been trying to kill me, again, it would have been good to hear the truth about Cel spoken aloud in open court.

I clung to Doyle, realizing in a strange way that I was right back where I'd begun three years ago. I'd left for fear that the next duel would be my last, and now here I was, challenged again. Challenged not just by a sidhe, but by the head of an entire house. There are three ways to be head of a house. You can inherit it, you can be elected into it, or you can challenge one after the other of a house until you either destroy them all or they concede that you are the better fighter, and they will not stand in your way. Guess which way Miniver had made her mark in our court?

Miniver had been one of the last of the Seelie nobles to ask admittance to our court. She had waited a handful of days until she found which of the noble houses was most respected for their magic, then she had challenged them, one after the other, until five duels later they had given her their respect, and their allegiance.

As the challenged, I could choose weapons. Before I'd come into my hands of power I would have chosen knives, or guns if it were still allowed, but now I had a hand of power that was perfect for this challenge. Before we fought, we would each nick our body, and taste each other's blood. A small cut was all the hand of blood needed. The problem was, if I chose magic and Miniver didn't bleed to death fast enough, she would kill me.

I spoke with my face pressed against Doyle's skin. "The sidhe never call it a duel to the death. What blood does she call?"

Doyle's deep voice cut across the murmur of voices. "The princess asks to what blood does her challenger call?"

Miniver's voice rang out clear and strangely triumphant, as if we'd been silly to ask, "To third blood, of course, and if I could ask for a duel to the death, I would do it. But the immortal sidhe cannot die, unless tainted by mortal blood."

I stood up, one arm wrapped tight around Doyle's waist. The men moved back to make a sort of curtain through which I could see her. The guards around her had done the same, though she was not being hugged tight by anyone. No, she stood tall and straight and full of that awful arrogance, that surety that was always the sidhe's greatest weakness.

"You will drink of my blood, Miniver, and if my blood truly makes you mortal, then you risk true death."

"I am content either way, Meredith. If I kill you, as I believe I will, then you cannot take the throne and contaminate this court with your mortality. If you by some oddity slay me, give me true death, then my death will show the entire court what their fate will be if they take you as their queen and make blood oath to you. If by my death or my life, I can keep your mortality from spreading through the Unseelie like a curse, then I am more than content."

One of the nobles from her house called, "Lady Miniver, she carries the hand of blood now."

"If she is so bold as to choose magic against me, then she will die all the sooner. She cannot bleed me to death from three tiny wounds, not before I have slain her." She stood there, supremely confident, and if I had had only the first part of the hand of blood, she'd have been right. But I could widen those three tiny wounds, spilling her life's blood a hundred times faster. If I could survive long enough, I had her.

Chapter 33

THERE ARE NO SECONDS IN A SEELIE DUEL. ONCE ONE OF THE combatants can no longer continue, the fight ends. There is no second to pick up the weapon and avenge you. But you can choose who wields the blade that draws your blood for the oath.

Doyle had borrowed a ribbon to pull his hair back from his face. He put the tip of his knife against my lower lip, the very point of his sharp knife against the soft skin of my mouth. He was quick, but it hurt anyway. It always did when you bled your mouth. It would be a kiss that sealed the blood oath: such a little bit of blood to mean so much.

If it had been only to first blood we could have worn armor, which was why the first cut was on the face. All you had to do was remove the helmet, and you could be cut.

He cradled my hand in his, baring the wrist to the point of his blade. Again, he was quick, but it hurt more this time, because it was a larger cut. Not too deep, but longer. Blood filled the wound and began to drip slowly down my skin.

Again, if it had been to second blood, someone could have kept a little armor on, but third blood meant no armor. No protection but your own skin and whatever clothes you were wearing.

Doyle touched his blade to the hollow of my throat, and made a tiny cut that stung. I could not see when blood filled it, but I could feel the first trickle of warmth as my blood began to slide down my neck.

All three cuts hurt, sharp and immediate, which was good. I knew from experience that if any of the cuts closed before the final part of the ritual, Miniver's blade wielder would get to redo my wounds. I did not want that. I didn't even have to know who it was, to know that you do not give your flesh over to your enemies' blades. I'd had Galen wield the knife once, and he'd been so squeamish about hurting me that two of the wounds had had to be redone. Cel's friends had damn near slit my wrist.

I looked up into Doyle's darkly handsome face. I wanted to say so many things. I wanted to kiss him good-bye, but didn't dare. We stood in a magic circle that the queen had traced upon the stones of the main court. Inside this circle was a sacred place, and one touch of mortal blood could contaminate, as I'd proven in other duels. But the last duel that I'd managed to kill someone in, I'd been armed with a handgun. They'd been outlawed after that duel. I thought that was unfair, since the gun had acted as the equalizer it was meant to be. The sidhe who'd died had outweighed me by more than a hundred pounds, and had had more than double my reach of arm and leg. He'd been a great swordsman, and I was not. But he hadn't been much of a marksman. Most of the sidhe weren't, the Queen's Ravens being the exception. Most sidhe still treated firearms as if they were some sort of human trick.

But there would be no guns today. No swords, no weapons. I'd chosen magic, and Miniver was more confident than ever of her victory. I was hoping she would be overconfident. She was Seelie enough for it.

She stood across the stones from me, in her dress of gold. Blood had begun to trace a thin dark line on the front of that dress, as her neck wound bled. The cuff of her dress was scarlet with her blood. Her blood was only a little darker red than her mouth, and it only showed crimson as it began to spill down her chin.

I fought the urge to lick my own lip as I felt the blood seep down my chin, but we were supposed to save that blood for each other.

"Are the wounds satisfactory?" the queen asked from the throne where she sat to watch.

We both nodded.

"Then make oath to each other." Andais's voice was neutral, but not perfectly so. Her voice betrayed a niggling sense of anger and unease.

Doyle stepped to one side, and the noble who had wielded the blade for Miniver did the same on the opposite side of the circle. It left Miniver and me facing each other over a space of stone floor.

We stayed unmoving for a heartbeat or two, then she started forward, striding in her full skirt like a confident golden cloud. I walked to meet her. I had to be more careful, because the high heels I was wearing were not meant for striding over old stones. It would ruin so much if I twisted an ankle. My skirt was too short to do anything, and all my clothes were still blood-soaked. Nothing about me billowed or floated like a cloud.

Her full skirts seemed to wrap around my nearly bare legs. She looked down at me for a moment, as if she expected me to finish it, but she was a foot taller than I was, and there was no way for me to close that distance without her help.

She stood there, blood running down her chin. Hands at her sides. I wasn't sure what was wrong at first; then I realized where she was looking. She was staring at my throat, at the blood that welled there. She was trying to stare as if she were horrified by the barbarity of it, and most of her face succeeded, but her eyes ... those beautiful blue eyes like three circles of perfect sky ... those eyes held something close to hunger. I remembered what Andais had said: that whoever crafted the spell had understood her battle madness, her bloodlust. Whoever had made the spell had understood Andais's magic. How do you best understand something, except by experiencing it yourself.

Miniver's eyes stared at the wound in my throat as if it was something wondrous, and fearful. She wanted the blood, or the wound, or the harm; something about it fascinated her. But she feared that fascination.

I'd spent my share of time being on the wrong end of Andais's hobbies. I knew that for her blood and sex and violence were all intertwined to the point that where one left off, and the others began, had blurred.

Miniver had never by action or word given hint that her power held anything akin to the queen's. If she was filled with the same hungers that Andais fed, then Miniver had the control of a saint. Of course, it's easy to be a saint when you are so terribly careful never to be tempted.

Miniver had spent my lifetime leaving the court when the entertainments were too bloody. She was too Seelie to enjoy such blood sport, so she'd said. Now I saw the truth in her eyes. She hadn't left because she was horrified; she'd left because she did not trust herself. Just as she did not trust herself at this moment.

I knew what it was to deny your true nature. I'd done it for years among the humans, cut off from faerie and from anyone who could have given me what I craved. I knew what it felt like to have that craving answered after so very long. It had been overwhelming. Would it be the same for Miniver?

I closed the distance between us, wading into that stiff gold cloth until I could feel her legs, her hips, against my body. She watched the blood at my throat, as if the rest of me were not there. I finally moved close enough that I had to put my hands around her waist to keep steady on my high heels.

She backed up then, and made a show of not wanting me to embrace her, but it hadn't been that, or at least not just that. I'd stepped so close she couldn't see the blood flowing.

"You are a foot taller than I am, Miniver. I cannot share oath with you, unless you help."

She stared down that perfect nose at me. "Too short to be sidhe at any court."

I nodded, and winced, made a show of touching my throat. It hurt, but not that much. She watched me touch the wound, watched me tug at the neck of my blouse. If she'd been male, or a lover of women, I'd have accused her of enjoying the flash of clean white breast I gave her, but I don't think it was anything as simple as flashing the top of my breast at her. I think it was the sight of clean white flesh with fresh blood on it.

I offered her my hand, the one with the cut wrist. "Come, Miniver, help me make this oath."

She could not refuse me, but the moment her hand touched mine, felt the slick play of blood, she jerked back. It must have been torture to her to watch first the goblins feed, and then the demi-fey.

"If you wish to call this duel off, I will not argue," I said, and my voice sounded utterly reasonable.

"Of course you wouldn't, because I am about to end your life."

"Will you bleed me?" I asked, raising the wrist so she could see how much blood was welling out of it. "Will you spill my body open across these stones?"

The first bead of sweat marred that perfect forehead. Oh, yes, she wanted to do just that. She wanted to slaughter as she'd made Andais do. She had filled that wine with all her own most fervent and hidden desires. If I stripped her of her pretense late in the fight, she would slaughter me. But if I could strip her now, immediately, if I could make her attack me during the kiss, then I could strike without any ceremony, too. I could open that white throat from end to end, and maybe, just maybe, I'd live through this.

She had two hands of power. The first worked from afar, and I didn't want that one. She could shoot a bolt of energy from a great distance, and one direct hit might be enough to stop my heart, but she had a second hand. The hand of claws. She had to put those slender fingers against my body, and it would be as if invisible claws shot out from those manicured nails. Invisible claws that cut through flesh like knives, and could be wrenched through the body without the resistance of metal. Doyle and Rhys had both seen her use it. It was her left hand, and it was the one I could survive. So it was the one I needed her to use.

I'd been afraid, but now there was no time for fear. Panic would get me killed, and what would happen to my men if I died? Frost had said he would die before going back to Andais. I was all that stood between them and returning to the queen's mercy. I could not leave them, not like that. Not helpless to protect themselves.

I needed to survive. I had to survive, and that meant that Miniver had to die.

I walked back into the rough embrace of her gold cloth, and as before when I was close enough to feel her body through the dress, I put my hands at her waist for balance.

This time she pulled me roughly against her, as if she'd make it all as quick as possible.

I raised my left hand, the one with its fresh wound, as if I meant to touch her face, but she grabbed my wrist to stop me. It didn't really hurt, her hand on the cut, but I made a small pain sound anyway.

Her eyes were just a little wider, and she pressed her hand into my wrist.

I obliged her, making another small sound.

I could see her pulse in her throat jumping under her skin. She liked the sounds. She liked them so much that she ground her hand into my wrist, and the next sound was real.

My voice came out breathy, and it wasn't pretend. "You're hurting me."

She pulled me in tight against her body, twisting my arm behind my back so that she could keep digging at the wound. She jerked my arm upward, sharp and hard as if she meant to pull it out of its socket.

I cried out, and her eyes were wild. She put her other hand against the back of my head, balling her hand into my blood-soaked hair. A sound came low in her throat, and I watched her fight against herself, watched the battle rage in her eyes from inches away. If I had misjudged this, I was about to die, and it was going to be slower and a great deal more painful. The thought brought fear in a rush over my skin, thundering my pulse in my head. I didn't fight it, and it was as if Miniver could smell it on me, could smell my fear, and liked it.

Her mouth hovered over mine, a breath from closing the space and sealing our oath. She jerked my arm again, and I screamed for her. A sound came out of her that was almost a laugh, but had nothing to do with laughter. I'd never heard anything like it. If I'd heard it in the dark, I'd have been afraid.

She whispered into my mouth, "Scream for me, scream for me as I drink your blood. Scream, and I won't hurt you while I do it."

I hesitated, because I could not decide in that split second what would be better: to give in and scream, or to make her work for it. Miniver made my mind up for me. She pressed her mouth to mine, and I didn't scream for her, so she made me scream.

She jerked my arm again, and that made a small sound, but she didn't want a small sound. There was no warning, no prickle of magic; my left hand was just suddenly pierced by knives, five blades slicing through my flesh and bones. I screamed for her then, I screamed, and screamed, and screamed, muffled against her mouth, trapped against her body. She drank my screams the way she drank my blood, and I defended myself.

The pain and fear translated directly into power. I didn't think, *Bleed*, I thought, *Die*. Her throat exploded with our mouths still pressed together, so that we both coughed on her blood.

I thought she would let me go, but she didn't. Her hand was still wrapped in my hair, and all she had to do was call her power, and I would die. I focused on the wound in her wrist, and she tried to scream with her ruined throat. Her hand fell away from my head, and the hand flopped, almost completely torn away from the arm. There was no hunger in her eyes now, only shock and horror, and the panic that only the truly immortal can show at death. That puzzled fear as they feel it begin to take hold.

She threw me away from her body, and I couldn't catch myself with only one good arm. The arm she had pulled behind my back was useless, numb and aching at the same time. I could not feel my shoulder, and distantly I knew that was probably a good thing.

I lay on the floor for a second trying to decide if I was too hurt to move. Then I saw her stagger toward me, trying to get her hand in line with her wrist, as if she was having trouble using her hand of power with her hand torn away. I had to do something before she figured out how to use it.

I stared at the gaping red mess that had been her throat, her spine shining wetly in the lights. I could see the bones of her clavicle just over her breasts. With all that damage, she was still struggling to kill me. She should have been dying by now. Why wasn't she dying?

I shoved my power into her. I could feel it like a huge balled fist just under the bare bones I could see in her upper chest. I squeezed that power, squeezed it, concentrated it.

A bolt of energy raised the hair on my body, and scarred the floor just beyond me. Miniver had torn her own hand off, and was trying to shoot energy out of her bloody stump, but she was having trouble finding the range.

I felt that huge fist of power in her upper chest, in the wound I'd made, and I opened it. I spread the fingers of my magic wide, and her upper chest exploded outward in shards of bone and flesh and blood like a crimson rain.

I had to use my good hand to wipe the blood from my eyes so I could see Miniver on her back, her arms scrambling at the stones as if she was trying to breathe without a throat, without a chest, without lungs. If she'd been human she would have been dead. If she had been mortal, she would have been dead. But she wasn't dead.

I heard the queen's voice distant, more distant than it should have been. "I declare this duel over. Do any of you argue this?"

There was no sound.

"I declare Meredith the winner. Do any of you debate that?"

I heard a voice, though I couldn't place it. It was a woman. "They are both on the ground. I think the princess is as hurt as Miniver."

I understood then that I would have to get up. I managed to push myself upright with my good arm. The world swam in colors, but if I braced my arm, I could sit. I looked up, slowly, and found it was Nerys who had spoken against me.

"Are you content now, Nerys?" Andais asked.

"The law says that to be victor you must leave the circle under your own power."

I was really beginning to dislike Nerys. I pushed to my knees, and the world swam in colors, but finally I could see again. I wasn't entirely sure I could stand, let alone walk. But if you have no pride to defend, then there are other methods of moving. I crawled on one hand, and my knees. I crawled toward Nerys. I crossed the magic circle just in front of her table, then I used my good hand to grab the edge of that table and pull myself upright.

I stared at her from not so very far away, and said, "Doyle."

He was beside me, and probably had been closer than I knew. "I am here, Princess."

"Tell the queen to tell the court what Nerys did."

He called to Andais, "The princess requests that you reveal what Nerys has done."

The queen did, and I watched Nerys and all her people push away from the table, and stand there. They could not run because the guards held the only door, but the moment they pushed to their feet in a mass, I knew they intended to fight, and not as Miniver had fought, not within the rules. They intended to fight everyone.

"Demi-fey," I said.

Doyle leaned close. "Let me carry you, Meredith."

I said again, "Demi-fey."

He didn't seem to understand, but I suddenly had a small cloud of winged people around me. "You called, Princess?" said the one with a voice like bells.

"I offer you sidhe flesh and blood."

"Yours?" she asked.

"No," I said, "theirs."

There was a moment where the cloud of bloody butterflies hesitated, then almost as a single mass they fell upon Nerys and her people. It was so unexpected that the demi-fey got their bit of blood and flesh before the sidhe began to swat at them, and use magic to burn one small winged creature out of the air.

Nerys's face was a mass of bloody scratches. All of them had been bloodied, hands, necks, faces, breasts. The demi-fey had done their work well.

It never occurred to me that I shouldn't try. It never occurred to me that it wouldn't work. Shock is a wonderful thing. I didn't even hurt; I just couldn't feel my arm. But I could feel my power. I whispered, "Bleed," and blood began to pour out of their wounds. Such small wounds for so very much blood.

That burning bolt came our way, but an armored knight was there to take the blow, to send the heat shattering into sparks.

"Goblins," I said, and the Red Cap Jonty was there, with Ash and Holly beside him. "Bring your brother Red Caps."

Jonty didn't argue, but brought back a wall of huge Red Caps, and they lined up around me. They helped keep me safe while I called blood from Nerys and all her nobles.

Some of them broke ranks and drew knives against the swords of the guard. I think they preferred to be cut down rather than go the way Miniver had gone. Then one of her nobles dropped to her knees, and called out, "Forgive us!"

Andais said, "You would have killed me, and made me slaughter my guards. What mercy do you deserve?"

The woman crawled out from under the table, and Doyle moved me back, out of her bloody reach. "Please, Princess, please, do not destroy our entire house, all that we are."

"Nerys must die, for she has led you into betraying your queen."

Nerys's voice came, all arrogance gone. "I will pay the price for my actions if you will spare my people."

Andais agreed, and Nerys came out from behind her table, to stand where Miniver and I had begun our fight. The circle was gone. It was not a duel. It was an execution. Except how do you kill the immortal? Miniver was still struggling on the floor surrounded by guards. How do you kill the immortal? By tearing them apart.

I had Ash do it, because I needed Doyle to keep me standing, and I would not have asked any of the other guards to do it. Ash cut her at her throat, chest, and stomach, and I thought that was enough. The Red Caps encircled her, and the demifey hovered overhead. I threw the hand of blood into those wounds, and split her open like a ripe melon thrown to the ground. The Red Caps and demi-fey were drenched in her blood. But she did not die.

My legs wouldn't hold me anymore, and Doyle carried me away from it. He carried me to the queen, and I was crying, and didn't remember it. "I can't kill them any more dead than this."

She handed her sword, Mortal Dread, to me, hilt-first.

"She cannot stand enough to wield it," Doyle said.

"Then I will give them to your allies, the goblins and the demi-fey. I will let them be eaten alive as a warning to our enemies."

I looked into her eyes and hoped she was joking, but knew she wasn't. I held out my hand for the sword, and she gave it to me. Doyle carried me back with the sword resting across my lap.

The queen stood and announced in her ringing voice, "Miniver drank of Meredith's blood, yet she has not died from mortal wounds. It seems to disprove her theory that Meredith's mortality is contagious."

Silence met her words, silence and faces pale with shock. I think that the Unseelie Court had seen more of a show than they'd bargained for this night.

"Meredith begs me to kill the two traitors and not to leave them as they are. I told her that they were her kills, and that I would give them to the goblins and the demi-fey to feast upon. Let them be eaten alive, and let their screams echo in the ears of my enemies."

They stared up at her like children told that the monster under the bed is coming to get them.

"But they are not my kills, and if the princess can bring them true death before they are fed to the goblins and the wee ones, then so be it."

Doyle carried me to the floor, then hesitated a moment before carrying me to Miniver. Her throat had begun to heal, the flesh filling back in. I realized that she would survive this wound. In fact, the hand that she'd torn off to try to kill me was half attached again.

"Doyle," I said, and he seemed to know what I meant, because he called my guards to me. If Miniver was healing, then that meant she was still dangerous. It would be foolish indeed to get myself killed doing an errand of mercy.

Andais called, "Why do you need extra guards, my niece?"

Doyle answered for me, "She heals, my queen."

"Yes, be careful that your act of mercy does not get you killed, Meredith. That would be a shame." She said it almost carelessly, as if it truly didn't matter to her. "You will find, niece, that no one here will respect you for being merciful."

I said too softly for her to hear, "I do not do it for their respect."

"What did you say, niece?"

I took a deep breath and did my best to make myself heard. "I do not do it for their respect."

"Then why?" she asked.

"Because if I were in her place, I would want someone to do it for me."

"That is weakness, Meredith, and the Unseelie will not forgive it. It is a sin among them."

"I do not do it for their pleasure or their pain; I do it because it matters to me what I do, not what they do, not what anyone else does, only what I do."

"You are like an echo of my brother. Remember what happened to him, Meredith, and take it as caution. It was most likely his sense of mercy and fair play that got him killed." She stalked down the steps, holding her black skirts out, and she looked as if she were waiting for a roving photographer to snap her picture. She always moved in front of the court as if she were on display.

"Strange then, Aunt, that it was your violence and love of pain that was nearly your undoing."

She stopped on the last step. "Have a care, niece."

I was too tired, and the shock was beginning to wear off, and my arm was beginning to hurt. I wanted to be somewhere where I could pass out when I could feel my arm completely again. The first twinges promised much, none of it good.

I looked down at Miniver. "Do you wish true death? Or would you go alive into the pots of the goblins?"

I watched thoughts slide through those blue eyes, some good, some bad. Some I couldn't even begin to understand. "What will they do to me?" she asked, at last.

I leaned in against Doyle's chest, and didn't want to answer the question. I wanted to be done with this. I did not want to be sitting here talking to someone who should have been dead. Someone who was, in a way, already dead. Miniver still held hope in her eyes, and she should not have.

"At the rate you are healing, the goblins will most likely use you for sex before they begin to cut off pieces of you for food."

She stared up at me, and I saw the denial in her eyes. She didn't believe me. She was rebuilding herself, not just her body, but her sense of self. I was watching that arrogance begin to take hold again. She did not believe that such horrors would befall her. She believed that she would somehow survive, as she'd survived my attack.

"You will wish for death long before it comes, Miniver."

"Where there is life, there are always possibilities," she said. The skin of her chest showed white and whole through the blood, as if this was new skin, freshly made, that the blood had not touched.

Doyle put two guards on her and carried me back to Nerys. She was not healing as quickly, because I'd been more thorough, but she was healing.

I gave her the same choice that I'd given Miniver, but Nerys said, "Kill me." Her eyes had flicked up to the circle of Red Caps, and Holly and Ash. Seeing them stare down at her had convinced her she did not want to be alive when they took her.

"Ash." I had to repeat his name twice more, before he turned his green eyes to me. "Take the Red Caps and stand around Miniver. Let her see what fate awaits her if you take her living into the mound."

"We will be staying here with you, so we will not be touching her."

I sighed. "Please, do not split hairs with me, just do what needs doing."

"How convincing do you want us to be?" he asked, and there was something in his face of anger. I'd spoken dismissively to him, and that is not a good tone to take with a goblin warrior, especially one who will share your body soon.

Saying I was sorry would be seen as weakness, and would make it worse. I did the only thing I could do: I grabbed his arm—not as hard as I would have liked, but as hard as I was able with the inside of my head feeling so fragile. "You and Holly are not to be convincing at all. You are mine, and I will not share you. Let the Red Caps be convincing."

Ash gave me a smile that managed to be fierce and lusty at the same time, a look you wore if slaughter was your idea of sex. "You played the first sidhe well, Princess." He leaned in close and almost whispered, "Helpless little noises. Will you make helpless little noises for us?"

I felt Doyle's body go very still, as if he didn't like the question, or what it meant. But truth was truth. "Helpless little ones, and probably great big screams."

He chuckled, and it was that masculine sound that all men make when they think of such things. It was almost reassuring that he made that laugh. Male was male, some of the time.

"Your screams will be the sweetest of music." He took my hand from his arm and laid a kiss upon the back of it. Then he motioned, and all the Red Caps, save Jonty, followed him away.

Jonty looked at me. "My king ordered me to guard your

body, not hers. I got distracted by this one's blood, and let you get too close to that other one just now. If she'd killed you, I'd have never heard the end of it."

He was well-spoken for a Red Cap, but I didn't say so out loud, because that would imply I was surprised that any Red Cap was well-spoken.

"You must strike the death blow from your own two feet, Meredith," Andais said, "or Nerys goes to the goblins as she is."

Real fear flared in Nerys's eyes, and she mouthed, *Please*.

Doyle pressed his mouth against my ear. "Can you stand?"

I laid my face against his and gave the only answer I had. "I don't know."

He set me on my feet, and steadied me that moment I needed. I looked at her chest. I was short enough that I could rest the tip of the blade over her heart. My legs began to tremble, but that was all right. I gripped the hilt with my good hand, took a deep steadying breath, and let my body fall upon the hilt of the sword, driving the point through her chest and into that still-beating heart. The blade rested against bone for a second, then slid home. I collapsed to my knees beside the body, my one good hand still wrapped around the hilt.

Nerys's eyes, almost a twin of the queen's, were open and unseeing. I'd done what I could for her.

Screams came from behind us.

I leaned my forehead against my good arm. I wasn't sure I could stand on my own. If the queen insisted on me walking to Miniver, then I could not do it.

Galen knelt beside me. "Take off the high heels, Merry."

I turned my head just enough to see his face, and managed a smile. "Smart you."

He slid the shoes off my feet while I stayed kneeling. I realized that I was swaying on my knees. Shoes or no shoes, that didn't bode well for walking. "What are they doing to her?"

"Playing," Doyle answered.

I raised my head enough to meet his eyes. "Playing?"

Doyle and Galen exchanged a look. That was enough.
"Take me to her." Doyle lifted me as gently as he could, and
the sword trailed from my hand. It felt so heavy. Apparently
being dead once today, and nearly having my arm ripped out,
was taking its toll. I was beginning to look forward to passing
out, the way you look forward to sleep after a long, hard day.

The goblins had moved so that the court could see what they
were doing. It was a show—and what good is a show without
an audience? One of the smaller Red Caps was kneeling beside Miniver. His fingers were playing in the healing flesh of
her chest. He traced and tickled her flesh, as if he were touching her genitalia. A touch here, a caress there, and it showed
skill, but his fingers weren't between her legs. His fingers were
inside the meat of her chest. He was caressing the top of her
heart as if that would finally bring her to orgasm.

Doyle carried me around to her head. "Don't let them take
you like this, Miniver."

"Get them away from me. Get them away from me!"

I looked at Ash, and he motioned the rest of them away.
The one who was playing in her body left reluctantly, and
squeezed her breast as he moved away.

Miniver lay there gasping on the floor, her eyes wild. She
looked up at Jonty, still standing over her, and said, "Get him
away."

"No," he said, "I am her guard, and I will guard her. I have
no interest in your white flesh."

Doyle put me on my feet, but my legs did not hold this
time. I collapsed to my knees beside her.

Miniver reached out toward me with her healed hand, beseeching. I had a heartbeat to realize that she lied with her
eyes and her body. Doyle hit her hand away, and the bolt of
energy sizzled outward to scar along the table on the other
side of the room. Jonty trapped her arm under his big knee. He
was shaking his head. "Do you want me to tear her arm off?"

I thought about it, then shook my head. "Bind her, and let
them take her."

"No," Andais said, "for that last, I think we should see

some of her punishment." The queen came in a hiss of black silk. She looked down at Miniver. "You are a fool. Do you not understand that the very fact that you are alive and healing means that Meredith is no longer mortal? I watched her die today, and breathe again. You have lost everything you are, for nothing."

"Lies," she said.

Andais leaned down, touched the other woman's face, a strangely tender caress. "You craved blood and violence. I saw it. We all saw it. You tried to destroy me with it. Now we will see you destroyed with it." She turned to me. "Do you see now, Meredith? You offered her mercy, and she tried to kill you. You cannot be weak among the sidhe, not if you wish to rule." She touched my face, much as she'd touched Miniver's. "Heed this lesson, Meredith, and wipe mercy from your heart, or the sidhe will surely cut it out." Her smile was half wistful, half something I could not read, and probably did not want to. "You look tired, Meredith."

She eased the sword from my hand. "Take your princess to my room, use my bed as if it were your own. I will send Fflur with you." She motioned and a sidhe as golden-haired as Miniver came forward, but Fflur's skin was also a pale yellow, and her eyes a solid black. She had been Andais's personal healer for more years than I remembered.

She gave a lovely curtsey and said, "I would be honored to tend the princess."

"Yes, yes," the queen said and waved it away, as if it were a given and Fflur had had no real choice.

Chains had been brought, and Miniver screamed as they shackled her. It was cold iron, and her hands of power would not work while she wore it. Goblins handle base metal better than the sidhe, probably because it interferes with magic more than the strength of arm.

"Take her, Darkness. Go." She turned and began to walk back toward her throne.

It was only when Sholto realized we were leaving for the night that he came to the doors. "The duty of the sluagh is to protect the queen, but when our bargain is done, we will also protect you." It was almost an apology for not having helped more tonight. Sholto is young for a king, under four hundred, and it keeps him more humble than most.

"I will not be striking any bargains with anyone tonight," I said.

"That is as well; I would not leave the queen's side this night." He glanced back at her. "The sluagh stand with Andais, and there are still those sitting here who need to be reminded of that."

He was right, and I was suddenly more tired than I could manage. I wanted no more politics tonight. No more games. My arm throbbed, sending sharp, shooting pains through my body like small knives. The muscles in it seemed to have a life of their own, dancing and twitching involuntarily. I fought not to cry out with the pain, for that was weakness, too, among the sidhe.

Fflur touched the arm lightly, and made a small *tsk*ing sound. "You've torn the muscles, and the ligaments that bind your bones. Dislocated, as well. The damage to the soft tissues will be harder to heal than bone." She shook her head, and made that faint *tsk*ing sound again.

"Can she be healed tonight?" Ash asked.

Fflur looked at the goblin as if she wouldn't answer, then did. "No, not tonight. She is part human, and that makes her healing slower."

Ash grinned at me. "Then we will leave you for tonight, Princess. I think we should stay and hear what else happens tonight."

"As you please," I said, and truly did not care what they did. I was fast approaching the point where the pain was all I could concentrate on. Soon nothing else would matter, and my world would narrow down to the pain. I liked a little pain in the right context, but I couldn't turn this to pleasure. This was just going to hurt.

We left the great hall to the sounds of voices, as the Unseelie began to murmur among themselves. It would be interesting to see how long it took this night's work to reach the ears of the King of Light and Illusion in the Seelie Court. I was due in two days to be at a banquet in my honor at his court. Two days to heal. Two days to finish my alliance with the sluagh and the goblins. Two days didn't seem enough time for all that.

Chapter 34

FFLUR WAS ENAMORED OF THE HEALING SPRING. SHE MADE ME drink a cup of the cool, clear water, and the pain lessened. She stripped me down and bathed the arm in the water. It didn't heal immediately, but the muscles stopped jumping and fighting, and the pain went from a sharp stabbing to a dull ache. I could live with an ache, could sleep with an ache.

The queen's room had been cleaned while we were gone. How the white ladies had gotten rid of all that blood, I didn't know, and perhaps I didn't want to know.

Galen helped me out of the rest of my clothes. His eyes were shiny with unshed tears. He leaned in and touched his lips to my forehead. "I thought I'd lost you today." I reached for him, but he moved away. "No, Merry, I'll do first watch. If you hold me, I'll cry, and that's so unmanly." He tried to make a joke of it, but it didn't quite work. I thought there was more going on than simply worry about what had happened, but I was in no shape to chase him down and make him tell the truth.

Doyle curled his nude body around me in the center of the queen's huge bed. It was larger than a king-sized bed. I'd coined the term *orgy-sized*, but never to the queen's face. I was sleepy from a draft that Fflur had given me. She said it would help me sleep and speed the healing. I settled into the first drowsiness of the potion and the velvet warmth of Doyle's body.

Frost kissed my forehead, and it made me blink my eyes open. I hadn't remembered shutting them. "I will help Galen keep watch. There is someone else who needs to sleep next to you right now." There was a look on his face, he wasn't pouting, or being childish. He looked, silly as it seemed for a being centuries old, grown-up.

I woke the next moment when someone crawled in beside me, moving carefully around my wounded arm. It was not a body I knew. I couldn't say how I was so certain, but I knew the men who shared my bed—the feel of them, the scent of their skin—and this was no one I knew that well. I opened my eyes and found Adair's golden-skinned face hovering over mine. "The queen says I am yours if you want me." There was a trembling look in his eyes, fear, uncertainty. Goddess alone knew what mood the queen would be in after our little show. I wouldn't have wanted to be on the receiving end of that mood.

"Stay with us," I whispered, "of course, stay."

He turned away from me and cuddled his body in against mine. A shudder ran through him, and it took me a moment to realize he was crying. The bed moved as Rhys crawled in on the other side of Adair, and Kitto crawled across the foot of the bed, and Nicca and Sage with their wings carefully back. We all touched Adair, letting him know with our hands and our bodies that he was safe. We fell asleep like that in a huge piles of warm bodies and comforting hands.

Two things woke me: Adair whimpered in his sleep, and Doyle went very still on the other side of me. I blinked awake, and his arm around my waist tightened enough to tell me not to move. I stayed frozen in the curve of his body, with Adair making his small helpless noises.

The queen stood at the foot of the bed, staring down at all of us. I could not read her thoughts, only that they were not light ones.

I stroked Adair's naked back until the noises ceased, and he fell back to sleep. I felt rather than saw that Rhys was awake on the other side of him. I think Nicca, Kitto, and Sage were actually still asleep; their breathing was even and deep.

Frost and Galen stood by the bed, behind her, as if they wanted to grab her, but were afraid to. How do you guard someone from the queen? The answer is, you don't, not really.

She looked down at us and spoke softly, as if she didn't want to wake those who slept. "I do not know who to envy more. You with all your men, or your men curled next to you. I have tasted your power and found it sweet, Meredith, very sweet." She turned her head, though I had heard nothing. "Eamon awaits, and the guards I have chosen for the night." She looked back down at me. "You have inspired me to choose more of them for my bed this night."

Adair's body tensed against mine, and I knew that though his eyes were closed, he was awake. He feigned sleep the way a child will: *Pretend hard enough and the bad thing will go away.*

She gave a throaty chuckle, and he actually jumped, as if the sound had struck him, though I knew it had not. She left the room laughing, but none of us found it particularly funny.

I wondered where Barinthus was, and Usna, and Abloec, and even Onilwyn and Amatheon. They were supposed to be mine now, and that meant I was supposed to protect them. I sent Rhys to ask about them. He came back a little while later trailing them behind him, all of them. Including Hawthorne, Ivi, and Brii. "I asked the queen's permission to bring all your men, and she gave the ones you hadn't fucked yet a choice. They all chose to come in here for the night." He looked both amused and tired.

Barinthus looked down at the bed and shook his head. "Not even this bed will hold us all." He was right, but they managed to get more of them on it than you'd think. When we'd settled down for the night, with more bodies than I'd ever shared a bed with, it was Amatheon's voice coming from somewhere at the foot of the bed that seemed to speak for most of the new guards. "Thank you for sending Rhys to find us."

"You're mine now, Amatheon, for better or for worse."

"For better or for worse," Rhys said from somewhere farther into the room.

"This isn't a human marriage ceremony," Frost said from near the door. He sounded a little disgruntled.

Doyle cuddled in tighter against me, and I relaxed in the curve of him.

"Marriage can end in divorce, or one can simply walk out," Doyle said. "Merry takes her responsibilities more seriously than that."

"So, what," I said from the darkness, "it's for richer or poorer?"

"I don't know about that," Rhys said. "I don't think I'd like being poor."

"Good night, Rhys," I said.

He laughed.

From somewhere near the door Galen said, "In sickness and in health, till death do us part."

There was something both comforting and ominous about those words.

Onilwyn's voice came out of the dark, far enough away that I knew he hadn't managed to find a spot on the bed. "So just like that, you bind yourself to us, to our protection and our fates?"

"To your protection, yes, but not your fate, Onilwyn. Your fate, like everyone's fate, is your own, and no one can take it from you."

"The queen says that our fate is in her hands," he said, in that quiet voice everyone seems to use in the dark as people begin to drift off to sleep.

"No," I said, "I want no one's fate. It is too much responsibility."

"Isn't that what it means to be queen?" he asked.

"It means I have the fate of my people, yes, but individual choices, those are your own. You have free will, Onilwyn."

"Do you truly believe that?" he asked.

"Yes," I said, and put my face into the curve of Adair's neck. He smelled like fresh-cut wood. No one had made him move, and it made me wonder what Andais had done to him besides cutting off his hair.

"An absolute monarch who believes in free will, isn't that against the rules?" Onilwyn asked.

"No," I said, my face buried against Adair's skin, "it's not.

Not against my rules." My voice was beginning to drag with that edge of sleep.

"I think I will like your rules," Onilwyn said, and his voice, too, was growing heavy.

"The rules, yes," Rhys said, "but the housework is a bitch."

"Housework!" Onilwyn said. "The sidhe don't do housework."

"My house, my rules," I said.

He and some of the others who were still awake began to protest. "Enough," Doyle said. "You will do what the princess says you will do."

"Or what?" a voice I didn't recognize asked.

"Or you will be sent back to the queen's tender care."

Silence to that, a thick and not very restful silence. "The sex had better be damn good if I'm expected to do windows." I think it was Usna.

"It is," Rhys said.

"Shut up, Rhys," Galen said.

"Well, it's true," he said.

"Enough," I said, "I'm tired, and if I'm going to be well enough to do anything with anyone tomorrow, I need sleep."

Silence then, and the small noises that bodies make as they move under sheets. Ivi's voice came soft and distant. "How good?"

Rhys answered from the door, "Very . . ."

"Good night, Rhys," I said, "and good night, Ivi. Go to sleep."

I was almost asleep, lost between the twin warmths of Doyle and Adair, when I heard whispering. I knew from the tone that one of them was Rhys, and thought the other was probably Ivi. I could have yelled at them, but I let sleep roll over me like a warm, thick blanket. If I insisted on all of them being quiet at the same time, we'd never get to sleep. If Rhys wanted to regale Ivi with tales of sex, then he was free to do it. So long as I didn't have to listen to the details.

The last sound I heard was a stifled and very masculine laugh. I would learn the next morning that Rhys had attracted quite a crowd for his erotic tales. He swore our most solemn oath that he hadn't lied or exaggerated. I had to believe him, but I vowed never again to let him stay up late telling tales to those who had not shared my bed. If I wasn't careful he'd give me a reputation that no one, not even a fertility goddess, could live up to. Rhys tells me I'm being modest. I tell him I'm only mortal, and how can one mortal woman satisfy the lusts of sixteen immortal sidhe?

He gave me a look and said, "Mortal is it? Are you sure of that?"

The answer, truthfully, is no, but how do you tell if you're immortal? I mean, I don't feel that different. Shouldn't immortality feel different? It seems like it should. Besides, how do you test the theory?

Pronunciation Guide

Most of the names used in the books come from two sources: *Celtic Baby Names* by Judy Sierra and *Celtic Names for Children* by Loreto Todd.

Abloec ab-LOCK
Adair a-DARE
Adaria AH-dare-ee-a
Afagdu a-fag-DUE
Ametheon A-math-eon
Andais ON-dee-ay-us
Artagan ART-a-gan
Bainidhe Dub Ban-ith DU
Barinthus BA-rinth-us
Besaba bet-SHA-ba
Bhatar VAH-tuhr
Bleddyn BLETH-in
Branwyn BRAN-wen
Briac bree-ACK
Bryok bri-OCK
Bucca BOO-ka
Carrow CARE-o
Cel KEL
Conri CON-ree
Creeda CREE-da
Doyle DOLE
Eamon AY-mon
Edain e-DANE
Eluned el-EEN-ed

Emrys EM-rees
Essus ES-us
Ezekiel Ee-zeke-ee-el
Fey FAY
Fflur FLEW-er
Firblogs FUR-blogs
Galen GAY-len
Gethin GETH-an
Griffin GRIF-in
Hedwick HEAD-wick
Ivi EYE-vee
Jonty JON-tee
Keelin KEY-lynn
Killian KILL-ee-an
Kitto KIT-toe
Kongar con-GAR
Kurag CUR-ahg
Maelgwn MAYL-goon
Maeve MAY
Miniver min-E-ver
Mistral MISS-tra-el
Nerys Ner-IS
Nicca NICK-uh
Niceven NIS-ah-ven

Nuline NEW-lyn
Onilwyn ON-ill-win
Pach PAH-ch
Pasco PASS-co
Phouka POO-ka
Pol PAHL
Rhys REESE
Roane Finn ROAN FIN
Rosemerta ROSE-mur-ta
Rozenwyn roh-ZEN-win
Seelie SEE-lee
Segna SEG-na
Sholto SHOLE-toe

Sidhe SHE
Siobhan SHE-oh-vin
Sithney SITH-nee
Siun sigh-ON
Sluagh SLEW-ah
Taranis TAR-a-nis
Uar ooh-ARE
Unseelie UN-see-lee
Usna OOSH-na
Uther OOH-thur
Yannick YAN-nick
Yule YOUL

BIBLIOGRAPHY

Often the question of which books were used for research in the Merry series is asked. So, here is a list (in no particular order). While not comprehensive, it contains the major sources.

An Encyclopedia of Faeries by Katharine Briggs

Faeries by Brian Froud and Alan Lee

Dictionary of Celtic Myth and Legend by Miranda J. Green

Celtic Goddesses by Miranda J. Green

Dictionary of Celtic Mythology by Peter Berresford Ellis

Goddesses in World Mythology by Martha Ann and Dorothy Myers Imel

A Witches' Bible by Janet and Stewart Farrar

The Fairy Faith in Celtic Countries by W. Y. Evans-Wentz

Pagan Celtic Britain by Anne Ross

The Ancient British Goddesses by Kathy Jones

Fairy Tradition in Britain by Lewis Spense

One Hundred Old Roses for the American Garden by Clair G. Martin

Taylor's Guide to Roses

Pendragon by Steve Blake and Scott Lloyd

Kings and Queens from Collins Gem

Butterflies of Europe: A Princeton Guide by Tom Tolman and Richard Lewington

Butterflies and Moths of Missouri by J. Richard and Joan E. Heitzman

Dorling Kindersly Handbook: Butterflies and Moths by David Carter

The Natural World of Bugs and Insects by Ken and Rod Preston Mafham

Big Cats: Kingdom of Might by Tom Brakefield

Just Cats by Karen Anderson

Wild Cats of the World by Art Wolfe and Barbara Sleeper

Beauty and the Beast translated by Jack Zipes

The Complete Fairy Tales of the Brothers Grimm translated by Jack Zipes

Grimms' Tales for Young and Old by Ralph Manheim

Complete Guide to Cats by the ASPCA

Field Guide to Insects and Spiders from the National Audubon Society

Bibliography 409

Mammals of Europe by David W. MacDonald

Wicca: A Guide for the Solitary Practitioner by Scott Cunningham

Northern Mysteries and Magick by Freya Aswym

Cabbages and Kings by Jonathan Roberts

Gaelic: A Complete Guide for Beginners

The Norse Myths by Kevin Crossley Holland

The Penguin Companion to Food by Alan Davidson

Read on for an excerpt from

A STROKE OF MIDNIGHT

by Laurell K. Hamilton

I'D SEEN MORE VIOLENCE IN THE COURTS THAN IN ALL MY years as a private detective in Los Angeles, but I'd seen more death in L.A. Not because I was included in murder cases—private dicks don't do murder cases, not fresh ones—but because most of the things that live in fairie land are immortal. I could count on one hand how many fresh crime scenes the police had called us in on and still have fingers left over. Even those cases were because the Grey Detective Agency could boast some of the best magic workers on the west coast. Magic is like everything else, if you can do good with it, some people will find a way to do bad with it. Our agency specialized in supernatural problems, magical solutions. It was on the business cards and everything.

I'd learned that the body is an "it," not he or she. Because if you think of the dead body as a he or a she, they begin to be real people for you. You can have sympathy for the victim later, but at the crime scene, especially in the first moments, you serve the victim better by not sympathizing. Detachment and logic, those are your salvation at a fresh murder. Anything else leads to hysterics, and I was not only the most experienced detective in the hallway, but I was also Princess Meredith NicEssus, wielder of the hands of flesh and blood, Baseba's Bane, Peace _____ . I was a princess and I might one day be queen. Future queens do not have hysterics. Future queens that are also trained detectives aren't allowed hysterics.

The problem was that I knew one of these bodies. I'd known her alive and walking around. I knew that she liked classical literature. When she was cast out of the Seelie Court and had to come to the Unseelie court, she'd changed her name, as many did, even among the Seelie. They changed their names so they wouldn't be reminded daily of who and what they had once been, and how far they had fallen. She called herself Beatrice, after the love interest in Dante's *Inferno*. She said, "I'm in hell, I might as well have a name to match."

Blood had soaked in a wide, dark pool around her body. Someone had come up behind her and slit her throat. To get that close to her, it had been someone she trusted, or someone with enough magic to sneak up on her. Of course, they'd needed enough magic to negate her immortality. There weren't that many things in fairie that could do both of those things.

"What happened, Beatrice?" I said softly. "Who did this to you?"

Galen came up beside me. "Merry."

I looked up at him.

"Are you all right?"

I shook my head, and looked down the hallway to our second body. Out loud I said, "I'll be fine."

"Liar," he said softly, and he tried to bend over me, tried to hold me. I moved away. Now wasn't the time to cling to someone. According to our culture, I should have been touching someone. Close physical contact makes a fey feel safer. But the handful of guards that had come to L.A. with me, had only worked at Grey's Detective Agency for a few months. I'd been there a few years. You didn't huddle at crime scenes. You didn't comfort yourself. You did your job.

Galen's face fell a little, as if I'd hurt his feelings. I didn't want to hurt his feelings, but we had a crisis here. Surely he could see that. So why, as so often, was I having to waste energy worrying about Galen's feelings when I should have been doing nothing but concentrating on the job? There were moments, no matter how dear he was to me, that I understood all too well why my father had not chosen Galen for my fiancé.

I walked toward the second body. The man lay just short of the hallway's intersection with another larger hallway. He was on his stomach, arms outspread. There was a large stain of blood on his back, and more of it curling down along the side of his body.

Rhys was squatting by the body. He looked up as I approached. The demi fey peeked out at me through his thick white hair, then hid her tiny face, as if she were afraid. The demi fey usually went around in large groups like flocks of birds or butterflies. Some of them were shy when on their own.

"Do we know what killed him yet?" I asked.

Rhys put his fingers just above the man's suit jacket, careful not to touch anything, but pointing out that there was a narrow hole in the man's back. "Knife, I think."

I nodded. "But they took the blade with them, why?"

"Because there was something about the knife that might give them away."

"Or they simply did not want to lose a good blade," Frost said. He stepped from the big corridor into the smaller one. He'd been coordinating the guards who were keeping everyone out of the crime scene. I had enough guards with me to close off both ends of the hallway, and I'd done it.

I'd sent Barinthus to tell the Queen what had happened. Of all of the men, he had the best chance of not being punished for being the bearer of such terrible news. The queen did have a tendency to blame the messenger.

"Possible," Rhys said, "just habit. You use the blade, you retrieve, clean it, and put it back in its sheath." He pointed to a smear on the man's jacket.

"He wiped the blade off," I said.

Rhys looked at me. "Why he?"

I shrugged. "You're right, it could be a she."

I didn't hear Doyle come down the hallway, but I knew he

was there a second before he spoke. "He was running when they threw the blade."

I actually agreed, but I wanted his reasoning. "What makes you say he was running?"

He started to touch the man's coat, and I said, "Don't touch him."

He gave me a look. "The wound in his shirt does not line up with the coat as it lies. I believe he was running, then when they retrieved the knife, they went through his pockets, moved his coat around."

"I'll bet they didn't wear gloves."

"Most here would not think about fingerprints and DNA. They will be more worried that magic will find them than science."

I nodded. "Exactly."

"He saw something that scared him," Rhys said, standing up. "He took off down this way to try and outrun it. But what did he see? What made him run?"

"There are many frightening things loose in the corridors of our sithen," Frost said.

"Yes," I said, "but he was a reporter. He came looking for something odd or frightening."

"Perhaps he saw the lesser fey's death," Frost said.

"You mean he witnessed Beatrice's murder," I said.

Frost nodded.

"Okay, say he witnessed it. He ran, they threw a blade, killed him." I shook my head. "Almost everyone carries a knife. Most of them can pin a fly to the wall with one. It doesn't limit our suspect pool much. Besides, you can't kill the immortal with a knife, but she's dead. It needed a spell, a powerful spell, and only a sidhe, or some few members of the Sluagh could have done it."

"The Queen forbid the Sluagh to be out this night. Simply to be seen while the reporters are in our sithen would raise suspicion."

The Sluagh were the least human of fairie. The nightmares that even the Unseelie fear. They are the only wild hunt that is left to us. The only frightening group that can hunt the fey, even the sidhe, until they are caught.

I shook my head. "I don't think a member of the Slaugh could have hidden themselves enough to wander about the sithen tonight. Not with all the spells we had on the corridors to keep everyone boxed into that one tiny section."

"Just as the reporter should not have been able to leave the area," Frost said. He had a point.

"Let me say what we're all thinking. A sidhe killed Beatrice and the reporter."

"That still leaves us with several hundred suspects," Rhys said.

I had an idea, an awful idea, because Queen Andais would hate it: What if it had been Prince Cel's people?

The trouble was that I couldn't see what Cel, or anyone serving his interests, would gain from killing Beatrice. The reporter seemed accidental, just in the wrong place at the wrong time.

"You've thought of something," Rhys said.

"Later," I said, and let my eyes flick to the backs of the men just a foot away from us.

"Yes," Doyle said, "yes, we do need some privacy."

"We should hide the body," said one of the men behind me. Amatheon's hair in its tight coppery red French braids left his face bare, but nothing could leave it unadorned, for his eyes were layered petals of red, blue, yellow, and green, like some multi-colored flower. His face was square-jawed, but slender, so that he managed to be both strongly masculine and vaguely delicate at the same time. Almost as if his face, like his eyes, couldn't quite decide what it wanted to be.

"The reporter will be missed, Amatheon," I said. "We can't just hide his body and hope this will all go away."

"Why can we not? Why can we not simply say we don't know where he has gone? Or that one of the lesser fey saw him leave the sithen."

"Those are all lies," Rhys said. "The sidhe don't lie, or did you forget that in all those years you hung around with Cel?"

Amatheon's face clouded with the beginnings of anger, but he fought it off. "What I did, or did not do, with Prince Cel is not your business. But I know that the Queen would want to hide this from the press. To have a human reporter killed in our court will ruin all the good publicity she has managed to acquire for us in the last few decades."

He was probably right on that last part. The Queen would not want to admit what had happened. If she even suspected that I suspected that one of Cel's people were responsible, she'd want to hide it even deeper. She loved Cel too well, and always had.

The fact that Amantheon had suggested disposing of the body made me wonder even harder if Cel's interests were somehow behind this. Amantheon had always been one of Cel's supporters because Cel was the last pure-blood sidhe of a house that had ruled this court for three thousand years. Amatheon was one of the sidhe who thought me a mongrel and a disgrace to the throne. So why was he here to compete to bed me and make me queen? Because Queen Andais had ordered it. When he refused the honor, she made certain that he got her point, her painful point, that she was ruler here, not Cel, and Amatheon would do as he was told, or else. Part of the *or else* had been to cut his knee-length hair to his shoulders, a mark of great shame for him. She'd done other things to him, things more painful to his body, than to his pride, but he hadn't shared details and I didn't really want to know.

"If Beatrice were the only one dead, then I might agree," I said. "But a human is dead in our land. We can't hide that."

"Yes," he said, "we can."

"You haven't dealt as directly with the press as I have, Amatheon. Was this reporter alone when he came here to the sithen? Or was he part of a group that will miss him right away? Even if he came alone, he will be known to other members of the press. If one of us had killed him out in the human world, we might be able to hide who did it, and let it be just another unsolved crime. But he was killed here on our land, and that we cannot hide."

"You sound as if you are going to tell the press of his death."

I looked away from his confusing eyes.

He reached out to touch my arm, but Frost simply moved in the way, and he never completed the gesture. "You will announce it to the press?" He sounded astonished.

"No, but we have to contact the police."

"Meredith . . ." Doyle started to say.

I cut him off. "No, Doyle, we'll never figure out whose blade killed him. But a good forensics team might."

"There are spells for tracing a wound to the weapon that made it," Doyle said.

"Yes, and you tried those spells when you found my father's body in the meadow. You did your spells, and you never found the weapons that killed him." I did my best to make those words empty. Just a fact, nothing more.

Doyle drew a deep breath. "I failed Prince Essus that day, Princess Meredith, and you."

"You failed because it was a sidhe that killed him. It was someone who had enough magic to thwart your spells. Don't you see, Doyle, whoever did this is as good at magic as we are. But they won't know modern forensics. They won't be able to protect themselves against science."

Onilwyn stepped away from the guards. He was tall but stockier than any of the other sidhe, and yet he always moved with grace. His hair fell in a long wavy ponytail over the back of his black suit and white shirt. Black, the Queen's color, and Prince Cel's color. A very popular color here at the Unseelie Court. His hair was a green so dark it had black highlights. His eyes were pale green with a star burst in the center around his pupil.

"You cannot mean to bring human warriors into our land?"

"If you mean human policemen, yes, that is exactly what I mean to do."

"You will open us up to that over the death of one human and a cook?"

"Do you think the death of a human is less important than

the death of a sidhe?" I looked him straight in the face, and watched him remember that I was part human.

"What is one death, even two, over the damage it will do to our court in the eyes of the world?"

"Do you think the death of a cook is less important than the death of a nobleman?" I asked, ignoring his attempt to fix things.

He smiled then, and it was arrogant, and so very Onilwyn. "Of course I believe that the life of a noble born sidhe is worth more than the life of a servant, or a human. So would you if you were pure sidhe."

"Then I'm glad that I'm not pure sidhe." I was angry now, and I fought not to show my power, not to start to glow, and raise the stakes of this fight. "This servant, whose name happens to be Beatrice, showed me more kindness than most of the nobles of either fairie court. Beatrice was my friend, and if you have nothing more helpful to add than class prejudice, then I'm sure that Queen Andais can find a use for you back among her guards."

His skin went from pale whitish green to just white. I felt a swift burst of satisfaction at his fear. Andais had given him to me to bed, and if I didn't, he would suffer. So would I, but in that moment, I wasn't sure I cared.

"How was I to know she meant anything to you, Princess Meredith?"

"Consider this as my only warning to you, Onilwyn," I raised my voice so that it carried down the hallway, "and for the rest of you, who don't know me. I spent a great deal of time with the lesser fey while I was at court. Most of my friends here were not among the sidhe. Apparently I was not pure-blooded enough for most of you. You have only yourselves to blame then, that my attitude is a little more democratic than usual for a noble. Think upon that before you say something as foolish to me as Onilwyn just did." I turned back to the guard in question, and lowered my voice. "Bear that in mind, Onilwyn, before you open your mouth again, and say something else equally stupid."

He actually dropped to one knee and bowed his head. "As my princess bids, so I do."

"Get up, and go stand somewhere farther away from me."

Doyle told him to go to the other end of the hallway, and he went, without another word, though the star bursts in his eyes were glittering with his rage.

"I do not agree with Onilwyn," Amatheon said, "not completely, but are you truly going to bring in the human police?"

I nodded.

"The Queen will not like it."

"No, she won't."

"Why would you risk her anger, Princess?" He seemed to be truly puzzled by that. "I would not risk her anger again for anything, or anyone. Not even my honor."

"Beatrice was my friend, but more than that she was one of my people. I want whoever did this. I want them caught and I want them punished. I want to stop them from doing it to anyone else. The reporter was our guest, and to kill him like this is an insult to the honor of the court itself."

"You don't care about the honor of the court," he said.

"No, not really. But no one gets to kill people that I have sworn to protect, Amatheon, no one."

"You are not sworn, not yet. You have taken no oath for this court, you sit on no throne."

"If I do not do my utmost to solve these deaths, to protect everyone in this sithen, from greatest to least, then I do not deserve to sit on any throne."

"You are mad," he said, and his eyes were very wide. "The Queen will kill you for this."

I glanced back at Beatrice's body, and I thought of another death so many years ago. The only reason the Queen hadn't hidden my father's body from the press is that they found him first. Miles away from the fairie mounds, cut to pieces. They found him and took pictures of him. Not only were his bodyguards too late to save his life, but too late to save his dignity, or my horror.

The police had done some investigating because he was

killed outside of our lands, but they had been stopped before they began because the queen was convinced we would find who had done this terrible thing. We never did.

"I will remind my aunt what she said when my father, her brother, was murdered."

"What did she say?" he asked.

It was Doyle who answered. "That we would find who had killed Prince Essus, and the humans would only hinder us in our search."

I looked at him, and he met my gaze. "This time I will say to her that the humans have methods that the sidhe cannot hide from. That the only reason to keep the police out is if she does not want these murders solved."

"Merry," Rhys said, "you will discuss this with the queen before telling the press or contacting the police, right?"

"Yes, and just the police. We're going to try and get the press out of here first."

"Thank the Consort."

"I'm determined, Rhys, not suicidal."

"You're hoping she loved her brother enough to feel guilty," Amatheon said, and the fact that he'd grasped that made me think better of him.

"Something like that," I said.

"She cares for no one except Prince Cel," he said.

I thought about that. "You might be right, or you might be wrong."

"Are you so certain that you are right?" he asked.

"About the Queen, no, but I am right about what we need to do to find our murderer, and I'm willing to tell the Queen so."

He shuddered. "I would rather stay here and guard the hallway, if you do not mind."

"I don't want anyone with me that's more afraid of the Queen than of doing what's right."

"Oh, hell, Merry, then none of us can come," Rhys said.

I looked at him.

He shrugged. "All of us fear her."

"But I will go with you," Frost said.

"And me," Galen said.

"Do you need to ask?" Doyle said.

It was Adair who finally spoke for most of them. "I think this is foolishness. Honorable foolishness, but it does not matter. You are our ameraudur, and that is a title that I have not let cross my lips for many years."

Ameraudur meant a war leader that was chosen for love, not bloodline. It meant that the man who called you so, would give his own life before he saw yours fail.

I didn't know what to say, because I hadn't done enough to deserve it, not yet. "I haven't earned such a title from you, Adair, or from anyone. Do not call me so."

"You offered yourself in our place last night, Princess. You took the might of the Queen herself upon your mortal body. Seeing you draw magic against her was one of the bravest things ever I saw, my oath on that."

I didn't know whether to be embarrassed or try to explain that I'd been afraid the whole time.

"You are our ameraudur, and we will follow you wherever that may lead. To whatever end. I will die before I let another harm you."

"You can't mean that," Amatheon said.

"She saved us last night," Adair said, "She saved us all. She risked her life to save ours. How can you stand there and not give her your oath?"

"A man without honor has no oath to give," Amatheon said.

Adair put his mailed hand on the other's shoulder. "Then come with us to the Queen, regain your honor, rediscover your oath."

"She took my courage with the rest. I am too afraid to go before her with such news." A single tear glittered down his cheek.

I looked at the despair in his eyes, and said the only thing I could think of. "I will use her guilt over never solving her own brother's murder. But if guilt won't work, then I will remind her that she owes me the life of her consort and her pet human."

"It is not always wise to remind the Queen she owes you a debt," Doyle said.

"No, but I want her to say yes, Doyle. I need her to say yes."

He touched my face. "I see in your eyes a haunting. I see in your eyes your father's death like a weight of injustice on her heart."

I closed my eyes and let my cheek rest against the warmth of his palm. With Doyle touching me, I could let myself remember that awful day. It's funny how your mind protects you. I saw the bloody sheet and the stretcher. I held my father's hand, cold, but not stiff, not yet. I had his blood on my hands from touching him, and it was cold, and it wasn't him. I felt a terrible emptiness when I touched him. He was gone. My tall, handsome, amazing father. He was supposed to have been immortal, but there are spells to steal even the life of a god; a once-upon-a-time god.

If I poke at the memory of that day too hard, try to make myself remember too much, it isn't my father's body or blood that I remember. It is his sword. One of his guards laid it in my hands, the way you lay a flag at a military funeral. The hilt was leather set with gold, and I spent much of that day with my face pressed to it. I breathed in the scent of good leather, the oil that he'd used to clean the sword, and over all that, was the scent of him. I could touch the hilt and feel where even this magical metal had shaped to the constant use of his hand.

I had slept with that sword for days, huddled around it as if I could still feel his hand on it, his body near it. I swore on the hilt of my father's sword that I would avenge his death. I'd been seventeen.

I was thirty-three now. Sixteen years had passed since I slept beside my dead father's sword. The sword had simply vanished about a month after his death. It had gone the way of so many of our great relics, as if without Essus to wield it, the sword chose to fade and vanish into the mists. Perhaps the great relics do not choose to go. Perhaps Goddess calls them home when they have done their work. Or perhaps she calls them home until someone comes again that is fit, or suited, for them.

I would try to use guilt to get Andais to allow me to call in the police, though I did not have much faith in her ability to be emotionally blackmailed. But she still did not know that one of the greatest relics of the fairie courts had returned. The chalice, the one that mankind's wishes had changed from a cauldron of plenty into a golden cup, had returned from wherever it had been. It had come to me in a dream, and when I woke it was real. The chalice had been one of the great treasures of the Seelie court, and one reason to keep its reappearance a secret was that the Seelie might try to reclaim it. The chalice definitely had a mind of its own and went where it would. I was almost certain that it would not stay at the Seelie Court even if we allowed them to take it back. And if it kept disappearing there, and reappearing here, the Seelie would think we'd stolen it. Or at least accuse us of it, because if the chalice simply found them unworthy, King Taranis would never admit it. No, my uncle would blame us, not himself and his shining throng.

If guilt and family connections could not sway her, then perhaps the fact that the chalice had come to my hand would. I still hoped, someday, to know who had killed my father, but the case was cold. Sixteen years cold. But for Beatrice and the reporter, the case was literally still warm. The crime scene was fresh. The suspect list wasn't endless. Rhys said a few hundred as if that was a lot. I'd helped the police in a few cases where almost the entire population of Los Angeles had been suspects. What was a few hundred to that?

We could do this. If we brought in modern police work, we could get them. Because they wouldn't be expecting it, and they wouldn't know how to protect themselves against it. It would work. All right, I was 99.9 percent certain it would work. Only a fool is 100 percent certain when it comes to murder. Either about committing one or solving one. Both can be equally dangerous, and hazardous to your health.

The time is right for another dark,
sensual Meredith Gentry novel

A STROKE OF MIDNIGHT

by Laurell K. Hamilton

I am Meredith Gentry, P.I., solving cases in Los Angeles, far from the peril and deception of my real home—because I am also Princess Meredith, heir to the darkest throne faerie has to offer. Enemies watch my every move. My cousin Cel strives to have me killed even now from his prison cell. But not all the assassination attempts are his. Enemies unforeseen move against us—enemies who would murder the least among us.

I need my allies now more than ever, especially since fate will lead me into the arms of Mistral, Master of Storms, the queen's new captain of her guard. Our passion will reawaken powers long forgotten among the warriors of the sidhe. Pain and pleasure await me—and danger, as well, for some at that court seek only death. The gentlest of my guards will find new strength and break my heart. Passions undreamed of await us—and my enemies gather, for the future of both courts of faerie begins to unravel.